LEGACY OF LUCK

BOOK THREE IN
THE DRUID'S BROOCH SERIES

CHRISTY NICHOLAS

GREEN DRAGON PUBLISHING

Table of Contents

Dedication

I lovingly dedicate this book to my husband, who has indulged me with many trips to my soul's home, Ireland. He has supported me through my growing pangs as a writer. And sincere thanks go to my publisher, editors, and beta readers, including Ian Erik Morris, Christina Lalama, David Parker, Julie Young, Catie Jarvis, Patty Tavormina, Caleb Wimble, and Samantha Benton—without your help, this never would have happened!

I also dedicate it to those who find fate has not worked out as they had planned. Sometimes this is not a bad thing.

Foreword

What we want and what we get are two different things in the world. Sometimes we can control our own lives and the others within it. Usually, we cannot. We drift on a tide of action and reaction, only occasionally poking our heads up above the chaos to see where the nearest shore might be.

Pronunciation Guide

Irish, a language in the Gaelic family, has several rules of pronunciation that are different from English. For instance, if some letters are followed by H, they are softened. An example from English is S, which softens to SH, or P which softens to PH.

In Irish, this is true of BH and MH, which become V, while DH becomes a very soft YH, barely discernible. TH becomes H, while GH and CH become a rather guttural H. FH is silent.

Another difference is in the slender vowels, I and E. When some letters are around these vowels, they become lenited as well. For instance, SÍ is pronounced SHEE, and SÉ is pronounced SHAY.

An accent draws out the length of the vowel and makes it slightly broader (like from cat to caught).

Below is a list of some of the words and names in the story that are pronounced in a way that might not be obvious to someone unfamiliar with Irish.

A ghrá rua—(uh ghraw ROOah) his red-headed love
An phìob mhòr—(an feeb vor) the great pipes
Arasaid—(AIR-ah-sed) a Scottish traditional shawl
As ucht Dé—(as oocht day) for God's sake
Cailín—(cawl-EEN) girl
Cailleach—(CAL-yukh) the Hag goddess
Ceanndána—(kyan-DAW-nah) headstrong
Céili—(KAY-lee) party
Cláirseach—(CLARE-shock) harp
Dia duit/Dia daoibh—(JEE-uh GHITCH/GWEEV)hello - singular/plural
Doit--(DOYt) a small coin
Édaín—(ay-DEEN)
Fionnuala—(finn-NOO-luh)
Geis—(GEE-ish) a curse or prophecy
In ainm Dé—(in AN-im DAY) in God's name

Hy-Brasil—(HI-brass-ILL)
Lus na mban sídhe—(loos na man shee) Plant of the fairy woman
Manannán mac Lír—(MAN-nuh-nahn mac LEER)
M'iníon—(MIN-yeen) my daughter
Mo chailín milis—(mow KHA-leen MEEL-ish) my sweet girl
Mo chailín rua—(mow KHA-leen ROO-uh) my red head lass
Mo chara—(mow KHA-ruh) my friend
Mo cheann dearg—(mow KHYAN dereg) my red one
Mo chroi—(mow KHRE) my heart
Mo leanbh—(mow lennev) my baby
Mo mhuirnín—(mow VOOYR-neen) my darling
Poitín—(po-CHEEN) moonshine
Righin—(REE-hin) rigid
Sí Bheag, Sí Mhor—(shee beg, shee more) small fairy, big fairy
Sídhe—(SHEE) the Faery Folk
Smúid—(smwidge) misty
Teàrlach mhic Seumas—(CHEER-loch vic SHAYmuss) Charles, son of James
Tír na nÓg—(CHEER nuh NOHG) the world of the afterlife

Part I
Chapter One

Ballyshannon, Ireland, April 1745

Éamonn:
Éamonn Doherty relished the clatter of bone as the dice rattled in the cup.

He prayed to Saint Cajetan for luck as he tossed them onto the dirt clearing. He didn't know if an Italian saint would listen to prayers from an Irish Traveler, but prayers never hurt.

Éamonn rolled a nine. A good start for the game of Hazard. Taking a deep swig of his small ale, Éamonn waited while the other player rolled the dice to determine their point. Faded pips on the carved dice faded in flickering firelight. The spring sun had set on the first day of the annual horse fair.

The second player didn't cast well. Éamonn smiled. This would be grand fun. He jabbed his brother in the ribs.

"What?" Ruari hissed.

"Pay attention!"

Éamonn's brother gestured at a gaggle of young women in bright-colored skirts, glancing and giggling and glancing at the gambling men. One woman with dark hair and long legs flashed him an inviting smile. "I'm more interested in the scenery."

"Hmph." At the age of eighteen, Éamonn had fantastic luck with lovely ladies. But when he enjoyed a good run, he got more pleasure from dice. He could always pursue the fillies later. He ran a hand through his short white-blond hair. The dice clicked again.

Occasionally, Ruari tried his chances with gambling. He didn't win often but enjoyed playing. Still, Éamonn liked him nearby in case things got ugly. A bad losing streak might turn the gentlest of men into an angry lout, intent on beating their money from fair winners.

Éamonn glanced to his other side at his cousin, Ciaran Kilbane. He was a better gambler than Ruari, but not as reliable. Éamonn rolled the dice again, hoping to beat the last roll.

An hour later, Ciaran stood without a word. His slim, dark form disappeared into the shadows behind the wagon, into the shadows. Éamonn glanced at Ruari, who shrugged. They grinned when Ciaran returned with a squat stone bottle. He'd brought out the *poitín*.

Since law required a tax on all spirits, many people distilled their own in secret. Ciaran handed the harsh spirit around. Éamonn took a long swig. He spluttered and coughed. This batch tasted rough. Still, strong drink might make his opponents sloppy.

Ruari didn't take a sip. Stolid and steady, Éamonn's brother rarely let himself get out of control. The Rock of Gibraltar, that one.

Staring at the dice, Éamonn blinked twice. His opponent beat him in the latest round. How had that happened? He glared at the *poitín* bottle. Surely he hadn't already gotten so drunk.

He grabbed the dice and rattled his cup with another silent prayer. He closed his eyes, cast, and then opened them. *Ah, there, a winning roll.*

Éamonn loved winning, and he'd been on a good streak since he got to the fair three days before. It thrilled him more than tumbling a fetching young lady or riding a spirited horse. Better than dancing or drinking. As much as he loved the gamble, he couldn't stop when on top. Always one more roll, one more chance to be even better.

He threw again, this time winning the round.

Éamonn couldn't escape.
Gloomy shapes clutched his ankles and arms as he slogged past in slow motion. Every step sank in the boggy ground, no matter how hard he ran.

He sat up with a small cry, panting and sweating.

He'd always suffered from chase dreams. Sometimes, he got away more quickly, but usually not. Éamonn shook the sleep from his head and stumbled to the cooking area, splashing icy water on his face. That shocked him awake, but his head still throbbed. He blew his hooked nose, which set his head pounding anew.

Éamonn hadn't had such a great night. He'd lost everything he won that evening, plus a good portion of his stake. Ah well, he'd win the money back again today. The ponies never let him down.

After he dressed, he wandered through the horse stalls, checking out the racers. With a gentle hand, he examined the muscular flank of a bay cob, then the sturdy neck of a roan, and the white Vanner with white feathers. The Percheron would be no good. Éamonn had no idea why the owner would even enter such a heavy draft horse in a race. The cob had the best chance, though the gelding appeared eager, ready to beat every other racer. He liked the horse's spirit.

Still gazing at the gelding, he turned to go find the betting stall and slammed into someone.

A slim, raven-haired girl with bright blue eyes glared up at him, her hands on her hips and a scowl on her face. She wore a faded blue skirt, a white blouse, and a cream-colored kerchief on her head. One of her eyebrows lifted. "Well?"

Éamonn forced his voice to be nonchalant. "Well, what? I was just walking along, minding my own business—"

"When you decided, with no warning, mind you, to turn on your heel and crash into me. You stepped on my foot!" Freckles stood out stark on her fair skin.

"Ah, well, we can't have that, now, can we? Shall I rub your foot to make it better?" He bent as if to take her shoe off.

The girl skittered back, her scowl deepening. "Don't you touch me."

She's as flighty as a filly. He straightened and arched his eyebrows, trying to keep the smile from his eyes.

She crossed her arms, but her dimples deepened. "Aren't you going to at least apologize?"

He grinned and bowed. "My abject apologies, Mistress—?"

"Deirdre. I'm Deirdre O'Malley."

"Mistress Deirdre. I am Éamonn Doherty, pleased to be at your service." He offered his hand. She placed a hesitant hand on top, so tiny in his own massive palm. When he bent to kiss her fingertips, she snatched her hand away. He still couldn't tell if she was angry or flirting. Perhaps some of both?

She flung her hair off her shoulders and turned to go.

"Wait, Mistress Deirdre, please, don't go just yet!"

The girl halted but didn't turn.

"May I have the honor of a dance this evening?"

Instead of answering, she turned her head, gave him a knowing smile, and skipped off.

He grinned and ran a hand through his hair. *Time to bring out the charm.* The day had brightened already. Regardless of lovely lasses with midnight hair and dimples, he still had to place his bet. He hurried to the betting stalls before the races started.

Éamonn found Ruari there, digging his finger into his ear as the broker took bets. His brother's dirty-blond hair stuck up, so Éamonn jumped up to ruffle it more. Ruari ducked and mock-punched him in the gut. They play-tussled until the broker shooed them off.

Turning to his older brother, Éamonn chucked him on the shoulder. "Which horse did you bet on?"

Ruari startled. "Me? You know I never bet. But Da wanted someone and sent me to fetch him. I thought he'd be here."

"Who does Da want?"

"Some horse trader named Donald. He's a Scot."

Despite his brother outweighing him by several stone, Éamonn stood a few inches taller than Ruari. He rose on his toes and scanned the dusty crowd, searching for plaid. Lots of folks wore checkered cloth, but plaid was rarer. A flash of red plaid showed near the ale booth. "I see him! Ruari, this way." He dashed off through the milling crowd.

Éamonn emerged from the sea of people near the ale booth. The bright-red plaid had disappeared. However, any day could be improved with beer.

His brother caught up, panting. "Where?"

He shrugged, handed the vendor a coin, and drank deep. "He's gone. Sorry, I tried."

"Are you sure you didn't just search for a drink?" With a scowl, Ruari stomped off.

The bell signaled the start of the race. He hadn't placed his bet in time. "Damn it to hell."

He swallowed the last dregs of his beer, wiped his mouth with the back of his sleeve, and stormed off after his brother. If he couldn't bet on the race, he didn't want to watch. Might as well help Ruari.

Despite scanning the crowd, he couldn't find Ruari. Instead, his gaze steadied on two heads of blue-black hair. He recognized his cousin, Ciaran. Could the other be his midnight lass from earlier?

Though they'd just had the brief encounter, he already considered her half-won. He didn't like his younger cousin muscling in on his territory. Éamonn made his way to the fence where the two spoke. The crowd jockeyed for vantage points as the race passed by on the course. He'd lost interest in the horses. While he loved gambling, he wanted to win a different sort of race.

Finally, Éamonn emerged from the crowd, disheveled and panting. Ciaran and Deirdre sat on the fence, speaking with their heads close together. The girl gave a bright smile, her tinkling laugh tugging at him.

Éamonn sauntered by like he hadn't yet noticed them and brushed her sleeve. He stopped as if amazed to find them. "Ah, my lovely Mistress Deirdre. How delightful to see you again and so soon after our earlier...tryst." He made another courtly bow. Women couldn't resist them.

Ciaran narrowed his hazel eyes at the girl. "A tryst?"

Éamonn smiled, showing off his own dimples. "Nothing untoward, I assure you."

Ciaran didn't look assured. The girl flashed a shy smile, which he took as encouragement. "Might I take you down to the river? The water is lovely this time of morning." Éamonn extended his hand.

With a guilty glance at Ciaran, Deirdre took Éamonn's hand and hopped from the fence. She hesitated and then gazed up at Éamonn with bright eyes. Her smile had a most alluring sensual curve, like a woman well-satisfied in bed.

Ciaran spluttered as they walked away, but Éamonn would deal with him later.

They found the path to the river, made muddy with many footsteps.

Éamonn turned to the lovely lass. "Have you traveled far?"

She shook her head, her long hair swaying in the summer breeze. "No, we're just up from Sligo this summer. Last summer, we traveled along the south coast."

Travelers often summered in different places, while wintering in the same location each year. "We usually winter in Donegal."

They spoke of places they'd been as they walked until he found the bend in the river.

His place. A secluded alcove next to the burbling river, embraced by two huge willows. Éamonn spread out his long coat on a flat rock, gesturing her to sit.

Deirdre clapped her hands together. "Oh, this is delightful!"

Taking her hand, he kissed her fingers again. This time, she let him. Her blush enticed him, dappled by the sunlight through the willow branches. Fetching pink blossomed in her cheeks, down her neck, and into the pale-blue kerchief tucked into her bodice. *How much farther does it go?*

She giggled when he turned her hand over and kissed the palm. "That gives me the shivers."

"Do you want me to stop?"

"Nooo—" She peered from under lowered lashes. Her smile curved again as she moved her hand up his leg and towards his manhood. Deirdre's earlier feistiness had devolved into brash sensuality. Éamonn returned the smile and kissed her wrist, light as a feather. She shut her eyes and let out a soft sigh.

He took her reaction as praise and kissed his way up the tender skin of her forearm, the crook of the elbow, and her shoulders. He moved aside the faded cotton shift and kissed more tender places.

Katie:
That afternoon, as Katie shook out a freshly washed blanket, her sister, Deirdre, rushed to their shelter with a flushed face.

In a sharp tone, Katie asked, "What's got you so flustered?"

Deirdre snapped. "None of your business." She pushed by Katie and entered the shelter they'd set up for the fair. The bow tent had saplings bent over and secured, covered in oiled canvas. Long enough to have semi-private sleeping areas, the central chamber had a table, a workbench, and a hearth.

The annual horse fair at Ballyshannon lasted three weeks every spring and drew people from all over northwest Ireland. Despite being for Traveling Folk, *settled* people set up booths selling food, beer, livestock, clothing, and luxuries. The area became a three-week city with several hundred people. Dances and gambling took place most nights, with races and contests during the day. Family groups and Traveler tribes set up camps around the perimeter. Some set up shelters like theirs, while others used their wagons.

The girls' mother, Saoirse, sat at her loom, fastidiously setting up her weft for a new project. The wooden frame only worked for small tasks, not the broadcloth that would sell for a higher price, but the larger loom wouldn't fit in the space. Their father,

Liam, sorted through a trunk in the back. He muttered curses as he pushed through the piles, banging and growling in frustration.

Katie put out her hand. "Ma, I need some pennies. Bread is more expensive this year, and I don't have enough *doit*."

"Nonsense, Caitriona. Just buy horsebread. That's cheap and filling."

Katie wrinkled her nose. Horsebread consisted of beans and dried peas. The dense stuff stuck in her throat and tasted like the horse feed it was.

Their father yanked a platter from the trunk. "Deirdre, come here."

With cautious steps, the younger sister approached.

He piled several dented tin platters on her outstretched arms. "Take this, this…and this, to be sure. Take those down to Sean. Get him to bang them out."

"Yes, sir." She clutched the platters to her chest and skittered out of his reach. When Deirdre spun around, she barreled into her sister. The platters clattered to the ground with an enormous racket.

Deirdre's eyes flashed. "Dolt! Get out of my way!"

"You should watch where you're going!" Katie shouted back, moss-green eyes bright with fury. A tray had landed on her foot, so she hopped back.

Deirdre bent to pick up the platters with a nervous glance at their father, but he paid no attention.

Katie let out a breath of relief. *Good.* As she inspected her toe for damage, Deirdre bumped her with a shoulder. Katie fell on her backside. "You bumped me on purpose!"

Deirdre smiled and opened her eyes wide, all innocence. "Of course, I didn't. Ma, tell her. I just picked up the trays as father needs them fixed. It's your own clumsy self that fell."

"Caitriona, let your sister do her errand. Come help me with this thread."

Deirdre flashed her a nasty, hidden smile. Katie hated weaving with a passion, though she had skill. The wool felt so itchy, and her hands always turned bright red afterward.

Deirdre made her escape and skipped to the tinker's stall.

She'd hoped to get back to the fair this afternoon. She wanted to watch the dance competition. *Damn Deirdre and her manipulations!* She always botched Katie's plans, without even seeming to try.

Katie took her frustrations out on the wool as she untangled the thread, rolling the string into tight balls. Her hands would itch horribly tonight, but she didn't care. She imagined her sister's head as being at the center of each ball and wound it tighter and tighter, cutting off all her air.

Her mother's voice cut through her simmering anger. "Katie! Undo that and rewind it properly. You'll stretch the wool."

She complied with a grimace, her lips pursed in displeasure.

"And stop making faces. You'll never get a husband if you scowl like a sour old maid."

Her parents exchanged a meaningful glance. What had that been about? Her father glared at her. "Katie."

What did I do now? "Yes, Da?"

"No running off tonight. I need you here."

Why? She'd finished her chores. What did he need her home for? Katie wanted to be out dancing and enjoying the fair. Besides, how could she find a husband if she didn't meet anyone?

Her crossness must have shown on her face. In two steps, her father loomed over her. Before she could react, the sharp pain of his fist slammed into the side of her head. Unbidden tears welled up. Katie fought hard to keep from being bowled over. If she kept her head down, she might escape another clout.

Another smack came, then her father stomped back to his trunk. Her right ear pounded. It might have been worse, and the pain would fade. Regardless, she still meant to slip out later, but she'd have to be canny about it.

Katie, as the eldest, had to be married off first. At eighteen, most girls her age had a babe or two. She'd had offers but had driven each one away with her sharp tongue, much to her parents' frustration. She had no wish to be saddled to a man like her father, someone who'd own her and control her entire life. If Katie wanted to escape his cruelty, she'd need to choose well. But none seemed right and, as her family had a poor reputation, her offers dwindled.

How would she escape this evening? They'd allow Deirdre out, of course. Her sister always got more liberties. Deirdre would charm their mother and get whatever she wanted. Katie gritted her teeth against the unfairness.

Father often indulged in drink in the evenings, but he might not fall asleep for hours. They could only afford small beer, which had little effect. Maybe if she found stronger spirits? Several young men drank bottles of *poitín* last night. She might get her hands on one.

With a straight back, Katie handed her mother the ball of wool. "Ma, I'm finished with these. Shall I fetch the horsebread for our supper? I'll come straight back, I promise."

Her mother narrowed her eyes, then reached into the pocket tied to her waistband, pulling out another doit. "Get your da something to drink, too."

Success! She even had funds. Not enough money for what she wanted, but she'd figure something out. Katie bobbed a quick curtsy to her mother and dashed out the door.

The sunlight burned bright after the dim hut, and she squinted, trying to remember the young man from last night. He'd been gambling and came back with a stone bottle, certainly *poitín*. What did he look like? She had a vague impression of black curls. Tall and slim, like one of the Fae. Katie stood too short to see over the heads of the crowd, so she scanned for a vantage point.

Climbing on a fence, she did a quick search. The few tall heads poking through the crowd all looked fair. She spied a young man with white-blond hair stuck up like hay, a ginger lad with frizzy, flyaway hair, there near the tanner's stall, and someone with curly, black hair, young and handsome. Flirting didn't come naturally to Katie, though her sister could charm the birds from the sky. However, when Katie tried hard, she could do well enough.

Katie used her elbows to jostle through the crowd. She hated being so short. At least she had too many curves to be mistaken for a child, and far more than Deirdre.

She found the tanning stall by the reek of the hides. Once inside, Katie searched the shop for her mystery man. He stood behind the counter, dickering with someone who caressed a bridle. Could he be a tanner, then?

Katie browsed the wares, stroking an undyed rabbit skin until he became free. When he completed his dicker, he turned his attention to her.

"Softest rabbit this side of Dublin, mistress!" He flashed a grin, his handsome hazel eyes crinkled in the sun.

She smiled back, fluttering her eyelids. She felt foolish but knew how this play-act worked. "I'm hoping for something… stronger." She peered up at him.

He blushed. How endearing.

Her next smile became more genuine. "To be sure," she glanced around and lowered her voice, "I noticed you had a wee bottle last night. I wondered if you had any to spare for a lass?"

The young man cleared his throat and glanced around, giving her a nervous smile. "Aye, well, yes, I *do* have a few bottles. I'll bring one out tonight at the dance if you like. We could share, uh, some of the drink Miss…?"

Tonight would be too late. "I'm Catriona, but most folks call me Katie. Well, to be honest—"

A wry voice from behind startled her, and she whirled around. "'Tis best to be honest, to be sure." Another of the gamblers loomed over her, the young man with the hair like hay. He bore a wide smile with white, straight teeth.

She glared at the interruption, crossed her arms, and turned back to the black-haired man. "To be honest, I won't come out at all tonight to share anything unless I can get my da to sleep with drink first." She raised her eyebrows and shrugged. "I haven't much coin, but I can pay some." Her fingers brushed her pouch.

The blond man put his hand over hers, his skin cool.

"No need for coin, my dear. Sure and Ciaran would be happy to lend you a bottle, on future consideration, as it were." He winked at her and smiled. She flushed and glanced at Ciaran. He blushed and ducked back into the wagon behind the booth.

Katie turned to the tall blond man. "And what's your name, then?"

He flashed a knowing smile. "Éamonn Doherty, at your service." He tried to bow, but a surge in the crowd jostled him.

His head bumped hers in a painful blow, right where her father had hit her. "Ow! Bloody be-damned eejit! What in Brid's name are you playing at?" She rubbed the sore spot.

A grin escaped as he placed his hand on her head. She batted it away. Ciaran returned with a cool bottle of the needed spirits. He handed the bottle to her, and she realized her act as a sweet, seductive girl had been broken. She schooled her scowl and flashed him a forced, grateful smile. "I'll come find you when I can escape to thank you properly."

This made Ciaran blush again, and her grin widened. He seemed very kind. She turned to glare at his friend. "You, on the other hand, need to move now. I have to get to the baker's stall and home again before I'm missed. Come now, you big oaf, out of my way!" She tried to push past him, but he filled the entrance.

He resisted for a moment but let her pass with a smirk and a mocking bow.

She tied the bottle to her belt, under her skirts, and rushed to the baker's stall, grabbing several loaves of horsebread. Those should last a day or two. The stuff tasted like rotting peas but filled the belly and cost very little. She hadn't even had to use the extra coin. Just as she left the baker, she spied Deirdre flirting with a dark-haired man. Just like her sister to find the handsome lads. Katie made a face and hurried home.

Katie returned to the hut, walking as tall as her short frame would allow. When she approached, two men left with her da. She didn't recognize them, but they looked her up and down as they left. One looked big and burly, older, with short brown hair and hard black eyes. The younger one seemed solid, but with flyaway blond hair and a distant look in his eyes.

She handed the loaves to her mother while still staring back at the door. "Ma? Who were those men?"

Her mother's tone sounded light. "Just someone your da is dealing with. They're hoping to sell a horse, I think."

"Horses? How can we afford horses? We can barely afford horsebread!"

Her mother's tone snapped back to its normal sharpness. "You leave the dealings to your da. Your place isn't to second guess his business."

Katie hid the bottle in a place Da would find it, but not Mam. Mam would keep him from getting too drunk. She'd need to distract her mother so her da would drink the *poitín*.

"Ma? I saw new fabrics in the stalls when I bought the bread. They had fine serge, not expensive at all. Would you come see? The fabric might work for the garments you're making to sell, to bring up the class, I mean."

Her mother narrowed her eyes before saying, "Grand, then, we'll go out. Your da will be back soon."

Her mother bought some of the serge, and when they returned, Da sat in his alcove. The bottle had disappeared, and Katie smiled to herself. Her plan might work, for once. She put the success down to Deirdre not being around.

She choked down her portion of the horsebread and washed each stodgy mouthful down with water. Her father didn't even glare at her throughout dinner. She retreated to her sleeping area, drew the curtain, and listened.

After her mother went to her alcove to sleep, and her father passed out from the drink, Katie slipped on a brightly colored overskirt and a shawl, escaping into the cool April evening air.

Chapter Two

Katie:

Dusk fell with intense indigo, a blanket snuggling around the fair folks, keeping them safe and sound against the outside world.

Katie searched for fire and noise and found several groups. Several musicians played for a crowd of reveling dancers near the racetrack.

She loved music, especially singing. At least, she used to until Deirdre mocked her. Their father had little use for such frivolities. But song took her away on wings of freedom. Besides, she had a duty to the sweet, blushing Ciaran. Would a kiss be adequate payment for his kindness? She grinned in anticipation of satisfying her debt, while twitching her sleeve down to cover a bruise on her arm.

Dust rose around the dancers as the musicians struck up a jig. Firelight glowed like the pits of Hell. Perhaps she'd end up in hell for her manipulations, but she didn't care how wicked she felt. She needed some fun.

Katie spied the dark curls of her quarry. He sat with the blond man—Éamonn?—and a bulky man about the same age. An older man with pale hair sat beyond them. She frowned as her sister's laugh pealed out. Perhaps she shouldn't join them. Deidre would just make the situation difficult. She turned to leave just as Ciaran called out to her, "Katie!"

With a sigh, she strode to the group. "Ciaran, how lovely to see you again." He scooted over to make a space for her as Deirdre scowled.

Katie returned her sister's scowl. "Da asked after you."

"You're a liar. He never did."

Katie shrugged. "If you want to risk that, be my guest."

Ciaran cleared his throat and gestured to the blond as he handed her a stone bottle. "This is my cousin, Éamonn. That big brute there is his brother, Ruari. And Turlough, he's my uncle." She greeted each man with a nod, but Éamonn's attention returned to something Deirdre murmured in his ear. Her sister's giggle grated on Katie's nerves.

Katie took a drink from the bottle. Ciaran must have an endless supply of the stuff. She passed the bottle to Éamonn on her other side. Before he could accept, Deirdre pulled Éamonn to his feet and dragged him into the dancing area. His blond hair glinted in the bonfire. He grinned as he sent an apologetic glance to his cousin. Ciaran shrugged and grabbed the abandoned bottle, took a swig, and passed it on to Ruari. Then he got up to go behind a wagon. Katie considered following him. She felt abandoned. But she realized he likely just needed to relieve himself.

Their father, Turlough, looked more like Éamonn. Not as tall, but with the same blond hair, a shade or two darker and worn in a long ponytail. As the musicians took a break, he regaled them with a hilarious tale about a donkey. His hand rested on his harp behind him. Perhaps later he'd play as well.

Her spine shot straight. A voice like her father's called out, and her heartbeat raced. When she looked around for the source, she found some other man. She stilled her speeding heart and took several deep breaths.

As Katie watched the dancing, she recognized two of the dancers. The men who'd left their tent after speaking with her father danced with two girls. They seemed too young for the men, at least a few years younger than herself. The girls looked like twins, with matching dark curls.

Katie played with her own red curl, sparkling cinnamon in the dying light. She dropped the lock as she'd always hated her hair. So different and bright, not elegant like her sister's straight, dark tresses.

Deirdre plopped down next to her, panting from the dance. When Katie raised an eyebrow, her sister scowled back. "What?"

Katie shook her head. "I didn't say anything."

"You looked at me as if you wanted to."

Katie rolled her eyes. "If I wanted to say something, I would have. You're imagining things."

Ciaran sat between them and turned to her with shining eyes and another blush. "Might I collect the reward you promised earlier, Mistress Caitriona?"

Katie liked the way he used her full name, making her sound adult and sophisticated. She dropped her gaze. The coy act always worked for Deirdre. "I suppose that's only right. You're the only reason I could come tonight, after all."

After leaning over, she planted a light kiss on his lips. His arm reached around her shoulders, controlling the length. He pressed his lips firmly to hers, holding the kiss longer than she'd intended.

When they broke contact, his eyes glittered. "Ah, a sweeter reward one could not ask for, to be sure." A stray curl flopped down his forehead, and he brushed the lock aside.

She grinned back, feeling silly. Despite his shyness, he must have a romantic heart. Deirdre made a rude noise.

Katie turned to her sister. "Did you say something, Deirdre? Or did a donkey join us?"

Deirdre rolled her eyes. "No, that was your own backside talking."

Katie clenched her fists, ready to smack that smug look off her sister's face when Ciaran placed a hand on her shoulder. She turned back to his liquid brown eyes and lost herself in their depth.

Their interlude shattered when a dancer passed too close and stomped on her instep. Pain shot through her foot. "Ow! Oaf!" Katie yelled. The blond horse trader stumbled, trying to regain his balance. Ciaran sprung to his feet, but Turlough pulled him back down. The dancer scowled at Ciaran as he careened into Turlough.

The other horse trader called out in a Scottish accent. "Pay attention, Lochlann!" His voice sounded low, gruff, and he carried himself like a fighter. He glared at Katie and Ciaran as he yanked on Lochlann's arm. They stalked off, muttering.

Why in Brid's name are they angry with me? That Lochlann was the clumsy eejit. She snorted and turned back to Ciaran, but he'd disappeared.

The circle grew silent as the musicians stopped playing. Turlough lifted his great harp, his *cláirseach*. The elegant instrument, as tall as she, had an exquisitely decorated sound box. Interlaced designs traced from the box up into the top, which held a double row of strings. Katie held her breath. She'd only heard harp music once, long ago as a child, like angels singing. As soon as Turlough plucked the strings, all conversation jangled to a halt.

Liquid notes sang across the silence like raindrops of honey. Notes melded and harmonized as Turlough's hands climbed up and down in a heavenly glide. When he stopped, Katie felt the halt like a sharp pain.

The older man spoke with a soft, musical voice. "Now that I have everyone's attention, I shall play a tune by my namesake, Turlough O'Carolan, the last true bard of Ireland."

Everyone knew of O'Carolan, a blind bard who'd traveled the countryside fifty years ago, composing and playing music. His music lived on.

The tune began slow and dreamy, with a majestic rhythm. the melody repeated faster, growing lively. The surrounding people danced to the enchanting tune. Katie's feet itched to join them. With a nod from Turlough, she rose and searched for a way into the circle of dancers.

Two people parted, grabbing her hands. Katie spun until her skirts billowed out, almost touching the fire in the middle of the circle. She turned until dizzy, the *poitín* buzzing in her ears, and fell laughing into someone's arms. Ruari's grin almost reached ear to ear. They shared a laugh as he brought her to her feet. He smelled of leather and soap.

Turlough began another tune, a sprightly jig. Ruari offered his hand. With a grin, she accepted, and he whirled her around. While she delighted in the sheer feminine feel of being spun about like a top, she underestimated his strength and stumbled. The next man caught her as she worked around the circle. She grew breathless by the time the melody ended. Fanning herself to cool off, she escaped to sit on a log.

Ciaran still hadn't returned, and she felt exposed with no one beside her. Where had everyone gone? Katie didn't see either Éamonn or Ciaran. Lochlann and the other man had also disappeared. Deirdre danced with a young redheaded lad. She kept glaring back at Katie.

Turlough took a break, sipping from his cup. A grunt from the darkness startled her. She peered into the gloom, trying to identify the sound.

Two grappling men burst from the shadows. Gasps rang out as they staggered close to the flames. They steered away from the danger just as another man joined the scuffle. Éamonn tried to pull the two fighters apart.

Ciaran punched the blond man who'd knocked into her earlier, Lochlann. Each struggled to get free. As they staggered, Éamonn scored a punch to Lochlann's kidney, but Lochlann kicked him away. A fourth man, Lochlann's companion, waded into the fray, striking Ciaran's ear. Éamonn tripped this new man but lost balance, tumbling into the ashes. Dust billowed and stung her eyes as the fighters collided with the dancers.

Katie glanced at Turlough, but he remained calm. This must not be the boys' first fight. Then she realized why Turlough appeared unconcerned. Ruari had arrived.

While large and slow, once he got going, no one could stop the giant of a man. He waded in, pounding his huge fist into the new man's nose. Katie winced at the sickening *crunch*. Ruari then shot a jab into Lochlann's shoulder, and the Scot spun away from Ciaran.

Lochlann stumbled toward the fire, pulling Éamonn with him. They both fell into the flames. Sparks flew up and chunks of wood scattered. Katie jumped up, a scream ripping from her throat. Other shrieks filled her ears.

As Lochlann rolled out of the flames, Katie rushed to Éamonn, yanking on his shirt to pull him out, but she couldn't budge him. His shirt ripped when she tried again. Why wouldn't anyone else help? She slipped and fell next to him, her legs burned from the heat, but she scrambled to her knees and tugged at his shirt again.

Someone lifted her like a toy and set her down away from the fire. She glanced up as Ruari extracted Éamonn. Her legs hurt.

Katie batted frantically at her skirts. They smoldered with embers. She slapped them until the glow died. She coughed several times, staring at the charred edges of fabric.

"Come, Katie, ye'r burned. I'll take ye to the healer's tent." Turlough drew her to her feet.

She must have whimpered. Turlough tightened his grip on her shoulders. "Ye'll be fine, my dear, to be sure. Just let Cormac look at those burns before ye go to yer bed, aye?"

The healer's tent sat on the north edge of the fair. Larger than most, the dark, cool interior soothed her. Several braziers lit the space. Ruari carried Éamonn, with no sign of Ciaran. Ruari's face looked ashen as he lay his unconscious brother on a cot with gentle hands. Katie glanced at Turlough, his own expression pinched.

Lochlann lay on another cot, conscious but quiet. His companion sat beside him, glaring at Ruari and Éamonn.

"Ah, then, let me get to the lad here first. He seems to have gotten the worst of the fire." A fluttering little man, no taller than Katie, fussed around Éamonn. *He must be the healer, Cormac.* After a few muttered oaths, he glanced up at Ruari. The older man's head barely reached Ruari's shoulders.

"Young man. I can be *much* more effective if you will move your enormous hulking self out of my light!"

Such a tiny man being so demanding of the young giant gave Katie an uncontrollable fit of the giggles. For a moment, her own pain faded. But the laughter started her coughing once more. Then her legs throbbed again, and she let out a whimper. Turlough brought a cup, and she sipped the cool water. She flashed him a grateful smile.

Ruari backed up but kept his eyes glued to his brother, who'd suffered enough burns around his scalp to make his blond hair patchy. Cormac fussed with jars and salves lined up on the shelves. He bent over his bowl, mixing several ingredients with a marble pestle. He sniffed the concoction, rubbed the salve on his skin, and added a pinch of something else. Eventually, he applied the concoction to Éamonn's skin. Katie smelled eggs and butter. "Are you treating burns or making a meal?"

The healer chuckled. "Aye, well, the butter both soothes the burns and forms a barrier to keep the dirt out. The eggs make the stuff stick." He muttered as he worked his way down his patient's arms and torso. He peered up, blinking several times before his gaze fell on Ruari. "You! Giant! I need you to flip this man over."

With Turlough's help, they turned Éamonn onto his stomach, and the healer continued his ministrations. A faint moan escaped from the patient. Katie's heart skipped a beat.

Lochlann's companion growled. "Hurry up, healer! He's not the only one hurt!"

The tiny healer halted, glaring at the man. "One patient at a time, good man, one at a time. Your man will bide, I'm certain." He bent to his task.

Lochlann's voice came high and reedy, like the wind whistling through a lonely moor, in contrast to his thick chest. "Donald, leave it. I'm fine for the moment."

Cormac finished his work on Éamonn, adding bandages to the worst burns. He asked Ruari to flip him back over, which resulted in more painful moans.

Moving to Lochlann, Cormac checked his wounds, but the Scot shook his head. "Attend the young lady first if you please. I'll be fine for a time, as you say."

Giving Donald a long, smug look, the healer came to Katie's side. He tsked-tsked at her burnt skirts, then applied the eggy salve to her calves. She let out a sigh at the relief, cool and soothing. She winced when Cormac touched a few places near her ankles. At one point, she almost kicked his face.

With a wry smile, he took firm grip of her foot. "You've done the nerves no damage, then. That's all to the good."

She giggled again, but then the laugh morphed into a cough.

"You'll be right as rain in a day or three, my dear. Now, to the young man." The healer turned to Lochlann.

As Katie gingerly stepped off her cot, she glanced at Turlough. "Will you let me know how he fares? I'll come visit in the morning if I may?"

Cormac clapped a hand on her shoulder and gave her a kind smile. "Of course, lass."

She kept her voice low. "Do you have any idea why they fought?"

"Sure, and the young lad there stepped on you. That darkhaired boy, Ciaran, he threw the first punch, but Éamonn took up the banner. At least, that's what Ciaran told me."

Katie glanced around for the young man. "Ciaran? Where is he? Did he get hurt? When did you speak to him?"

"While you acted the hero and pulled Éamonn from the fire. I thank you for trying to save my bull-headed son." He sketched a bow to her and this time, her blush was genuine.

"I shouldn't have tried, I know. But I couldn't just sit and wait for someone else to help."

"That's all to the good. You go along home, now. I'm certain yer parents will be worried sick about you."

She snorted. "That's how much you know. They'll both be dead to the world."

While picking her way back to the tent in the near darkness, she glimpsed Deirdre leaning into Ciaran's shoulder, staring at the smoldering remnants of the fire. Well, isn't that the way things always went? She got burned and bruised while Deirdre got the man. This night had been a total disaster.

Katie:

Late the next afternoon, Katie stood by Éamonn's cot, holding a cup. Despite her red cheeks, his smile brightened the room. Her heart beat faster. "I brought you some cider."

He couldn't drink lying down. Should she offer to help him sit up? One big burn marred his tanned cheek, already turning red and black with a scab. A bruise showed on his temple, and her cheek throbbed in sympathy.

Éamonn managed a weak smile. "Thank you, Katie. That's kind of you. Can you place the cup on the table?"

She put the drink out of the way and sat on the stool, picking at her nails.

Éamonn started. "Why did you leave—"

"I hoped you'd come—" Katie said.

They both stopped and shared a chuckle. He smiled, taking her hand. "Thank you for what you tried to do. Da's regaled me with tales of your bravery. And you such a wee thing."

"It was stupidity, is what it was. I couldn't do much good, after all."

"Ah, but you tried. A more gallant champion no man could ask for." His grin lit up his face, and his blue-green eyes shone. She fell into those eyes.

Ciaran wasn't the only one in the family with a romantic streak. Her face grew warm, and she stared at the floor. When had she turned into this fragile flower? "I only saved a fool from being foolish. Did Cormac say how long you'd be off your feet?"

The gleam returned to his eyes. "I won't be dancing for a day or two, if you're asking."

Turlough lifted the tent flap and peeked in. When he saw Katie, he turned to leave, but she gestured him over. "No, Turlough, come sit with us."

With reluctance, the older man pulled up a second stool. He cocked his head at Katie. "Are ye feeling well, dear one? Are your burns healing?"

"They itch horribly, but Cormac gave me more salve."

"Burns? Da, you didn't tell me Katie got hurt!" Éamonn struggled to sit up, but his father pressed him down to the cot.

She put a hand on the cool skin of his arm. "I'm not hurt, Éamonn. My skirts got crispy."

Éamonn glared at his father. Turlough returned the accusatory look with raised eyebrows and a shrug.

Katie changed the subject. "Turlough, what's the name of the last tune you played before this eejit started a fight and make himself a walking bonfire?" She still didn't know where she recognized that tune from, only that the music reminded her of flowers.

He glanced at the tent roof for a moment before snapping his fingers. "The last one… Ah, 'twas *'Sí Bheag, Sí Mhor'*. O'Carolan's first composition, so the tale goes."

"I enjoyed the tune very much. So light and airy." Katie tried to hum it, but the tune eluded her.

The older man clasped his hands in his lap. "There's a legend about the tune, so they say. Y'see, O'Carolan had spent the night out on the road when a storm blew through. He found no shelter but an ancient stone dolmen out on the open moor. The bard sat shivering under the three stones while the storm whipped and twisted around him." Turlough's voice turned gentle. "He drifted off to sleep while the wind raged."

Katie's eyes grew wide. Falling asleep near the Fae stones never turned out well.

"He woke in a place he'd never seen, with no sun and no moon. With a sky neither bright nor dark, but trees glowing with their own light. Mist drifted everywhere and muffled music filled the air."

"The Otherworld?"

Turlough nodded. "Aye, the land of the Fair Folk, as some call the Fae. He knew, from other legends, how dangerous it could be for a mortal in the Otherworld. Many never came back. Others returned hundreds of years later, only to turn to dust, like Oisín. And some escaped with horrible disfigurements, like a clubbed foot, blind, or deaf."

Katie leaned forward. "And they blinded him?"

Turlough nodded. "Indeed, so the story goes. But the Fae didn't take his eyes out of spite. They bestowed their music upon him, the very music he heard amongst the trees. They say he then wrote dozens, hundreds of tunes on paper. And those tunes he learned from the Fair Folk themselves."

Katie would never choose to be blind, even for such a gift. To never gaze upon another sunrise across the glittering sea. Or the sweet smile of a young man. "How did he escape?"

"No one's certain. Some say he slept again and woke under the dolmen. Others claim he entertained the Fae Queen at her court, and the Fae music became a reward for his entertainment. Others say he never returned at all, but a changeling replaced him." Turlough's face faded as if remembering a long-ago dream.

"And you're named for him?"

Turlough nodded. "So I'm told."

Éamonn jumped in, an impish grin on his face. "Don't let him fool you. O'Carolan's his father."

"Your father? Truly?"

Turlough shook his head with a chuckle. "That may be true or may not. I'll never know. He visited my mother often, though, and they say I've some of his talent. Perhaps my mother wished to honor a dear friend. Or perhaps not. She didn't marry until I turned three, to Peadar Doherty. She'd never say who my father was, and she passed on long ago before O'Carolan married at age fifty, to be sure."

Katie had never met anyone famous. Or the son of someone famous. "I love the old tales, like the one you told last night. Do you know many?"

Éamonn let out a laugh. "Katie, my da knows all the tales in Ireland. He'll talk your ear off if you give him the chance. And mine, too, so don't ask here! I'm trapped, a prisoner without parole."

With a grin, Katie cocked her head. "And have you learned no stories yourself? Are you daft after all?"

He rolled his eyes. "I have indeed, by force! I prefer the battle tales, truth be told."

"Of course you do. Men love fighting, as you proved last night." She glowered at him, but a smile twitched free. "My favorites are the ones with magic. Like the boat that could hold as many people as needed but looked like a tiny curragh."

Turlough nodded. "That would be Lugh's boat, *Wave Sweeper,* young lady."

"That's the one!"

The older man studied her for a moment. "My mother, she bore the O'Malley name, like you. Perhaps a distant relation, even?"

"What was her name?"

"Maeve O'Malley, she was. From County Clare. Somewhere in the north, across the bay from Galway."

Katie shook her head. "I don't know of any family in that area. Most of us are Travelers, though, so we could be from anywhere."

"No, she was Settled Folk. Peadar had been the Traveler. Ah, well. That would've been a pleasant coincidence." Katie noticed he didn't call Peadar his father.

She glanced outside and saw the long shadows. "Well, I should get back home. My mother will miss me soon."

Éamonn grabbed her hand, his grip stronger than she expected. He stared deep into her eyes. "Thank you again, Mistress Katie. I am indebted to you."

"It's just being neighborly, to be sure."

What had made her so prone to blushing? She nodded to Turlough as she rushed out.

Éamonn:

Turlough's mouth curled into a half-smile as he watched the short redhead flee the healer's tent. "That one is a handful, so she is."

The girl entranced Éamonn. She grew hot and cold in turns, like his gut when he spoke with her. Half the time, he couldn't tell if she hated him or loved him. "She might well be. I wouldn't mind trying to tame her." He tried to sit up to drink the cider, but that bumped his burned skin. He let out a hiss.

His father leveled a look at him. "Don't trifle with that one, son. She's the all-or-nothing sort. You either marry her or forget her, mark my words."

"Sure, and tell that to Ciaran. He's the one who's kissed her. I kissed her sister, Deirdre. Of course, Ciaran got *her*, too." Éamonn couldn't keep the sour jealousy from his voice.

"Ciaran isn't strong enough to handle Katie. She's too spirited for his gentle soul. As much as I love my nephew, he simply tries too hard to please."

Éamonn snorted. "He just wants to be loved."

Turlough chuckled. "We all love him, even if he doesn't realize it. He's family, after all. His problem is he wants to be worshipped."

He chuckled but didn't argue. Arguing with his da never worked. His father might be the true son of the Last Bard, and may even be Fae-touched himself, but he didn't play the fool, either.

"Éamonn, I wanted to ask you, did you fetch something from my music bag yesterday? Or Ruari?"

"Music bag? You know I don't touch that, Da."

Da didn't write everything down, but some tunes deserved saving. Turlough took careful note of anything composed by

24

O'Carolan, either out of sentimentality or sheer appreciation of the music. He kept these treasures in a leather shoulder bag.

As a lad of twelve, Éamonn found his father's music bag. He lifted the soft, worn leather flap. His hand tingled, stronger than the spark from stroking animal fur on a dry day. Strong enough to knock him back a few feet. He'd never touched the bag again.

Éamonn took a sip of his cider, wincing as the skin on his cheek stretched. "Do you think Ciaran might have gone through the bag?"

Turlough shook his head. "I don't know. Some papers are missing."

"Which ones?"

"Some of O'Carolan's music. They took tunes I didn't yet know by heart, too. Well, the music is precious to me. See if you can ask around, aye? Someone might have heard something."

"From my sickbed? I'll not be much use here, Da."

His da patted his leg, well away from any burned skin. "Well, I can't ask Ruari, can I? He's not got the wit to ferret out such things. And Ciaran—"

"Why would Ciaran want them?"

While staring at the ground, Turlough's eyes turned sad. "I don't know, son. Truly, I don't. Perhaps he wanted to trade for them. Perhaps he wanted the music for himself, though God knows why. The man can't play an instrument to save his life. Maybe he is playing some game of stealing them so he can find them and be the hero. Just see what you can find, aye?"

"I'll do what I can. Cormac said I should be up and about tomorrow."

Turlough slapped his hands on his knees. "That's grand, then. I'll send Ruari in with dinner for ye later, so."

"Will you need help with the booth, Da? Ruari isn't the best trader—"

"We'll be fine. Ciaran is good with a dicker if nothing else. And his leatherwork is high quality." With a pat on Éamonn's shoulder, a part with no burns, Turlough struggled to his feet.

"And do be careful with the girls?" After lifting his hands high to crack his back, Turlough left the tent.

Chapter Three

Deirdre:
She couldn't believe Katie had been so bold. Well, she'd paid for her audacity, true enough. And if Deirdre had anything to say in the matter, she'd continue to pay. After all, she'd spied the tall, blond lad first. Éamonn had taken _her_ to the riverbank, not Katie. Her older sister always managed to ruin everything. This time, Deirdre wouldn't let her ruin things.

With a few judicious hints to their parents, Deirdre ensured that Katie was kept at the tent over the next few days. She used this time to flirt with Éamonn and Ciaran. While she would much prefer to snag Éamonn, Ciaran was sweet enough. Besides, flirting was fun, and having two men to play off each other improved her chances with her desired target. Jealousy was a powerful tool, and she'd used it many times in the past to increase her own desirability.

Besides the sheer fun of their flirting, it gave her a chance to get away from their father. While he was far harder on Katie for any infringement, Deirdre had felt his heavy hand too many times to count. She meant to find a way to escape him once and forever.

Éamonn would be an excellent escape plan.

Éamonn:
Two days later, Éamonn made a plan, determined to spirit the fair Katie away for a private tryst. His favorite spot by the river would be perfect. He packed his bag with cider, cheese, bread, and a soft blanket. When he reached for the bread, he winced as the bruises on his arm twinged. He rubbed at the still-healing scabs.

After a search, he found her sitting on a fence, already deep in conversation with Ciaran. Clenching his fist tight around the basket handle and flashing his cousin a scowl, Éamonn joined them. Why, under the sun, must Ciaran muscle in on his women? And why did fair Katie flutter her eyelids at him? No matter what Turlough said, the lass was a lovely blossom for some lucky bee.

Just as he opened his mouth to say something angry to Ciaran and make a fool of himself, he realized he needed to be gracious. "Are you both hungry? I brought some food."

Éamonn pulled out a wheat loaf and broke the bread into thirds. "I hoped to lure Mistress Catriona away for a walk along the river?" He hooked his arm out in invitation.

Katie glared at him. "Are you so sure of yourself, then? That you can just sweep me off my feet? Not with that smarmy smile on your face!"

"Uh, well I…"

She raised her chin. "I'm not a prize to be won, nor am I one to be led all innocent to a life of sin, Éamonn Doherty. You'd best keep that in mind."

He caught a tinge of uncertainty in her voice, the quick flick of her eyes from him to Ciaran and back again.

Turning to his cousin, she smiled sweetly. "Ciaran, would you do me the kind honor of escorting me to my tent?"

With a gloating grin, Ciaran hopped down and offered his arm. She hooked her hand into his elbow, and they marched off.

But she came to visit me in the healer's tent! Did she like Ciaran better? He wished she'd make her feelings clear. This isn't fair at all.

As Éamonn's anger and jealousy faded into rueful regret, he crafted a different plan. This might be more difficult than he'd expected, but her recent disdain only fanned the flame of his desire.

The next day, he sought out her family's tent with a fresh pack of food and drink. Katie worked in the communal space behind several wagons, hanging laundry, her face soaked with sweat and the cloth dripping with soap. Lines had been strung across trees, with about half the space left. Her hair frizzled, escaping her kerchief and framing her face in a russet glow. Disheveled and gorgeous, she took his breath away.

A rare fine day, with the sun bright and hot. Not a cloud showed in the sky. A light breeze kept the weather cool but not strong enough to be cold.

He should approach and offer to help. But for some reason, he stayed hidden in the bushes, watching her work. He admired her lithe body and smiled as she stretched tall to pin the fabric to the line.

Katie bent to grab the next piece of laundry, and Éamonn recognized the skirt burned in the fire. The charred edge showed clear on the bright fabric.

Éamonn hadn't even noticed her father approaching before the older man snatched the skirt out of her hand and brandished the sopping garment in her face. "What's this? How can you be so careless with your clothing? And you woman old enough to marry? You clumsy oaf!"

He hit her, an open-handed slap against her cheek, and she fell into the dirt. She stared down, unwilling to look up. Finally, he threw the skirt into the mud and stomped off. As he disappeared into their tent, she struggled to her feet.

Éamonn hid deeper into the bushes, horrified at what he'd just witnessed. Sure, and people hit their children all the time, and husbands their wives. But Katie's father's blows had been so random, so unfair. Guilt washed over him for being the cause of her burnt skirt and, therefore, at her beating.

Katie brushed her skirts and touched her cheek gingerly, already turning red. She heaved a deep sigh and reached for the next piece of clothing to pin. To his surprise, she hummed. Perhaps she did so in defiance of her father's discipline. Regardless, the lighter mood gave him a welcome reason to emerge.

He shouldered his bag and strode from the bushes. "Your sweet voice could call the angels down from Heaven, so it could."

She whirled around at the voice over her shoulder. The sopping wet skirt in her hands slapped against Éamonn's hip, making a smacking sound. He jumped back in surprise.

"By all that's holy! What are you trying to do, drown me?"

"You shouldn't sneak up on people!" She visibly trembled. She must still be wary of her father's wrath.

"That's the fine thanks I get for giving you a compliment."

With a narrowed gaze, she cocked her head. "Oh, compliments, is it? Is that what they call spying these days?"

He sighed. "Can we start again?"

She glowered but gave him a reluctant nod.

"Mistress Caitriona O'Malley, I came to ask if you would care to walk with me on this fine day. May I escort you?" He patted the strap of his pack and offered his arm, posh and polite, as a lord of the manor might ask a lady. She chuckled, a welcome respite from Deirdre's giggling.

She placed her hand in the crook of his elbow with a grin. "Very well, sir. Shall we? Oh, but…I have to do the laundry first."

He let out a laugh and dropped his arm. "Here, I'll help you finish. Then we can be away more quickly."

With raised eyebrows, she drew back. "A man? Helping with the washing? How does that happen?"

He gave a shrug. "I help out often as a matter of fact. The men outnumber the women in our household, so I'm used to lending a hand. Besides, the more quickly you finish, the more quickly you can escape." He dropped his voice to a bare whisper, "And your da is less likely to hit you again."

Her face burned bright red, and she glanced back at the tent.

Éamonn took her hand. "Come. You hand me the pieces, and I'll pin them. I'm taller."

She handed him the skirt she had held when he'd surprised her. With a chuckle, he took the garment and pinned it to the line. "Does my help mean I can entice you with lunch afterward?"

Katie gave him a side-long glance. "Like I said before, I'm no man's prize."

After witnessing her getting hit, he wanted to make her smile. "No, surely you are not. You are a fair flower, and I'm but a buzzing bee, hoping to drink of your sweet nectar."

Instead of smiling, she narrowed her gaze. "Hmm. If we get done in enough time, perhaps."

He'd have to try a different tack if he wanted to cheer her up. "And what if I just—" Éamonn splashed the rinse water on her. She'd already been well-soaked, but her color rose. He itched to touch the heat of her skin.

"If you keep playing like that, the answer will be no."

He complied with mock submission but grinned. "Yes, Mistress Katie." Though she looked fierce, the corner of her mouth twitched up. He hid his own smile, knowing he made progress.

Once they finished the laundry, she glanced back at the tent. "I really ought to return home. My father…"

He rubbed his head but had forgotten about his burn scabs and gave a grimace. "Your father won't miss you yet. I'll get you back in good time."

Still, her eyes flicked back over her shoulder. He lifted her chin and saw fear in her eyes. "Hey, now. You've naught to be afraid of. I'll never hurt you, Katie. I promise you."

"No, I'm not worried about you." She gave a nervous glance toward the tent. "But Da's got a fearful temper."

Éamonn remembered the anger on her father's face when he cuffed her. His blood grew cold at that memory, and he fought the urge to spirit her away immediately, but he daren't. He spoke gently. "Would you like to talk about your da?"

She shook her head and tried to pull away, but he held her close, drawing her into a warm embrace. Her body trembled, and he gripped harder to quell the fear.

This had turned into more than a summer conquest. His desire to help Katie escape her father itched his soul. "Would an hour be all right? Would you be safe?"

Katie:

The laundry went more quickly than Katie had imagined. They worked through the basket and off in no time. She grabbed her woolen shawl in case the wind picked up.

They climbed through the wooded hills into the marshland beyond. As they picked their way through the bog, Katie asked, "Where on earth are you taking me? Should I be worried?"

"No, no, just a spot my father likes to go when he wants quiet. A special place, I assure you."

"It had better be. This isn't a trek for the faint-hearted!" Her breath came shorter as they climbed through the fens.

"Not much longer now."

They came around a large bush filled with light green spring buds, and she gasped as she spied the stones, like someone had built a flat hill in the center of the marsh and plopped the stones evenly in a circle. *Well, and perhaps they had.* Legends of the Fair Folk and giants swam through her head, a jumble of tales and songs. Her mind spun with too much imagination.

The stones felt warm from the sun, and she took comfort from that. Éamonn sat next to her and took her hand.

Katie finally caught her breath. "Standing stones. They say you can ask the faeries a favor at standing stones."

"You said you liked the tales with magic. What's more magic than faery stones? But I'd be wary of asking for any favors. You might not like the price they ask."

She let out a rueful laugh. "I suppose you're right. I'm surprised you remembered."

"I remember everything you said, *mo chara*. I've also got a surprise for you."

She narrowed her eyes. While she liked him a lot more when he acted genuine than when he pretended to be a man of the world, she didn't trust which mask he'd wear today. "What sort of surprise?"

Her suspicion must have amused him because he chuckled. "A tasty one!"

After slinging the leather bag from over his shoulder, he unpacked their feast. He brought out several pears, a couple of goat's cheeses, two stone bottles, a fresh loaf of barley bread, and spicy sausage.

Éamonn picked out two pears, shined one on his shirt, handing the fruit to her with a grin. She nibbled as she watched him, relishing any meal other than the stodgy, disgusting horsebread. The warmth from the stones made her pull off her woolen shawl.

This Éamonn, he's an odd one. He seemed smitten by her sister but treated her with such kindness. He remembered her fondness for magical stories, and that warmed her heart. But a polished player would act so, wouldn't he? He'd planned this interlude and designed the romance to compromise her.

Well, unlike Deirdre, she wouldn't be bought so cheaply. "You said your father comes here?"

"Mmhm." He finished swallowing a slice of pear. "He especially likes to come here in the morning before the mists lift. He says the stones sing to him."

Katie shivered. She liked the tales but messing about with the Fae would be right dangerous. She crossed herself.

Oddly, this didn't amuse Éamonn as everything else seemed to. He simply nodded and crossed himself as well.

After he finished his pear, Éamonn picked a flower, twirling the stem in his fingers. In a casual tone, he asked, "You seem to like Ciaran a lot."

Katie didn't answer but plucked the flower from his hands. With a grin, he picked two more and tucked them behind her ear.

"What about your mother? Does she not come to the fair?"

He shook his head, the first time she had ever seen his face sad. "She died after she bore my little sister, Síle."

A flood of sympathy came over her, and she regretted asking such a painful question. She placed a hand on his arm in apology. "Oh, I'm that sorry. How old were you? Do you remember her much?"

Éamonn stared at his hand. "Ten. I remember her clearly, though usually only flashes and scenes. She looked pale and frail, like a changeling. She had eight, with five living children."

Tears fell down his cheeks. Katie dabbed the wetness with her kerchief. He blinked several times and sniffed. His nose, already a prominent hook shape, now shone red. She handed him the kerchief.

He honked into the cloth a few times until he got back under control. He peered at the piece of cloth and then at her.

She shook her head with a sympathetic smile. "Keep it. I have others."

"Thanks, *mo chailín rua*." He tucked it into his bag and placed a hand on hers.

The endearment made her unaccountably warm inside. Normally, she disliked people mentioning her bright red, unruly hair. But to be called *my red one* made her skin tingle.

"That's when Da started wandering."

Katie's eyes grew wide. "Wandering? With five children and a newborn babe?"

His voice sounded flat, a far cry from his usual jovial tone. "No, no, he left most of us with our aunt and uncle. He did take Ruari with him, the biggest. I don't think he could handle seeing Síle every day, knowing she killed Mam."

She sniffed back impending tears. "That's one of the saddest things I've ever heard."

Éamonn squeezed her hand. When she looked into his eyes, they looked eternally blue. For a moment, the world around them froze.

The wind picked up and whistled around the stones. Newly sprouted grasses shifted in the breeze. A raven squawked in the distance, several others answered, and the spell broke.

Éamonn sighed. "Well, that's all past history, so it is. I'm meant to be dazzling you with my winning personality not depressing you with tragic tales." He handed her one of the stone bottles.

Her sharp tone returned, unbidden. "Oh, and so what *had* you wanted?" She unstopped the bottle and cautiously sniffed, mindful of his access to Ciaran's *poitín*. However, she smelled small ale. She took a grateful gulp, washing down the bread and pear.

"Just to have rare time alone with you."

This didn't sound like the typical Éamonn to her. She narrowed her gaze.

His hand on his chest, he said, "No, truly! I much prefer your company to that of your sister, you know."

She stung with jealousy, and her tune turned sharp. "I don't know, actually. You seem to enjoy her company quite well enough, from what I've seen."

"Ah, she's just a grand bit of fun. I would much rather—"

Her blood grew hot with jealousy. A grand bit of fun! Well, he could keep his fun. "I can imagine what you'd *rather* do, Éamonn Doherty! And you can just *rather* with someone else for all I'm concerned!"

She snatched her woolen shawl from where she'd draped it on the stone behind her. With angry strides, she escaped with purpose and indignation. Had Deirdre been some sort of *practice* for her? The man had seduced her sister and now thought that qualified him to woo her? Anger pulsed through her with every step.

Katie cursed him in earnest as she got lost in the marshes. She couldn't remember the path and must have taken a wrong turn. While peering into the mist, she searched for a sign of the fair. Her ears caught voices. She made her way carefully in the muck in that direction, hoping the wind didn't play with the sound.

The more she tramped, the more lost she got. The Fae must be leading her astray. Time to ignore what might not be and concentrate on what must be. She looked up at the sky, scanning the gray expanse. *A bright spot. That must be the sun burning through the cloud cover. So, then, the fair should be this way.*

Clapping and cheering grew stronger as she finally burst from the boglands into the sidelines of a horse race. Grimacing at her muddy shoes and skirt, she slunk back to her parents' shelter to clean up.

And she'd keep out of that Éamonn's way. At least long enough for him to miss her.

Éamonn:

As Katie stomped off, Éamonn flung several stones against the tree. The romantic interlude wasn't supposed to end with Katie stomping off into the bog. It was supposed to end with... Well, that obviously wouldn't happen now. After cursing his own idiocy, he returned to the fair in a foul temper.

After only catching tantalizing glimpses of Katie over the next two days as she hurried by, Éamonn just about gave up. Instead, he threw himself into some work. Éamonn whistled while he brushed his horse. The bay mare whickered at Éamonn as he applied a stiff brush to her flank. "Ah, like that, do you, then? Here, I'll do the other side." He dipped the brush in cool water and scrubbed harder.

Taking care of horses always relaxed Éamonn. Brushing down the horses lacked the glamor of the dice but getting immediate appreciation for his care left him satisfied.

He whistled a jaunty tune his father often played. As he put his back into the work, his whistle grew louder.

A woman's voice startled him, "Are you calling the birds from the sky, so?"

He whirled around, splashing soapy water from his brush as the horse nickered from the sudden movement. The water hit Katie, who gasped, her mouth opening in surprise. Her eyes flashed mossy-green above her frown. Had she no joy in life? He yearned to make her laugh and forget everything she feared.

He put on his most heart-melting grin. "Ah, Katie! I'd been hoping for a wee Fae girl with fiery hair to come help me. And see, here's my wish granted!" He spread his hands wide, the suds dripping from the brush.

Katie narrowed her eyes, but the corner of her mouth twitched. "Fine, then. I suppose that's an apology. You shouldn't work so hard while your burns are healing, anyhow." She reached for the brush, but he lifted it out of her reach.

Instead of jumping as he'd intended, she kicked him in the shin. "Ow!" He dropped the brush and bent to clutch his leg.

She retrieved the brush with a smug smile. "When you're as *wee* as I am, you learn a few tricks in dealing with tall folk.

Especially those who believe themselves superior." With a sniff, she brushed the mare, standing on tiptoes to reach the spine.

Giggling behind him made him turn. Deirdre and his little sister, *Édaín*, a thin girl with long bones, watched them.

Deirdre's taunting voice asked, "Would you like another kick? I'm sure the mare would accommodate."

"I'd rather be struck by a lovely lass, Deirdre. Come here and wallop me!" He puffed his solid chest and slapped it three times.

Deirdre sauntered to him, her hands on her hips, while Katie made a rude noise.

As he stepped away from the horse, the dark-haired girl walked around him once, as if inspecting a purchase. Then she poked him in the torso. Not a sharp blow by any means, just a soft push, but he stepped back, holding a hand over his heart. "Struck down by a lovely lass! Surely, you're a goddess, here to steal my heart and soul!" With exaggerated theatrics, he staggered as if teetering on the edge of balance.

This performance received giggles from Deirdre and Édaín. Katie made another noise, brushing the horse harder. The mare whickered. Then she stopped and turned to her sister. "Why is it, whenever I am actually enjoying myself, you must shove yourself in? Can't you just leave me in peace?"

Deirdre's grin turned to an ugly glower. "Not everything is all about you, Katie!"

"No, because you always make everything about *you!*"

Édaín spoke in a loud voice. "Are you working the leather booth today, Éamonn? Or are you helping Da with the horses all afternoon?" Édaín had married last summer but still helped at the family booth when she could. Éamonn guessed her husband, Tor, must be with the other journeyman metalsmiths.

Éamonn gave a shrug. "I'm on horse duty for the duration. Ruari and Ciaran are fine in the booth by themselves. I'm sure they'd love a visit from such fine young ladies such as yourselves. Why don't you bring them ale?"

Deirdre batted her eyes and lowered them, the very picture of a demure young *cailín*. His desire ached as he remembered the afternoon they'd enjoyed by the river. Her soft lips seemed as alluring as Katie's fiery eyes. After he finished with the horses, he might tempt her away from the bustle of the fair.

Her tone softened into an alluring invitation. "Should I come back later with your meal, then?"

Just as he imagined what he might want to eat, a sharp pain burst on his temple. "*Ow!* What in the name of all that's holy?" He clapped his hand to his head. The horse brush lay in the dust, oozing soapy water. If Katie could hurt him with her gaze, he'd be writhing in exquisite pain. He stumbled back from her naked fury.

"That's for playing with my emotions! That's for pretending to like me when you really want my sister!"

Deirdre rolled her eyes. "Oh, don't be so dramatic, Katie. You'd think the world revolved around you. We're just talking." She placed a soft hand on Éamonn's chest and gazed up at him. He gulped as his body reacted, despite himself.

Instead of angry words, Katie stomped away. As much as he loved flirting for its own sake, he'd just thrown it in Katie's face, flirting with her sister. His heart dropped as she got farther away. "Katie!"

Deirdre placed a gentle hand on his arm, stroking his skin until it pebbled. "Let her go. No man wants to deal with her temper, not when she's in a froth like that." The corner of her mouth curled up. "What would you like to eat, then?"

Édaín rolled her eyes. "Come, Deirdre. Leave the man to his chores. We'll come back later." As his sister dragged Deirdre away, he kept his gaze locked with the midnight-haired lass. As she turned the corner, he sighed and bent back to the mare. He rubbed his head where Katie threw the brush and stared in the direction she'd gone.

If only Éamonn could decide which sister he wanted more.

Éamonn:

The sun had barely kissed the horizon when Éamonn arrived at the Hazard game. He spied a tight-knit group of five players already staring intently at the smoothed circle, waiting for the next player to toss his luck. He needed to apologize to Katie and wanted to get her something pretty. A bracelet, perhaps. But first, he needed some funds.

A chilly breeze kicked up the dust and made the men cough and sputter as Ruari rattled his cup. Not a great roll, but a decent enough start. Éamonn shoved in between Ruari and the man next to him.

The other man glanced up, startled. Éamonn found himself gazing at the unfocused black eyes of Lochlann MacCrimmon, the lad he'd fought with the other night. He stopped in case Lochlann intended to renew their tussle, but the Scot only gave a curt nod. Éamonn returned the nod and concentrated on the game, giving his scalp a hearty scratch. Those burns turned to scabs and his head itched constantly.

He'd have to wait until the next game to join but, in the meantime, he assessed his opponents. Ciaran sat next to Ruari, already in his cups. Lochlann's brother, Donald, shifted his glare between Éamonn and Ciaran. He didn't seem to consider Ruari as worthy of his regard. That angered him. Sure, Ruari moved slowly, but his brother measured a fair match for any man in a fight. Éamonn kept his simmering resentment hidden. His father always told him the gambling pit had no room for anger.

The fifth man, Éamonn hadn't met. He didn't speak and looked older than the others. His black hair grizzled to gray near his ears, a big, gruff man with an enormous pot belly like a prize pig. Éamonn thought he might fall into the dice pit.

The piggish man rolled a fantastic point. Éamonn thanked Saint Catejan he'd sat out this round. He glanced at Ruari's and Ciaran's coins. They'd offered little ante.

Donald grabbed the dice next. He closed his eyes when he shook them in his bone cup. They hit the dirt, revealing an out.

"Glaikit bastirt!" He spat to the side and stomped off, forfeiting his bet. Éamonn hoped he wouldn't return. That man had no hold on his temper.

Ciaran rolled next and did well enough. Not nearly good enough to beat the old man, so he pushed his stake in and sat back with a frustrated scowl. Briefly, Éamonn remembered Turlough's music, but he'd have to ask later. Ruari already bowed out, as he gestured for Lochlann to take the dice next.

Lochlann rolled well. He matched the old man, but Éamonn hadn't seen the first round. He didn't know what the point showed. From the expression on Lochlann's face, he didn't know, either. Could the man be a daftie? Surely, he could keep track of the caster's point? Then how the hell had he been winning so easily? Éamonn smelled a rat.

The piggy man's voice came gruff and sharp, "Roll the tie-breaker, Lochlann."

Lochlann rolled a twelve. The piggy man cursed, threw his own casting cup on the ground, and stomped off.

Such blatant disregard for the dice cup made Éamonn gasp. Most gamblers took better care of their cup than their own child. The cup represented a vessel of luck, the very thing which provided their winnings. He peered at the bone cup, lying in the dust. One edge had a nick.

They started another round without Donald and the piggy man. With only the four players, the rounds went quickly, though Lochlann won often. He had a fool's luck. Éamonn watched him roll carefully, alert to any sign of pocketed dice or other cheating.

Ciaran kept staring at Lochlann and Éamonn, as if expecting an explosion. He seemed disappointed no one threw a punch. While shaking his head, Éamonn cast the first point of the next round.

Several bottles and several rounds later, Éamonn had to admit Lochlann played an excellent game. But the lad's luck had to give sometime, didn't it? Éamonn bet again, against his better judgment. Lochlann won again. How could he win so steadily? Éamonn tried to discern if he had dice hidden in his sleeve but couldn't tell.

Éamonn felt his pouch, but he knew exactly how much coin he had left. Not enough to buy Katie that lovely bracelet he'd spied at the bronze-smith's booth. He needed to earn enough back to afford the gift.

Lochlann didn't flaunt his winnings but quietly gathered the bets to his own pile. He put some into his belt bag and left the rest for future bets. A canny gambler, then. Lochlann must have been chased off from his winnings before. Someone who cheated would never leave their entire pile on the ground. Which meant he might just be cheating now and getting prepared to leave in a hurry.

Lochlann cast next. Everyone tossed their ante into the ring. The blond man put the dice in his own cup, rolled an eight, and that became the fader's point. He then rolled his own caster point, succeeding with a twelve. A winning roll. The others didn't even get a chance.

Now, he'd never afford that bracelet for Katie. This simpering little idiot couldn't be this lucky. He must be doing something shady.

Éamonn growled, "Cheater!" Swinging his hand, Éamonn brushed the dice out of the circle and the gambling pit. They scattered outside, drawing the attention of a couple passing by.

Éamonn wanted to knock the polite confusion off the Scottish eejit's face. When he stood, he towered over the Scot, fury lashing through his veins. Ruari growled something behind him, and Ciaran shouted his name.

Lochlann slowly rose and stared at him. He took a deep breath, nodded, and turned to go.

The man couldn't cheat his way into a win and walk away unscathed. Éamonn clutched Lochlann's shoulder and swung him around. Lochlann glared at him with steel in his eyes. *Good. Perhaps I'll get a good fight out of this, after all.*

A hand fell on his shoulder and by the solid weight. He tried to shake Ruari off, but that proved futile. The hand held firm.

Ciaran clapped a hand on his other shoulder. "Come, Éamonn. It's no big deal. I've another bottle in the wagon."

Éamonn didn't want to be talked down. "He's got to be cheating! He couldn't be so lucky as that!"

Ciaran tightened his grip. "Éamonn! Leave him. He lost steadily enough before you got here. He just had a good streak, is all!"

Éamonn wrenched away, but Lochlann had disappeared. With a snort of disgust, he turned to Ciaran. "Well then, cousin, you'd better break out your bottle! I feel the need to drown my sorrows."

Éamonn:
The sun burned high when Éamonn stumbled out of his wagon the next day. His head pounded like a herd of kine stampeded within. His mouth tasted the same, and his scalp itched. He squinted through the dust at the misty sun and rubbed his hands through his hair. He'd had to trim the patchy parts the day after the fire.

Éamonn took a long drink from his waterskin, swished the cool water around his mouth, and spat into the dust. After he poured more through his hair, he splashed it on his face and arms. After a good scrub, he felt more human.

Éamonn pocketed a few apples and left the Traveler's tent site to wander the horse stalls. He looked forward to placing a bet on a good race today. Besides, he needed to make up for his losses and get that bracelet for Katie.

First, however, he had research to do. He'd heard about some fine horses on offer at the east end stalls. Éamonn wanted to check out the stallions. His da said he'd been looking for a good stud for their mares.

Éamonn strolled as his head still pounded from last night's *poitín*. He didn't remember much other than being angry at someone. Who or why eluded him. As he passed their leather stall, he waved at Ruari.

Ciaran came up behind him and yelled in his ear. "How's the head, Coz?"

"Gah!" Éamonn grabbed his hands over his pounding skull and ducked away from his annoying cousin. "You're a right arse, you are!"

Ciaran trailed after him, screaming in a falsetto voice. "Éamonn! Come home for supper! Éamonn! You shouldn't drink so much! Éamonn!"

Éamonn swung out to catch Ciaran in the mouth to shut him for good, but he missed horribly. Ciaran laughed like a screeching donkey's bray.

"God damn your soul to hell, Ciaran Kilbane!"

Ciaran halted in his tracks. With a dead earnest face, he admonished, "Éamonn…you shouldn't say such things."

Éamonn cocked his head, ignoring the blood pounding in his ears. "Ciaran, will you stop being so silly? I swear, you're more superstitious than an old witch. Now, bugger off and leave me to my misery." Ciaran frowned, and Éamonn stalked away. If he couldn't take it, he shouldn't dish it. *Bloody hell, I forgot to ask about the music again. Ah, well, Da's sure to have asked by now.*

When he finally reached the east stalls, the dust made him cough. Hawkers sold goods, both livestock and sundry. Noise pummeled his head, and he winced. The aroma of roasting pig made his mouth water, but his stomach warned him in no uncertain terms he shouldn't eat.

He heard the whinny before the horse came into view. A magnificent pale gray stallion with white spots along his flank shook his head. With beautiful conformation and a sleek coat, his long, sinuous neck stood out from the milling crowd. Éamonn made a beeline to that stall.

Such a magnificent creature in too small a stall. This grand lad needed room to burn off his energy. Éamonn grabbed an apple from his pocket and offered the treat as a greeting. With a snuffle of his velvet muzzle, the stallion accepted the proffered gift. He crunched the succulent treat, spraying bits of apple as he chewed. Éamonn stroked his nose. "Ah, you're a grand lad, you are. Are ye racing today, then?"

"He is, and I'll thank you not to fatten him up before time."

Éamonn twirled around to find Donald MacCrimmon glowering at him with black eyes. His heart sank. "The horse is yours?"

"He is. Come away, now, Smúid." The older man drew the horse away with a practiced hand. Did the creature run like his namesake mist?

Éamonn sauntered through the stalls, but no horse caught his fancy as deeply as Smúid had. Damn the man to hell, why did MacCrimmon have to own the best stallion on offer? Anyone else he might bargain with. But the fight between Éamonn and the MacCrimmon brothers killed that notion.

Perhaps his father would strike a decent deal. Of course, if the horse did well in the races, the price would rise. He might hedge his bets. After finding the betting tout, he placed a few judicious wagers. Then he judged his belly had settled enough to break his fast.

While he munched on a hot pork bridie, mopping the dripping juices and licking his hand to catch the last of them, he pondered on how he'd ask his father. Turlough traded in horses but didn't tolerate underhanded tactics. He had a fantastic reputation as an even dealer, which was all to the good. His father preferred playing his damned Fae-touched harp to dealing with horses any day of the week.

Earning a living with music wasn't easy, though Turlough tried. He'd traveled the land as his namesake had, drifting from grand house to grand house. After Éamonn's mother died in childbirth, the grief had been too much. His da had dumped four of his five children on a cousin and went tramping across the land. Only Ruari stayed with him.

The vagabonds returned two years later, dressed in rags, stooped and defeated. He'd kept his harp but little else. Nothing on God's green earth or beyond could pry that sacred instrument from Turlough's talented hands.

Éamonn remembered the rainy day they'd returned. He'd been twelve, but he'd barely recognized his own father, this ragamuffin creature walking up the sodden trail to their wagons. Two years felt like an eternity to a child. The harp, wrapped in a bag on his back, had made him look hunchbacked. Da's dread at his reception showed with every step, even to a child. Éamonn ran to get Uncle Pat to save them from the approaching spook.

Éamonn hadn't been willing to accept this broken creature as his father. His aunt used to describe his da as a shining creature of Fae enchantment, off to regale the land with magical tales and music. Not this shattered creature smelling of wet dung.

With Uncle Pat's help, his da started a *real trade* and joined their Traveler band as a horse trader.

Éamonn sighed. Such a long time ago. He'd spent most of his adult life trying to amend that mistrust of his father. Turlough would never hold such a thing against him, which made things worse. His little sister, Édaín, had been eight at the time and loved everyone, while Fionnuala's shyness kept her silent. Síle had been barely two and played with Turlough's beard.

Éamonn loved and respected his father. But sometimes a touch of wild confusion still shone through Turlough's eyes, an echo of his time on the road. Éamonn often wondered what caused that madness but never dared ask.

Perhaps Turlough wouldn't be the best person to buy the gray stallion from the MacCrimmon's, after all. Ruari had little skill as a trader, though he broke beasts well and knew how to handle the high-strung ones. Ciaran did well enough at trading, but his skill at working leather trumped any trading talent. Maybe Ciaran's relationship with the MacCrimmon brothers would work better than Éamonn's.

Lost in his assessments, a hand against his waist startled him. He spluttered the last few crumbs of his bridie and spun. The bright eyes and freckles of Deirdre O'Malley gazed back. She giggled and brushed the crumbs from his shirt. She brushed slowly, her hand lingering on his chest with exaggerated care. He wished he had a drink to clear his mouth of bread so he could talk without showering her with more pastry.

Giggling, she kissed stray crumbs from his chin as a cloud darkened the sun. Éamonn's desire flared. The bloody thing had a

42

mind of its own and damn the rest of the world. He tried to shift his leg to relieve the discomfort, but she noticed the movement.

"Restless today, are you, my sweet man?" Her hand brushed crumbs lower. This made him squirm more, and he flushed.

Katie's sharp voice cut through the fog in his mind. "Deirdre! Mother wants you. Now!"

"*As ucht Dé!*" Even as she stalked off, he watched her pretty bottom sway. Éamonn sighed with relief and regret. Deirdre's mouth looked so sweet and kissable. That raven hair, silky and smooth. He shook his head. That sort of thinking would make him more uncomfortable.

Katie glared at him, her arms crossed. "And you! Don't go messing about with such as her!" Her mouth formed angry lines. He couldn't tell her anger was jealousy or being protective of her sister.

Éamonn still wanted to kiss hers as much as Deirdre's, maybe even more. "Oh? And are you her mother, then? She can look after herself, that one." He placed the back of his hand on his forehead. "But, alas, I hoped to go for a lovely walk by the river and now I've no companion. Would you join me?" He proffered an arm, all gallant gentleman. After staring at him for a long moment, she growled, spun on her heel, and stalked away.

Éamonn:
The lovely gray stallion Éamonn coveted had placed second in the race. He'd hedged his bets, placing wagers on first, second, and third, and made a tidy sum. In addition, the horse not winning meant bargaining power.

When he brought Ciaran in on his intentions, his cousin gave a wide grin and flipped a large coin. "I've just the lucky *doit* to seal the deal!"

Éamonn sent his cousin off to the stalls while he sought out his father. Once he shared their plan, Turlough gave him a long, lingering look. He let out a deep sigh, slapped his thighs, and rose. "Let's walk, son. I've got to get you away from the people."

They took a path north from the fair, into the brushy moors. While they picked their way through tussocks and grasses, Turlough strode with purpose as if he had a destination in mind. After twenty minutes, they came to a solid island in the bog. A circle of ancient faerie stones jutted out of the island, forming a crooked crown.

No one knew from where standing stones came or who built them. Many had tool marks or carvings. Some said they'd once been druids, turned to stone by Saint Patrick. Others claimed they'd been hapless souls of folks who had angered the *Sidhe*. Still others reckoned giants placed them, like an ancient game of marbles left and forgotten in the mists of time.

Éamonn believed in the Fair Folk, of course. Only a fool would risk angering them. But he also believed in the power of God. He'd often wondered if the two beliefs were compatible and never came to a satisfactory answer.

Turlough settled on a standing stone and patted the space next to him. "Come, Éamonn. Sit by me. The damp is getting into my bones, and I need a rest."

Éamonn stared into the swirling mist. Turlough would talk when ready, but the silence grew heavy. "I asked around about your music, Da. I overheard someone talking in a hushed voice about *music papers*. As far as I know, you're the only one at the fair with written music. When I turned to ask questions, they'd disappeared. A young man with a gruff voice. Did you ask Ciaran?"

Turlough perked up at his first words, but then deflated with a shrug. "No, I never talked to Ciaran. At least you'd recognize Ciaran's voice, so that wouldn't be him. I found nothing in the gossip. I began to think the faeries took them back, so I had. But no, this tells me I've a mortal thief to deal with."

Éamonn resolved to do some digging to find them. But what if fairies really had stolen the music back? He had no desire to mess with the likes of them. "Do you really think the Fair Folk gifted O'Carolan their music, Da? Truly?"

"I truly do, son. The *Sidhe* are real, I can guarantee that. And I believe his music to come from their mystical land." Turlough caressed the stone as if stroking the cheek of a favorite child.

"How could you possibly guarantee that?"

His father gave a smug smile. "I've heard the music, lad. I've heard tunes when no earthly musician stood nigh. I've heard melodies in the mists of the morning and behind the moon shadows. The music surrounds us. And it sounds like that music stolen from my bag."

Turlough might have lost what few wits he had left, but Éamonn knew better than to argue when his father took that tone.

"I wanted to give you a fair warning, though. Even beyond the stolen music, you're messing with dangerous things at the fair."

The change of subject took Éamonn by surprise. "What dangerous things?"

"Several. The MacCrimmon boys, for one. I've asked about them. They're over from Scotland, with strong clan connections."

"Bah. They're Travelers, like us. What connection could they have to a powerful clan?"

"Their father holds a position with a Clan Chief. That's all I heard. Tread canny now, to be sure."

Éamonn huffed but nodded. "What other dangers do you see?"

"The two wee O'Malley girls. You're courting disaster there, in so many senses of the word, my son."

"Ah, we're just having fun, Da. They're both—"

"They are *not* both fun. Caitriona's the strong one. If you want her, fine. But don't toy with her! She's worth the keeping. The other one…what's her name, Deirdre? That one's trouble, and not in a good way."

"She's no trouble at all, Da." He thought of Deirdre brushing off crumbs, and his body warmed to the memory.

"Éamonn! Pay attention. That one'll be a girl her whole life. You don't need a girl. You need a woman."

He grinned and waggled his eyebrows. "She's plenty woman, Da, trust me."

Pain exploded in his ear. His father rarely struck him, but the cuff stung. "Da!"

Turlough gave a fierce scowl. "You may be taller than me, but you're still my son. If I have to beat sense into you, I will. Stop messing about with her. She'll make you sorry. I can tell the type. And you aren't her first love, I'll warrant. She's got her ways down pat, so she does. I remember a young lass before your mother, all polish and no substance. Lucky for me yer mother shone bright enough to cloud the other's false gold."

Éamonn didn't want to defy his da, but Deirdre tempted him sorely. Then again, so did Katie. Perhaps she made the better bet, temper and all. Her fire made her more interesting. Like a fractious mare to be broken. *Best not mention that to Da, though.*

A powerful spark flashed behind his father's eyes. "Mind me, now. I'm not fooling one bit about this. I want to see you well married off before I shed my mortal coil."

"Da, stop being gloomy. You're not about to die anytime soon. You're only, what, forty-five?"

"Forty-seven and stop arguing. I feel the winter in my bones, no mistake, and it's already April. Those years of wandering did damage. They sunk into my marrow and never truly let go."

Turlough sighed, his shoulders slumping. His father appeared frail, as if he'd aged overnight into an ancient, wizened man.

Éamonn's blood grew cold. What if Turlough wasn't just being morose? "You'll never be old, Da. Your music keeps you young."

"Aye, I suppose it does at that. Perhaps we can find the missing bits and set everything to rights. Come. We've chatted long enough. Let's go check on that brother of yours. Hopefully, he's not traded the best stuff away for pennies."

The walk back seemed oddly tense. His father's words wound through his mind. Old? Plenty of folks grew older than his da, practically dancing jigs in the streets. But if Da grew old, that meant so did he. Turlough's words of settling down gripped him. Perhaps he should grow more serious and choose a lass to marry.

Deirdre and Katie. While Deirdre tempted him, Katie fascinated him, and few women had that talent. She beguiled and delighted him. The more he thought of her, the more he agreed with his father. Katie'd be a much better choice as a partner.

He'd lived eighteen years, after all. Time to settle down with a wife. His father married late and lost his wife after just twelve years.

Later that afternoon, he invited Katie for another walk by the river, but she outright refused him. He helped her with her chores several times, caught up with her as she ran errands at the fair, but each time she turned away with nothing but a blur of her copper curls.

And yet, the half-smile she flashed him as she stomped off in a huff gave him hope. Perhaps she couldn't admit her interest, even to herself. Grim determination set in. He had a mission.

Chapter Four

Katie:

Katie grunted under the weight of the water buckets. Deirdre should have filled them, but her feckless sister had disappeared at first light. Of course, she wouldn't get in trouble for it. She had learned how to manipulate her parents and turned those skills to everyone else she met. Her sister had been cuddling up to Éamonn yesterday, so she must have run off with him. Katie's blood burned at the betrayal. Well, he could have her and take her away forever. Bloody eejit.

As she approached their tent, she shifted the buckets for a better grip. Voices inside made her slow. The gruff voice of the older MacCrimmon man, the fighter. She paused, listening. Yes, she heard Lochlann's light voice, speaking in low, urgent tones. She still hadn't figured out how her da could afford to buy their horse.

She walked in with her head high and nodded, polite as she could be. Her mother had already left so only the men remained. They all stopped talking as she placed the buckets next to the hearth. Lochlann watched her with an odd expression. Did she have dirt on her face? She turned her back and wiped her cheeks. She hadn't tucked her skirt in her belt, and her stays looked fine. She patted her hair, but her curls remained modestly bound by the kerchief.

Regardless of what he found odd, time to play the hostess. "Hello, Donald, Lochlann. May I get you a cool drink? We've cider in the back."

The younger man gave a polite smile. "I'd love some, Mistress Caitriona, thank ye kindly." His words made her pause. She'd never heard him be rude, but he seldom offered much in conversation.

She cocked her head to Donald, but he waved her away. "I'm fine. Get his drink."

Hiding a snort at his rough command, she walked outside to the back storage bin. The cider jug hid under a flap of canvas. She poured a mug and re-entered the room. They spoke in whispers. Whatever plan they hatched wouldn't be for her ears.

"I'm off to collect some firewood. I should be back in about an hour."

That would give them a timeline for whatever shady deal they worked. She didn't think ill of Lochlann, even after that fight. He'd acted rather sweet. But she shivered whenever Donald stared at her. *As if I was a pork shoulder that wanted marinating.*

Out past the horse stalls lay several wooded hills. While so many people camping nearby had practically denuded the area of deadfall, a windy storm last night had brought down fresh branches. The wood needed drying, or it would smoke, but at least they'd have some.

Katie made several trips to the hills, piling up the green branches behind their tent before she spied the two men leaving. She studied their backs as they disappeared behind other family tents. The soft grass hid any footsteps she might have heard, so when her father hit her ear, she let out a surprised grunt. She fell to the ground, holding her head.

"Stop gawping about like a child! It's about time you grew up. Ye're well old enough to know how to finish your work!"

Katie didn't remember the first time Da hit her. They swam in her memory like a series of endless blows. But she'd learned how to respond to them to keep them from getting worse.

She knew better than to duck when he hit her a second time.

Éamonn:

Ciaran closed the stall when Éamonn returned. His cousin raised his eyebrows. "What's all this, then? We missed you today."

Éamonn didn't feel like discussing his continued failures, so he shrugged.

Ciaran let out a chuckle. "Oh, things went that well, did they? Deirdre came searching for you, so I know she didn't reject you. Who are you after now?"

"None of your damned business."

That made Ciaran laugh louder. "Oho, the great Éamonn, seducer of women from Bantry Bay to Derry has failed! This is a memorable day, indeed! Come, now, tell us the name of this paragon of virtue, Éamonn. What fair lass is strong enough to resist your uncountable charms?"

Éamonn's color rose. He punched his cousin's left shoulder. "I said, none of your business! Now, feck off."

Ciaran shoved back, on the right shoulder. "Just having a bit of fun, *cousin.*"

Éamonn pushed him again, this time in the center of the chest, and the lighter man stumbled back. Ciaran's brows knit into a scowl and his face flushed.

With a grunt, Éamonn balled his fists. *Good. Now they were both nice and angry.*

Ciaran swung at Éamonn, but the taller man ducked in time, ramming a shoulder into Ciaran's stomach. As they both fell to the ground, he twisted around to punch Ciaran in the face. Instead, Ciaran grabbed his fist and wrenched it around.

Now too close for effective punches, the fight devolved into a wrestling match. The two young men writhed on the muddy ground until a huge hand grabbed Ciaran by his shirt collar. The cloth ripped when Ruari jerked him from the fray. Ruari then pushed himself between the two combatants. They panted, red-faced and filthy.

The big man held them apart. "Stop!"

Éamonn darted under Ruari's outstretched arm for another push at Ciaran. They both toppled into a fence around the stables, and Ruari had to wade in again. By the time he held them apart, red scratches covered their arms and faces. Ruari sported a deep gouge on his upper arm from a nail in the fence post.

Éamonn glared at his cousin and wiped his hands through his hair. He winced as half-healed scabs caught on his hand. "He pushed me!"

"What are you, five? You shoved me." Ciaran's eye shone red. He'd have a nice shiner by this time tomorrow.

"You deserved it!" Éamonn's face fell when his father approached.

Turlough's expression looked pinched. "I can't believe my ears. Éamonn, you're a grown man of eighteen, but you're acting like a spoiled child. Ciaran, wipe that smug smirk off your face now. You're twenty and should know even better. I can't even trust you to close the booth without a war. Éamonn, where did you wander off to all day? No, don't answer now. Get off and clean yourselves up. Together, if you don't mind. And no fighting."

Chastened, Éamonn stalked to the river to wash the worst of the mud. Ciaran accompanied him in stony silence.

Deirdre showed up as they climbed the banks. With a sweet smile and a giggle, she ran a soft hand along his arm, caressing Éamonn's still-wet shirt. "Éamonn, I needed you earlier. I couldn't find you anywhere." Her tone turned to wheedling. "Will you be at the *céili* tonight?"

Ciaran snorted but said nothing.

Thinking of how Katie had stomped off, he had to come up with a way to put her off. Éamonn answered in a brusque voice. "I had business. What did you want?"

She pressed against him, her hand on his chest, but didn't answer. Her giggling and simpering grated his nerves. He preferred Katie's warm chuckle and powerful will. Éamonn must get her alone again. He couldn't just leave things like that. She made his blood run hot and cold with both her temper and her smile. Éamonn loved how her moss-green eyes had flashed when angry. They seemed magical, sparkling in the sunlight.

Deirdre had asked him a question and waited for his answer. He hadn't heard a word she had said.

She put her hands on her hips. "Well?"

"Uh…I'm not sure." *A safe enough answer, no?*

"You're not sure? But Éamonn…Éamonn, I'm so looking forward to tonight. Please? I want to dance with you." She wrapped her arms around his waist. His spine stiffened.

Well, that couldn't happen. Katie would get even angrier with him. He wriggled out of her embrace. "Uh…well, my da won't want me to have much fun tonight. I'm sort of in trouble, you see."

"In trouble? You're a man grown, aren't you? What's a little trouble? Trouble can be fun sometimes." Her tone settled just on the edge of whining. Strange how a week ago, that tone sounded sweet. Now, he just wanted to get away. She locked her arms around him again.

With firm determination, he removed her arms and backed away. "Deirdre, maybe I'll see you, but I may not come at all. Here, Ciaran will dance with you. Won't you, Ciaran?" *Please, save me here.*

Ciaran brought out the charm and bowed to the dark-haired girl. "I'd be honored if you would consent to be my guest this evening, Mistress Deirdre."

Éamonn sighed with relief. Ciaran may be an annoying git, but he had loyalty, to be sure.

Deirdre blushed with a fetching smile, and Éamonn momentarily regretted his choice. She lowered her lashes, glanced at each, and rushed off into the setting sun.

Should he avoid the party? He couldn't, not if he wanted to talk to Katie again. He must find her and explain. Or apologize. Or whatever she wanted from him. He had no idea, and that's part of what made her so enticing. Deirdre's flirting seemed so transparent he didn't have to figure out what she wanted. Katie intrigued him. She represented a mystery, a puzzle. Just thinking about her made his blood warm in anticipation. And other parts.

After washing in the river and returning to their wagon, he stepped out of his wet clothes and hung them on a drying rack. He pulled on his best outfit. A deep russet vest, trimmed in cream embroidery, with a cream shirt underneath. The colors on the new vest remained vibrant. He only had one pair of clean breeks left, but the fine gray wool felt soft and inviting. He smiled at the thought of Katie touching...

Ruari entered their wagon, looking him up and down. "What are you up to, Éamonn?"

"I'm off to the *céili*, of course. Aren't you?"

"Da says you need to take Fionnuala."

After wiping away a crease in his breeks, he glanced up. "Fionnuala? Won't she be going with her fiancé?"

"You know they aren't official yet, and she's only fifteen. So, she needs an official escort from the family."

Éamonn sighed. This must be his penance for today's truancy and the fight. Escorting his sister wouldn't be such a bad thing. Fionnuala had a young man who loved her but wanted to wait to marry until he had a larger part in his father's wool trade.

He cupped water in his hands and ruffled his hands through his hair. The scabs no longer hurt, at least. Even before the fire, he liked to keep his hair short, but growing it longer might be a pleasant change. Would Katie like him better with long hair?

Fionnuala waited for him in the next wagon. She stood straight and fidgeted with her fingers. Her straight auburn hair fell down her back and glinted in the twilight.

He took her hand and kissed her fingertips. "Ah, you are lovely, my dear sister. You'll be the shining star of the party, to be sure."

She blushed and glanced at her feet, her freckles noticeable even in the dim light. He put a finger under her chin. "Fionnuala? Is everything all right? Is Malachy making you sad?"

"No, no, Malachy's grand. I just don't like *céilís*. So many people."

"I'll make sure you have fun at this one, sweetling. Come, let's stage an entrance, shall we?" He held out the crook of his arm.

Fionnuala placed her hand, and he clapped his other hand upon hers as they strode to the gathering. As they arrived, he sought out the others. Ruari sat next to Ciaran. Deirdre sat just past Ciaran, glancing up when Éamonn arrived. She pouted, but Ciaran whispered in her ear. Her mouth went round with understanding. She gave Fionnuala a patronizing smile. Well, at least he dodged that trouble tonight.

He glanced around for his Caitriona, but he didn't catch a glimpse of her red hair.

His Caitriona? What was happening? Such attachment usually frightened him. But his realization of his father's mortality made him determined to get his own love life in order. At the same time, fear murmured behind that decision. He shoved the thought away for now.

The players started a fast jig, though they weren't yet in harmony. The tune jangled before they got used to each other's rhythms.

Only a few people danced, though one man staggered from place to place in what he must have thought formed a dance. His actions prompted a couple of giggles, but everyone jumped out of his way. With a start, Éamonn recognized Lochlann MacCrimmon. The Scotsman hadn't seemed the sort to get legless.

The fair-haired man stumbled toward them, his flyaway hair mussed and a vacant look in his eyes. He made his way back around the circle, and Donald arrived, guiding him to the sidelines.

What prompted all that? A poor trade? Had they sold off that lovely gray stallion? Ciaran had made no headway with purchasing the magnificent horse. He said the brothers had no interest in selling them the beast. Which meant Éamonn lost that chance to please his father with a grand new stud for their mares.

More dancers formed a ring as the music settled into a more harmonious cadence.

Éamonn stood and bowed to his sister. "Fionnuala, would you do me the great kindness of accompanying me on the dance floor?"

She tittered behind her hand. The sound didn't annoy him from his little sister nearly as much as from Deirdre. Fionnuala took his arm, keeping her eyes lowered. They joined in the circle dance. As he swung her around, she let out a delighted laugh.

He loved his sister. She'd always been kind to others. Her own passion was dying cloth, and that's where she'd met her fiancé, Malachy. They'd make a grand pair, despite both being so shy. Éamonn glimpsed Malachy at the far end of the circle. Malachy stared at Fionnuala with sheep's eyes. Yes, they'd be grand together.

A glimpse of fire caught Éamonn's attention. He steadied his gaze to find Caitriona. Dressed in a pale-green dress with a darker green corset, she was the loveliest thing he'd ever seen. She stared at him with a wide smile, standing tall in the flickering firelight, making his breath catch in his throat. Éamonn stumbled as he forgot his steps in the dance. When he caught her eyes again, her smile had turned into a frown.

Was she still upset from this afternoon? He whirled Fionnuala, trying not to step on her skirts while watching Katie. He spun his sister, and when he glanced back, Katie had disappeared.

Where had she gone? She'd just arrived, for the love of... Then the realization struck him. *Oh, by all that's holy. She doesn't know Fionnuala is my sister.*

Éamonn had to finish the dance. He owed that much to Fionnuala. But as soon as the music faded, he shoved his sister into Malachy's arms. "I know you aren't official yet, but I must go for a moment. I'll be back, I promise!" He tossed a kiss at his sister's cheek and dashed off in the direction he had last seen Katie.

Most of the fair either danced or slept in their tents and wagons. The revelry grew distant as he searched. He cursed his rotten luck and timing. Éamonn regretted his reputation with the ladies. She must have heard stories of his conquests.

He caught no tantalizing flash of a green skirt or a glimpse of sunset curls. Had Katie gone back to her parents' tent? He found his way to the quiet, ramshackle shelter. If she'd retreated to her home, surely she'd be throwing things about and cursing. She wouldn't be one to mope or sulk. Or she may need to stay silent around her father. Only faint snoring came from the tent.

Defeated, Éamonn returned to the party. He'd have to apologize to Fionnuala. But when he stared at the dance circle, he spied Katie dancing with his brother, Ruari. She put her hand on his arm where Ruari had cut himself on the fence breaking up

Ciaran and Éamonn's fight. After she touched the knot in the dirty bandage, she laughed and smiled up at Ruari.

Ruari? He didn't have the wit for many jokes. Dependable, strong, and solid, yes. Great in a fight. But not clever or funny.

Not that Ruari had ever been competition for the ladies. They admired his build and strength and he got a fair amount of attention but seldom took advantage. But Katie looked like she enjoyed his company. Éamonn's blood turned hot and cold and his hands curled into fists.

Well, two could play at this game. He sought out Fionnuala, who spoke to Malachy in intense tones. Without preamble, he pulled on her arm.

"Éamonn! You're hurting me!"

"Sorry, sis. I need to dance with you. It's only my duty, after all. C'mon."

"But, Éamonn—"

"You wanted to have fun tonight, right? Besides, Malachy can't claim you entirely yet, you know."

As she glanced back at her intended, he knew he acted like a heel. Éamonn considered giving her back, but then Ruari laughed at something Katie said, and his resolve firmed. He spun Fionnuala into the dance circle, her russet hair fanning out behind her.

His smile grew plastered on his face. He wouldn't let Katie know she'd upset him. He nodded coldly to her as they passed in the circle. She sent him an angry glare, and he gritted his teeth.

As the music drew to a close, he caught Katie frowning at him. He indulged in a scowl himself and escorted Fionnuala back to Malachy. When he turned back to find Katie, she'd disappeared again.

He seldom got angry with his older brother. Frustrated, sometimes, but not angry. This time, however, his blood roared in his ears. He stomped toward Ruari. "What are you playing at?"

"What do you mean?"

"Dancing with Katie! Why did you do that?"

He gave a happy grin. "She asked me. She's nice. And pretty."

Shame flooded through him. How could he think Ruari had planned anything sinister? He let out a deep sigh and clapped his brother's shoulder. "Ruari, Katie is my girl, all right? If she wants to dance, she should dance with me."

The bigger man shrugged. "Shouldn't she dance with who she wants to?"

Éamonn didn't have time to discuss the finer points with Ruari. He must find her. "Where'd she go?"

Ruari shrugged again. "Don't know. She told me to clean my arm."

"Your arm?" Éamonn frowned, glancing at the knotted cloth. "We cleaned it earlier."

Ruari squinted at his bandage. Leakage seeped through the cloth. "She said to do it again."

"Yeah, she's right. Go see Cormac, he'll know what to do. But I need to go find Katie. Can't you remember which direction she went?"

Shrugging again, Ruari bit his lip. "Is she upset? What did I do?"

"Nothing. I'm sure she got upset with me not you. I said something earlier she didn't like." Éamonn patted Ruari's good arm and marched off in search of the girl. *Blast her.*

Chapter Five

Katie:

Katie didn't know why she felt so angry. She had no claim on Éamonn. They'd never even kissed. Why should she care so much about who he danced with? Besides, when he pretended to be some worldly lover, she hated the false act. Stomping off into the darkness, she'd had enough of parties for the night. She craved solitude, away from giggling women like her sister.

That girl with the lovely waterfall hair. She looked so elegant, dancing with Éamonn. They moved well together, as if they'd danced many times before. Her heat rose again, and her shoulders tensed.

While sitting on a fence in the darkness, she steamed, running the images through her mind. While she had familiarity with feelings of rage and betrayal, the intensity frightened her. For a short time, she'd imagined Éamonn different from the others. Katie might enjoy spending more time with him. But he showed his true colors in the end. She just wished her mind would convince her heart of that.

Footsteps approached. She glanced around, but she didn't spy a hiding place. She expected Éamonn, but Ruari emerged from the gloom.

The big man had no guile or deception in him. Katie felt like she could talk to him about anything, and what's more, he listened. He might not give her sparkling conversation, but she could relax with him.

After he settled next to her on the fence, he said, "Éamonn's searching for you."

"You found me easily enough. If he wants me, he can find me." Even to her own ears, she sounded petulant.

"He's upset."

That set her off again. The ire bubbled up through her blood. "And so am I! He pranced around, showing off his new conquest—"

Ruari's brow furrowed. "What conquest?"

58

"The tall, thin girl with lovely red-brown hair. He danced—"

"That's Fionnuala. She's our sister."

Three simple words. Their sister? She'd stormed off in a huff about his sister? Her shame and cheeks burned. Katie stared at her hands clasped in her lap. "Oh, Ruari...I've made a right mess of things, haven't I?"

Ruari put an awkward arm around her. "That's grand. He'll find you, and you'll be friends again."

It felt lovely to snuggle into a big, manly arm. Even if she had no physical attraction to him, he gave her the comfort of a good friend. She'd never had a close friend like that. He protected as her father never had.

"You're easy to talk to, Ruari."

"Ah, well, that's because I don't talk much myself. I let others talk more."

Katie giggled and hugged him, enjoying his strength.

Éamonn emerged from the darkness. He took a good, long look at Ruari's arm around Katie. After spinning on his heel, he pelted away.

Katie jumped off the fence, her heart in her throat. "Éamonn! Wait!"

But he'd disappeared into the darkness, and Katie realized she had to get back to her tent before her absence was discovered.

Katie:

Two more days passed before Katie escaped her father's list of chores to seek Éamonn. Her father's temper had grown worse and her body ached from his clouts. She could hide most of the bruises with her long sleeves.

When she did escape, she rushed to Éamonn's family's booth, but only Ciaran and Ruari worked the stall. Maybe they'd know where to find him.

Waiting for Ruari to finish a trade with a mousy woman, she sneaked a look at his wounded arm. The skin around the gash looked red and inflamed. He should go visit Cormac for a salve.

While he completed his trade, a lovely saddlebag with intertwined knotwork caught her eye. She lifted it from the peg and traced the lines with her finger. Expertly tooled leather with blue and red painted lines. She loved the serpentine designs sometimes carved on high crosses, or the old book the priest kept. The vivid colors and exquisite drawings enchanted her.

Ciaran's voice at her shoulder interrupted her musings. "That's my own work, it is."

Katie grinned up at him. "This is stunning. Do you do the painting as well?"

"No, that's Éamonn's job." A curl of black hair fell into his eyes. He pushed it back absently. "Your sister isn't with you by chance, is she?"

Katie's good mood turned sour at the mention of Deirdre. "No, she isn't. If you want her so bad, go find her." She slammed the saddle bag onto the counter and spun around, intending to walk off in righteous indignation. Instead, she turned right into the chest of Éamonn Doherty.

After opening her mouth, she closed it again, at a loss for words.

The tall blond man chuckled and gave her a half-smile. "If you're going to keep popping your mouth open and closed like a fish, I should throw you back into the river."

Taking a deep breath, Katie swallowed the angry retort that rose to her lips. "Éamonn, can you get away? I'd like to talk to you."

He took both her hands in his. "For you, *mo chailín rua,* any time."

Her flush at his sweet words made her skin tingle. Éamonn steered her away from the stall to a knoll behind the stables.

Katie opened her mouth yet again, but he put a finger to her lips. "Not here. Let's find a private place." He led her down a path, to an enormous willow tree on the riverbank. Buzzing bees and a few arguing crows rustled in the bushes. The distant sounds of the fair got lost in birdsong.

The river flowed by, and the water smelled fresh and mingled with the fragrance of the surrounding wildflowers. A sunbeam pushed through the canopy of trees and dappled Éamonn's face.

As she sat on the grass, she searched her mind for how to start. What would she say? That she felt sorry for getting angry? She'd never been in the habit of apologizing, except to her father, and then only for her own safety. Her father's face loomed in her imagination, and she shuddered.

Éamonn put his arm around her shoulders, giving a squeeze. "Now. Would you like to tell me what in the name of all that's holy has been going through your lovely head these last days? I know you were angry with me, and then avoided me. What happened?"

"I'm not angry! Well, not anymore. I *did* get the wrong end of the stick about the girl you danced with. Ruari said she's your sister?"

The edge of his mouth curled up. "Yes, wee Fionnuala. She's engaged to Malachy, but she's only fifteen, so they aren't yet official. I had a bit of trouble earlier so, for my penance, I took her to the dance." He brushed his hand through his hair, his expression turning sheepish. "I waited for you, you know."

She lowered her eyes. "Your sister is a lovely girl. I got jealous."

"And my brother is an impressive man. So did I."

Katie's eyes grew wide. "Ruari? He's just a friend. I'd never—" She shook her head, dislodging a tree blossom that had fallen in her hair.

"And why would you never? My brother isn't good enough for you?"

She couldn't tell if she'd offended him or if he teased her again. "No, he's a fine man. But he's not for me. I need someone who I can talk to. I mean, I can talk to him, but he can't, I mean, he's not… Oh, bloody hell." Katie threw her hands up and shook her head. "I can't say this right, Éamonn. I need someone smarter than Ruari. I—"

"I know my brother is no scholar, Katie." Éamonn squeezed her shoulder again, his tone tender. "Still, I don't like hearing others dismiss him for that."

"I don't dismiss him. I value him. He's a friend. And I enjoy talking to him. He's a wonderful listener. But father insists I must marry soon. And for a husband, I need something more."

Éamonn smiled. "That's crystal clear, *mo chailín milis.*"

She let out a chuckle. "It's been a long time since anyone called me sweet."

"Ah, but you *are* sweet. And I long to taste of that honey." He brought her hand to his lips.

His polished worldly lover mask had returned. She jerked her hand back. "Stop right there, Éamonn Doherty. I want to make myself perfectly clear, right now."

He blinked, reminding her of a startled owl. Despite her resolve, she fought the urge to laugh. "I am not the sort of girl who will lie with you on the banks of a river no matter how romantic. If you're serious about courting me, you're to do it properly. Am I understood?"

He straightened his spine and gave a roguish smile. "Aye, Mistress Caitriona. Perfectly clear. I hear and obey, mistress mine!" He saluted her.

Katie gave in to the urge to laugh, and he answered with a whoop. A flock of startled birds burst from the trees, making them both duck and cover their heads. That just made them laugh more.

As the laughter died, he cracked a wide grin. "Aha! I did it!"

"Did what?"

"Why, I made you laugh, sweet girl."

Wiping tears from her eyes, she said, "Oh, Éamonn, you do a girl good, you do."

"Always at your service, milady. Say, are you hungry? I'm fair starved. Stay here, and I'll fetch us something to eat."

Éamonn dashed off to find food. Sorting out their misunderstandings had been easier than she'd thought it would be. The world brightened, and birds sang more sweetly now. This man might just be someone she could stand for more than a week. Someone she might even enjoy spending her life with. Katie smiled in secret anticipation.

After about twenty minutes, he returned with bread and butter and settled next to her, placing a chaste kiss on her forehead. They spent a delightful afternoon, talking about everything and nothing.

"So, I've met Ruari and Turlough. You have sisters other than Fionnuala, yes?"

"Sure, and I do. Édaín, she's married to a smith. Then there's Síle, the baby of the family."

Katie remembered his story about Síle being the last child before their mother died and swallowed back unexpected tears. Her mother might not be the most loving parent, but she lived, at least. "And you all work in your family trade?"

"We all work with leather, but Ciaran and I are best at tooling. Ruari can shape it well. We trade horses and other things. Da will sometimes sing for our supper, whatever we need to do. Tell me of your family? Obviously, I've met your sister."

She wrinkled her nose. "Aye, you have. Well, there's just the two of us, with Mam and Da. Mam does some weaving and sewing. Da trades, but nothing expensive like horses. Sometimes Deirdre and I used to gather flowers to sell bunches in town. Roses are my favorite. As you say, whatever we need to do. I love horses, but we can't even afford one of our own."

Katie remembered one suitor she had, Tomas. He'd been a lovely man but talked so much, he never let her get a word in edgewise. And he never asked her anything. Loved the sound of his own voice, to be sure. She'd rather spend her life with someone who actually let her talk.

As she told him of her sister and parents, Éamonn shifted to face her, avid interest sparkling in his eyes. He seemed genuinely interested in her, a novel feeling. He took her hand and kissed the knuckles. "You are a rare treasure. Your eyes light with a thousand stars when you speak, Katie."

He spoke with flowery poetic skill. Perhaps his grandfather had been the great bard after all. Katie tried hard not to fall into those earnest blue eyes. Still, she couldn't shake the notion of Éamonn's attraction to Deirdre despite his declarations of devotion.

For the rest of the afternoon, they spoke only of the past. They avoided the future, leaving that subject wide open and full of possibilities. The future excited Katie the most. As they parted, he bowed over her hand, kissing her knuckles like a fancy gentleman. Warmth flooded her cheeks as she rushed away.

Katie didn't normally give in to optimism, but the world felt joyful as she walked home that evening, like a new dream, despite the darkening sky.

When she walked into her family's tent, her parents stopped their conversation. Her father sat near their sleeping area, whittling a piece of wood, while her mother set up her loom. With tense shoulders, Katie walked over to her bed and removed her pack from her shoulder.

After she sat at the central hearth, her mother played with a curl of her reddish-brown hair. The way her mother gazed at her with a sort of appraising evaluation meant she planned something.

Da could be trusted to be blunt and honest, if cruel. Mam would smile sweetly to your face while stabbing you in the back. Deirdre learned her tricks from Mam. When her parents exchanged a sideways glance, the hairs on Katie's neck prickled. Then Deirdre came in, oblivious to the tension.

Supper tasted better than usual. Instead of horsebread, they had a loaf of rye with sweet butter, followed by a thick stew of peas and hamhock. Katie still felt full from her meal with Éamonn, but to refuse food would have drawn attention.

Deidre wiped her mouth and cocked her head. "Katie, I searched for you this afternoon. Where'd you disappear to?" Her mother scowled, and the tension ramped up again, but her sister remained oblivious.

"Off doing mending. My skirt ripped when I did laundry the other day." She pulled up the hem of her skirt to show where she mended the tear. *Just not today.*

"All afternoon? That must have been a mighty rip."

Silence, Deirdre. Eat your stew. "I didn't go far. Where did you search?"

"Oh, here and there. I thought you might be at the tanner's booth."

Her father glared at Katie.

Was Deirdre a total eejit or intent on getting Katie in trouble? Probably both. "No, I've not been to their booth for a while. No need for me to visit. We've no horse to saddle, after all."

Her parents exchanged another long glance, and her mother smiled. Not a pleasant expression.

What in Brid's name is happening? Katie longed to question Deirdre, to see how she liked being interrogated. Wisdom and self-preservation kept her silent.

Her father washed down a mouthful of stew with his ale. "Don't run off tomorrow, Katie. We'll need you in the morning." He spoke in quiet words and simple finality.

Even Deirdre finally caught on to the tension. The younger sister glanced between her father and Katie, questions in her eyes. Katie prayed she'd keep quiet and, for once, her prayers were answered.

Curiosity and dread crept into Katie's mind and kept her awake through the night, tossing and turning. The sounds of people carousing outside beckoned to her. She yearned to escape the stifling environs of her tent. Yet her parents remained awake, murmuring in their cot across the room. She tried to relax her muscles, but they ached from clenching. Someone stumbled just outside to the hilarity of his friends. They came close enough that she smelled sour ale.

Grunts and chuckles signaled the lads fell into a tussle, and then the drunken group drifted off into the night.

Tomorrow would bring nothing good. She rarely got anything nice from her parents. Anything nice went to Deirdre, not *her*.

As long as Katie could remember, her sister had gotten the benefit of the doubt in arguments, the best gifts, and the softer hand of discipline. Katie often suffered at her father's hand but didn't beat Deirdre as often. A couple times he'd beaten Katie almost senseless. She bore scars on her arms and back. Katie didn't even remember what she'd done the last time. She did remember not being able to move without sore muscles for weeks.

Fellow Travelers didn't approve of violence against children but rarely acted in censure, except in the most extreme cases. Even if the tribal council fined him, her father would be too stubborn to change. Most trades needed children to work. Sons worked at trades while girls managed the household. The Traveler way of life had rules.

Parents negotiated marriage contracts to guarantee a good match. Girls could always say no, in theory, but a sense of duty often prevented them. Katie's father had made several negotiations in the past. However, the chosen men always broke off negotiations after meeting her. Her father always chose men like him, violent and brutal. Katie spoke her mind and refused to be saddled with a husband like her father. Her sharp tongue would be no prize in an obedient wife, especially from a poor family. Each time, she'd received a beating worse than the last.

Memories of recent transgressions marched through her head, along with the subsequent punishment. What had she done wrong this week? Anything that warranted more beatings? She struggled to remember any slight, even imagined. She had, but nothing her father knew about. He'd already have beaten her if he'd learned of her trysts with Éamonn. Her father hit hard but fast. He didn't dither around. What about her mother? Perhaps she'd learned some gossip, juicy tidbits about Katie's misbehavior. If so, she'd wait for a time to bring everything into one massive sinful charge. Her father would beat her to within an inch of her life. She gave a violent shudder.

Should she leave? Tonight? No, she'd be on her own in the dark with nowhere to go. Her conversation with Éamonn had given her a glimmer of hope she might escape with him, but even if he liked her, she mustn't assume he'd spirit her away to safety. Besides, she might just be imagining problems.

Curiosity and dread crept into Katie's mind and kept her awake through the night, tossing and turning even as Deirdre slept like a babe next to her. *Drat that Deirdre.* She'd refused to share any information on their parent's plans, if she even knew.

Exhaustion took her to the land of sleep. Katie dreamed of a giant standing stone chasing her around the dance circle, trying to crush her with every step. She tossed and turned.

She must have moaned or cried out, for Deirdre poked her. "Shut your gob, Katie."

Katie:

The morning dawned with dim light filtering through the chinks in the tent. Rain poured outside, some dripping through the thin tent walls. Several drops fell on Katie's face as she tossed, still trying to find solace in slumber.

After giving up, Katie flung the covers off, crawled out from beside Deirdre, and dressed. She splashed icy water on her face and tackled her hair. Brushing her hair often soothed her but, today, her locks tangled as soon as she touched them, even where she'd already brushed. Katie cursed under her breath, low enough to keep from waking anyone.

She longed to escape, but her father had told her clearly to remain. Blatant disregard for his orders would ensure a beating.

Last night's stew pot remained on the hook next to the banked fire. She stoked the peat and swung the pot over to warm the rest.

Deirdre emerged from their shared cot, rubbing sleep from her eyes. She stood in her shift, the dim morning light shining behind her. Katie envied her sister's height, slim figure, and long legs. What would it be like to be almost as tall as a man, to just cock her head a little bit to kiss? Éamonn stood so much taller than she did.

Her mother's sharp voice brought Katie back to earth. "Don't burn it, Katie. Can't you do anything right?"

After swinging the pot off the fire, Katie stirred the soup, letting her hair fall to hide her face, but her mother shoved her aside. "Useless girl! Get eggs from the henhouse."

She stumbled outside and breathed deep of the cool, fresh dawn air despite the rain. Freedom, if only for a moment. She quickly got soaked despite her wool shawl. The rain cleared the odor of scorched peas, replacing it with wet wool, mud, and sweet grasses.

While staring into the misty distance, Katie once again thought about running away into the rain, but she had no place to go. Her heart grew as heavy as the rain weighing down her woolen shawl.

Inside again, her mother spooned the scorched stew into bowls and snatched the egg basket from Katie. Cracking them into a pan, she sent a glare toward Katie. "Put a dozen aside. We can sell them for a few *doit.*"

Katie had always respected her mother's talent with the family's finances. Their father earned little enough to work with, but Saoirse managed what resources they had, stretching the meager funds to cover their needs. Katie often wished her mother had been as creative with showing affection. Still, now and then, her mother's anger seemed to shield something more vulnerable. A shadow of fear. Da never hit Mam, but perhaps he used to.

Deirdre escaped after breakfast. Katie stared after her sister with bitter envy, wishing she had half so much freedom. Katie was the eldest and unmarried. Her parents hoped she'd marry well and take care of the whole family. But she'd scared off any suitors so far. She wouldn't submit to a marriage with a man like her father.

After breaking her fast, Katie perched on a stool and carded wool. Combing and untangling the wool took little thought. Her restless night left her with no power of concentration for fine embroidery work, and weaving would be out of the question. The rhythmic clicking and clacking of the loom would only lull her to sleep. To keep her hands from turning red, she tried something Éamonn had suggested. She dripped a bit of melted candle wax onto her palm, slathering the mess over her hands. That helped.

The morning stretched long. Her mother stayed silent while her father slept late. She endured a special sort of torture, waiting for whatever he had in store. Even if her mother knew, she'd never tell Katie. If that was allowed, she'd have done so last night.

The rain slacked to a drizzle by midday. Katie carded all the wool they had in the shelter and began spinning. Despite the wax, her hands grew red and raw by the time her father finally stirred. He grunted for food, and her mother jumped to comply. Katie shrank back to blend into the tent wall.

Spin, spin, pull, twist, spin. Repeat. She almost forgot her parents sitting at the table, keeping sullen company. Spin, twist, pull. Spin more, a soothing rhythm. The drip of water inside the tent eased, and then stopped all together.

She risked a peek. Her father stared right at her. What had she done now? She behaved like a model young lady, doing her chores. He wouldn't punish her for behaving well, would he? Katie gritted her teeth.

He glared at her with intense malice. Katie gulped but daren't look away. Her jaw ached, and her blood raced. What in Brid's name had he planned?

Like a thunderclap, her father spoke. "I've made another match for you. This time, you will agree. We've already shaken on the bargain."

The words made no real sense to Katie. A match? He meant a husband. Her heart leapt into her chest, thinking Éamonn must have talked to her father without her knowing. A sudden surety flashed through her, a certainty she wanted to spend the rest of her life with Éamonn. But no, he couldn't have. And what had her father meant, already shaken on? A daughter could always say no.

"The priest will begin the ceremony this evening. Have your mother get you ready. He's paid a hefty price, and he won't be cheated."

He stood to leave the tent, but Katie grabbed his arm. "Da! Who? Who is it?"

Her da glared at her hand on his arm. She dropped her hand and cast her gaze to the ground, heart racing. The anticipation made her shrink back, but he didn't strike her. "The MacCrimmon lad. He's traded a fine stallion for you. Make sure you earn it. And ye'll marry with no protest, or I promise you'll not live to protest again."

She stared at his feet as he left the tent.

Katie stood stunned. A horse? *He sold me for a horse! What am I, a wagon to be traded off to the highest bidder?* Anger flooded through her now her father had gone. Her face turned red.

Her mother's slap burned her cheek. "Don't you dare, Katie. You behave yourself like a proper girl ought, or I won't be the one delivering the next blow, d'ye hear?"

"But Ma, he can't force me to marry, can he? I'm allowed to refuse! That's our law!"

Her mother went back to her weaving. "He's had enough of your refusals. And enough of you running perfectly good husbands off with yer serpent's tongue."

Now she stopped her shuttle and glared at Katie. "Ye're eighteen, for the love of Mary. Ye should have been married off years ago, and Deirdre besides. Now, get yourself clean and back after midday. I've a new dress for you, at least."

Her fists clenched in fear and rage, Katie shook her head. "Ma, I can't!"

"You will. You'll do as you're told, young lady. Obey your father until you're married. Then obey your husband. We've given you far too much freedom. It's high time you learn your place."

After escaping once more into the cool April air, she took several deep, long breaths. Cool mist caressed her skin but, this time the water felt oppressive. Éamonn's face flashed in her memory, and she reached for that dream before it faded into the mist. For a moment, she felt freedom, rather than a rapidly closing snare. With a gasp, she realized she didn't know which "MacCrimmon lad" her father had sold her to.

Oh, please don't let it be Donald. Please, please, please! Not that she would walk quietly to her fate, but at least Lochlann seemed kind. Donald reminded her far too much of her father. Perhaps that's why he'd made the match. What a neat little trap, to escape one brute only to fall into the arms of another.

What should she do? Her idea of running away sprang up but, again, to where? Éamonn might help. Could she find him in a half-hour? She'd still have to wash or her mother would know.

Rushing to the river, she slipped several times in mud and wet grasses. She didn't care. On the way back, she'd be more cautious.

She removed her shoes and walked right into rushing water. Gasping from the chill, she dunked her head. The water rushed high and washed her clean in no time.

With some mad scrubbing in her hair, she loped back to the fair. Her haste rewarded her with several precious minutes to search for Éamonn.

First, she checked the tanner's booth. She spied Ruari, but not Éamonn, and his absence made her heart sink. Wait! She spied his blond hair. Ruari's bulk had eclipsed his slender brother.

She rushed to him, grabbing his arm as her clothing dripped. "Éamonn, I need your help!"

"Katie? Why are you soaked? Are you hurt?"

"No, I'm fine but please, come away! I must speak to you."

With a confused nod to his brother, he allowed her to pull him until they reached behind the booth, away from prying eyes and curious ears.

"What in the name of all that's holy has gotten into you? What's going on?"

Katie's gaze flicked all around, searching for any sign of her father, mother, or Deirdre. "I said I need your help."

His grin showed off his dimples, and he took both her hands. "Anything, my sweet. Shall I fetch you a carriage? A rose?"

Katie clenched her jaw against his silliness and kept her words low. "My da is marrying me off today."

He took a moment to digest the news, then his eyes grew wide. "Marrying you off? But you can say no! Please refuse, Katie. I can make a counteroffer! Wait… who is the groom?"

Her skin crawled as she shuddered. "One of the MacCrimmons. He didn't even say which. I don't think he cares. Éamonn, if I don't do this, he'll kill me. I can't refuse him. And…and he traded me for a *horse*!" Her indignation flooded back, rage filling her blood.

Éamonn scratched his chin, gazing toward the horse stalls. "Hmph. I'll bet I know which horse, too. He's a beauty, I'll grant you."

She jerked her hands out of his grasp. "Are you saying you *approve*?"

Hastily he shook his head. "No, no, of course not, *mo mhuirnín*. Nothing of the sort. Just an admiration of the beast in question. I'd wanted to buy him myself. He'd make a grand stud."

She put her palms on his cheeks. "Focus, Éamonn! I need to rush back. Mam is expecting me at any moment. To dress me like a prize for my new husband."

Éamonn gripped her shoulders. "I'll find your da and offer him… I don't know. I'll offer him something. He must be more interested in a love match if I can just give him what he wants."

Her father's list of needs had never included Katie's happiness. That must have shown on her face.

"Hey, now, my love. My own true dear love. I'll find a way. I promise. I promised to protect you, remember? I'll do so now. I swear I will protect you with my body, my name, whatever I have to give. Do you believe me?"

"I want to, I do! But—"

He placed a finger to her lips. "Shh. I'll find a way."

Katie glanced over her shoulder. "I'm counting on you, Éamonn. I must fly. The wedding is in a few hours." She dashed off, careful not to slip again in the mud.

Part II
Chapter Six

Éamonn:

Éamonn paced the stall, wearing a trench in the mud with his anxious footsteps. What *could* he offer? His family had some wealth, but a horse remained an expensive commodity. They had two sturdy mares to pull their wagons, but the old dears came nowhere near the same class as that gray stallion. Ciaran had a beautifully tooled saddle, a piece they put out in front of the booth to draw customers in. But what use would such a gorgeous saddle be to a man with no horse?

He halted, glancing at the stall door. Could he bribe the priest into marrying them now? He and Katie, once wed, would be forever together. Lochlann would have no claim on her, and she'd be away from her father's heavy hand. But no, that seemed silly. The priest would be an honorable man, and he'd never go along with such an underhanded scheme.

Maybe Turlough had some ideas. But after a quick summation of the situation, his father shook his head. "I don't know, son. Our wealth is in our music not in coin. I don't suppose the fact you love the girl carries weight with her father?"

"She says not. He doesn't seem to care for either girl from what I've seen."

Turlough stroked his chin, gazing toward the horse stalls. "How about arranging a deal with the MacCrimmon lad? Convince him to back out of the agreement? After all, who wants a bride whose heart is already given?" Turlough narrowed his eyes at Éamonn. "Only the heart, yes?"

Éamonn waved his hand. "Yes, Da. We've not even kissed yet. I swear. Da, she doesn't even know which brother she's to marry! If that's Lochlann, I might have a chance. He seems a decent sort, despite all. But Donald—"

"This is a right fine mess, no doubt. Here, let's go approach Lochlann."

While staring at his shoes, Éamonn swallowed. "I don't think I'll be much help with him after that night at the dice ring."

Turlough shook his head. "No, I'll not do this for you. Perhaps you'll realize your actions have consequences. I'll come with you, though. And if things get dicey, I'll speak up."

Éamonn heaved a sigh of relief. He'd have no chance at all on his own. But Turlough had the skills of a bard. Traditionally, bards advised chiefs, and Turlough could talk his way out of most situations armed with nothing but charm and sweet guile. Not a large chance, especially if Donald was the groom, but a chance.

He couldn't find Lochlann at the horse corral. The gray stallion stood tall, coat shimmering in the late morning mist. Éamonn experienced another tug of envy at the beast.

Next, they checked the MacCrimmons' wagon on the other side of the fairgrounds. Lochlann washed his face at the water barrel out front. Éamonn hoped that meant he would be the groom.

Éamonn took a deep breath. "Lochlann, how are you this fine, soft day?"

Lochlann glared at Éamonn but answered pleasantly enough, "Just getting clean. I've important business to take care of this afternoon."

"I don't mean to pry into your business, certainly. However, I think I know what the business involves, and we've a suggestion."

Lochlann stared at Éamonn for several long moments. He stole a quick glance at Turlough. "And what would the likes of you have for me, then?"

After swallowing an angry response, Éamonn took a deep breath. "I'd like to make a bargain with you."

Éamonn held his breath as Lochlann gave him a long look, up and down. "Not you." He turned to Turlough. "I'll talk to you, Turlough. You've always been fair to me. But," he flicked his hand as if shooing a fly, "I'm not interested in discussing anything with that arse."

Éamonn glanced at his father. Turlough took a deep breath and turned back to Lochlann. "The matter concerns Éamonn, Lochlann. I need him to be part of this. Please reconsider? This is important. Otherwise, I wouldn't ask. I realize my son has been unjust to you in the past."

Éamonn kept his peace, his jaw aching as he gritted his teeth.

Lochlann spat to the side. "Fine. Let's sit inside, then. No need to let the rest of the world know we're talking. Just you, though. Not him."

Éamonn tried not to seethe. He paced outside like an eejit while Turlough and Lochlann discussed his love for Katie, the marriage contract, her father, the horse, all as if none of this had anything to do with him.

How had Katie reacted when her father had announced his *bargain?* Had she flown at him in a rage? Simmered until she burst? After comparing her to a hot pot of stew made him grin, he schooled his expression.

The Scotsman's voice filtered out, "But we've already made the deal, Turlough. We've shaken on the bargain. Liam owns the horse, and I'll wed Katie this evening."

So Lochlann will *be the groom.* He held onto that morsel of hope, at least. Éamonn shuddered at the idea of either man touching Katie, but Donald would have been so much worse.

Turlough clasped his hands together. "You could refuse to marry her."

Lochlann's eyes grew wide. "Jilt her at the altar? I would never do such a thing to a lass! Besides, that would mean I reneged on a deal. I'm a horse trader. My reputation is my livelihood."

Turlough spoke in a soft tone, and Éamonn leaned closer to the tent to make out the words. "Katie is no ordinary lass, young man. You're headed back to Scotland after this, aren't you? Who cares what they think of you in the backwoods of Ireland?"

"We're Travelers. Gossip moves faster than a racing horse."

"We have to find a way. She's already in love with my son, Lochlann. You can't want to marry a woman who's already given her heart to someone else?"

Lochlann hesitated before answering, "You're right, I'd rather marry a girl who liked me. But who does that? Parents arrange marriages so their children are well-cared for. I have a decent business and a respectable family on Skye. My father is the piper for a great clan. Katie'll be well taken care of. While I didn't originally want this marriage, I'm bound to go through with it."

Éamonn couldn't wait outside any longer. He rushed into the MacCrimmon's tent. "You didn't want this? Who wants it, then?"

He stared at Éamonn now, eyes wide as if asking forgiveness. "That would be my brother."

"Your brother? Why does he care?"

Lochlann shrugged. "He promised our father he'd see me married, to ensure the family line. He's a man of his word, too."

Turlough cleared his throat and placed his hands on his knees. "What if I offered a trade in exchange for your refusal?"

Lochlann blinked and wrinkled his nose. "Trade? Trade what?"

"Well, I'm sure you've seen the fine saddle Ciaran made at our booth."

The Scotsman's eyes grew wide. "The saddle? 'Tis indeed a work of art. Clearly, hundreds of hours of work went into the crafting of that piece. You'd trade that, just for your son to have a shrew for a wife?"

Turlough nodded. "His happiness means everything to me."

Tears prickled behind Éamonn's eyes. A surge of love and gratitude for his father almost overwhelmed him, but he must not allow them to leak in view of Lochlann.

Lochlann glanced at his feet again, his mouth moving as if he spoke to himself. Finally, he shook his head. "I can't, Turlough. This is Donald's deal, and I canna break the bargain. He's the eldest, and Da put him in charge."

Éamonn threw up his hands. "Then Donald should find his own wife! Why this complex plan?"

With a shake of his head, Lochlann stared at his hands again. "My brother had a wife. When she couldn't bear any bairns for him, he… Well, she died last year."

Silence descended on the tent. Turlough brushed his hands through his long hair, a gesture Éamonn recognized as his own.

Éamonn made a final, desperate offer. "Can I offer aught to change your mind, Lochlann? Anything at all?"

Éamonn expected resentment, but he saw only defeat in the other man's eyes. "No, Éamonn. I wish we could find a way. I'm fond of the girl, and I don't want to hurt her any more than you do. But Donald and her da are determined to make this happen." His shaky tenor voice sounded choked.

Turlough, Éamonn, and Lochlann all sighed at the same time. Éamonn gave a nod to his erstwhile rival, and Lochlann returned the gesture. At least they'd repaired some of the damage he'd caused with the cheating accusation.

As they returned to their own booth, Éamonn gripped his father's arm. "Da, I can't just leave things like this. I can't! I promised Katie I'd protect her."

"Éamonn, I can't think of what else to do. I tried everything with Lochlann. And he doesn't seem a bad sort. Sure and he'll not mistreat her. She'll have protection, though not your own."

Desperation turned Éamonn's mind frantic. "We could run off together. I'd take her before the wedding, far away, where we'd never be found."

His father gripped his arm. "Son, that would never work. Life on your own, without a Traveler family? You could never contact them again. Word would be out. Any Traveler would turn you in. You'd be on the run, like the tales of Diarmuid and Gráinne. And what would you do for a living? Your skills are gambling and horse trading. You need people for both."

Éamonn clenched his jaw, unconvinced.

"And when she is with child? How would she do all that alone? Or when she's ill? Look at Fionnuala, for instance. She isn't feeling well this morning, so we have Cormac looking after her. If you're alone, you'll have no one. No, Éamonn, that's no solution. Remember, I've been on my own on the road. Wandering isn't nearly as romantic as the tales might lead you to believe." His voice turned sad on the last words.

Éamonn kicked at a stone in the path. "We must be able to do something, Da! I'm ready to go to the stones and ask the Fair Folk for help at this point."

Turlough halted, staring at him with wide eyes. "Don't even joke about it, Éamonn. The Fair Folk are not to be called upon lightly. Asking the wrong way is folly."

The younger man threw his hands into the air. "This isn't lightly! This is my life and my love!"

With a roll of his eyes, Turlough started walking again. "Sing me another song, son. You'll have another 'love of your life' next fair. I've seen it happen. Nothing in this world is stronger than young lust."

"No, Da. This is the one. She's the match for me, I swear to you!"

Turlough turned back to him. "Éamonn, calm down. I know this seems like the end of the world just now, but in a few years, you'll—"

Éamonn grabbed his father's shoulders and gave them a shake. "You don't understand, Da!" He paused to take a deep breath. "I won't be here in a couple of years unless I'm with Katie."

Turlough pulled free and held up his hands. "Stop, Éamonn! Get hold of yourself. Heed me now. If you're that certain she's your one true love, there's one more thing we can try, but I need time to prepare. This may not help at all but may be worth a gamble."

Hope sprung in Éamonn's heart. "What? I'm always up for a gamble, Da. What'll you do?"

"You'll see. Meet me out at the standing stones in an hour."

His heart raced, unwilling to wait. "An hour? We don't have much time. We should go now!"

"Not now. Go."

Éamonn slunk away, anxious to do something, anything. Should he go find Katie? They wouldn't allow her to talk to him. Deirdre! Maybe he could convince her to carry a message, for Katie's sake if not for his. Where would she be? He went in search of Ciaran, despite the drizzly gloom.

As he came close to the leather booth, he thanked Jesus Christ and all his saints when he spied the raven-haired lass chatting with his cousin on a fence. They giggled over a flower Ciaran had in his hands.

He broke in without preamble, "Deirdre! I need your help. Would you do a favor for me?"

Ciaran scowled at the interruption, and Deirdre glared at him. "And a good morning to you, as well, Éamonn Doherty."

With a bow, Éamonn relented. "Good morning, Deirdre, I'm sorry for the rudeness. But I need your help."

Deirdre smiled and jumped off the fence and spoke in a lilting tone. "Of course, Éamonn. I'm at your service." Ciaran's scowl deepened.

"I need you to take a message to your sister, right away. Could you?"

Her eyes grew wide, and she cocked her head. "To Katie? Whatever for? She's busy this afternoon, anyhow. Family matters." She flicked her hand and gave him a coy smile.

"I know what she's busy with. I must get her a message. Can you tell her?" He poured urgency into his voice. His need must have gotten through, for her light tone hardened.

"I could, but I won't. And if you truly know what she's busy with, then you've no business sending her secret messages. Perhaps you should contact her *fiancé* if you've business with his bride."

With a sniff and flick of her hair, she turned her back on him and gave his cousin a sweet smile. "You were saying, Ciaran?"

He yanked on her arm. "Deirdre! Please, I need your help. What do you want from me? Anything, just let Katie know I've not given up."

She glanced back at him with a contemptuous sneer. "Why does that matter? The deal's done. If you knew my father at all, you'd know he never goes back on a bargain shaken upon."

Éamonn pulled back, looking at the dark-haired girl with fresh eyes. His skin prickled. "I do believe you are a spiteful wench, Deirdre O'Malley. You're jealous of your sister, is that it? You want to see her suffer?"

She drew herself up to her full height and placed a hand on her chest as Ciaran scowled. "Me, spiteful? You don't know Katie half as well as you think you do if you call *me* spiteful."

Éamonn narrowed his eyes and clenched his jaw. "You should find yourself a looking glass, Deirdre. You'll see what I'm talking about. Ciaran, have your fun with her, but I wouldn't keep her. She's spoilt."

He stalked off to find the stone circle and his father.

Despite his determination, the mists conspired to confuse him. He remembered where the circle stood. He even brought Katie there. But the drizzly day made the fog as thick as soup. Swirling and circling him, the mist taunted him with odd smells and echoes. His footfalls sounded flat and distant. The bushes and trees faded in and out of the light.

Éamonn arrived soaked to the knees from wet grass. He shivered and pulled his cloak around his shoulders. His father perched on the large flat stone at the center of the circle. When he saw Éamonn, he hopped off, cradling something in his hand. "Come, Éamonn. I've something to show you."

As Éamonn approached, his father held out a large, penannular cloak brooch. Exquisitely made from silver chased with gold knotwork, several rose-colored stones studded the piece. The interlaced design had birds and other animals. Éamonn let out his breath in an appreciative whistle. The jewelry covered the palm of his father's hand.

Éamonn met his father's gaze, the possibilities racing through his mind. "Do you think Lochlann would take this to refuse Katie?"

Turlough caressed the edge. "No. We can never trade this away."

"I don't understand."

"Nor should you. Let me tell you a story."

Éamonn frowned, staring at his father. Sometimes, Turlough didn't seem to have a firm grasp on reality. "Da, we don't have time for a story!"

"This won't take long, and I must."

While stomping to the largest stone, Éamonn crossed his arms and leaned against it. "Grand, tell your damned story, then."

After hopping back on his perch and adopting his storytelling posture, Turlough began. "Many generations ago, our family helped a druid in distress."

"Father! Seriously, what does this have to do with Katie?"

Turlough snapped in a sharp tone, "Be quiet and listen, Éamonn. You'll find out."

With a deep sigh, Éamonn settled on the stone across from his father with poor grace. They sat on the enormous, low altar stone, like two monks at prayer. The surface felt strangely warm.

Turlough caressed the jewelry while he spoke. Éamonn fancied he saw blue sparks as Turlough touched it. "Family legend says Christian monks hounded the druid, before Saint Patrick even arrived on our shores. We don't know what our family did to help him, but help him we did. He rewarded our family for our assistance. This brooch," he held up the jewelry, "he gave as reward. This piece is tied to our blood and gives the bearer a gift."

The younger man wrinkled his brow. "A gift? Father, stop being vague. What gift?"

Turlough gave a shrug. "That depends. Each person is different. For me, I received the music of the Fae."

For once, Éamonn held his tongue. This brooch gave his father his music? Whether Turlough O'Carolan was his father or not, he sang the angels down from the heavens. Perhaps his father wasn't just telling tales. Éamonn reached for the brooch.

His father pulled away, holding his hand up. "Wait, I'm not finished with the story yet. Each person gets a power. Nothing dramatic, like lightning out of the sky, or the ability to fly like an eagle, but subtle. However, not everyone is suitable for the brooch. Ruari, though I love him well, could never hold the power. Neither could Ciaran, bless his feckless soul. My mother passed the brooch on to me."

Éamonn's mind had been racing with plans, but that halted him. "Your mother? Not O'Carolan?"

"No, no. If O'Carolan received his music from the Fair Folk, then he didn't get that gift through this brooch. That must have been a separate magic. No, the brooch came to my mother's mother, through her kin."

"What was her gift?"

"She had a dangerous gift, one of illusion. Foolish use almost got her killed more than once and may have driven her mad in the end. That, with my own experiences, taught me to keep this secret. The church wouldn't be happy to see such a pagan artifact, and people get mad about stealing power."

Éamonn remembered stories of a witch burnt at the stake in Ulster, just fifty years earlier. He shuddered at such a horrible death. And Ruari wouldn't be clever enough to keep that secret. Ciaran would brag about such a gift.

"How do you decide who should get the brooch?"

"So I was taught, and so I shall teach. The person must be clever enough to keep the secret. They must be on a quest. That's an important part, the seeking. The brooch might help you find your gift. But until you're attuned to the brooch, you don't know what gift you will receive. Then you must perform a ceremony and ask to be accepted by the Fair Folk."

Éamonn's blood chilled at the serious mention of the Fair Folk. He'd been half-joking when he spoke of asking them earlier, but his father took the notion seriously. "And you're thinking I might get a useful power?"

"You might. And you might not. The brooch might bring you the ability to heal, or find things, or hear voices of the dead. Or something else we can't think of."

Éamonn eyed the brooch warily. "How do I attune to the magic?"

Turlough raised his eyebrows. "Do you want to try? It's not a gentle process."

Éamonn thought about Katie, dressing at this very moment to marry someone else. He swallowed. "I must try. This might be the only chance Katie and I have left."

Nodding, Turlough stood, his knees creaking with age. Éamonn stood ill at ease.

His father led him outside the circle. "Wait here. I'll walk around the circle with the brooch, and then we'll walk around together. Then we enter the circle, drink wine, and offer some to the Fae."

This sounded so wickedly pagan, like a witches' sabbat. Fear and Catholic guilt gripped his heart, and he crossed himself.

His father slapped at his hand. "None of that, Éamonn. This is Fae magic. You will not doubt that when you see. They don't take kindly to such gestures."

Guiltily, he dropped his hands. He glanced toward the sun, but it remained shrouded in fog. How much time did they have left?

Turlough marched around the outside of the circle while holding up a silver cup. He walked widdershins, opposite of sunwise, chanting under his breath. Not quite Irish, not English. Not even Traveler's Cant. Éamonn couldn't make out the words and didn't think he wanted to.

Something shone in the mist. No, he hadn't imagined it. A glow came from his father's hands, greenish-blue like his own eyes. He rubbed them, certain he dreamt. Despite his respect for his father, he hadn't believed him. *This must be a load of superstitious tripe.* No, the jewelry glimmered, pulsing and moving like northern lights in the palm of his father's hand.

An unearthly hum rumbled beneath him. Did the ground shake? Or his own knees? He knew in his bones this was no dream. Something inexplicable and magical had awakened. Something to do with the Fair Folk, the *Sídhe.* Those creatures that lived below the ground, full of magic and mischief.

Every child heard stories of the Fair Folk. Crafty, cruel, and sometimes downright nasty beings who lived in the hills. Even powerful men who feared nothing in the mortal realm would leave a saucer of cream out for the Fair Folk. To insult them might result in being plagued by disaster and disease for generations. To please them sometimes meant a precious gift. Like the brooch.

Éamonn's skin crawled as his father chanted in the strange language.

Turlough finished his circuit and reached for his son's arm. Éamonn couldn't abandon this frightening ritual. He must try, for Katie's sake. He shut his eyes tight and walked next to his father.

Without being able to see, the ground felt like it disappeared under his feet as they paced around the stones. Éamonn rose higher and higher, treading on nothing but good intentions and ghostly laughter. When he cracked his eyes open, the mists swirled and churned. Dancers gyrated in the fog.

Dancers?

Figures spun in elegant, nebulous formations. They glowed with a mix of pale blue, deep green, and purple light, trailing sparks like a shawl blowing in the wind. Bits of light emanating from the brooch danced with them. The sparks and dancers frolicked through the stones, swirling around behind them like ribbons.

Turlough's chanting turned to song. His voice smooth and true, his tone grew strong. Years fell from his face whenever he sang, but now he appeared younger than Éamonn. He sang as the lights danced, finishing the song as Éamonn and Turlough completed their walk around the stones. Éamonn had never heard a sound so beautiful and heartbreaking in his life.

Time lost all meaning as the shining sparks swirled in precise patterns. The stones glowed in different colors, too. Pinks and yellows joined blues and greens for an iridescent rainbow. Piercing points of white sparkled around him, like glow worms on a lazy summer evening. Éamonn squinted as his eyes ached from the shimmering spectacle.

The dancers joined Turlough's song, their descant rising far above human voice. The sound passed through the marrow of his bones, ripping through his body like a winter storm.

Turlough held out the brooch to him, flat in his palm. Éamonn took several deep breaths and grasped the glowing object.

A force slammed him back. He fell onto the marshy grass, his bones aching. He couldn't see or breathe, as if ten burly men Ruari's size had stomped on his chest. Éamonn choked, trying to get one good breath into his lungs. His fingers and toes burned, and his blood boiled. Battle sounds rang in his ears, a mighty war between a vast host of warriors. Death cries and shouts of triumph ripped through his brain. Ravens cawed and pecked at his eyes. Hoofbeats pounded through his skull, and the icy kiss of a deadly bronze blade caressed his neck.

The sounds faded as he tried to slow his heart. Finally, he could breathe again, but the air seared his throat. Someone screamed. He recognized his own voice. That's why his throat hurt.

He tried to open his eyes, but they refused to obey him. He tried again, squinting against the painful light, then shut them again.

Slowly, he cracked one eye, and his father knelt over him, surrounded by swirling white mists and a few sparkles of color. Turlough's ponytail draped over his shoulder, near Éamonn's face. A few long, blond locks of hair tickled his nose. He sneezed.

Turlough patted his chest. "Ah, well, that's better, then. As I recall, the magic packs quite a punch, but you'll recover well enough. Better to do this when you're young and strong."

"Gahkk!"

"Yes, I expect so. Come on, I'll help you up." He stood and offered his hand.

Even with Turlough's help, it took a great deal of creaking and groaning to get Éamonn back onto the now ice-cold altar stone. Bog dew soaked his back. He shivered despite his good wool cloak.

What happened? Something swirled in his mind. His faith in God did battle with the fae, and a great goddess rose from the mist. No, that must be Katie.

Éamonn's fingers hurt. When he glanced down, he realized he still clutched the jewelry tight. When he loosened his grip, prying each finger away from their position, the stones glowed purple rather than rose. A thread of ice shot down his spine.

His father chuckled. "The magic is always powerful the first time. This gets much easier later."

The younger man glanced up, eyes wide. "I have to do this again?"

"No, no, not like this. The first time is the worst. Later, you can come back to the stones. Any standing stones will do, mind you. You can get more power or a good soul rest. That's why I come here to meditate. The stones help me relax and heal. Any fairy stones, really."

Éamonn nodded, though he didn't understand. "How do I know what my gift is?" He breathed in deep and tasted something ancient, loamy, even primeval in the air.

Turlough grimaced and glanced away. "I'm afraid we have no one way to tell. That depends on what you received."

"So, I just try things and see if I can do them better? Or is there a test?"

"No, just trial and error."

Éamonn stepped off the stone to pace. "But that might take weeks. Months! And we don't even have an hour left!"

Turlough looked him up and down, searching for changes. "I said this would be a gamble. I thought you might receive some obvious gift, which would manifest quickly, but I can't see anything different, I'm afraid."

Éamonn considered what might have changed about him. His mind blanked just as the sun shot a beam of light through the mist.

Panic bubbled up fast. "It's getting late. I've got to get back, Da. I can't waste any more time on this Fae shite."

Turlough pulled back as his gaze darted around, naked fear on his face. His voice dropped to a fierce whisper, "Éamonn! You can't insult the Fae in their own place! I've taught you better than that! They were just here! Surely you saw them? Heard them? You must be more cautious! Just because our ancestor helped out a druid doesn't mean we're immune to Fae revenge!"

Éamonn scowled at his father. Sure, and Turlough had done his best to help but, in the end, nothing helped. He stormed off as well as he could on marshy land. When he glanced back, his father shook his head. Éamonn left him behind in the mists, amongst the fairy stones.

Turlough had wasted so much precious time on this mad dream. Such a trifling chance. Even if he *did* receive some mystical gift, he had no idea what it might be.

He wanted to hit everything as he hurried through the bog grasses. Turning his frustration into a test, he tried to push each stone he passed with his mind. He jumped a few times, flapping his arms. Maybe he could fly?

Several more ideas flitted through his mind as he pushed through the reeds. He tried lifting things and creating lightning, he listened for music or voices.

What if he got nothing? Éamonn's irritation returned as he walked. How could he figure out such a thing so quickly?

His father caught up with him, panting. "Éamonn! Have you lost your senses? You need to apologize for your disrespect to the Old Ones. You'll call down their mischief."

Biting back an angry retort, Éamonn saw the fear in Turlough's expression. Mischief was a much too mild word for the revenge folks had suffered from angering the Fair Folk. Chastened, Éamonn relented. "Fair enough, Da."

Lifting his voice to the still-thick fog, he said, "I apologize for any offense I may have offered in my ignorance." He bowed awkwardly to the surrounding marshland.

Calmer, he asked, "Da, will that work?"

Turlough glanced around. "You'll have to hope so. But if not, you'll know soon enough, to be sure."

Éamonn swallowed and gritted his teeth. "Do have you any idea how to help me find this gift?"

Turlough shook his head, a sad smile on his face. "Time and patience, perhaps some experimenting. That's the only advice I can give."

Éamonn's eyes grew wide as a notion struck him. "We'll go back and ask them!"

"That seems like a good…" He'd already half turned when his father grabbed his arm. "Wait, Éamonn! No, you can't go and ask them. They aren't a friendly neighbor or a landlord, but…" Turlough stared at him with narrowed eyes. "Try to convince me of something."

"What?"

"Make a case for some horrible idea. Try to force me to believe."

Éamonn narrowed his eyes and wondered if the Fae had stolen the last of his father's sense, but he shrugged. "We should sail to America tonight."

Turlough rolled his eyes. "Is this the best you can do? Feel the power, man. Pour energy into the sale. It'll tingle in your skin. You've seen the best traders at their craft." He snapped his fingers. "I know, pretend you're convincing Katie's father to let her marry you."

After taking a deep breath, Éamonn gripped his father's arms and said, "America's streets are paved with gold, Da! Everyone knows that's true. Come with me tonight, and we'll arrive by morning."

"Right, good! Now, tell me that's a terrible idea."

Éamonn pulled back. "Have you lost all your senses, Da?"

"Just do it!"

"Uh, sure and that's a horrible notion. We'd be poor in America without our family around us on a cold winter's night."

Turlough hesitated, a series of emotions flashing across his face, and then laughed out loud, echoing strangely in the thick mist. "That's it, lad! You've got it!"

Éamonn had to smile at his father's hilarity, but in the back of his mind, the minutes ticked away. "Got what? Have I caught insanity from you?"

"Persuasion, son. When you first suggested we ask the Fae about your gift, I actually considered doing so despite knowing full well it's a horrible idea. When you put your heart into the magic just now, the urge to run off to America and become wealthy beyond our wildest dreams surged in my heart."

He pressed his hand to his temple as his head ached. "Persuasion? You mean, I can convince people to do what they don't want?"

Turlough lifted his eyebrows. "At least for a short time. A kernel of truth in the desire might be needed. Certainly, I've no wish to go to America now, and yet, I felt ready to hop on a boat a moment ago. If your power is persuasion, that might help win the lass."

Éamonn scratched at his scalp. "Hmm. That has possibilities. But if the power fades so quickly…"

He might convince Katie's father he'd be a better match than Lochlann, but not for long. Could he persuade the priest they weren't a legal match? Again, the temporary nature of his gift made that a silly notion. "Da, if I could count on any length of time, this would help. But anything we try will fade too quickly. I'll just have to try something else. I must get back. Will you come with me? Maybe we can still stop this wedding after all." He gave a wan smile, hoping Turlough would forgive him for his earlier dismissal of the brooch's power. Still, the back of his mind churned with idea after idea.

With a resigned sigh, Turlough put his hand on his son's lean back. "All right, son, let's go see what we may do."

By the time they reached the fairgrounds, the sun hugged the horizon, and they hurried to the chapel area. The summer fair had no church, but the local priest consecrated a clearing, and Father Byrne conducted Mass every Sunday.

The wedding and Mass would be held today, the last Sunday of the event. This would be the culmination of three weeks of racing, trading, dealing, wooing, and finally, marrying before scattering to all points of Ireland.

Now that the rain had stopped, someone had decorated the clearing, draping the surrounding trees with colorful bunting and garlands of spring flowers. Dusk hadn't fallen, but lanterns already shone around the altar, draped with white vestments. A procession of young children passed halfway through the center aisle. Ten couples would be joined today, and the nuptials drew several hundred spectators.

Éamonn scanned the crowd for his Katie but didn't spy her red, curly hair amongst the brides. He searched for Lochlann, the kernel of a plan forming in his head. A desperation move, but he had no other choice.

He glimpsed flyaway blond hair and steadied his gaze. Lochlann fidgeted with his fingers with Donald glowering next to him. His expression deepened as Éamonn approached.

Ignoring the older brother, Éamonn spoke to Lochlann. "I have a proposal for you."

Donald growled. "That can wait, Doherty. We have a ceremony to attend first."

Éamonn put his hand on Lochlann's arm. "No, we can't. This is about the ceremony. Lochlann, can I speak with you in private?"

Donald shoved his way in front of his meeker brother. "No. Now bugger off."

Lochlann placed a hand on his brother's arm. "Donald, let's hear him out."

"We've nothing to say to the dirty beggar. Now, clear off, or I'll make sure you do." Donald balled his fists and leaned toward Éamonn before Lochlann pulled him away.

They'd turned to leave when Éamonn blurted out, "Lochlann! I'll play you for her."

None of them spoke for a long moment. Lochlann turned, his head cocked. "What? What do you mean?"

Éamonn spoke the words in a mad rush, pushing his heart into every word. "We'll play dice for the privilege of marrying Caitriona O'Malley. If I win, I can marry her, but you still get the saddle Ciaran made. If you win, you get the girl anyhow. Her father keeps the horse either way, so the deal is still honored, and your reputation is intact. You win no matter what. What do you say?"

Now, he held his breath, waiting for an answer to this last, desperate chance. He needed his luck to hold true.

Lochlann's brow furrowed, blinking like an owl. Then he shook his head.

Éamonn gripped him by the upper arms and gave him a small shake, pushing his Fae power through as much as he could, until his skin tingled. "C'mon, Lochlann. You can't lose! You know this makes sense."

Katie would murder him if he knew she'd used her as a bargaining chip, but that's how these men thought of her, and he had to speak their language. He sent a silent apology to her and a heartfelt wish she'd never find out, even as his stomach roiled.

Donald scowled at him. Éamonn tried to push his influence toward the older brother, instead. "You could have your choice of any single woman here!" His power slipped aside, like water off rocks. As he tried to push again, the tingle in his skin died to a whimper.

"I've been married, and I'm done with that. It's Lochlann's turn." The older Scot turned to the younger brother. "I don't trust him. Don't even try."

While glancing at Donald, the younger brother shrugged. "This might not be a bad idea. Have you seen that saddle?"

"No! We have the girl. No sense in gambling her away." He spun back on Éamonn, thunder clouding his eyes. "Now, feck off, Doherty!"

Rage sparked from Donald, more than his words or actions could account for. Éamonn squinted, not sure he actually saw the red maelstrom of vicious hostility swirling as a wave of nausea swept over him.

Lochlann lowered his head. He'd go along with his brother's dismissal. In Lochlann, he sensed calm, blue water, a shallow pond. But Éamonn didn't care about red storms or blue waters. He wanted Katie. His stomach churned and he grew dizzy. So much for the much-vaunted gift from the Fae.

The brothers left, and Éamonn started after them, but Turlough held him back. As the Scots got farther away, Éamonn's shoulders slumped. He'd tried his last gambit and failed. What else could he do? He stumbled off to the bushes and vomited.

When he returned, his expression must have shown his despair. Turlough raised his eyebrows as he clapped a hand on Éamonn's back. "Did you try to use the power at all?"

"Of course, I did, Da! Do you think I wouldn't? But nothing worked. The magic just makes me ill."

"Aye, that's the price. The harder you use the power, the sicker you get. Did you get even a glimmer of result?"

"With Lochlann, maybe, but not a bit on Donald. I might have seen something else. A vision, a glimpse of something. Donald seemed covered with anger and hate, red and swirling, while Lochlann looked like a still, blue pond."

"Hmm. Sort of a painting of their feelings, perhaps? Or their intentions?"

Éamonn shrugged. He didn't know what he'd seen, intentions, feelings, or insane apparitions brought on by his nausea.

Ruari and Ciaran joined them. He told them about Katie and his failed efforts, defeat coloring his voice. Ruari clapped a hand on Éamonn's shoulder, while Ciaran just pursed his lips.

The procession marched down the aisle. The brides came last, dressed in varying shades of blue. Most were young, but two older women stood in dark blue. Widows remarrying, or the lucky spinster who found someone to suit her.

Each girl found her groom and stood beside him. Some gazed up at their prospective mates with love-sick eyes, others with calm affection or nervous smiles. Katie didn't glance at Lochlann at all. She stared straight forward as if withstanding torture.

Éamonn's own anguish screamed in his mind. Katie hadn't even searched for him as she marched. She must have decided he'd abandoned her to her fate. The idea stung him to the quick.

Father Byrne intoned the service in Latin. Though most Travelers couldn't read more than their name and some figures, most understood the Latin well enough.

Éamonn stared, numb with indecision. He couldn't let this happen. In all the old tales, didn't the hero swoop in and save the damsel in distress before she succumbed to a fate worse than death?

He must save Katie. Frustration boiled up behind his eyes.

Father Byrne glanced up from his altar and called for the rings. Éamonn couldn't take this anymore. He had no plan, he just wanted to grab Katie and take her away. But as he surged forward, Ruari gripped one shoulder and Ciaran the other. He wrenched free of his cousin, but his brother wouldn't let go. Despite his injured arm, Ruari had far more strength.

With pleading eyes, Éamonn turned to Ruari. "I've got to take her away!" He sobbed, but Ruari wouldn't budge.

"Da said you'd try something. He told me to stop you."

Éamonn wriggled, trying to break his brother's iron grasp. "This is my last chance!" His shouts drew angry glances from the wedding party. Katie turned to him, entreaty in her eyes.

Ruari shook his head, his eyes sad. "You're too late. Look, they're done."

Éamonn didn't want to look. He didn't want to see Katie bonded to that feckless Scot. He didn't want to imagine him touching her. But he gave in and looked just as she glanced over her shoulder, and their gazes locked. All his hopes and dreams flooded into her blue eyes and shattered as she turned away to face her groom.

Éamonn wrenched himself free but didn't go toward Katie. Ruari was right. They were done. The priest said, "What God has joined together, let no man put asunder."

Éamonn held his stomach and stumbled away from the clearing. *Oh, God, how did I let it happen!*

Before he bawled before hundreds of onlookers, he rushed out of the crowd and headed… *Where?* What could he do to get rid of the pain?

He knew how to dull the pain, at least. Ciaran's *poitín* called to him. Éamonn didn't want to remember this day at all. He found his cousin's wagon and rummaged through the mess, searching for the hidden stash. Ciaran supplied one or two bottles each night. He must have an enormous supply hidden away. Éamonn flung things around the wagon. Soiled clothing, a bridle for mending, a half empty food bowl, hay for Ciaran's mule. Where would he hide the precious cargo?

With a click of his tongue, Éamonn climbed out of the wagon and crawled underneath. He tapped several sections until one sounded hollow. Éamonn examined the wooden planks, pressing and pushing each edge until he found the clever trap door. A *click* and a slide revealed two empty bottles.

He'd just risen to his feet and wiped off his breeks. He gripped the purloined treasure as Ciaran, Ruari, and Turlough approached. Grim lines painted their faces. Stealing alcohol was almost as bad as stealing a horse.

Or a bride. Éamonn squared his shoulders.

Turlough gave him a kind smile. "Éamonn, that's not the answer. Here, let me take those for you." His father reached for a bottle, but Éamonn pulled it back, despite it being empty. Ciaran plucked them both from his hand, having flanked him. Éamonn's shoulders slumped. He couldn't even do a proper liquor raid.

Turlough gripped his arms. "Éamonn, you have channels of complaint. By our customs, she should have been allowed to refuse. I'll take the case up with the council on your behalf. If you still want to, that is, after…"

"After he beds her, you mean? He's probably doing so as we speak." Éamonn spat in the dirt beside his feet.

Ciaran spoke in a low tone. "No, not yet."

Éamonn rounded on his cousin. "What? Why not? What do you know?"

Ciaran gave a smug smile as he imparted his juicy gossip. "Katie's refused him until they get back to his home. She screamed as much after the ceremony. She'll not give her maidenhead until she's met his father. And he's back on Skye!"

Turlough clapped him on the shoulder. "Oh, ho! Well, we have hope, then, don't we, son? Marriage isn't official until consummated!"

Hope. A slight one, to be sure, but still hope. But his mind refused to come up with any sort of plan. He glanced at his father, drained from his emotions. "What should I do, Da?"

While tapping his lip, Turlough stared into the distance. "I'll stay here and fight the marriage contract with the tribal council. When they leave, you follow them. Try not to catch up to them, though. Not until they're almost home. I'll send a messenger with any news. If I can get a decision before they reach Skye, that's grand. We can't stop them from going, but if the council annuls the marriage, you can pluck her away from them."

Cold and hot ran through Éamonn's veins as his father spoke. "And what if you can't break the marriage?"

"Ah, well, we'll burn that bridge when we get to it, won't we?" The twinkle in his father's eyes made Éamonn smile. This fight gave him vigor. "Besides, I must stay here anyhow. Fionnuala's come down with a fever."

"Fionnuala? She felt fine the other night at the dancing."

His father shook his head. "She's been running hot since this morning. Malachy hasn't left her side."

"But I should stay, then. She's my sister—"

Turlough shook his head with a frown. "You will not. Look, you go chase your bride, Éamonn, while I work on the council. By the time you catch up with her, I might have good news, and you can rescue Katie legally."

Ruari's bear paw settled on his shoulder. "I'll come with you." A warm glow spread through Éamonn at his brother's loyalty.

Ciaran clapped his hand over Ruari's. "Me, too."

Lochlann:

They had to hurry back to Skye, but Lochlann didn't look forward to returning home. Their father lived as Settled Folk, but their mother had Traveled before she married. Both Lochlann and Donald continued her Traveler ways, trading horses up and down the Western Isles. This trip had been the farthest they'd ventured.

After Katie embarrassed them with her strident diatribe, Lochlann brought his lovely bride back to the wagon. She'd walked beside him but refused his proffered arm. She wouldn't let him touch her at all. Her coldness cut him to the quick, making his cheeks burn.

Donald scowled at him. "She's your wife now. Make her behave like one."

Katie clenched her jaw and said nothing. Lochlann grabbed her hand and stuffed it into the crook of his arm, yanking her when she wouldn't walk.

After surveying their campsite, Donald grunted and crossed his arms. "I've business to finish before we leave. Start packing. Get her to do the washing up." Lochlann usually kept their campsite tidy, but the wedding preparations had disrupted his routine. He hadn't even put away their sleeping rolls from the night before. He leveled a knowing look at Lochlann.

Katie's voice came sharp, "You needn't leave us alone. We will have no *wedding night.*"

Lochlann stood, flabbergasted. "What do you mean, no wedding night?"

"Exactly that. Are you completely daft? Did you not hear me at the wedding? I refuse to submit to you. I am in this marriage against my will."

Donald spat to one side. "Lochlann, just take the wee bitch into the wagon. She's tiny. She won't be too much trouble."

Katie shrank back from them, eyes growing wide. Her gaze darted to each of the tents, the wagon, and then back toward the fair.

Lochlann shook his head in disgust. "Donald, I don't hold with rape, even of my wife. She'll come around."

"Good God, ya bampot! Command her! She has to obey. It's the law. Get yerself a backbone, will you!"

No, Lochlann took his vows seriously, and he'd promised the priest he'd protect his wife. "And what sort of marriage will that be, then? No, she may take time, but she'll come around."

Katie let out a snort. "Don't hold your breath, now."

Donald growled deep in his throat and raised a clenched fist.

The girl blanched but stood her ground. Donald took a step toward her. She flinched back but didn't cower. Lochlann took a step forward and reached for Donald's arm. Donald spun on him, glaring, forcing Lochlann back a few steps.

Katie's eyes flicked between the two brothers, and she squared her shoulders, as if she'd come to some decision. "I said I'll bed him, and I will. But I said earlier, not until I meet your father on Skye. That's only proper in our traditions, after all." She raised her chin.

Lochlann held his breath and glanced at Donald. He and his father didn't part on the best of terms, and a reunion would be sure to be rocky.

Donald stomped off, grumbling to himself about fractious mares. Lochlann turned to his bride. "Don't antagonize him, Katie. He's got a fearful temper."

"And so your duty is to protect me, is it not?"

Lochlann couldn't bear her haughty tone, and his patience ran thin. "And if you goad him, you've yourself to blame when he snaps!"

With that, he climbed into the second wagon. They had a lot to organize before they could leave. Several trunks held clean clothing, next to a neat pile with the dirties. Now that he had a wife, she could take care of that. He'd already packed their trade goods in the second wagon, while they slept in the first one. Now, they needed to shift things now for a third person. He'd have to survey what they could move and how much she brought with her.

Stepping from the covered red-and-blue painted wagon, he glanced at his bride. Katie sat on a stool in front of his wagon. She still wore the pale blue woolen dress she'd married in, but she'd loosened her hair. Red curls danced in the breeze. The thin rope from the handfasting part of the ceremony dangled from her wrist, but they'd untied their wrists before leaving the altar. She looked so fierce, like an avenging goddess.

Katie refused to look at him as he organized the trunks and cases. At least she held her tongue now. His mother had never been so fiery, but she always got her way in the end. Lochlann sniffed, missing his mother intensely. She should have been here on his wedding day.

He didn't want to go home. Going home meant facing his father. He hadn't spoken to Calum MacCrimmon since they'd fought a year ago. In remorse, Lochlann remembered their last harsh words, when their fight had made clear, for both, they'd been cut from separate bolts of cloth.

In his father's study, surrounded by leather-bound books and the stink of stale pipe smoke, Lochlann had asked his permission to take the string of horses to Ireland. Their father refused.

The whole family was pledged to the laird. Their father had told them to join the MacLeod's army as soldiers, to support King Geordie in London. As much as he wanted to, Lochlann couldn't bring himself to support the usurper. His heart lay with the Jacobite cause. But he could never tell his father he believed Prince Charles to be the true king of Scotland. He couldn't lie to his own conscience, though.

"But Da, the horses need selling. No one on Skye needs horses just now. We can't just let them sit in this godforsaken edge of the world!"

"I've already promised the chief your time. You're to serve with the MacLeods for the king, son. Do you defy my decision?"

Lochlann threw up his hands and started pacing around the room. "Da! It's not a matter of defiance. How can I take up arms? I can't even play the bloody pipes!"

"And you'd rather gallivant across the Isles and trade like a common merchant? Have you no pride in your name?"

He stopped pacing, turning to stare at his father. "Mother Traveled all her life, Da. Did you consider this life beneath her?"

His father's face had clouded with red-rimmed rage. He gripped the arms of his chair and rose to his feet. "Don't you dare bring your mother's good name into this! She mended her ways."

Despite his own frustration, Lochlann took a step back. His father had a heavy hand, and he'd felt it more than once. "Traveling isn't a crime! It's our way of life."

"Not for a MacCrimmon."

Lochlann and Donald had left anyhow, without their father's blessing or permission, taking the horses to sell in Ireland. Now that he faced the prospect of seeing his father again, Lochlann felt relieved he had a wife. That accomplishment should defuse the anger and punishment for their defiance. He clung onto that hope with all his might.

Katie's sister, Deirdre, had joined her, and they spoke in whispers. They stared at him when he emerged. *If looks could freeze, I'd be a glacier.*

He hoped Katie would grow to like him, despite Éamonn's hurtful words. Everyone told Lochlann they considered him a likable chap. Lochlann didn't fool himself that he had fine looks, but he got along well with folks. He loved his horses and they responded well. He'd never made an enemy, unless he counted his own father. Shouldn't that enough for her?

Donald wasn't good with people, but he fought well and stayed loyal to the family. While his brother had a better head for making plans, Lochlann preferred to take things as they came. That approach didn't always work.

He hadn't come to this festival planning to marry. The brothers intended to sell the gray stallion, Smúid, for a top price They had three mares and a gelding, all fine cobs, but the stallion remained the prize.

Donald warned him that returning to their father, even with a sack full of silver, would be difficult. He contrived a plan to mollify their father with a wife, tangible proof of Lochlann's intention of settling down and continuing the family. It sounded like a plausible plan, so he'd agreed to the match with Katie.

Well, they had gotten far more than they'd bargained for. They sold the stallion for a wife. The transaction bothered Lochlann, especially with Katie so opposed. But her father agreed to the deal, and she still lived under his roof. He had the right to arrange her marriage. To be proper, their father should have negotiated, but his older brother must do.

Deirdre left, with one contemptuous glance over her shoulder, flicking her lovely black hair. Lochlann stared at her as she walked away and let out a sigh. He had a wife now, and his thoughts should linger on her, not her sister. He'd like to do more than think about Katie, but she'd made her position clear. They'd have a long, frustrating trip home.

Lochlann placed another set of breeks in the trunk and shut the lid, clicking the latch. After he pulled the box into the wagon, he pressed his hand into the small of his back. He ached from bending over. Katie still sat on the stool, staring into space like a statue.

After jumping from the wagon, he knelt next to her. "Katie?"

She lifted her head, but her eyes didn't look at him. They looked at nothing. He bowed his head and let out a sigh. "Never mind." He returned to his packing with a guilty heart.

A boy ran to him, ragged and dirty. He carried a wrapped package. "Are you Donald MacCrimmon from Skye?"

"I'm his brother, Lochlann."

The boy, about eight, narrowed his eyes. "I'm to give this to Donald."

"I'll take it. Here." He flipped a *doit* to the boy. The messenger caught it out of the air and handed over the packet. Then he ran off, back toward the fairgrounds.

The leather wallet had been tied with several pieces of twine with an oilskin pouch tucked inside. Unfolding this, he found the letter.

Lochlann scanned the scrawled writing and blinked several times. He read it again, more slowly. He glanced at his motionless bride and walked off, searching for his brother.

Chapter Seven

Éamonn:

Éamonn knelt by the cot in the healer's wagon. Fionnuala slept, but her skin still looked angry, red and dry. He gently wiped her forehead with a cool, wet cloth and placed his hand on her cheek.

Éamonn had never seen Cormac so worried. The healer pressed his lips together as he mixed a salve. "Her body won't take much more of this. We've got to break the fever."

Turlough paced back and forth, his hands pushing through his hair in frustration. Síle stood in a corner, singing to her sister in a soft, high voice. She sang a sad song about love lost.

"So many ways to share a love
With words and touch we promised much
Do we understand
The footsteps in the sand."

Éamonn's throat choked with suppressed tears. "What can we do?"

"Keep her cool, make sure she drinks the honey water, and pray. Pray to St. Brigid to heal her and give her strength."

Édaín sat with her husband, Tor. The blacksmith appeared out of place in this crowd of Dohertys, but he brought food for those sitting vigil.

Despite his frantic worry about Katie, Éamonn wouldn't leave his sister's side. *How can I even consider going off to chase a dream when my sister might die?*

Ciaran arrived wearing a dour expression, with Deirdre in tow. Éamonn frowned at Katie's sister, but she gave him a sweet, sad smile. While he remained reluctant to forgive her for not taking Katie his message, his heart softened.

Éamonn cocked an eyebrow at his cousin, worry about Katie flooding his mind. "Ciaran? Did something happen?"

Ciaran shook his head and pointed up. When he glanced at the sky, three crows circled overhead. Crows flying over a home meant death. They both shuddered.

Ruari had been here all afternoon, but not attending Fionnuala. He lay on the next cot, his arm burning with fever. The healer had packed the festering wound with honey and herbs. They worried he might lose his arm.

Síle finished her song and glanced up, tears glinting in her eyes.

Éamonn gave her a hug. "Why don't you go make her a Brigid's Cross, *mo leanbh*? That'll help the saint find her and send healing blessings down from Heaven, aye?" That should keep her mind occupied, away from worry.

With a bound, the girl went to find straw to weave the charm. Brigid had been a goddess in Ireland long before she became a saint. Both had healing powers, so Éamonn didn't care which she'd been. Children often wove Brigid's Crosses, small even-armed crosses made from rushes or straw. Folks made them in early February, on Brigid's Day, and hung them in kitchens to ward off evil or fire.

As he sat between his sister and brother, Éamonn's mind searched for a puzzle, desperate to stop worrying about them and Katie. Something to keep his mind busy.

He'd done some experimenting with his newfound talent that day. He could give a simple request, as he just had with Síle, with nothing odd happening. If he *pushed* with his mind, a tangible shove, someone might agree to something they normally wouldn't, but only for a few moments.

The full push often left a colored shadow around the person he pushed, but that faded, and since he had no idea what the colors meant, he ignored them. The rapport didn't last long, and he always got a wicked headache or an upset stomach. Even a tiny push left him with a throbbing head.

Some people seemed less susceptible to his suggestions than others. Donald, for instance, remained beyond persuasion, while Lochlann might be more pliable. Just not pliable enough. Éamonn hung his head at his failure.

Síle handed out handfuls of straw to each person. "Here, I brought enough for everyone. We can make an army of them!"

Deirdre came in to check on the family, and Éamonn flashed her a grateful smile. Perhaps she had a kind heart, after all. When she spied Síle weaving, she knelt next to her. "I can help, but I don't remember how, sweetling. Can you show me?"

Éamonn smiled, pleased she kept Síle occupied. The girl crafted a simple woven square in the center, with four arms tied at each end. His little sister had been just a baby when their mother had died. *Oh, please be to God, don't make her watch Fionnuala die, too.* His smile faded.

That night remained clear and warm, a lucky thing as all the patients didn't fit in Cormac's tent. The stars peeked out of the velvet indigo sky, one by one. They winked in and out, dancing behind scattered clouds. Starlight sparkled on the river like those dancing faeries at the standing stones. Éamonn shuddered at the memory. Had it all been a dream, or had he seen dancing Fae? The events of that day jumbled together into a confusing mess. He needed time to sort everything out, and he didn't have that luxury.

He finished his own Brigid's Cross and hung the charm from the corner of Fionnuala's cot. She moaned and stirred in her sleep. He placed his hand on her forehead, still hot and dry. He went to dip the cloth in cool water.

As he returned, he put all the power he could behind his words. "Please, get better, sweet sister." Éamonn welcomed the resulting headache.

Katie:

Katie had tried hard not to let hope take root, hope that Éamonn would come and save her at the last moment. That's how love worked in the tales and legends, to be sure. The hero swept down to save the fair maiden from a fate worse than death.

But he hadn't come, and he hadn't saved her, and she now had a husband she didn't want. And neither man nor priest could change that. Yet she'd escaped her father's heavy hand, and she married Lochlann not Donald. Perhaps this wouldn't be as horrible as she thought.

She hadn't resigned herself to being his wife, but at least her insistence on meeting their father bought her some time, and maybe that was enough. With feigned nonchalance, she asked Lochlann what they might see on the way to Skye. While he didn't answer at first, he finally described a few places that might be of interest.

He only let her bid farewell to Deirdre. They stood, facing each other, neither sure of what to say. First Deirdre opened her mouth but said nothing. Then Katie reached out to take her sister's hand. Finally, they embraced, holding each other more tightly than they had in many years.

Katie pulled back and looked at her sister with urgent hope. "Can you tell Éamonn goodbye for me?"

Deirdre nodded, a tear showing in her eye. Katie regretted all the sniping of the last week and wiped it from her sister's cheek. Her sister looked up with mournful eyes. "Katie, I'm so sorry. Éamonn wanted me to bring you a message before the wedding, and I refused. I should have helped."

Through gritted teeth, Katie said, "That doesn't matter now."

"Sure, and it does. He still wants to try. And Turlough is determined to argue your case in front of the council."

Katie let out a snort, and they shared a sad smile. "I have little faith in them. The priest blessed us. What will they do?"

"Maybe nothing. But in case they do, Éamonn will come for you."

Katie glanced over her shoulder, toward the wagons where the MacCrimmon brothers packed. She turned back to Deirdre and spoke in a fierce whisper, hope returning to her heart. "I learned some details from Lochlann on the route we're taking to Skye. If I tell you the details, can you tell Éamonn?"

As her sister walked away, Katie grasped onto that hope like the last strand of an ever-unraveling rope, holding on for dear sanity. She held on while Lochlann packed around her. She held on while he and Donald had a furious discussion in shouted whispers and furtive glances. She held on as she perched on a stool next to the trunk of her own clothing, not bothering to unpack before they left for Scotland.

Scotland. A foreign land. Far away from her beloved emerald hills. Filled with savages and war. Lochlann explained about the Rising, a revolution to oust the current king of England from his throne and replace him with the son of the former King James. The Bonnie Prince. What was the son's name? Donald talked about him. *Teàrlach mhic Seumas.* Charles, son of James. Battles and dangerous men swarmed the Highlands of Scotland. And they'd be heading straight into war.

Ireland had its share of battles, but not in her lifetime. The last major war here had been over fifty years ago. Her people had either been too beaten, too servile, or too hungry to fight the English since. The Scots still imagined they had a chance. Katie let out a snort at that fancy. *As if anyone could fight off the King of England.*

She'd travel from her home to this strange land. Traveling would be no novelty but voyaging across the Irish Sea into the mountainous wilds of west Scotland frightened her. The Isle of Skye, Donald said. Most likely a desolate, barren place, despite its poetic name.

Donald growled and cuffed her on the shoulder. "Come on, girl. Get yer lazy arse up and help us load the wagons."

She hadn't even noticed his return. He'd left earlier and came back with their two remaining horses and the mule. She just stared at him, unable to move.

"Move yer arse! We're leaving in an hour!"

"Tonight? But the sun will set soon! I thought we'd leave tomorrow?" Éamonn wouldn't know. Could she get a message to him? Her eyes darted to the edges of the camp, but no one lingered.

"Now! Put yer trunk over here. Get yer cloak out. We've a brisk breeze tonight, and I don't want ye dying before we get to Skye." That hint of consideration almost humanized him. Almost.

She stuffed several boxes into the two wagons. They'd have no room inside either wagon for sleeping. Would they have tents on the road? The prospect of sleeping unprotected in the cold rain made her shiver. As she secured a rope to one corner, she considered sabotaging something to slow them down, but felt Donald's eyes on the back of her neck, and her skin crawled.

Katie picked up a trunk, grunting at the unexpected weight. Lochlann took the heavy box from her hands. "Here, I'll take that…Katie." He spoke her name shyly.

She still didn't know what to make of this man, her husband. Husband. She tasted the word, rolled it around in her mouth. Katie had imagined her own wedding as most girls did, but the reality had fallen far short of her fantasies. Sure, Travelers had mass weddings, but she'd wanted the weeks of planning, giddy anticipation, time to sew a lovely new dress. She'd gotten none of that.

Lochlann didn't seem to be a cruel man, or an old, ill-favored drunk. He was young, attractive, and even sweet at times. He had no ambition and lacked strong will. Katie might even control him with some effort. She didn't want a man she could control, though.

She craved a partner, a man she'd live with as an equal, but she'd have to work with what she had. Until Éamonn came for her. If he came. Her faith in his perseverance waffled between certainty and dread with every passing minute.

They tied the last strap on the wagons as the day's glow faded over the western horizon. Katie had spied a worn spot but didn't dare cut the strap further. Lochlann noticed the spot a few minutes later and made quick work of replacing the rope. A blanket of deep dusk curled around them. Fog rose to swirl between the horses' hooves.

As they drove away from the fairgrounds, Katie stared into the growing darkness, encroaching upon her like a monster from her worst nightmares. This morning she'd been full of plans with Éamonn, and now she had a husband she neither wanted nor loved. She still couldn't get her head around the whirlwind change.

Their mule, well-laden with food and provisions, brayed just as a bird flew out of a bush. The roans, *Ceanndána* and *Righin,* were nowhere near as beautiful as the stallion Katie had been sold for.

Her anger rose again at the notion of being traded. She'd heard of horses being part of a dowry or a bride price, but this felt obscene, like blasphemy. And yet her father had a duty to find her a husband. Perhaps she'd brought this on herself for driving away all other offers.

Katie thought of her earlier suitors. Donnell with his ridiculous gait and idiot grin. Timothy with his angry scowl and heavy hand. If she'd accepted one of them, she could have stayed in Ireland. And she'd have had a choice.

The darkness closed in on them along the road. Donald held a small lamp, but it did little to fight back the gloom. Katie drowsed with the cart's swaying.

After a few hours, they stopped to camp. The wind picked up, and Katie shivered, glad of her cloak. Lochlann started a fire, so she ought to cook supper. "Where are the provisions?"

Donald nodded towards the mule. "Up near her shoulder, the one closest to the fire. Soup from yesterday still in the pot, with bread on top. Heat that up."

She nodded and retrieved the pease porridge. After wrinkling her nose at the grayish mass, she extracted the iron tripod to hang the pot over the fire. Katie wanted to add some seasoning, and while she had good, plain cook skills, she had no supplies. Her mother hadn't even gifted her a customary dowry of cooking tools, unless she'd stuffed them in Katie's trunk, but she couldn't go rummaging for it now.

She turned to Lochlann. "Do you have any seasonings I can add?"

Her husband shook his head. "Not with us. There will be plenty when we get home, though."

"Not even salt?"

He just shrugged and stirred the embers.

After nestling the iron pot into the coals next to the cheerful fire, she stared at the glowing embers. Her hands had grown numb, so she stretched them toward the flames. Dancing figures in the fire had always mesmerized her. As a child, she'd imagined Fire Folk lived within, dancing a merry jig, and beckoning to join them in their warm realm. She'd never dared do so. Tales of folks who visited the Fae realms seldom ended well.

All day, she'd shoved away her anguish. Now, when she'd stopped to rest, the despair caught up to her. Katie stared deeper into the flames, longing for the release fire might bring her, but too frightened to take the leap.

Katie stirred the gloppy mess of the stew as it bubbled. Lochlann retrieved bowls, cups, spoons, and a bottle of small ale. She tasted the food and grimaced. No seasoning whatsoever, not even salt. They weren't two leagues from the ocean, and salt came cheap. Only the laziest folks had none for cooking.

Lochlann crouched next to her. "You'll like Skye, Katie. The island is beautiful. When the mists roll down off the mountains, you'd swear you lived in Heaven."

Mountains and mists. Poetic, but not practical. She continued to stir, not glancing at her unwanted husband.

"Our house is decent-sized, with stables and a kitchen garden. It's close to the ocean and commands a splendid view. We've a herd of wild horses nearby, on the lands near Dunvegan Castle."

Horses. Like the one he'd traded for her. She glanced at her new husband, caressing the horse's flank. Exactly what he'd be doing to her once they met his father. Her earlier surge of fear and anger welled anew with a vengeance. She spat on the ground.

"Hey! Why'd you do that?!"

She shot him a glare, her blood burning as hot as the fire. "Because you bought me with a horse. Like I'm a mule or a bolt of cloth. I am a woman! Not some trade goods you can just pass around like a pipe of tobacco!"

He pulled back, blinking with owlish eyes. "Most marriages are made with some sort of arrangement like that—"

"Not without asking the bride! I'm a slave, is what I am. I had no choice, sold to the highest bidder. So, what is your next command, master?" She put her hands together to mimic a solicitous servant. "Shall I shine your boots for you? Or lick the soles? Or perhaps you would like to rest your weary feet on my back?"

Her hair had already been a fright, and the windy night hadn't helped. In the firelight, she must look like an incarnation of the Morrigan, a goddess of war intent on defeating her enemy.

Lochlann stared at her as if she'd grown another head.

As she concentrated on her fury for Lochlann, something solid slammed into her head, taking her by surprise. She keeled over, away from Donald's fist, almost falling into the fire. She rolled away, beating out sparks on her skirt. Her head throbbed.

Her brother-in-law loomed over her, thunder in his eyes. "You'll keep a civil tongue in your head, woman! I'll not tolerate such talk in my household!"

She curled her lip. "I'm not in your household. I'm in your brother's!"

"And I've charge of him as he's the younger. Now shut yer trap, or you'll get another." He raised his fist. She didn't intend to cower, but her body understood this routine and her head bowed. She couldn't do it. Even if she learned how to control her husband, this brute would always be her brother-in-law. He'd *correct* her behavior whenever he liked, and Lochlann had no spine to stand up for her. Donald had too much physical strength to defy.

She'd just have to escape. If she could get away from the MacCrimmon brothers and find Éamonn, he'd protect her.

But if Éamonn never came, and she remained tied to Lochlann for life… Katie fought back a sob.

Éamonn would still be at the fair, but once it closed tomorrow, she'd have no idea how to find him. The kernel of a plan formed in her mind as she considered the obstacles and opportunities. Katie forged a dozen plans and discarded most as impractical. No matter what path she chose, she'd have to wait until the brothers fell asleep.

She'd insisted on a separate sleeping area until she met their father, so Lochlann built a tent for her, a simple lean-to against a tree trunk, canvas hanging from a low branch while the brothers slept in the second tent.

Katie kept her dress on, not even loosening her stays. Men never paid attention to clothing unless it revealed something, so she hoped they wouldn't notice. Lochlann might not be clever enough to puzzle out her plan, but Donald had cunning intelligence.

As she waited for them to sleep, she stared at her trunk. Did it hold anything she'd care about losing? Heirlooms, clothing, childhood memories. Best travel as light as possible.

She waited a long time before moving from her cocoon of warmth into the still night air. Katie crept out, careful not to make a noise, wincing as her knee pressed on a sharp pebble. She couldn't risk taking a horse or the mule. Her head spun with how many things might go wrong.

Katie only walked a few feet when the mule sounded off. She caught her breath, turned to watch the brothers' tent, and froze.

Donald stuck his head out. "What in the name of God are you doing, woman! Get back in your tent!"

"I've got to relieve myself."

He snorted and pulled himself out of the tent and glowered over her. "You should have done so before bed. Go, then. I'll wait for you."

Her body remained frozen, fear gripping every muscle.

He raised his hand in explicit threat. "Well, go, already!"

Katie swallowed and made her legs move toward the bushes. She rustled about and returned in short order. As she slunk back, he stared until she entered her tent again.

"Hmph. Hardly seemed worth it." He ducked his head back into his own. *Well, that was a complete failure.* She'd have to find a way of quieting the mule and the horses. Not tonight, though. Donald might stay awake for some time. He'd looked too wary.

Katie didn't think she'd be able to sleep, but after the past two days and all their hectic chaos, eventually tangled, disturbing dreams overtook her.

Éamonn:

Éamonn stared in disbelief that bordered on outrage. The wagons, and his fair Katie, had disappeared. A few broken pieces of pottery, a scrap of broken twine, the blackened ring where their campfire had been, and an abandoned broken bucket. All other traces of the two wagons, the two brothers, and his beloved, had vanished.

He fought a rising panic. Éamonn knew they'd go but didn't understand why they'd left so soon. He had made all his travel plans for this afternoon, but now he had to shift everything around.

He vowed to chase the MacCrimmons halfway up the coast of Scotland if he had to. Éamonn must include Katie in that group, as she bore that name now. They'd head toward Stranurler and Coleraine. Next, from the harbor at Ballycastle over the Irish Sea to Scotland. Éamonn had been to Coleraine, but never as far as Ballycastle. At least, that's the way he hoped they'd go. What if he took a different road and missed them?

Deirdre returned with a smug smile as she patted his packed horse. "I'm going with you."

"Absolutely not! This is not a romantic adventure. This is a dangerous journey, and not suitable for young girls!"

With a fetching pout, Deirdre lifted her chin. "Katie is my sister! Besides, what happens if her marriage is annulled? She shouldn't travel alone with *you*. That wouldn't be proper."

Katie didn't have a monopoly on haughty. Her sister matched her, tone for tone.

Éamonn shook his head, gazing toward the north trail. "And what makes you think it's proper for *you* to come? You'll be traveling alone with two unmarried men. Your parents would never allow that."

"That'll be permissible because I'm rescuing my sister. Besides, my parents only care about losing my bride price." She wrinkled her nose, then gave him a half-smile, peering at him from below lowered lashes.

He suspected her parents would be frantic, and that she was lying through her teeth. But he had no way to be sure, and he didn't want to brave her father, or risk getting her beaten. Éamonn squeezed his eyes shut, willing himself to resist the power of her petulance, too flustered to argue. "You'll slow us down."

She laid a hand on his chest, back to her seductress act. "I can ride better than you can. Besides, I'm the only one who knows the route they'll take."

He wished she wouldn't touch him like that, especially when speaking of riding. He removed her hand. Her skin felt warm and soft. "I doubt that." But he no longer had the strength to say no.

By her deepening smile, she knew she'd won.

Éamonn wanted his brother to come, but when he asked, Ruari shook his head. He remained pale, his arm still red and raw from the nail gash. "Go, Éamonn. Find your girl. I'll catch up when I'm doing better, I promise."

"No, you stay here and help Da pack the wagons. I'll manage. Ciaran will be with me, and we'll move more quickly with fewer people. And keep good care of Fionnuala?"

"Of course. She's my sister, too."

Fionnuala's cheeks had gained some color. Éamonn still felt guilt over leaving, but Cormac assured him she was healing. Perhaps his persuasion power had some use after all. He glanced at her cot. Had her illness come from his angering the Fae with his disrespect? Her forehead still felt warm, but she'd woken and gave him a tired smile.

Turlough clapped him on his shoulder. "Éamonn? A word before you go?"

He followed his father off to the fence behind the healer's tent. "Da? Is something wrong?"

"Besides your sister being ill, your brother's arm, and you set to run after your lost love into the wilds of Scotland? No, of course not. I'm drowning in the blessings of the Fair Folk."

His father rarely gave in to bouts of sarcasm. He must be feeling the strain. Éamonn's worry and guilt increased.

Turlough let out a long breath. "Son, I know you've your heart set on this. I promise I'll do what I can, but this might all be for naught. We may get no decision from the council. They may rule against you. They may take weeks, even months, before they come to any sort of decision."

"Are you saying I shouldn't go?"

"I'd never tell you that, son. You must follow your dreams. They are all we have, in the end. I'm only saying, don't pin all your hopes on your luck, that's all. You must create your own fate."

Éamonn didn't know what to say. His father usually spoke with shining optimism. He woke with the brightest dawn in his heart before anyone else had rubbed the sleep of doubt from their eyes. "Da, about what happened at the stones. I may have been wrong. I shouldn't have gotten so angry."

Turlough gave his arm a fierce squeeze. "You're fine, son. I understand a lover's heart. Remember, I loved your mother more than life itself. How can I stand in your way with your own true love?"

Da had loved her so much, he ran away when she died. Turlough still looked sadly at Síle, the child whose birth had killed her.

He heaved a deep sigh and hugged his Da. "Thank you, Da, for everything. I will come back, I promise."

"See that you do, son. We still need you, you know."

"I know, and I will."

"*Taisteal ádh sábháilte agus go maith, mo mhac.*"

Safe travels and good luck, my son. If only he had the power to ensure safety and luck. Éamonn blinked back a tear as the hug broke apart.

In short order, they packed the three steady horses Ciaran brought, packs for provisions, and Deirdre, damn her eyes.

He gave the dark-haired girl a narrow gaze. "What did you tell your mother?"

She held her head high, her black hair shimmering in the late morning sun. "Nothing. She won't know where I've gone."

"What? You have to tell her! She'll go mad with worry!"

Deirdre waved her hand in a dismissive gesture. "Pfft. Not that one. just wants my bride price, as she wanted Katie's."

"We don't want your parents following the trail and interfering."

She rolled her eyes. "They wouldn't stir themselves. But if you insist, I'll leave a note that I've gone with Katie, and that I'll return with a Traveler caravan when she's settled. They'll be glad of one less mouth to feed."

Éamonn didn't like it but said nothing. She wrote her note, and Turlough promised to deliver it. With a nod to his father and Síle, they set off past the marshes.

In the tales, there would be horns or drums to celebrate the start of a quest. A faint sound filtered through the bog. Fae music? He craned his head back. His father played the tin whistle, a slow, martial tune, well-suited for the steady plod of the horses' hooves.

Katie:

Rain pounded on her head, *pitpatpitpatpitpat.* Each drop hammered away at her sanity. Mud mired the wagon wheels, making them stop several times to get unstuck. If Éamonn caught up with them on the road, there might be a fight, and Donald was a strong fighter. If she could just get away and find Éamonn first, he'd be safe. Tonight, she'd try again to escape, while they still traveled the one road north from the fair.

Katie prayed the rain wouldn't stop Éamonn as much. Would he come? The rescuer always came in the stories, but she didn't have the best history with men. At least he wouldn't be bringing wagons and all his worldly goods, so should move faster than they did. Would Ruari or Ciaran be with him? From their tussle with Lochlann, she knew well and true that Ciaran and Éamonn could fight, but she hoped the brawny Ruari would come and lend his strength to their fight. Ruari would be than a match for Donald. The older MacCrimmon man stood tall but couldn't compare to the giant Ruari. Her brutish brother-in-law made up for that lack of height in cruelty and rage.

Rain might help her slip away as the men slept. And if her trail showed, what would that matter? She'd head back to the fair, and they'd know that. Rain might keep the horses and mule quiet. They'd be just as miserable as the humans and not notice sounds. As much as she hated it, she prayed for the deluge to continue.

When they stopped for the night, mud splattered every surface below the waist. It was like camping in soup.

Donald scowled at the sucking morass of mud at the roadside, tapping his lip. "Lochlann, let's pull some of the stronger trunks out of the wagon, cover them with tents, and sleep in the wagon tonight."

In her mind, Katie urged Lochlann to say no. Sleeping in the wagon would scupper all her plans.

As she held her breath, her bridegroom picked at his lip. "No, no, it'll be fine. The trunks will get covered with mud tomorrow when we put them back in. We're already filthy. It won't do us harm to be filthier."

"Well, if *milady* doesn't object, I'm fine with sleeping in the tents. Lochlann?" Donald's tone dripped with dry sarcasm.

Katie ignored it. For once, she became conciliatory and accommodating and gave him a curt nod. "Fine. Less work all around, then. I'll fetch firewood." She took a few strides toward the wood.

Donald grasped her arm, his fingers digging into her muscle. "You'll find nothing that'll burn. We'll just eat bread and dried fish for supper."

They set up the tents under a large tree, which deflected most of the rain. Heavy drops still pounded the tent, but not a constant shower.

Exhaustion dragged Katie down. As late as they'd stopped the night before, they'd left again with the dawn. She might have been lying down for five hours, but she'd been unable to sleep. Tonight, she had to stay awake. Before she entered her tent, she petted and spoke to the horses and the mule. The more familiar they were with her, the more likely they would be to stay quiet if she emerged in the night.

She stared into the blackness when Lochlann took her hand. "Katie? You must go in the tent. Donald'll not sleep until you're inside."

Katie bit back angry words and complied. Having set her own tent up as far as she could from the brothers' tent, citing a deep wallow of mud, she hoped the distance would be far enough away to mask noise.

The next hour crept by. Perhaps just one brother slept, after all. Once, the snoring man snorted and coughed, while another snore kept going. *Good, both are finally asleep.*

She wound her woolen cloak tight, slipped her boots on, and grabbed a chunk of bread. She poked her head out and strained her ears. Snoring.

Katie tiptoed across the clearing and past the wagons. She just reached the edge of one wagon when Ceanndána whickered.

"Shh, *mo chara*, all is well." She stroked the horse's neck. The mare snuffled but made no more sound.

Despite the squelching mud, Katie found the trail back toward Ballyshannon. As she got farther from the camp, she strode with more confidence. Had she escaped? She shouldn't need to keep quiet now. With a long breath to release the tension in her body, she tugged her cloak around her shoulders and rushed through the still-pouring rain.

Katie stepped on a sharp stone, hurting even through her boot sole. As the pain shot through her leg, the other foot slipped in the mud. Her legs split, and she fell on her backside in a deep mud puddle, soaked and bruised. With a groan, she struggled to her feet, wiped her hands off on her skirts, and kept moving.

She spied two groups of people sleeping in tents along the road, but none of the horses looked like Éamonn's, so she kept moving.

One foot in front of another in the dark. Over the next hour, the rain had settled to mist. Moonlight shone from behind clouds, giving a faint, diffuse glow to the countryside. Light limned leaves with a silver lining, as if someone had painted the edges with faery light. They rustled as raindrops splattered.

Despite the hard work of treading down the muddy path without falling, pride surged through her. She'd escaped! Katie would be no trade good for her father to buy and sell at a whim. She'd grasp her own fate, for once. Once she found Éamonn, they'd make their life together without her father, without Lochlann, and without Donald.

What if Éamonn had camped to the side of the track, out of sight? She halted, wiping the water from her face. She'd never find him in the dark. The rain and the night would hide any horse sounds or a trail from the main track. She might have already passed him.

Katie glanced back down the track. If she'd passed him, she'd never find him. If she hadn't, she must keep going. And if she returned to Ballyshannon, Turlough might shelter her until Éamonn returned.

Hoofbeats splattering in the mud. Turning with her heart full of hope, expecting Éamonn, she gasped at a glimpse of Donald and Lochlann, both riding their horses in the dim moonlight.

Panic surged through her blood and she darted for the brush. Branches and brambles tore at her cloak. Roots tripped her, but she scrambled through the thick undergrowth. The horses couldn't follow her. They'd have to dismount, which would give her some time. Katie pushed on until the edge of a large lake blocked her.

Damn! They'd find her along the shore. She must hide in the bracken. Even the best woodsmen would have difficulty tracking her in the rain and the now hidden moon. She should hole up and hide. She plunged into the brush again, this time to the left.

Thorns tugged at her hood and scratched her cheeks. Katie pushed headfirst into the darkness.

112

Voices cursing behind her, made her stop, listening. The sound grew fainter. She picked her way in the opposite direction concentrating on stealth rather than speed.

Katie found a fallen tree but, with one side rotted away, she'd be seen easily enough. She moved on.

A large rock had a cave underneath one edge. She tried to squeeze herself in, but she wasn't as slim as Deirdre. Katie daubed mud and fallen leaves over her face and hands and dragged a fallen trunk in front. Then she slowed her breathing until her heart stopped pounding. Her sweaty skin and panting shifted to chills and shivering.

Sounds in the darkness taunted her. A whinny from a horse, shouts from the woods, a splash in the lake. Then other voices shouted. Had Éamonn arrived? She almost emerged from her hiding place, but some instinct kept her still. A female voice? Had Deirdre come with him? It didn't sound like her sister. Who in Brid's name could that be?

She listened for more clues, but only the dripping of rain answered her.

Katie trembled in her hiding hole, but daren't emerge. She shivered so violently now that she had no movement to warm her and the cold of the ground seeping her last bit of warmth away, and her teeth chattered. The soaked wool cloak offered no warmth any longer.

A strange snuffling sounded in the darkness, with leaves rustling. The *crack* of a twig. They came closer. A dog bayed.

Oh, damn their eyes. Where'd they find a dog?

In mere moments, the dog barked next to her. She tried to spring from her refuge and run away, but Donald's hand snaked out of the darkness and snatched her arm. She couldn't wrest free of his iron grip. Three strangers and an older woman stared at her. The woman lifted a lantern high as one man held the leash of a bloodhound. The dog yipped and barked, straining to get free, excited at his discovery.

Donald handed the woman a coin pouch. "Thanks to you."

She hefted it and peered inside, squinting in the lantern light. With a nod, the group faded into the brush.

Donald yanked hard on her arm. "Come on, you stupid bitch. This time, I'm not taking any chances."

Chapter Eight

Éamonn:
Whenever they passed other travelers, Éamonn, Deirdre, and Ciaran asked about folks traveling north, but most had joined the muddy trail recently and encountered no other wagons. Two horses, two wagons, and a mule. Three travelers. How many groups could there be who matched that description? One wagon had red and blue stripes over the roof. The other might be green and blue.

Some Travelers let their wagons turn shabby out of poverty. Others let them fade on purpose to appear less wealthy. Most took great pride in their wagons, though, and painted them often and with delicate designs of flowers or birds. The MacCrimmons' wagons had no designs, though not in bad nick. Perhaps they'd break down on this mad flight to Scotland, and he'd catch them soon. And find Katie.

Éamonn's plan had been to follow them until his father sent word of success with the council, but that wouldn't work. He must rescue Katie and hide her until all the danger fell away.

Would she be willing? Perhaps she wanted to be Lochlann's wife, after all. She might not wish to career across the countryside, hiding in a different place each night like Diarmuid and Gráinne.

To keep his mind from worrying, Éamonn told the tale as they walked. "Gráinne had been the beautiful daughter of the High King Cormac mac Airt. He arranged a marriage for her to Fionn, an old but powerful man. Horrified to discover his plans, she fell in love with a handsome young warrior, Diarmuid."

Deirdre used his pause to give him those sheep's eyes again. He cleared his throat before he continued, "After using a sleeping potion on the castle guests, she begged Diarmuid to take her away. He resisted, but she threatened him with a *geis,* a magical promise, so he complied. They hid across Ireland as Fionn searched for them across hill and dale, over mountains, and beside rivers."

Ciaran snorted. "Like we're doing? Yeah, that's grand fun."

Éamonn leveled a glare at his cousin. "After many years and near misses, Diarmuid's foster father, Aengus Óg, negotiated peace with Fionn. The two lovers settled and raised many children, content in their love."

Would they chase him and Katie all over the land, only finding peace after years of desperation and guile? That didn't matter. Éamonn needed Katie, *a ghrá rua*.

Everything else paled beside his aching desire. His need pounded in his head, his heart and, of course, his manhood. He'd never even properly kissed the girl. Such an insidious longing confounded him.

A group of people approached and Éamonn bowed his head in greeting. "*Dia daoibh*, good folks. Can you help me? I'm searching for some friends."

They stared at him with narrow gazes. An older man with a younger couple wearing packs on their back. A black and white hound poked his head from around the younger man's legs. They had no wagon or livestock and looked thin and worn.

"I have food to trade for information if you can help?"

The woman glanced at the man. He nodded and cocked his head. "What do they look like, yer friends?"

Éamonn sighed with relief. The last group wouldn't even answer. His people could be garrulous or taciturn as they saw fit, but most ignored strangers.

"Two wagons, one painted red and blue. Two horses and a mule. Two men and a young woman with red curly hair."

They exchanged glances again. The young man shrugged. "I saw such a group with horses, but no wagons or mule."

Éamonn tried to quell his excitement. "The young woman had red hair? Did she seem very short?"

His informant nodded with a leer. "Aye, a wee thing, and her hair might have been red, at that. The men rode draft horses. One had light hair. T'other might have been brown. Couldn't tell much more, from the mud and darkness."

"How far back along the road?"

The woman looked at the older man, holding her hands out. "About four hours' walk, I'd say?"

"And headed on towards Londonderry?"

She shook her head. "No idea where they went. But they didn't pass this way, so I imagine they're going north, aye."

"Ah, thanks to you, kind lady. Here, I've some bread and cheese for your help." He rummaged in his pack, pulling out a sizeable chunk of cheese wrapped in burlap and a loaf of horsebread.

The woman hesitated, giving him a suspicious look. But then she snatched the offering, and they moved past Éamonn's horse.

Ciaran furrowed his brow. "Well, at least we've gotten word of them. Wonder what happened to their wagons? We didn't see any abandoned on the road, and that lot would have mentioned such a sight. They'd have pilfered them and would be groaning under the weight of their plunder."

Éamonn glared at his cousin. "You are a cynical one, aren't you? Perhaps they backtracked for something? Regardless, we'll catch up with them by nightfall, if they're that close."

Deirdre remained silent. Éamonn still regretted letting her come along. He wanted to send her back, but he'd tried twice. She refused to leave, and Ciaran reminded Éamonn only she knew which direction Katie would go. She seemed as determined to escape her parents as he was to find Katie. Did they beat her, as well?

At least the rain had eased. The morning brought heavy mist, and the road faded into the fog as if leading to the Otherworld. Éamonn couldn't suppress a shudder at that notion.

After an hour, hoofbeats splashed in the mud somewhere in the mist. Had Katie escaped? Éamonn couldn't even tell from what direction the sound came, but then, from behind, an enormous form loomed out of the dim light, transforming into his brother.

Éamonn pulled back on his horse as she stamped in the mud. "Ruari! Why are you here? Shouldn't you be back with Fionnuala?"

The big man, pale, drawn, and sweating in the morning mist, reined in his mount. Spots of blood seeped through the bandage on his arm.

Éamonn's brow furrowed with concern. "You look awful. Why are you out here? Let me look at that arm."

Ciaran glared at him. "Éamonn, if you shut your mouth long enough, maybe Ruari can answer?" Éamonn ignored him and glanced at his brother.

Ruari swallowed, the lines on his face stark in the diffuse light. "I've got bad news."

Their horses chose that moment to exchange whinneys, and both brothers reigned in their mounts, pulling side by side. Éamonn grabbed his brother's shoulder. "News? What news? Is Da alright?"

He shook his head. "No, no, not Da. Fionnuala."

His heart gripped with fear. "Fionnuala? She's worse? I knew I should have stayed. We'll go back now!"

He had pulled his horse's reins around before Ruari blocked his progress. "Fionnuala." He swallowed. "She's gone, Éamonn."

"Gone? Gone where? Did she and Malachy get married, then? I thought they wanted to wait until his masterhood?"

Tears shone in his brother's brown eyes. "Gone. Passed on. She died, Éamonn. She died."

Panic twisted in his mind. His horse, sensing the chaos, whinnied and tried to rear. He pulled hard on the reins to keep her feet on the ground as she wheeled around. "Gone? Gone? But she was getting better! You must have gotten that wrong, Ruari. Ciaran, we've got to get back."

As Éamonn gripped his reins, ready to ride, Ruari grabbed hold of them to stop him, shaking his head. "No, Éamonn. You can do nothing now. Da said to tell you, go find Katie. But Fionnuala said something before she passed."

Éamonn couldn't move, as he clenched his teeth so hard to keep his sobs back. "What did she say?"

Ruari leaned forward and awkwardly kissed his cheek. "She said that was for you."

He didn't try to stop the tears, his mind a maelstrom of emotions. Dear, sweet little Fionnuala, so young and in love. His awkward, thin little sister. Ciaran sniffed behind him. Even Deirdre looked stricken.

Éamonn wiped his face. "Da? How's Da doing? And Síle? Édaín?"

"He's tired. He's not feeling well, but he said to go tell you. The girls are crying, but they'll be fine. I'm coming with you now."

Éamonn shook his head. "If Da is sick, he needs you. And you aren't well yourself. How's your arm? You never answered."

Ruari shrugged and glanced at the bandage. "It feels better. Cormac says I'll be fine."

"That's still bleeding. I don't like that at all. The wound could fester again. Go on back to Da, Ruari. He needs you more than we do. And see Cormac about the arm, right?"

His brother hesitated, his eyes flicking between Ciaran and Éamonn. "All right but be careful. Donald's a good fighter."

"I will, brother." Éamonn sniffed in his tears, shoving away the guilt at leaving. "Take care of the family for me. I'll be back when I can."

Fionnuala had lost her chance at a lifetime of joy. That dear, sweet child, gone forever. Seizing his own joy suddenly became more important than ever.

Katie:

After her attempt to escape, Donald tied her hands behind her back as they rode. She struggled, of course, but the knots stayed tight, biting into her wrists. She begged Lochlann to speak for her. To his credit, he'd argued with his brother, but with no success.

Her wrists chafed as she jounced in the wagon seat. She couldn't steady herself and kept falling over. After the third time, Donald let out a string of curses and tied her to the wagon itself.

Two more sodden days passed before blue sky returned. Londonderry seemed like a wet blur as Donald hurried them through. He insisted on camping along the road. As much as Katie longed for a dry bed in an inn, she realized arguing would do nothing.

The first night, she asked him to tie her hands in front, instead of behind. "I can't sleep like this! I can't even feel my arms."

With a growl and much muttering under his breath, he worked the knots free. They grew tight with use and rain. She waggled her arms once free to get feeling back into her fingers. Once the tingling stopped, she stretched tall with her arms straight up and sighed in pain and pleasure at the freedom.

When she dropped her arms, Donald's leer made her shiver. Her stays shifted around during her imprisonment, so her breasts popped out when she stretched. The shift still covered them, but the rain made the fabric translucent. With an embarrassed blush, she fixed her clothing until decent again.

She walked to the edge of the clearing, but Donald grabbed her arm. She cried out in pain.

"Where the hell are you going?"

"To relieve myself. Unless you prefer to watch?" she snapped, snatching her arm back.

Donald watched her with an eagle eye as she ducked into the bushes. When she re-emerged, he grunted. What now? She checked her shift, but nothing seemed amiss. She set up her tent, and Donald still glared at her with a scowl. Katie froze, like a frightened bird. Despite her disgust with herself, she backed away from his menacing countenance.

Lochlann finished setting up their own tent, then cocked his head.

Donald narrowed his eyes but didn't turn away. "Lochlann, you need to consummate the marriage. Once that's done, she won't try to escape again."

Katie backed against the tent, desperation rising in her throat, tasting like bile. "Oh, no! Not until I meet your father!"

Lochlann knitted his brow. "But she can't escape again, not tied up. She'll be fine, Donald. I'm not forcing myself on her."

Katie breathed a sigh of gratitude.

With a grunt, Donald waited while she removed her stays. Once she finished, he re-tied her hands. Then he commanded her to sit in the tent and started to tie her feet.

"No! You don't need to do that! I can barely get up with my hands tied. What happens if I need to relieve myself in the night?"

"You call for us, and we'll untie you. I'm not taking any more chances." He grabbed one foot while she kicked to keep the other from his grasp.

"Lochlann! Please! Not my feet!" Lochlann shrugged, glancing at each of them before turning away. She scrambled back, trying to escape. "Stop! No, I won't let you!"

Donald's hand fell upon her head swiftly, making her ears ring. She blinked a couple times to get her bearings. He'd bound her ankles tight. Tears burned, but she choked them back. Katie refused to give him the satisfaction of seeing her weep.

With another grunt, he shoved her feet into the tent and secured the flap with another tie. Katie inched into the center of the tent, curled into a ball, the only position she could manage other than flat on her back. She found her cloak and buried her face to muffle her sobs. *Oh, God, where is Éamonn?*

Every snapped twig, every stray breeze, made Katie hold her breath, hoping against dying hope Éamonn had found her. Such a possibility seemed further and further away as each hour passed in the dark, horrible night.

In the morning, Donald untied her to relieve herself. She changed into fresh clothing for the day, and he came to re-tie her. "Couldn't you just tie me to the wagon? I can't jump off while we're moving."

"We have thirty miles to Coleraine. That's almost two days, even with fair weather. I don't want any delays."

"My wrists are bloody from yesterday! You don't want them to fester, that would slow us down more." Katie steeled herself from sighing. That would only result in being hit, and all chances for clemency would disappear. She lowered her voice to a reasonable tone. "Then tie me in the front seat instead of the back. I won't fall over as often."

He agreed, but when he tightened the ropes, they bit into her skin. She gritted her teeth and celebrated the tiny victory with a secret smile.

They passed a few people on the road, single travelers or couples, once a group of four elderly women. One or two glanced at her, and they must have noticed her tied hands. But when a middle-aged couple with three strapping sons passed, she called out to them.

Katie blurted out, "Help me, please! I'm being kidnapped! These men stole me from my parents!" She held up her tied hands as proof.

The couple stopped, exchanging glances with each other, their sons, and then with Donald.

He glowered. "The woman is mad. We're taking her to the sanitarium in Belfast."

The woman's brow furrowed, but her husband pulled her along the path while muttering in her ear. Katie let out a deep sigh at her failure.

"Right. That's enough of that rubbish." Donald yanked a sweaty kerchief from his pocket and jammed the dirty cloth into her mouth. She struggled and spat, trying to get the horrible thing out. Her lip caught in the gag, and she bit down, choking. He secured a rope around the wad. She couldn't hold back the tears this time.

"Well, that's your wages for your little stunt, ye fecking shrew. You don't know when to quit, do you?"

Lochlann's thready voice drifted from the other wagon. "Is that necessary, Donald? She did no harm."

"Lochlann, listen to yourself. She might have gotten us arrested as kidnappers! She doesn't care what happens to us. Your heart is too tender by half, little brother." He wrinkled his nose, looked Lochlann up and down. Then he shook his head and whipped at the reins. Katie lurched back as the wagon moved. Her tears of despair turned to anger.

Katie kicked sideways, connecting with Donald's shin despite the awkward angle. Her nose clogged from the crying, and she couldn't breathe through her mouth, so she blew her nose. By a quirk of fate, he'd moved his head at just the wrong moment. A huge glob of snot landed in his mouth.

Donald spat the glob out and turned to glare at her. His face turned a dangerous red, and his eyes glittering black with rage. She didn't even see Donald's arm swing, but she fell sideways, seeing stars. The rope holding her to the wagon must have loosened as she slid to the ground.

"Donald, no!" Lochlann's protest came too late.

Katie couldn't move or breathe from the impact. While trying to spit the gag out, she wriggled and flipped. She couldn't get the vile thing out. The rope around the gag had slipped when she hit the ground. She stuck her tongue to the edge to get space to breathe.

Donald kicked her in the stomach. Agonizing pain shot through her guts. Curling into a ball to avoid another clout, she waited for the next blow. Flashes of her father's heavy hands made her tense her entire body. The sobs had disappeared. She tried to retreat to a numb neverland of escape, the place she'd created in her head years before, without success. Every blow felt as painful as the last.

Donald kicked her back and legs with savage fury. Lochlann shouted and tried to pull Donald off her, but still the pain came. She cowered further into her hidden refuge.

Only ringing ears and dull throbbing remained. Katie's entire body ached, but he finally stopped. She didn't uncurl, but she returned to the real world, opening her senses. Lochlann yelling at Donald. So, he'd finally found his backbone, had he? But Donald shouted back. Skin hitting skin. Would Donald beat his own brother? A horse whickered, and the mule joined into the cacophony. More voices. She peeked through squinting eyes just in time to see Donald pull his foot back and kick her in the head.

Deirdre:

Deirdre descended into a miserable silence. Soaked to the skin, shivering, her hair straggly and tangled, streamed down her back. Éamonn turned away every time she tried to speak to him, and even Ciaran remained silent.

And what would they do if they found Katie? Wrench her away from her lawfully wed husband? What then? Would Éamonn and Katie run for the rest of their lives?

Despite the rough trip, Deirdre had no plans to return to her parents, even after this mad quest had finished. Deirdre watched Éamonn's back sway on his horse, walking in front of her on the trail. She'd much rather wed Éamonn than help him find Katie. Sure, Ciaran had a sweet smile, but Éamonn made her blood run hot with desire. She needed time with him, to make him realize she'd be a better choice than Katie.

Deirdre questioned her decision to stay, but as much as she fought with Katie, they remained sisters. And if Deirdre stood for Katie being sold off, would she be next? Being the favorite meant nothing to her mercenary mother. And while Katie got in trouble more often, Deirdre received her share of blows from their father. Besides, she needed time to convince Éamonn to love her.

They'd heard word of the MacCrimmons from several travelers along the road. One said the woman acted mad, blathering about kidnapping. Another described her ragged blue dress. A third spoke of her bedraggled hair. Éamonn's face grew red with this news. Had Katie lost her mind? Deirdre wished she knew the truth.

As they passed Londonderry, dusk fell. Ciaran's eyes darted into the dark woods and his voice wavered, "We'll have to stop for the night. The clouds rolled in and we've no moonlight to guide the horses." His face settled into a frown.

Éamonn waved away the suggestion. "They'll be grand, Ciaran. We can manage well enough."

"Do you want them to stumble? How fast will you catch your lady with a lame horse?"

Éamonn heaved a sigh. "Fine. Find us a decent campsite. I'll scout ahead."

Deirdre didn't have much of a chance to talk to him. As soon as they'd stopped to camp last night, the rain let loose in a downpour, and they retreated to their tents.

Later that evening, the rain moved on, and they'd been able to chat around the campfire. She started the fire and a pot of soup. They still had horsebread, stale but edible. Moisture hardened the bread into a brick but soaking in the soup might help. Better than chipping a tooth on the stuff. She crumbled the remaining loaves into the pot.

Deirdre sprinkled salt and dried seaweed from her bag. While she loved cooking, she rarely liked doing so for her parents. Her mother had always been full of criticism and spite. Now, she was free to prepare food as she liked and she'd grabbed her supplies when she left. She'd brought clothing, a comb, and a few personal keepsakes. A necklace from an admirer, her looking glass, a prize from another young man, and her herbs. She left her other things in Turlough's care. No matter what happened, she trusted the sweet bard far more than she trusted her own parents.

She might never see her parents again. This notion filled her with conflicting emotions. Her explanation had some hard truth and some bravado. Her mother wouldn't really care she'd gone but that she'd lost Deirdre's potential bride price. Marriageable women remained scarce among Travelers, and men paid high dowries for young, attractive brides. Sometimes, matches got made when the girls had but ten or eleven years, though the ceremony wouldn't take place until they became women.

Katie's reputation had grown to the point she'd had no new offers in the past year. She'd perfected the art of offending her suitors before they formalized, and Deirdre noted where that had gotten her. Well, Deirdre wouldn't be so stupid. She'd choose her husband and pursue him until he became well and truly hers.

Why had Katie decided on Éamonn? Deirdre found Éamonn first, after all. She and Éamonn had already enjoyed that lovely afternoon by the river. That had been a sweet day, with the bees buzzing around them in the fragrant spring flowers. Deirdre shivered at the memory of his gentle touch on her skin, causing her to smile. She ached for more and meant to win.

Ciaran came to sit next to her as she stirred her soup. "And to what do I owe such an enchanting smile? Whatever caused that, I'm grateful."

She must be careful not to alienate the young man. "Just remembering a lovely day." Ciaran liked her, but he acted too moody. Still, he'd be her second choice if she couldn't turn Éamonn's heart. A better option than returning to her parents' care, especially after disappearing.

He peered into her iron pot. "What are you concocting for us? A brew to bewitch our hearts?"

"As if I needed such things, Ciaran Kilbane." She flashed him a coy smile from under her lashes. He flushed and ducked his head.

His teasing gave her a dangerous idea, though. Several years ago, they'd stayed in a Mayo village over a brutal winter. The old herbwoman had taught Deirdre about herbs and flowers, potions and concoctions. Deirdre didn't know if the woman had been an actual witch and didn't care. She could use that knowledge to achieve her goals.

Deirdre needed clover, but that grew everywhere. She already had rose petals in her pack, and lavender. A pinch of carrageen moss might help. Old Moira had been a big believer of carrageen for all sorts of magic. They drew close to the coast, and she could restore her supply.

Lost in her preparations, she failed to notice Éamonn return from scouting. He sat on the other side of her and glanced into the pot as she stirred in the last ingredients.

Ciaran piped up. "She's brewing a potion for us, Éamonn. Care to become bewitched?"

The comment matched her plans too closely. She glared at Ciaran. From his wide, innocent eyes, he'd been jesting.

With poor grace, she switched her glare into a grin. "No, nothing like that. Here, Éamonn, have some bread. Soak that first, mind you, it's like a rock. It would be tastier with a few hours to simmer, but at least it will be hot." Deirdre scooped the soup into a horn bowl to hand to him. She waited until he placed his hands over hers and gazed into his eyes from under her lashes. She held the bowl a moment too long, and he flushed.

Pleased she could get a reaction, she turned and served Ciaran. "Eat well, boys. We need to conserve our strength for the journey."

She'd have to steep an herbal tea in the morning. But then Ciaran would drink the potion as well, and he'd already fallen for her. She didn't want him tripping over his own drool. However, if Éamonn came down with a cold, she might nurse him with her potion.

Éamonn slurped his soup and wiped his mouth with the back of his hand. "We shouldn't be too far behind. If we can't travel at night, neither can they, aye? We might catch up tomorrow and find them before they reach port."

Deirdre took a sip of her soup, letting her lips linger on the spoon as Éamonn watched. "Katie said they planned on shipping out from Ballycastle."

"They'll like as not take the road through Coleraine, and along the coast through Bushmill. The smugglers are busy in the area and keep the roads clear. Unless the English are nearby, then convenient rock falls and washouts happen."

"A bit more soup? We should finish the rest off. No sense wasting good food." Old Moira had assured her a man didn't stray from a good cook's hearth.

He held out his bowl, and she scraped the last bit in. Ciaran pouted, so she handed him the last crust of horsebread. The dark-haired man grimaced and gnawed on the heel.

Traveling without her parents felt so wicked and free. Why, she might do whatever she liked and not fear her father's hand. She could play with Éamonn, with Ciaran, go screaming in circles, or kick off her clothes to swim in the ocean. Well, perhaps not that last one. In May, the ocean would be frigid. She shivered at the thought.

"Are you cold, Deirdre? Here, take my cloak." Éamonn draped his heavy fur cloak over her. The fabric smelled of him, still warm from his body heat. She snuggled into the warmth and leaned her head against his shoulder. Startled, he placed his arm around her. He went stiff, but she cuddled in and, soon, his muscles relaxed. Ciaran frowned and stared into the fire.

Deirdre fluttered her eyes at him. "Ciaran, would you mind fetching me a drink? I think I salted the soup too much." Ciaran went off to fetch a bottle of ale for each of them.

Éamonn pulled back from her and raised an eyebrow. "The soup tasted fine, lass. Are you still cold?"

Deirdre snuggled back into his arm. "Just a little, but I'm warming up." She caressed his knee, and he flinched. "Is aught wrong?"

"No, nothing wrong, you just startled me, is all." As Ciaran returned with his bottle, Éamonn stood, leaving his cloak around her shoulders. "Here, Ciaran, why don't you sit and warm the poor girl? I've got to tend the horses."

She sighed when he rose, but she'd made progress. Ciaran sat and put his arm around her as Éamonn had. However, he wasn't as tall as his cousin, and she didn't fit the same. They shared the campfire's warmth as she sat in sullen silence.

Chapter Nine

Éamonn:
The small town of Coleraine looked full of English soldiers. Since the English often harassed Travelers, they journeyed around the place. Éamonn reasoned the MacCrimmons must have done the same. Niggling doubt preyed on his mind, though. He must scout ahead. If he could find a handy cliff, he'd climb to have a look. He remembered several along the north coast, most with ancient stone towers for long-dead lookouts.

Heading along the road, they approached a steep hill with a lone white stone on the summit. Just what he sought, a vantage point to survey the area for any sign of fair Katie. The highland must command a fantastic view of the coastline and down the road.

After scrambling up the side, almost slipping twice, he panted when he reached the top. The white stone he'd spied wasn't a tower but an ancient Fae stone. Bits of white paint flaked off from the weather.

Éamonn approached with caution, remembering his last experience at the fairy stones. He half-expected to find sprites dancing in the sunlight, reminding him of when his father gave him the brooch, and his heart clenched for missing his family. For a moment, he thought he spied faint lights sparkling around it, but that must have been his own active imagination.

Should he touch it? His father had mentioned using the stones as a way to heal, to regain strength. This pursuit had exhausted him, body and mind. He could use some strength, even if it was a fairy gift.

Before laying a hand on the stone, he braced himself for the onslaught of noise, light, and confusion as when his father gifted him the brooch. None of that happened. Simply a warm, calming wave of pleasure washing through him as he stared out across the horizon.

Éamonn took comfort in the calm, breathing in and out in measured beats. The power melted the jagged edges in his head and heart. His anger and suspicion eased. He even grew a warm spot for Lochlann, the poor lad. The Scot might already regret his trade. He didn't envy the man Katie's temper for marrying her against her will. Éamonn gave a half-smile, imagining how much she'd harangue the hapless soul.

The sky cleared as he peered down the road. Shafts of silvery sunlight pierced the clouds like arrows from Heaven. Dappled light danced across rolling hills and rocky cliffs, and a glimmer of the ocean flashed in the distance, light sparkling on the waves.

He didn't know how long he stood next to the stone. Ciaran shouted his name from the bottom of the hill. Éamonn waved to Ciaran, but when he hastily scanned the road for his quarry, the whole reason he'd come up here in the first place, he couldn't find anyone who might be the MacCrimmons. Some of his calm peeled away, for without a clue of which way the lass had gone, how was he to know where to follow? With a frustrated curse, he climbed back down the hill.

Ciaran glanced up at the stone with a furrowed brow. "What took you so long? You stood up there a good half-hour. Did you see anything?"

"A half hour? There's no way I was there that long. You've been out in the sun too long."

Deirdre and Ciaran exchanged a worried glance, but Éamonn decided they must be playing a joke, and gestured along the road. "Just the coastline. No wagon parties. Either we've passed them, or they're halfway to Ballycastle. An excellent view from that standing stone, though."

His cousin took a few steps back. "A standing stone? You shouldn't have touched something like that."

Éamonn waved his hand. "It's grand, Ciaran. Just an old stone someone painted white."

Ciaran blanched. "That means it's sacred to the Fae Queen, Éamonn. Did you touch the thing?"

"Well, sure. I wanted to keep my balance."

The other man shook his head, staring at the ground. "No good can come of this. We should go back!"

"For the love of…we're not heading back, Ciaran. Certainly not because I touched a bloody be-damned stone!"

Ciaran grew paler and exchanged another glance with Deirdre. "Hush with those words, Éamonn! Here, let me find hawthorn. It might protect you from Her wrath." He scrambled into the bushes on the other side of the road.

He knew better than they did that the Fae were real. What if Ciaran had seen him at the stone? The idea that Ciaran and Deirdre might discover this bit of magic his father gave him, and maybe take it away, fueled his anger into frustration and resentment. "We don't have time, Ciaran! Get back here, we're off. You're being foolish. You should know better, and you a grown man."

With curses and rustling, Ciaran returned, a prickly sprig of hawthorn in his hand. A few early buds of white blossoms hung on. With a cry, Deirdre sprinkled water over the branch. "Never cut a hawthorn in the day, Ciaran! Only by the full moon."

"In the name of all that's holy, will you two stop? We don't have the whole host of the Fae behind us in an angry mob. It's just a bloody stone!"

After he leapt back on his horse, they started off again. *Hawthorn and full moons, my arse.* Still, he touched the sprig Ciaran had tucked into his belt as he glanced back up the hill, the white stone shining like a beacon. A shiver ran down his spine as the echo of fairy music danced in his head.

Thinking back to the MacCrimmons, since he hadn't seen them on the road, he'd have to find their trail again. What if they headed towards Belfast instead of Ballycastle?

Without better information, Éamonn pushed along their original route. Portrush didn't lie far away. As they came to the docks, they saw all sorts of working men lingering along the shore, such as sailors, fishers, and traders.

When he glanced at the lowering sun, Éamonn had an idea about increasing their limited resources. Turlough had given them a few coins. Travelers relied more on trade and barter. Boatmen preferred cash. Éamonn preferred dice.

Besides, he might do worse than to have a drink and perhaps a game or two. Finding out information worked easier when playing dice with a man.

However, when he tried to leave Ciaran and Deirdre at the inn, Ciaran grew stubborn. "Why can't I come with you? I'm just as good at the dice as you, cousin mine!"

Except Éamonn now had his new talent for persuasion. He considered using it on his cousin but dismissed that as a cheap trick. Still, he couldn't tell Ciaran why he must do this alone. "Because Deirdre needs watching. This is a rough place."

"Bah. She's a Traveler, no blushing aristo. She can handle herself."

Deirdre straightened tall in response to this compliment. "I can, indeed! I need no protection from the likes of you, Éamonn Doherty."

"Neither of you have been to this place before, but I have. I know the sorts who roam the streets. Please, be smart, aye? Just one evening, while I'm searching for information. If I'm alone, folks are more likely to talk to me."

Deirdre crossed her arms and pouted her lips. "I want to see the town!"

"And so you will, tomorrow! Not tonight."

She narrowed her gaze. "We're leaving tomorrow."

Éamonn rolled his eyes. "Deirdre. Please. We need to find out if they've been through here. I can't be distracted. Can't you understand?" He considered pushing her into agreeing with the brooch's magic but didn't want to waste the headache on her.

Ciaran took her arm with a gallant gesture. "Come with me, Deirdre. I'll keep you company while His Highness delves into the depths of the docks."

As they walked toward the inn, Éamonn's eyes lingered on Deirdre's shapely backside before he tore himself away and stalked toward the pier.

The docks looked even rougher than he remembered. Grizzled men with scowls and muscles teemed along the pier. The stench of fish and unwashed men permeated. He wandered, stopped to watch a dice game, resisted the urge to jump in, then moved on to the next knot of players. Every now and then, he'd catch a man's eye and nod in silent greeting.

As velvet night embraced the town, he took out his own cup, cradling the precious tool in the palm of his hand. His dice rattled inside, catching the attention of a group finishing a game. When he gave them a grin, they invited him in with a gesture.

His talent worked on the gamblers even without words. He pushed at them to place unwise bets, or to hold back when they had a strong position. It worked too well at first. He had to make a few obvious mistakes himself to allay suspicion. Did he cheat when he used a Fae-granted gift? Sure, and he'd insult the Fair Folk more to waste such a gift.

After a few calculated losses, he'd built fragile camaraderie with the group. Time to test that bond. He turned to the man next to him, who had an enormous nose like a blotchy potato and no hair at all. "Are ye local, then?"

The short answer didn't encourage discussion. "Aye."

"I've just come from Ballyshannon myself. Did some trading."

That raised some eyebrows. "Oh, aye? And whatcha trade, then?"

"Horses, mostly."

The man spat to the side. "Land creatures are no use to me."

"You fish each day?"

He hawked and looked as if he would spit again. "When t' weather allows, aye."

"I'm searching for a man who sold me a lame horse and my cousin. Perhaps you've seen them come through?"

The gambler shrugged. Éamonn took the plunge. "Two men and a woman, all about my age. Two horses, two wagons, and a mule. Sound like anyone you've seen in the last day?"

The other man raised a fuzzy eyebrow, interest now sparking in his eyes. "Pretty lass? Red hair?"

Éamonn couldn't control his excitement, his spine straightening. "That's them, yes. When did they come through?"

He scratched his bald pate and shrugged. "This morning, sure enough. She looked in awful shape, though."

His heart jumped into his throat. With difficulty, he swallowed, unsure he wanted to know more but desperate to hear news. "Did she look ill?"

"Nay, nay, but she'd been beaten right proper. Big bruises on her face, and a purpled eye. Her face looked bonny enough around that, though puffy from crying, belike. I remember thinking such a shame she be used so."

Fury rose within Éamonn like a phoenix from warm ashes. He tamped down on the rage. "She's...she's my cousin. I aim to get her back."

The man raised an eyebrow, interested despite himself. "Did she run off with the men?"

Clenching his teeth, Éamonn shook his head. "No, she was sold to them."

With a frown, the gambler cocked his head. "Sold? By whom?"

"Her father." Éamonn couldn't say much more without bursting from the anger. He snapped his mouth shut and clamped his jaw.

"Ah, that's not right, that isn't. A fair match is all well and good but selling your daughter to a brute. That's not on."

Éamonn nodded, fighting back both rage and tears.

The other man clapped his shoulder. "I wish you luck on your search, lad. I do. And if you find them, give the brute a good wallop for me, aye?"

Éamonn gave another nod, unable to speak. Now, more than ever, his resolve to rescue Katie pounded in his heart. Any hesitation in him died when he pictured her bruised face. He couldn't just abandon her to the tender mercies of beasts like the MacCrimmons. Even if he had to steal her away, he'd rescue her. He'd promised to protect her, after all.

The bald man rose from the circle with a grunt. Éamonn watched him disappear into the gathering gloom.

"Your turn, mate."

Éamonn grabbed his cup and rolled. He didn't care any longer if he looked suspicious. Time to win. If the MacCrimmons passed through here this morning, he'd have to make tracks at the break of dawn. The inevitable headache pounded in his skull as he decided he needed boat fare, right quick.

Katie:

One mare stepped on a stone and went lame as they traversed the coastal road. They had to unhook the wagon while Lochlann found a replacement beast at a nearby village. By the time he returned, the sun already touched the ocean. As always, Katie listened in vain to hear the faint sizzle as the sun touched the water. Such a foolish notion, one Deirdre teased her about to no end as children. That's when she had learned to keep her more fanciful notions private. While she loved stories of magic and fairies, most people didn't appreciate the everyday magic. She'd learned that letting someone else into those fancies always invited pain. She glanced at Lochlann and let out a deep sigh.

The sky turned dark blue by the time they reached Bushmills. The streets thronged with people, jostling their wagons, and alarming the mule. He voiced his distress loudly and so often Donald kicked the beast several times, which set the horses off.

A strong sour odor of fermented mash hung heavy in the air, a sure sign of a huge nearby still. Smugglers must frequent this port, despite the English soldiers. How did they maintain their secrecy when the stuff stank so much? Any soldier searching for contraband whiskey could trace the stench. Someone must pay them well to ignore the smell.

Her own light-headedness had little to do with the fumes. She'd barely slept in the last week. Had she been wed a week? She'd lost track of the days. It didn't matter. She felt numb, aching, and exhausted. She'd tried to wiggle her muscles into a more comfortable position a thousand times, to no success. Her arms ached from being tied, and her head was one big throbbing mass from Donald's kick.

Donald had landed a good blow to her eye, and the rest of her body felt like one giant bruise. Not much broken skin, but cuts would've healed more quickly than the massive purple blotches on her back, legs, and arms.

Almost worse than the pain was the pitying glances from passing folk. They'd glance at her as if she was but a simple child, no smarter than a stone. And perhaps she hadn't been to have aggravated Donald so.

As the last blue light faded, water shimmered in the distance, the Irish Sea in all its splendor. Soon, they'd reach Ballycastle and go aboard a boat. That idea terrified her more than another beating from Donald.

When living in Ireland, one never got far from the sea. Water surrounded everyone, in rivers and burns, in lakes and pools, and hanging in the air they breathed. The domain of *Manannán mac Lír*, the god of the sea, surrounded them.

That god's fury manifested whenever a storm hammered the coast. A fierce tempest caused horrible damage on land. What could that wind do to a tiny boat, bobbing on its surface?

Even Scotland and all the unknowns she'd face didn't compare to her fear of the open, hungry ocean. Violent shivers ran over her body.

Lochlann draped his plaid across her shoulders. "Are ye cold, lass? Here, take my cloak." The fabric had a soft blue and green faded checkered pattern, with narrow stripes of red and yellow. Katie wanted to rage at Lochlann for letting Donald hurt her.

She wanted to fling the offered cloak into the sea and laugh at his measly attempt. Instead, she continued to stare at the black sea, and her shudder had nothing to do with the brisk wind whipping the cloak and her hair.

The last bit of light died in the ocean as they stopped. Katie wanted to climb down, but her hands were still bound. Lochlann took her by the waist and lifted her to the ground. He tried to be gentle, but the landing jarred every muscle and ache in her body. She stumbled into him, and he held her against his shoulder as she sobbed.

Donald removed the gag with her promise she'd behave herself. Katie had been ready to promise anything to have the horrid thing removed.

She searched the face of every person they passed. What had happened to Éamonn? He should have been able to catch up, especially after the delay with the lame horse. He must have given her up as a poor gamble. Katie let out a sob as her last shred of hope fluttered away in the ocean wind. She'd have no knight in shining armor galloping down the dock to rescue her at the last moment. She had no choice now but to resign herself to her fate.

Donald chose a simple, bare inn near the docks for their rest. At least he bought hot stew and fresh bread for supper. She chewed tiny bites, careful not to move her jaw more than necessary.

Several people in the room glanced her way, their gazes sliding from her as if guilty for seeing her. Her eyes traveled to the door.

Donald's whisper grated in her ears, "Don't even think it."

Katie bowed her head and rubbed her chaffed wrists. Her skin still burned, and her waist stung from the rope. Tomorrow would be her last day in her own country. She tried to clutch onto her memories like charms against the future. Each hill and river, every wildflower, the aroma of sweet grass on the breeze. She prayed on each image like a talisman, locking them away in her mind.

Éamonn's face floated into her imagination unbidden, a rakish half-smile splitting his cheeks. The image came so sudden, she sobbed with the impact. She must forget him. He'd abandoned her. He wasn't worth the remembering. That hurt worse than her bruised back.

Éamonn:

A black cloud angled over the sea from the west to form an impressive storm. Curls and eddies swirled as wind sheared the clouds. The sun struggled to beat back the encroaching storm. The few beams that pushed through the storm got devoured, replaced with sheets of wind and rain.

Éamonn prayed a tempest would keep the MacCrimmons from embarking today.

The squall might be an hour off, but Éamonn picked up the pace. From the cliff track above the Clare Road, he spied the town and natural harbor. Ships and sailors scrambled like angry ants around the pier, either speeding out of the harbor or battening down their crafts.

Hopefully, the MacCrimmons remained with the latter.

Éamonn goaded his mare faster along the cliff road. A blast of wind tugged at his cloak as his horse stumbled. The burnt smell of lightning hung in the air, and the temperature plummeted. Ciaran and Deirdre fell behind, but he no longer cared. He'd find Katie and extract her from the clutches of those malicious brutes. Never mind Katie had legally wed. Lochlann had no right to her heart. That remained hers alone to bestow.

Éamonn felt the crinkle of her red curls in his hands. The fresh scent of her skin teased him in every passing breeze. Her low chuckle beckoned him whenever he passed a stream.

Once at the pier, he scanned the people on the dock, searching for the telltale red hair of his love. A few redheads caught his eye, but nothing like her blazing glory. He saw another and steadied his gaze, all the way at the other end of the docks.

Two wagons, three horses? Two men rushing to sail before the storm. They'd already moved the wagons onto the boat, and the taller man coaxed the first horse up the plank. A redheaded woman slumped on the dock, a blurry smudge so far away. He recognized her form, and his heart leapt.

Éamonn clicked and dug his heels into his horse's flank. His teeth chattered from the icy wind. He must reach her! He couldn't come this close and still miss them.

Donald—for that's who the taller man surely was—led the second horse aboard, damn his eyes. And Lochlann, who pulled a struggling Katie into the craft. *No!*

"Katie! Katie! Wait!" His throat burned, but he was still too far away. Hoofbeats and wind stole his voice. His cloak whipped behind him as he rushed down the road, his progress halted multiple times by people in his way, even as the sails on their craft billowed madly, and the captain glanced up. With the horses all on board, Donald glanced back one last time from the dock.

The Scotsman must have glimpsed Éamonn in his mad race to the docks. Éamonn came close enough now he saw the man break into a nasty, self-satisfied smile.

"Katie! Kaaatieee!!"

She turned toward him, her mouth agape in shock. For one glorious moment, their eyes locked. "Éamonn!" her faint voice reached him. She tried to rush to the edge of the boat, but Lochlann and Donald held her tight. She struggled to wrench from their grip. The captain stood on the deck as his hands untied the craft from its moorings. The ship creaked and groaned, eager to race in the wind of the open sea.

By the time Éamonn's horse reached the dock, heaving and sweating, the boat had escaped. The dwindling craft took his dreams away.

When Ciaran and Deirdre caught up, they stood next to him as he watched the ship disappear into the rousing storm. Winds howled, but Éamonn stood still as if carved from stone.

Ciaran took an arm. "Come inside, cousin. Out of the wet. There's no point in catching your death on top of losing your love. Come, we'll sort this all out."

Éamonn cast a longing gaze towards the callous sea. Tears ran down his cheeks, mingling with the first heavy drops of rain. No other captain would risk their craft in this storm now. *Too late. Much too late.*

He stumbled back to the horses and let Ciaran led him to an inn, just a ramshackle dock building some enterprising soul had walled off into private rooms. The wind howled through gaps in the planking, but the worst of the fury stayed outside. Burning peat crackled in the hearth as Ciaran pulled stools up to a nearby round table. "Here, man, have a seat. I'll pay for rooms, and we'll find a boat after the storm has passed, aye?"

Éamonn numbly stared at the table.

Deirdre caressed his knee. "Maybe this is how things should be, as Ciaran said. After all, they *are* legally wed, are they not?" Her warmth seeped through his wet breeks, burning the skin beneath. He grunted, unable to admit even that.

"We'll eat something and have a drink. You'll feel better once you're warm and dry." She gave a fetching giggle. "I thought you would pitch headfirst over the cliff a few times. How you stayed on your horse, I'll never know."

He glared at her as her chatter annoyed him, but he had neither the energy nor the will to stop her.

Ciaran returned with a large loaf of bread and cheese to share. "We've two rooms, one for you and me, Éamonn, and one for Deirdre, and supper as well. Here."

Deirdre placed her hands on the table, pushing to her feet. "I'll fetch something to drink."

Éamonn took the bread and cheese, breaking off hard bits and tossing them on the floor. Perhaps ale would blunt his pain.

When Deirdre returned, she had a single cup of tea, which she handed to Eamonn while placing the packet Eamonn recognized from the road back into her pocket.

"Where's my ale?"

"Drink the tea first. It will help. Drink it all. They say," she added with a sly smile, "that it will heal the most broken of hearts."

He took the tea and began to drink. It did warm him, that much was true.

Ciaran asked. "Hey, what about me?"

"In a moment, greedy guts. Éamonn needs to drink first."

He pouted. "I got rained on, too."

Deirdre rolled her eyes, returned to the tavern's kitchen, and came back with tea for Ciaran, as well as ales for them all. "Here, silly man. Be happy you got any."

The storm raged outside, buffeting the shaky structure with steady winds. A slow drip formed above Éamonn's head, but he wouldn't move out of the way. Deirdre glanced up at the splatter of the drops and pulled him closer to her. She studied him as he sipped his drink.

Ciaran glanced at her over his steaming cup. "The tea is tasty, Deirdre. What's in it?"

"My own secret blend. Good for what ails you."

Éamonn sipped his tea in silence, staring at the flickering and glowing of the peat in the hearth. He might have gotten better rooms with the money he'd won the night before, but he deserved to suffer for his failure. His head still pounded from using the brooch's magic the night before. The pain didn't always come immediately, but he paid for each use of the faery-gift. One or two small pushes, and his head ached. If he pushed harder, he'd be sick most of the next day.

Moping, he rose to get more ale. When the barkeep held his hand out for payment, he placed a doit in it and trudged back to the table. The man gave him a narrow look, then closed his hand around the payment. Éamonn heaved a sigh and returned to the table, intent upon drinking himself into numbness.

That night, sleep came fitful and scarce. At one point, Éamonn heard Deirdre stirring in the next room. She mumbled or sang to herself. The wind drowned out her words.

As he dozed, he once again found himself in the dream bog. This time, he recognized his hunters. Faerie forms with grotesque faces, twisted by nature or magic. Horrifying and disgusting, he pulled away from their spindly, gnarled fingers, but he had nowhere to run, and his heart raced in panic. They surrounded him and forced him into the murky marsh.

The next morning, Éamonn woke in a cold sweat. If only he'd been a few minutes quicker. He'd spent too much time gawking about on the hill near the standing stone. What if they'd left earlier in the morning? What if the MacCrimmons moved slower? What if they hadn't found a ship so quickly? What if the storm had come sooner, or late enough that he found a ship before the wind came? What if I had begged their captain to come back? What if the storm drowned Katie?

The *what ifs* swirled in his head as he cursed himself, Donald MacCrimmon, the Fae, God and all his saints, and both Ciaran and Deirdre.

That idea brought him up short. Why did he curse Deirdre and Ciaran? The girl *tried* to help, but he kept having to fend off her flirting. Éamonn didn't want Deirdre, he wanted Katie. And Ciaran, he'd never steered Éamonn wrong. *Maybe,* he thought with a mix of resignation and despair, *they have a point. Maybe I have lost.*

He rolled the idea around in his mind. A life without Katie. Married to someone else. Whom would he marry? Not another redhead. Such a girl would always remind him of Katie. He glanced at Deirdre's midnight waterfall of hair. Éamonn remembered the silky smoothness against his skin. That afternoon by the river, he'd enjoyed playing with it, the sleek way her hair fell on his chest. His body ached to take her into his arms. But then his cheeks burned with memory of Katie. His promise to protect her from her father, from anyone who'd harm her. With his name and his body, he'd vowed. And he'd failed her.

He rose, dressed, splashed chilly water on his face, and waited for the storm to ease, pacing in the common room. At every sound outside, he peered through the dingy window, hoping to see clear skies, but the storm still howled. He begged the gods to bring him sky clear enough to sail across the Irish Sea.

Ciaran sat with his tea, relaxing by the crackling fire while Deirdre slept in. "Will you sit already, Éamonn?"

"I can't relax, Ciaran. I feel trapped."

"A trap of your own making then, cousin. Hell, she can't be worth all this, can she? I mean, you've not even—"

The punch sounded loud in the quiet room. Ciaran shook his head and stood with a glower. "That was uncalled for, Éamonn Doherty."

"Don't you speak so about Katie."

"Like what? Like she's a married woman? Like she's got a husband to bed her each night?"

Ciaran was ready this time and ducked, getting a shot of his own into his cousin's stomach. Éamonn bent over in pain. He swung around to knock Ciaran on the head, but only landed a glancing blow. Ciaran tripped him and they fell to the floor. Éamonn grabbed Ciaran's shoulders, pulling his elbow back to punch him in the gut, but Ciaran wriggled away.

With a quick kick towards Éamonn's face, Ciaran scrambled to one corner of the common room. "She's not yours, Éamonn! She never…was! Give her…up!"

Éamonn scuttled after him, his blood boiling with frustration and rage. "I can't leave her…to them!" He grabbed Ciaran's foot, pulling himself closer to his cousin's face. He wanted to choke Ciaran until he just shut up. His cousin's face turned red, and then an alarming shade of purple before Éamonn came to his senses.

Backing away, his eyes grew wide. "Oh, God, Ciaran. What the hell am I doing?" He sat with his head in his hands.

Ciaran coughed and sat up. "I have no idea, Éamonn. What I do know is that you're headed for trouble."

"I can't leave her to them, Ciaran."

Ciaran spread his arms. "Why? I've supported you so far, but the fates are making themselves pretty clear. Besides, don't you want to get back to your father? Why is she so important you must be the conquering hero? Are you so arrogant you need to be the king in every castle? You can snap your fingers and have a half-dozen lovely women fawning over you like a bard."

Éamonn stared at his cousin in astonishment. "No, Ciaran. It's not like that, not at all. It's…it's her father."

Ciaran flung his hands up. "What in the name of all that's holy does her father have to do with anything?"

"He beat her. Possibly both of them."

Ciaran shrugged. "That's common enough."

Éamonn shook his head. "He terrified her, Ciaran, and I promised her I'd take care of her, that I'd never let him beat her again. That I'd protect her from harm. And then, well, they beat her on the road here. One of the dock men said she looked in horrible shape."

"Beaten? By Lochlann?"

Closing his eyes, Éamonn covered his face with his hands. "I don't know. More likely Donald, but does it matter? I promised to protect her, and I failed. Can't you see? I must make sure she is safe."

Ciaran didn't answer, and they both stared at the fire.

Éamonn:
After almost going mad, Éamonn leapt out of the inn as soon as the sky brightened, combing the docks for any willing sailor.

The first captain looked ninety years older than God himself. "Nay, I'll not be takin' anyone across today, nor yet tomorrow. Yonder storm cracked my mast. I'll need to do repairs first."

The second captain, another older man with skin like mahogany, tapped his chin several times before refusing. "For just the three of you, a trip ain't worth me time, aye? If ye had perhaps a half-dozen passengers, then all'd be well. I'll have to wait until I'm full up."

After shaking his head in disgust, Éamonn tried yet another captain. A younger man, perhaps ten years older than himself. With a weather eye on the clouds, which still loomed dark on the horizon, he shrugged. "I'll go if it's worth my time, to be sure."

Éamonn hefted his belt pouch. "I'll make sure the trip's worth your time, you can be sure of that."

The captain grinned, showing three gold teeth. A man who liked to keep his wealth mobile. With some dickering and a price agreed upon, Éamonn rushed back to the inn to fetch the others.

Deirdre wrinkled her nose, staring at the dark horizon. "I don't know, Éamonn. The sea is still rough."

Ciaran hugged her shoulders and nodded. "Besides, either God or the Fae are out to keep you in Ireland. I wouldn't trust my skin to their revenge on the open sea."

Deirdre echoed his nod. "You *have* had a string of bad luck."

With a sigh of exasperation, Éamonn stared at them. "I'm going. If you prefer to stay here, then stay. I'm off across the water."

Ciaran clutched at his arm. "Wait! Éamonn, wait. At least get the ship blessed. Better to hedge your bets, aye?"

The fool believes this malarkey. And yet, I know for a fact that fairies are real. Maybe he's not full of shite, after all. "Fine. Do what you must but be quick. I mean to sail within the hour."

Between Ciaran finding a priest and the subsequent haggle about a price, the three of them set sail from Ballycastle Harbour two hours later. The sky had almost cleared by then, in the fickle way of Irish weather. A strong gale pushed them across the bay into the ocean and toward Scotland. And Katie.

Part III
Chapter Ten

Katie:

The sight of Éamonn galloping headlong down the cliff road toward the dock had made her spirit soar. *He came! He still loves me!* But as his form dwindled into the distance, and his face, full of anxious longing, faded, her heart sank again. He'd come too late. For a long, aching moment, she wanted to jump into the ocean to swim back to him, but her fear of the deep water and Donald MacCrimmon's iron grip on her arm kept her still.

For a mad moment, she considered shoving Donald into the icy water, even if they both went in. But fear paralyzed her.

The wind whipped up, slapping her face with seawater. The sky had turned a preternatural gray-green as they raced from the shore. After that, one nightmare after another slammed into her. Katie's stomach let her know in no uncertain terms it didn't like the pitching ship. Even Lochlann looked green.

The storm tossed their ship about like a toy. Katie lived in dread that each wave would engulf them and drag them to the watery depths. *Manannán mac Lír,* the god of the sea, seemed to laugh in the wind, mocking her hope and her fear.

Mist and rain surrounded them as they stood on the deck, with Donald on the other side, facing their destination. How could the captain navigate in this? Would they land in England or Wales? Or would they sail into the dusky mist, into the unknown. The land of *Tír na nÓg,* where gods lived in everlasting youth and beauty. Or *Hy-Brasil,* the mythical land west of the waves, a land only visible one day every seven years.

She tried to distract herself and imagine what the land of ever-young would be like. What sort of trees grew in the Otherland? What sort of fruit would she pluck? But thinking of fruit reminded her of Éamonn by the riverside, and her throat closed as she gripped the railing. At least Donald hadn't rebound her hands.

The captain said the trip would be two hours, depending on the weather. Two hours. What a long time to—She bent over the rail to throw up.

After her stomach emptied, she stared at the agitated water below. A dangerous fascination, like a bird gazing into the eyes of a snake. Patterns and movement of sea spray and whitecaps swirled and danced. Beautiful and terrifying.

The black depths beckoned to her, but Katie couldn't swim. She'd only be ending her own life. *Would it be so horrible?*

Katie swallowed down a lump in her throat. No, she'd never have the gumption. Giving in would be a mortal sin. No, Caitriona O'Malley would never take her own life. Well, Caitriona MacCrimmon now. Katie shuddered, pulling her shawl tighter.

Lochlann walked to her side, pitching his voice to be heard over the wind. "Are ye well, lass? I've brought another cloak. Here, the fabric's dry on the inside, at least." He wrapped her in his cloak, still warm from his body.

She didn't recognize her own meek voice. "Thank you, Lochlann. That's kind of you."

"Ah, and what sort of husband would I be if I let you freeze to death? We'll be in Scotland soon."

Katie's stomach churned, either from the ship's motion or his mention of Scotland. While keeping a tight grip on the railing, she stared back toward the invisible Irish shoreline. "You're a sweet man, Lochlann. I'm sorry I've been so difficult. You don't deserve that."

He placed a tentative arm around her shoulders. "I do understand, Katie. You had no interest in this match. I hope you'll give me a chance to change your mind. Will you… D'you think you can give me that chance?" He gazed at her with black eyes, glittering in the rain, his thin blond hair plastered like a helmet on his head.

She returned to staring at the waves. The choppy water couldn't erase her memories of Éamonn. More than that, she could never look at Lochlann and not see someone who bought her for a horse. And yet, if she didn't try to make the best of this life, she'd never be free of the pain. "I can try, Lochlann. That's all I can promise. But my heart—"

"Yes, I can tell where your heart lies." He spoke in a sour tone as he followed her gaze back towards Ballycastle. His voice rose as he scowled at the shore. "Bloody arse. What can he think to do?

We're married. The deal is done. Does he think he can steal you away in a grand gesture?"

She bowed her head, unwilling to say what she really thought. "I don't know what he thinks."

Lochlann grasped her upper arms, his grip tight. "Well, I'll not let him. You're mine, by law and church. I'll treat you well. I'll provide for you and care for you, but I won't let yonder villain take you." Her teeth clacked as he gave her a shake, his voice steely.

That steel gave her a modicum of strength back, her voice rising to match his. "And what about the villain in your own house? What about your own brother, beating me to within an inch of my life, and you not lifting a hand to stop him? You're nothing but a coward, Lochlann. So much for 'I'll treat you well.' You can start by protecting me from *him!*"

Fresh wind shoved the craft sideways. They both clutched at the railing, but Lochlann didn't get a firm grip and slid down the deck. He lost his footing and skittered toward the stern. The ship yawed, and he slammed against the back railing. With a desperate grab, Lochlann latched onto the weathered wood.

Katie clutched her own railing, fear gripping every inch of her body. The ship rocked back the other way, and she let out a sob and shut her eyes tight, praying to God she'd live through this. Salty spray slapped her face, mingling with her fearful tears.

As the wind eased, she let out a shuddering breath. The deck turned horizontal again. Her putative husband still gripped the railing, soaked but alive. For a wonder, relief washed through her. As much as she wished to be out of this marriage, Lochlann was a kind enough man, and his dying would only leave her at Donald's mercy.

Lochlann didn't move, staring as if afraid of her. Frustrated by his cowardice, she turned away from him in disgust. He didn't return to answer her challenge. She couldn't stand to look at the spineless wretch. Kindness might be lovely, but a man needed strength. Even Donald had more manly traits, if he hadn't been such a vicious swine.

She whirled away and they passed the rest of the journey in silence. The captain, bless his very soul, brought the craft into a small harbor just as the storm dwindled. Katie wanted to shout with rapture at their safe arrival. Instead, she shivered as Donald turned around and scowled at her. She stiffened her spine and walked past him to the wooden dock and past three other boats.

As soon as she reached the stony shore, she tripped, her legs not believing they were on stable ground again.

Land. Blessed, firm land. She didn't want to move from where she lay, sprawled out on the damp stone. Moss tickled her cheek, but she didn't care. Oh, sweet, unmoving rock.

Land had never felt so wonderful.

Katie stroked the sweet, solid rock and rejoiced in its firm comfort. Her stomach settled, and the terror which had gripped her soul from the moment they left Ballycastle Harbour faded.

Donald's gruff voice broke into her reverie of the earth. "Get up, lazy girl. Help us hook the wagons." Resentful, she nevertheless rose to help. Katie well knew the penalties for disobedience.

Katie hoped he wouldn't retie her hands this time. She couldn't run back to Ireland. She had no coins to pay for a sea voyage. Besides, if she never entered a boat again, it would be too soon.

They trudged from Campbeltown to Tarbert and planned a route through Fort William to the Isle of Skye. Islands meant more boats. Perhaps a miracle would happen between now and then. Éamonn might catch up with them. Lochlann may decide she wasn't worth all the trouble. Or the earth might open up and swallow Donald.

At least he didn't tie her hands this time.

Katie stared at the wagons before she climbed into the seat. A week on the road would be no hardship for a Traveler. However, she wished the wagons had enough room for beds. She'd been a Traveler all her life, but her parents always kept one wagon to shelter from storms. Tents morphed into wet sacks dripping with water. No matter how oiled the leather, rain seeped through the seams.

On their left stood a tall standing stone in a bare field. Nothing grew near the stone, no trees, no bushes, not even other stones. The monolith leaned at a jaunty angle, about Éamonn's height. Everything reminded her of Éamonn. She gritted her teeth and tore her eyes away from the stone.

A couple of miles outside Campbeltown, they stopped for the night. Dusk fell fast this evening, as the horizon still loomed dark with storm clouds. Crossing the peninsula, farmland stretched on either side, with mountains to the north and low hills disappearing into the mists to the south. Everything seemed subdued, as if waiting.

In the past, Katie had met Scots, Welsh, English, and sometimes traders from farther away, like Portugal or France. Once she even met a Greek with an exotic accent. The Scots she'd met tended to be dour and brave, while the Welsh loved to sing and made beautiful wood carvings. The English, well, most of the English she'd met had been soldiers. Most Travelers avoided them. Soldiers blamed Travelers for anything wrong for a week before and after their visit. Settled Folks liked to blame transients before accusing a local of villainy.

Donald chose a sheltered clearing off the main road and set up the tents. Katie set up hers and made a ring of stones for the fire.

Donald kicked a stone away. "No fire tonight."

"No fire? But I'm chilled through to the bone! And we need to eat!"

He growled and cocked his fist back. "No fire, I said! Your silly little paramour might still follow, and I'll take no chances."

Katie cowered, but he held his blow. Éamonn couldn't have followed them with that storm on their backs. Would he persevere and come across to a strange land for her? She had no way to know. Peering into the sparse trees around the clearing, Katie tried to conjure her lover.

She pictured his face but panicked when she couldn't recall his features. His hair came first, messy and pale blond, cut short since the fire. He always ran his hands through it, making the hair stick up in spikes. He had a long, thin face and a wide smile with big, white teeth. His prominent nose, and the twinkle in his blue-green eyes when he made a joke. The line on his cheek that dimpled just so when he smiled. She relaxed as the details fell into place, the image forming. Closing her eyes to preserve the memory, she smiled. Pain on the back of her head made her stumble.

"Stop dreaming, you stupid thing. Lochlann, she's gone daft. They cheated you. Bringing that horse back home to father would have been far less trouble than this one."

Images of that blasted horse haunting her mind, she grabbed her tent and finished her camp preparations in sullen silence.

Katie always had difficulty keeping quiet, even with her father's heavy hand. She'd often spoken out of turn and seldom cowered. Perhaps she didn't learn quickly. The fact that men could treat her this way made her furious. But society granted fathers and husbands the right to do with their women as they chose. Folk may frown upon beatings, but law permitted them. If the beatings seemed to work, people didn't protest.

Most men found no pleasure in beating their wives. Lochlann must be like that, and while a more compassionate woman might feel grateful for small favors, anger seethed through her blood. Some hit only at extremes of bad behavior, believing it the only way to teach. But those like her father and her new brother-in-law enjoyed dealing pain. They loved the power, a lust feeding on itself. This lust shone in their eyes.

Well, she might be a weak woman, but she had her wits, didn't she? With no one else to help her, she'd fight back in other ways.

Women had fewer weapons than men. She couldn't beat Donald in a physical fight, but she might win by guile. She'd sometimes dreamt of slipping something noxious into her father's stew but never gathered the courage. Alcohol left near him worked fine. He poisoned himself with the drinking and fell into a stupor.

Donald didn't drink much, but she had less sentimentality about him. She could never kill a man, but she might make him ill. Perhaps too ill to beat her.

But Katie had no poison. Several plants would do the job, but she'd have to gather them. And if, by some miracle, she found some, how would she feed anything just to him? They ate together, sharing stew, game, and ale.

Poison was a fool's dream. Perhaps she could beg for help along the trip, though Donald's reaction to her last attempt made her leery. Her new father-in-law might even be sympathetic, but waiting until they reached Skye would be a dangerous gambit. She only remained a maid due to her insistence on meeting their father before consummation.

Chilled, exhausted from the boat trip, and her stomach roiling with cold, dried fish, Katie didn't sleep well. Memories from the ocean dragged her from sleep. Waves tugged at her arms, and sea foam choked her breath. Gasping in a cold sweat, she bolted awake, images of underwater hell swirling in her mind. The nightmares retreated only when she stayed awake, so she stopped trying to sleep.

Her bladder insisted on a visit outside. Katie pulled on her cloak, stepping into the clearing. Twin snores came from the other tent, so she slipped away to take care of her business.

Cold, wet leaves slipped under her feet in the darkness. As Katie turned to head back, she halted. The horses and mule hadn't liked the voyage any better than she had, and they slept fine. They hadn't made a peep when she'd emerged from her tent. Campbeltown had been just down the only road. She might reach the town under the cover of dark.

And then what? Donald and Lochlann would search Campbeltown first. Katie had no place to hide. Even if she found a champion to protect her, he'd return her to her lawfully wedded husband. She had no money for bread and ale, much less a voyage back to Ireland, even if she had the courage for the harrowing journey. Despair flooded her mind, and her knees buckled. She sat on the ground with a *thump*. Her tailbone smarted from the impact, and after a single, racking sob, she yielded to despair.

Wiping her eyes and nose with her cloak edge, she stood again. *You're being ridiculous, Katie. Get hold of yourself.* While she must face the reality she couldn't escape, she still had some power. She'd search for something to add to just Donald's stew and dull his love of brutal blows.

The half-moonlit night offered slim options for foraging. Nettles brushed against her hand, but while they irritated the skin, they were edible. Nettle soup was her favorite treat. Horse-chestnut grew under the oak tree, but the leaves only grew buds.

Katie wished for Deirdre's help. Her sister knew plants well. While Katie remembered a few, most trees and bushes seemed unfamiliar, especially in the dim light.

A pale, yellow-green, leafy root shone in the moonlight. The bud of one flower sat on the end of the last fork. Thorn-apple? Her sister used it in medicines, but Deirdre told her once not to use it herself as the flower could kill if prepared wrong. Besides, the bitter taste would make it difficult to hide in stew.

A thin cluster of purple flowers pushed through their buds on a spike rising from the bushes. Foxglove? Yes, no mistake. *Lus na mban sídhe*, plant of the fairy women. The whole plant, though used as a medicine, could kill.

Would she kill Donald? Katie recoiled from the idea. No, she couldn't kill him, because to do so would damn her soul to hellfire, but she might make him ill.

She gathered the leaves but left the flower. They'd be too identifiable. She broke the leaves into pieces and secreted them in a larger leaf, placing that in her pocket. She'd find a better hiding place tomorrow. If she added a little to Donald's food, she had a weapon. On her way back, she gathered some chives as well.

Nothing stirred in her absence, but a faint light in the sky shone in the east. Katie let out a mighty yawn and soaked dried travel bars into three bowls. In Donald's, she sprinkled a bit of the foxglove as a test. Not too much, but enough to get him used to the flavor. And adding fresh chives to all three bowls should conceal the change.

By the time the men stirred, each bar of hard tack, preserved meat and grain for eating while traveling, had softened to something edible. She stirred the mixture into a thick, cold soup. Katie sipped hers and pulled her cloak tight against the morning chill. The horrible stew tasted like week-old shoe leather but, without fire, she couldn't provide much else.

Lochlann emerged from the tent, rubbing his face to wake up. When Katie handed him his bowl with a false smile, he sat on a log and dug in with gusto.

When Donald stumbled from his tent, he growled at the world before taking his bowl. Trying not to stare at him while he ate, Katie kept her nose in her own bowl, eating tiny spoonfuls. Donald shoveled his meal into his mouth and thrust the empty bowl to her just as Lochlann finished. After sighing with relief, she took their bowls to the stream to wash them.

Lochlann had just pulled down his tent stake when she returned, repacking the bowls. "Thank ye, lass. Do you need help with your tent?"

"No, I'll manage fine. But I thank you, Lochlann."

As they left the clearing, Katie glanced back. They left obvious signs of recent use, but few clues as to whom. Except for the strip of bright blue fabric from her wedding dress, tied in a knot around a branch at the edge of the clearing, out of view of Donald and Lochlann as they harnessed the horses. To Katie's eyes, the strip glowed like a bright lighthouse on the moors, shining through the dreary mists. She prayed Éamonn found the fabric when he passed on the trail. If he still followed.

Éamonn:

Why had Ciaran wasted his money on that blasted priest? Despite clear skies, the water tossed the craft about like a toy. The captain blathered on about crosscurrents, but Éamonn paid him no mind. He had one goal, to get to Scotland.

He'd never been to another country, though his father had visited Scotland several times on his wanderings. Éamonn tried to recall Turlough's tales of Scotland, but his mind turned blank. He wished he had his father's incredible memory. Turlough learned a piece of music and retained the tune for years. That reminded Éamonn about the music pages that had gone missing from his father's bag. Had Turlough ever found them?

The craft didn't move fast enough to suit Éamonn. He stood at the prow, hands gripping the railing as if by will alone he could shove the ship through the waves. He tried to use his mind to push the sails out faster, but nothing changed. He could only influence people's thoughts, not boats. He chuckled to himself at his silly notion.

Éamonn gazed at the horizon with growing impatience. A purple smudge formed in the distance. A new country, the land that held his prize.

His mind raced from Katie's face to Lochlann's smug smile. The marriage ceremony intruded on his memory, no matter how often he banished the images. Her red, unruly hair bound under the veil as she said vows to that man.

Deirdre had turned green with nausea and didn't want to watch the waves, so Ciaran took her below deck. Waves meant wind, and wind meant speed. He glanced at the sails, only half-filled. *Damn the sea god and his fickle ways.*

Would a sea god be angered at such a curse? Éamonn had second thoughts and tossed bread into the water to appease any listening entity. He shouldn't anger any sea god, not when he needed all the luck he could get. Damn it all, he'd become as superstitious as his cousin.

Had the purple smudge gotten closer?

After an eternity, they arrived in port just as the sun kissed the western horizon, blazing the waves with orange. Éamonn shouldered his pack and glanced around the small fishing village. As Ciaran led Deirdre to land, Éamonn turned to them. "I'll go ask if Katie's been through here. Find us a place to stay, will you?"

As much as he wanted to keep moving, traveling in the dark in a strange place would be unwise. He noted two roads out of town, one due north along the west coast and one northeast, crossing to the east coast of the promontory.

Deirdre refused to go with Ciaran, but wore a sullen frown as she followed Éamonn. He asked a couple of dock workers, but none remembered Katie's group. Frustrated, he gazed back out to sea, wondering if maybe he had angered that sea god. In stark silhouette against the dying light, a single stone stood on a hill north of town. A standing stone?

Maybe a visit would help him settle his mind. "Deirdre, let's go find Ciaran. I've got something I need to take care of alone."

"Alone? What in the world are you on about?"

"Just something I need to do, Deirdre. Don't argue, there's a lass."

She pouted but didn't argue further as they searched for Ciaran. When they found him, he'd secured rooms at an inn better than last night's lodging. At least this place had a decent common room and a warm peat fire.

Once they'd all settled and had a bit to eat, Éamonn slapped his hands on his knees and rose. "I'll be back in when I'm done."

He strode along the darkening north road. In the last shred of light, the stone beckoned to him. The half-moon rose as he climbed the hill. Limned in silver, modest farmsteads, and stands of forest dotted gentle slopes. The two roads out of town shone bright. Éamonn searched along these silver ribbons, hopeful to glimpse Katie despite knowing she must be much too far ahead of him.

With a sigh at his folly, he sat with his back to the standing stone. Éamonn closed his eyes and breathed in, the solid stone bolstering his flagging spirits. Imagining a line of energy pulling from the earth and into his bones, he breathed in deep and then expelled slowly as his father taught him to. He leaned forward, tension sliding away from his bones. He repeated this process several times until he felt rested.

When he opened his eyes, Deirdre's face hovered inches from his own. He yelped and jerked back, bashing his head on the stone. Bright light flashed, and he let out a groan of pain.

While rubbing the back of his skull, he scowled at her. "Deirdre, what the devil are you doing here? I said I needed to be alone!"

She stood straight, hands on her hips and eyes flashing with anger. "Yes, and you're just sitting here, snuffling like a pig. You could do that anywhere! What are you *really* doing?"

Éamonn matched her glare. "I'm just getting peace, woman! I needed to think and relax." He struggled to rise, but she sat on his outstretched legs.

He let out a long sigh. "What are you up to, Deirdre?"

"I can relax you." She kneaded the muscles of his thighs. Her eyes glittered in the moonlight, and her hair brushed his arms.

He closed his eyes and prayed for strength. "Deirdre, stop." If he moved, he'd dump her on the ground. But if she kept doing that... Her hands got closer to his groin. They felt warm and pleasant, and his body responded.

Éamonn put his hands on hers. "Deirdre, please." He couldn't articulate what he asked for, but his body cried out for what his mind didn't want.

She leaned forward to kiss him. Her lips pressed against his, incredibly pliable. He didn't remember them being so supple. Her breath smelled sweet, her buttocks warm on his thighs.

He pushed her away. "No! I can't!" She resisted his efforts, and he couldn't get leverage with her pinning his legs.

She shifted to straddle him, kneeling and leaning forward. "Does your head hurt, Éamonn? Here, a kiss will make everything better." Her breasts pressed against his face as she stroked his hair. She kissed the top of his head.

As he closed his eyes, he imagined Katie's lips caressing him. He froze in panic. Despite his reluctance, his desire betrayed him. He embraced her soft curves and held her close. She felt so warm and willing. The memory of Katie's smile stopped him.

Disgusted with himself, he shoved Deirdre to the side. She fell with a muffled curse. "Éamonn! Why did you do that? My hip hurts." She whined and rubbed her hip in seductive invitation and opened her legs.

He tore his eyes from her. "I've got to get back, Deirdre. Come, I'll help you up." He reached his hand out, and she placed hers in his. She didn't rise but tugged him toward the ground. With a sigh, he bent and lifted her by the waist. As she got to her feet, Deirdre snuggled into his arms, pressing her entire body against his.

He fought his desire once again and pushed her firmly away. "You smell like herbs. What have you been concocting?"

154

Her lovely smile shifted to a frown. "What the hell is the matter with you, Éamonn Doherty? You liked me well enough before. Have I turned into an ugly witch in the meantime? Éamonn, I'm *here*. You have no need to chase faery dreams when you have a warm, willing woman already in your arms."

She shifted so easily from hellcat to seductress. He caught movement out of the corner of his eye. Ciaran had climbed the hill and stared at them.

He shoved Deirdre away again. "Deirdre, I've told you before. I'm in love with your sister. Can't you get that through your thick head?"

Ciaran grabbed his shoulder and spun him around. "What do you think you're doing with her? Isn't Katie's heart enough for you?"

Rage bubbled inside Éamonn, disconnected from logic and family duty. He pulled his arm back and punched Ciaran's scowling face.

The look of sheer surprise on his cousin's face cooled some of his anger, but then Ciaran let out a roar and tackled Éamonn. As his back hit the ground, he let out a grunt and scrabbled to get Ciaran's arms off him. Instead, they rolled around on the grass, while Deirdre made distressed noises. Finally, he extracted himself from Ciaran's grip and stumbled to his feet, running his hand through his hair.

Éamonn harbored no guilt now about stomping off and leaving her to her own devices. Ciaran would care for her. As Éamonn picked his steps down the hill, Ciaran's mumbled words of comfort faded, followed by her angry, gushing sobs.

Éamonn thanked all that was holy he'd left the hill before she cried. He'd never been able to resist comforting a crying woman. Women wielded powerful, confusing magic, to be sure. He berated himself for his weakness. As his father had said, Deirdre was no good for him. Let Ciaran comfort her.

He didn't go back to the inn, instead strolling along the docks. When he spied a few workers, he made a few inquiries and eventually found someone who remembered the MacCrimmons' party. He'd helped unload the Traveler wagons. According to his source, they took the northwest road the evening before, so they'd be a full day behind Katie. He'd been so close! How much time had he lost from that cursed storm?

He stared out at the ocean. Silver glittering on the now calm water. Bits of white light reminded him of the dancing faery lights in the standing stones in Ireland. Did the ocean have Fair Folk as well, skipping across the waves? He fancied he heard a giggle in the distance, but likely only heard the water murmuring against the pier. Éamonn stared at the undulating water without seeing it until Ciaran returned with Deirdre, and they all retired to the inn.

As dawn's light peeked over the horizon, the group left. With modest mountains to the north and gentle farmland to the south, the road wound up to the west coast and along the white beaches. Deirdre wanted to stop to pick some plants, but Éamonn crushed the notion. Her precious tea would have to wait. He must make up the time they'd lost from the storm.

They approached Tarbert by sunset, forty miles in one day. Just as the sun kissed the water, four English soldiers came out of the town.

Travelers never got along with soldiers. Soldiers often blamed Travelers for any number of evils, and usually meant trouble.

The first soldier reined his horse in and looked them up and down with a wary eye. "Here, what's this? Where are you off to, then?"

"We're on a journey to visit some kin. They live on the Isle of Skye." An easy enough tale. True enough and nothing to verify, and far enough away they wouldn't be tempted to *offer an escort.*

"Skye, is it? And you're Irish from your accent. You're a fair way from home."

Éamonn shrugged and kept his mouth clamped shut in case something sarcastic emerged. He glanced at Ciaran and Deirdre, but they sat still.

The soldier raised an eyebrow. "Just the three of you, then?"

"Aye, me and my cousins. Grandmother is dying, you see. We're traveling to see her before she passes on." Now he'd established they were on an urgent mission that they shouldn't delay.

The officer clicked his tongue a few times, staring at him. Then he glanced past him at Deirdre and whistled. "Now she's a nice piece if I do say so. Higgins, go and help the lass from her mount, will you? I'd like a proper look at the girl."

Éamonn clenched his jaw to keep from yelling at Ciaran to gallop away. The soldiers' beasts looked far superior to theirs, and they'd be caught. He tensed and peeked at Deirdre, but she stayed astride the horse.

Come on, Deirdre. Please, don't antagonize them. Éamonn didn't know what the soldiers planned, but Deirdre remained under his protection. Ciaran dismounted instead.

The other two soldiers then dismounted. One walked toward Ciaran, only stopping when they stood face to face. "He didn't ask to see a proper look at you, you dirty turf sucker. Move aside so he can see the girl."

After letting out a long breath, Éamonn got off his own horse. He inserted himself between Ciaran and the soldier and spoke with his most charming voice, pulling on the brooch's power, "Surely, you're not interested in a scruffy Irish lass, now, gentlemen."

Éamonn's head ached already from the unpredictable brooch— or the surly fae, upset with his curses. He planted his feet, kept his shoulders back, and pushed harder on his suggestion, despite the growing pain.

After a moment, the other man's lecherous expression slid off his face and he backed off, shaking his head. "Well, she's no queen, that's certain!"

However, the third soldier had dismounted now. "She's pretty enough for me!"

Éamonn pushed at that one. Could he affect several people? He widened his concentration to include both, and a wave of nausea swept over him. "Sure, she's nothing special. You'll find better lasses at the docks."

Still, the soldier came towards Deirdre's horse. She froze, eyeing the man as if he were a bug.

Éamonn pushed harder. "She's not worth the trouble."

The soldiers glanced at each other, confused, but didn't get back on their horses. Even Deirdre glared at him. What was the point if he only delayed action? Éamonn struggled to keep from doubling over and spewing.

Éamonn topped the tallest of the group, but one soldier had Ruari's bulk. Four against two would make for a quick fight, and they'd not be the winners.

With a whisper, Éamonn turned to Ciaran. "Stand your ground, but don't start anything." Deirdre's skirts rustled behind him. He itched to reach for his knife, strapped to his side under his coat. But the slightest movement would be folly. While the fight remained fists only, they stood a chance.

The first soldier strode to Éamonn, chest to chest. He stood a good six inches shorter but made up for any lack in height with attitude. "Stand aside, you filthy Mick."

Éamonn lifted his chin. "I cannot, as I have the charge of my cousin's protection."

"And I command you to stand aside."

Any answer would be the wrong one. "We mean no trouble. We're just peaceful folk traveling to our grandmother's."

He put all his power into the simple words, weaving calm and peace over the soldiers. He imagined calm blue pools of water around them all, beatific and serene. And again, as before, confusion lit the lines of their faces, their tense lines eased, and one actually cracked a smile. Éamonn let out a cautious breath.

Absorbed in his magic, he didn't see what started the conflict. Ciaran and the second soldier grappled, and the two others egged them on. With a huge sigh, Éamonn put all his strength and height behind his fist as he punched the soldier before him.

The man didn't stay down, but a few more blows from Éamonn changed his mind. Scowling, he turned to help Ciaran.

Éamonn and Ciaran had fought in many brawls, while the soldiers would be more used to swords and muskets. He'd just gut-punched the second soldier when Deirdre screamed.

The first soldier, the one who'd stopped them, had jerked her off the horse. She beat him with her hands. He cursed but tugged at her bodice. When it wouldn't rip, he grabbed both wrists. Then he kicked her legs out from under her.

She dropped with a whoosh of breath and shock. He jumped on her, pushing up her skirts. She kicked up, nailing him between the legs. This made him moan, but then he growled, "That's enough of that, you Irish slut!"

Éamonn flung himself at the man, pulling him off and rolling with him, off Deirdre and into the bushes. He punched the man's smarmy face. Once, twice, three times, with a satisfying smack each time. He couldn't stop. When he rose, the man lay unconscious. Blood and dust smeared on the soldier's face, and Éamonn's knuckles were sore and torn. He shook his hands out as he walked away.

As he returned to the horses, Deirdre sobbed in his arms. Ciaran had knocked the third soldier to the ground, though the man groaned. With a nod to his cousin, they helped Deirdre back on her horse.

Tarbert would be the first place the soldiers searched. Instead, they went back the way they had come until they found a path off the road. If they stayed in the woods, they'd be much safer. In the morning, they'd rush through town and continue north.

Deirdre still sobbed softly. When they dismounted, Ciaran tried to comfort her, but she pushed him away and clung to Éamonn. He glanced at Ciaran and got a glowering look. Ciaran went to set up the tents. They didn't dare risk a fire.

He held Deirdre and stroked her hair. "Now, that's over now. He didn't get to you after all. You're grand. Shh, shh. Come on, now, I've got to tend the horses. Here, sit and have a drink, aye?"

Deirdre's breath came in short, pitiful gasps. Her eyes were red and puffy, and her hair tangled. "A drink?"

He pulled a leaf from her hair and flicked it away, lifting her chin. Giving her tasks to do might help. "You'll be fine, now, won't you? Go, steep your tea. I've a fierce headache from all that."

She spoke more softly than he ever remembered. "I can't without a-a fire."

Éamonn stroked her hair as he would a child. "Just let the tea steep in the water. It won't be tasty, but it'll give us strength. I have cheese and bread in my saddlebag. Fetch those for our supper."

At least the task would get her out of his hair as he prepared the horses for the night. Removing the saddles and brushing the beasts calmed his racing heart. When he returned to the campsite, Deirdre was stretching her arms in the air, but when she noticed him, she stopped stretching and sat on one of the logs she'd placed as if they had a fire. Her shoulders drooped as Ciaran sat on the other log wearing a sullen expression.

As Éamonn drank the bitter, cold potion she handed him, his mind blanked on what to say to her. The evening's events kept them all subdued.

In his tent, he lay awake, his stomach still roiling from using his magic and thinking what he might have done differently. He couldn't find a better solution, try as he might. The soldiers had been intent on mischief. Complying would have gotten Deirdre assaulted. Resisting would have had the same result. They'd taken the only option unless his power had been stronger. Could he have used his powers in a different way? His head hurt too much to think any more. What use is fairy magic if it didn't work when he needed it most?

He'd just about drifted off into sleep when the tent flap rustled. Ciaran left. He must need to relieve himself. Then Deirdre's shadow entered the tent.

Her body nestled pliant next to him. She wriggled until she got under his blanket.

Éamonn bolted up. "Deirdre, go back to your own tent." He tried to push the power into his voice, but he didn't feel the flow of the magic.

Deirdre shook her head. Though she seemed a bare shadow, her silken hair brushed his arm. "I'm frightened, Éamonn. I can't sleep in my tent. Every time I try, I wake up, afraid the awful soldier would…would…" She buried her face in the crook of his shoulder and began to weep again.

By Christ and all his saints. How should he handle this? "Shh. Shh. Deirdre, you can't stay here. Ciaran will be back soon."

"No, he won't. He's gone to scout around."

Bloody hell.

She wrapped her leg around his, pulling one apart from the other. Her bare flesh pressed against his. *Bare flesh? Where are her skirts?* Had she come in naked? His body responded, and her skin burned against his own.

Her soft whisper tickled his ear. "Please, protect me, Éamonn."

Deirdre caressed his chest, inching her hand under his shirt and played with his nipple. Éamonn moaned and pushed her hand away. In answer, she pushed his shirt up and took the closer one in her mouth. Her hand moved from his nipple, along the trail of hair in the center of his chest.

He squirmed but couldn't make his body leave.

Her hand inched further down, teasing as it went, dancing circles on his belly with her fingers. When her delicate fingers touched intimate flesh, he could no longer control his own need. Éamonn moaned, hating himself, but giving in to the vixen and her demands.

Vague impressions of sweat-soaked skin and beautifully painful scratches overwhelmed him until Katie's face flitted through his mind. Before he gave in completely, he sat up abruptly, dislodging her capable hands.

Deirdre cried a protest. "Éamonn, what's wrong? Don't you want me?"

He grabbed his coat and rushed outside. He curled up next to a log, leaving Deirdre to the tent. Though his desire burned for a long time, she didn't emerge, and he fell into a fitful slumber.

The next morning, Éamonn still smelled her scent on his skin. He covered his face with his hands. What in the name of all the saints in Heaven had he done last night? Even if he hadn't coupled with Deirdre, guilt washed across him. Unfair to Deirdre, and a betrayal of Katie.

Chapter Eleven

Lochlann:

They woke to a sodden world, with the wagon wheels stuck in muddy ruts. The rain hadn't been heavy but constant. Still, Donald refused to wait.

Lochlann worried about Katie. She'd lost all her spark, that intense fire she'd had when he first met her. She huddled in forlorn despair, like a rag doll on the bench. After several heated arguments, he convinced Donald not to bind her again. Katie rewarded that trust with good behavior. She spoke with a civil tongue rather than insult, another small victory. Lochlann smiled at the notion that his new wife could be sweet when she put her mind to it.

When Donald struck Katie, Lochlann seethed with frustration at his own cowardice. Lochlann ached to stop him, but Donald always triumphed over him in sport or sword practice. Donald always beat everyone. He beat older cousins as they grew up, even their own father once, with no quarter given for the weak. Their father always rewarded such prowess.

Though their father, Calum MacCrimmon, had a position as piper to the MacLeod, he was no wandering minstrel. The Great Highland bagpipe, or *an phìob mhòr*, counted as a war instrument, with pipers honored members of the army. Pipers led the troops to battle, sustained them through the fight with martial music, and then marched them home from a victory. It took courage to stand on a chaotic battlefield with no sword or musket, though no Scot would dare to strike a piper in battle.

Lochlann could coax a tune from the massive, unwieldy instrument, but Donald had a true talent. He composed his own music, a skill that fascinated and baffled his younger brother. Thus, Donald became the golden son, and Lochlann would ever live in his shadow.

What would their father make of his new bride? He appreciated such fire and temper in mares. Would he approve of feistiness in women? His mother had been feisty, once, when he was a boy.

Their mother had died of a fever when he turned twelve. He remembered her in vague flashes, with hair like spun gold in the sunlight, and a sweet, sad smile. Since his mother's death, his father grew farther from him in both deed and sympathy. They argued often, including the last one about Lochlann settling down with a wife and a family and abandoning his mother's Traveling habits.

With a swallow of memory at that last fight, Lochlann clenched his teeth. Donald and Lochlann left the previous August to travel with several mares, a gelding, and the magnificent stallion named Smúid. Named for the silver mist which hugged the mountains on Skye, the horse had been the prize of the year. He'd fetch a fantastic price amongst the Irish, so they took a boat to the island and wintered with several Irish Traveler groups.

They'd decided that the spring horse fair would be the best place to find a buyer for such a unique creature. And find a buyer they had, but they'd accepted a bride rather than hard coin. That would take care of two purposes; finding Lochlann a bride so the family line would continue, and prove to their father that they were good at trade.

Donald's coughing interrupted his reveries. His brother looked poorly today. He retched that morning, but Lochlann had offered no sympathy to his brother. Donald would call him weak for caring. Lochlann would never wish ill on his brother, but he nursed a secret smile about heavenly justice.

Wiping spittle from his mouth, Donald turned to Lochlann. "We'll stop at Kintraw tonight."

Lochlann turned to Katie, but she slept on the cart seat. She'd wilted in the rain like a dying flower, slumped back against the wagon, her hood over her head. Kintraw might mean a dry bed, at least. Even Donald must concede a night at an inn would be better than this muck if he felt ill.

Kintraw had very little, not much more than a stopping point for travelers. A coaching inn, a trading post, and a few farms. The village stood at the head of Loch Craignish, a cluster for the fishing trade, on one of the few main roads north.

He shook his bride's shoulder. "Katie? Katie, are you awake? We're stopping." She moaned but peered up with red, swollen eyes. She must have been crying again. His heart ached to comfort her, but she'd rebuffed all his earlier attempts. He couldn't blame her. If he wanted her to accept him, he'd need to tread slowly and gain her trust, like taming a wild animal. Lochlann had no interest in a slave-wife. He dreamt of a willing mate, someone who'd work beside him. Someone to bear his children and make a home.

When Donald had been married, he'd treated his wife as a servant. He beat her, ordered her about, and in the end, she'd died from his blows. Lochlann had to help him bury her, and while his brother had been silent, only Lochlann wept for the poor lass. Now it was his turn to be wed, and his chance to carry on the family line. His last chance to prove himself to their father.

Lochlann sighed with his idealistic dreams. How many marriages truly had that? His parents' marriage hadn't held much love. He remembered one farming couple in their village who had real affection for each other. Lochlann had craved that closeness and would work hard to get that.

As Katie dismounted from the wagon, Lochlann offered his hand and led his bride into the warm inn. A peat fire glowed in the hearth, and the savory smell of hearty lamb stew wafted by. Odors of stale beer and unwashed men warred with the stew.

Lochlann sought a landlady as Donald secured the wagons. "Have you two rooms for the night?"

A short, round woman with dark skin and hair turned from the kitchen door. "Aye. Two shillings. Three." She amended her total as Donald came in.

Still holding Katie's hand, he shook his head. "No, I'm only asking for the two rooms."

"You'll be wanting three suppers, no?"

"No," Donald answered. "I'm not hungry."

The woman stared at him a moment and shrugged. "Fine, then. Two shillings. Top t'stairs, to the right and left." She held out a soot-stained hand for her coins.

Once they stowed their bags, Lochlann brought Katie down for stew and ale. Donald remained in their room. Donald rarely missed a chance to eat. He'd best give his brother some time to feel better. "Katie? Katie, I think I must sleep with you tonight."

Her head snapped up, and her eyes flitted around the room like a caged creature.

Lochlann held up his hands. "No, not for that. I'll set a pallet on the floor. But Donald's not feeling well. I don't relish him retching on me in the middle of the night, at least."

The panic faded from her eyes, and she let out a snort. Laughter? Derision? Understanding? Whichever, her icy manner melted a tad.

She gave him a small smile. "I suppose so. I don't have a worry about my reputation, after all. You are my…my husband." The word choked out and her smile disappeared.

He let out a breath of relief at the minor victory. "Thank you. I swear, I will never force myself on you."

Katie arched one eyebrow. "Never? Be careful what you promise, Lochlann."

"Never. Until you invite me to your bed, I'll not force you."

She narrowed her gaze. "And if I never invite you?"

Lochlann gave a shrug. "Well, then, I'll be unrequited forever. But I like to think I'll not be such a horrible husband, for all that." He took her icy hand in his.

She stared at their hands on the table and blinked several times. Something glinted in her eyes, perhaps the beginnings of tears. "And I promised I'd try, Lochlann. I can promise nothing more, but I will try. You've shown me kindness, and I treasure that."

"That's good enough for me, my wife." He whispered the last word.

The landlady brought two bowls of stew and a half loaf of crusty bread. Not fresh, but not moldy, at least. Lochlann broke the loaf in half. Katie tore chunks from hers and dropped them into the stew. The peat shifted in the hearth, and a carriage passed on the street outside.

Katie stirred her stew, staring into her bowl. "If Éamonn comes for me—"

Throwing his hands up, Lochlann rolled his eyes. "Éamonn again. Éamonn, Éamonn, Éamonn. What the hell am I supposed to do, Katie? You're my wife, not his. I don't know what you two shared before, but your father assured me you were still a maid. You are, aren't you? You didn't give yourself to Éamonn?"

She gave a nervous nod, still staring at her supper.

"Then why can't you forget him? Love and pain fade with time, Katie. Learn that now, and it will help you in the future." His own mother's death had taken a long time to fade, and pain from her loss still stabbed him often. He swallowed and lowered his voice, "If he comes for you, you must send him away. If he won't go, well, you've seen Donald fight. Do you want your precious Éamonn killed?"

Katie's eyes flashing with a hint of their former spark. "Éamonn can fight, too!"

"Aye, and well I know that! Remember our fight at the fair? I came too near to you while dancing and stepped on your toes. I didn't like how close you sat to Ciaran and Éamonn. I wanted to interrupt. We'd already started talking to your da."

Her head snapped up, and her eyes in full fire now. "So, the conspiracy is that old, is it? You're no husband, Lochlann. You're nothing but conniving, sneaky, meddling brigand! In actual fact, you're a slave master! You bought me. Well, you may have bought my body, but you'll never get my heart. I'll keep that locked away well and good from you forever!" She upended the bowl of lukewarm stew over his head and ran up the stairs, slamming the door to their room.

Lochlann sighed and wiped the mess from his face. Women possessed an incredible talent for twisting an innocent comment into an unforgivable insult.

He finished his own meal and checked on the horses in the stable. The mares weren't high bred like Smúid, but sound enough to pull the wagons. They seemed content with the night's shelter. Lochlann brushed them down, taking comfort in the task and calming his own frayed nerves.

Still loathe to intrude on Katie, he checked on the wagons. Donald had locked and parked them behind the stable. With nothing left to do, he wandered up to the room. After easing the door open, he tiptoed in. The scents of old tallow and musty bedding hung in the air.

Katie had disappeared, along with her bag. The bed didn't look slept in.

Bloody hell. That foolish woman. What had she done?

He rushed into the street and looked in both directions. She'd have a decent head start, but he must try. She'll have headed back south. Lochlann ran to the stable and harnessed and saddled a mare. "Sorry, Ceanndána. You'll get rest soon, I promise. But first, we must find my wife."

He burst from the stable and galloped down the road, south towards Tarbert. He rushed down the road, shrouded in darkness. Whenever he spied something bright glinting to the side, he reined in to examine the glint in case Katie had gone to ground.

Twenty minutes later, he glimpsed her shadowy form in the darkness. Her pale skirts winked out from under her darker woolen cloak. She turned and ran into the bushes. He leapt from the horse,

166

ran to her, and clutched at her arm, but she slipped from his grasp, burrowing deeper into the undergrowth.

"Katie! You know this won't work. Come out, Katie. I'm sorry I upset you, but you must come back."

She answered with muffled cursing and rustling in the bracken. *Blast the girl.*

He pursued the sounds, cursing at the sharp branches, which caught at his face and cloak. When he found her, tangled in a hawthorn bush, trying to pull her skirts free, he grabbed her arm.

She spun on him, acid in her tone. "Feck off, Lochlann MacCrimmon! I'll not stay here and be your wife. I need to live my own life without you and your monster of a brother!"

With patient hands, he extracted her garments from the clutches of the thorn bush. Branch by branch, he freed her. Once she climbed from the bracken, they glared at each other. When he reached for her hand, she pulled away, her voice softer, "I just can't. I can't go with you."

Lochlann grasped her shoulders, staring into her eyes. "And where else should you go? Your man is still back in Ireland, and he'll have long since given up on you. You've no friends or family here but me and mine. Come, lass. Am I such a monster you'd rather starve on the moors than be my wife?"

She dropped her gaze, several emotions flickering across her face. He tucked her hand in the crook of his elbow, as English gentry did. He led her back to the road, holding back branches so they wouldn't snap into her face. Katie kept her head bowed until they reached the road.

In the moonlight, tears glinted on her cheeks. Lochlann pulled her into an embrace as she sobbed on his shoulder. He didn't understand such a volatile woman, but he treasured the ability to comfort her. After helping her mount behind him, they returned to town.

Lochlann hoped Donald was still sleeping in his room. He couldn't imagine what his brother might do if he found Katie had escaped again. The prayer became a chant in time with the hoofbeats. *Let Donald be sleeping. Let Donald be sleeping.* The refrain kept his mind occupied the entire trip back.

He led his wife up the stairs toward the room they shared, gazing into the gloom. Donald glowered at the top of the stairs.

"I just took Katie out to—"

Donald's voice sounded grim and loud in the sleepy inn. "Be quiet, Lochlann."

"We only—"

"I said be quiet. Your excuses are useless."

"That's not an excuse, that's—"

Donald's fist hit him square in the face. A blinding shot of pain exploded in his head. He tumbled down the stairs.

Katie:

The sky shone bright blue the last two days as they approached Fort William. The fair weather should have lightened her mood. She still ached all over from Donald's beating in Kintraw. Her face healed slowly, bruises blooming purple with yellow edges wherever Donald had found his target. Lochlann's broken nose swelled, both his eyes puffed deep purple, and he'd sprained his wrist, but nothing worse.

Katie didn't dare dose Donald with more foxglove. The last dose had made him ill for two days. But being sick the same way twice would lead to suspicion, so she must wait. At least she had a notion of how much she needed. Not that she felt brave enough to try again, but she must.

She'd been so certain of her escape. Striding down the road in the starlight had been incredible, as if she hadn't a care in the world. Éamonn might be right around the next bend. They'd run into each other's arms, and he'd carry her away to safety. England, France, any place Donald and Lochlann wouldn't follow.

But Lochlann came, and the very trees helped him recapture her.

At least her new husband had tried to shield her from his brother, though he'd received blows for his efforts. He still tried in little ways. Lochlann stood between them when they set up camp and answered for her when asked a question. He'd grown into a sort of armor she needn't take off. Katie's anger softened to gratitude at his gallantry.

Perhaps no true freedom in the world existed without bonds. To remain safe, I accept certain levels of imprisonment. Marriage, willing or not, can be both prison and protection. Even on a grander scale. If it wasn't for my father, I'd be free to do what I like in a Traveler tribe, within certain rules. I can't kill anyone or the tribe brings justice. The tribe protects me from outsiders but protects their own, too. The only true difference is if I shoulder the protective armor of my own free will or have it foisted upon me.

Such grand philosophy on a warm day. Katie stretched her back, despite her aching muscles. As she took a sip from the waterskin, she relished the cool liquid trickling down her throat. While Donald insisted on tying her hands again, Lochlann made sure she had food and drink handy before they set out. Donald tied her feet to the wagon, and the stout rope around her waist chafed as the seat jounced on the rough track.

Despite what faced her at the end of this journey, she wished this trip over. She didn't want to fulfill her promise to Lochlann, but everything hurt. She'd traveled across the countryside all her life but never trussed like a pig, ready for the slaughter.

Swallowing to keep her gorge from rising, she took another sip. Katie snuck a glance at Lochlann just as he winced with a jolt of the wagon. His nose must be painful, swollen to almost twice its original size. She glanced at his bruised eye and wondered if they'd have their own household. What if they had to live with Donald for the rest of her life?

As they crossed the mouth of Loch Leven on an old, rickety ferry, the wind whipped up. The horses whickered, and the mule brayed loudly enough to be heard for miles. Nonetheless, they got the beasts and the wagons across. Storm clouds glowered on the horizon.

Katie pulled her cloak up. During the warm day, she'd let the garment fall behind her. She twisted around to grab the cloak with her tied hands, draping it over her shoulders. Lochlann reached out to help her. She rewarded him with a grateful smile.

Despite her cloak, the chill shot through as a storm rushed toward them. Biting wind darted under, making the fabric edge flap and flutter. The sky dimmed, and she peered up nervously.

Lochlann followed her gaze and shouted over the roar of the wind. "Donald! Donald, we need to find a place to shelter."

"It's barely midafternoon. We've miles to go before we rest for the night. I want to get to Fort William before dark."

"The sky is dark already. Can't we find a place to brave out the storm?"

His voice sounded so childish and pleading, Katie wanted to give him some of her own backbone. How could a man, a true man, sound so weak? His sweetness seemed like a liability. Lochlann showed no mettle. With a sigh, she tugged the edges of the cloak back over her arms, now covered in goose flesh.

The first big drops splattered in the dirt before they found a rocky overhang along the hillside edge. Landscapes shifted from farms and woods into rocky peaks of gray mountains. The storm slapped against stubborn rock, running down in rivulets. A cascade of water outside the cave.

While the wagons and horses stood outside, Lochlann, Donald, and Katie retrieved their saddlebags and huddled below the overhang before the full fury hit. Earth's blood flowed down the wall through a million vessels. Water sluiced in front of them like icicles, almost solid. Very little splashed into the cave. Katie stared out at the violent storm, shivering.

Donald deigned to untie her, correctly assuming she wouldn't risk running out. After rubbing her wrists, she pulled out bread they'd bought in the last town, passing a loaf around. A hunk of cheese and dried fish completed their simple meal.

Katie wanted something hot, but they had no wood nor space for a fire. She shivered again, pulling her cloak tighter.

Lochlann came behind her. "Your teeth are clattering, lass. Let me help?" Confused, she nodded. He opened his own cloak and wrapped one arm around her, pulling her into his cocoon of warmth. "Better?"

"Yes, thank you." Her shivers eased. Lochlann might be spineless, but he did have a kind heart. He'd promised to take care of her. If Éamonn never came, perhaps she might even learn to like him.

Would Éamonn travel to Scotland for her? For all she knew, he'd turned tail at Ballycastle and returned to his family. She couldn't blame him. They'd had such little time together, their chances so slight. She'd never even kissed him. Regret seemed too pale a word. *What should have been* kept her awake at night, imagining more intimate acts she'd never share with him.

Éamonn:

Éamonn hadn't found a trace of Katie or the MacCrimmons since they'd left Campbeltown, but he pushed doggedly on toward Skye. Chartering a boat would have been faster but too expensive, and difficult to find one who would take the horses as well. With just horses, they'd move faster than the two wagons. They'd catch up.

Ever since that night with Deirdre, Éamonn had been miserable. He'd betrayed Katie with his desire for her sister. Deirdre, in contrast, bounced along beside him with bubbly enthusiasm. She touched him constantly, but Éamonn moved away each time. He wouldn't give her a chance to breach his defenses again.

Ciaran retreated into a sullen pout and seldom spoke. He stewed like a skulking thief, staring at Éamonn or Deirdre. Parry and riposte, touch and rebuff.

Once they stopped for the night, Deirdre went to forage for food while Éamonn and Ciaran set up camp. "Ciaran, help me with the tents."

After a few moments of silent work, Ciaran turned to him. "Do you want to tell me what you're doing with my girl?"

Éamonn snorted. "Nothing I wanted."

"It doesn't look like that to me. Why are we even on this trip if you're just going to bed every girl you see?"

Éamonn let out a bark of rueful laughter. "I don't bed every girl I see! Ciaran, don't be a fool."

Ciaran scowled, his arms crossed. "Why can't you just leave her alone?"

Praying to the saints above for fortitude, Eamonn took his cousin by the shoulders.. "Ciaran, I'm not the one sneaking into tents at night. That's your sweet, innocent Deirdre's doing, so it is. If you want her so bad, why don't you court the lass properly? Gather her some flowers. Kill her a wee rabbit."

Thunder crossed his cousin's face. As soon as Ciaran threw the punch, Éamonn ducked, but instead of returning the blow, he just glared. "Ciaran, can you get this through your thick head? I love Katie, not Deirdre. You obviously want Deirdre, so do something to win her. Show her! I'll not fight you in the slightest. In fact, I'll help all I can. Here, I'll get the damnable flowers myself while you finish the fire. Deal?"

His cousin scowled at him and made a noise in the back of his throat. Rustling bushes nearby heralded Deirdre's return, and both men fell to their task in silence.

Éamonn:

After bringing the horses onto a ferry across the mouth of Loch Etive, Éamonn concentrated on the view in the early morning mists. He tried to think of anything other than Deirdre's gaze on the back of his head. Her eyes burned into him.

Fog clung to the glass-still waters, diffusing the orange morning glow of the sun into an otherworldly haze. The land of the Fae might have this strange light, coming from nowhere and everywhere all at once, bathing everything in the odd luminosity of time.

Ripples spread from the ferry as the last passenger boarded the large, flat raft. The ferryman collected his tolls while his assistant pushed from the dock with large poles, shoving against the shore. A mighty creak and nervous stamping from the horses, and they drifted across.

This gentle drift was a far cry from their tumultuous voyage from Ireland. A long rope lay across the channel, allowing the ferryman to pull the craft across. A major inlet to a long, narrow loch and a beautiful one, but still one more barrier to finding Katie.

They should reach Fort William by the day's end. Fort William had a garrison with English soldiers in a massive block fortress on the shore of Loch Eil.

Fort William had been a site of carnage. A month ago, Scottish rebels in the Jacobite cause laid siege at the fort. War never treated soldiers kindly. Officers sent men to their death without a second thought. Even today, Katie could be forcibly married and beaten with few batting an eye at the injustice. A chill ran through him as he resolved to find her quickly.

Civilians would always be the true losers in any war, caught in the middle of the conflict, unable to flee the violence. Armies trampled crops and burned farms for spite. They stole livestock with no compensation to the poor crofting family. Houses burned, women raped, and children killed. War never meant good news for the common folk. Even a war on foreign soil meant young men pressed into the army, sometimes as young as twelve or thirteen years, and never seen alive again.

Thinking of Cromwell's slaughter in Ireland, Éamonn remembered tales of salted lands and burnt towns. What craven idiocy, to destroy the soil for generations to come. Would the English be any better or worse in Scotland? Éamonn wanted no part of finding out.

A jolt jerked him from his thoughts. They'd reached the north side of the inlet, and the ferryman unloaded his craft. Éamonn hurried to help, thankful he once again had a physical task. Forced idleness allowed his thoughts to wander to painful places.

Remounting, they resumed the northward journey. Perhaps they'd catch up with Katie this day. What if she had resigned herself to marriage with the Scotsman? What if she didn't want Éamonn now? They'd had so little time together. The dark clouds gathering on the horizon matched his mood.

As they passed a clearing, Éamonn spied a thin shred of light blue cloth. With a shout, he jumped off his horse and snatched the strip from the branch. The same color as Katie's wedding dress and tied deliberately. He picked the knot open and held it in his hand, his heart soaring with resolve and relief. Katie had been here, and she wanted him to find her.

Clutching the scrap of fabric to his chest, he closed his eyes and prayed that he'd find her in time.

Katie:
Gentle farmlands and green pastures of the lowlands gave way to massive mountains on narrow passes through the highlands. At Fort William, Lochlann pointed out Ben Nevis. Even in late May, snow capped the summit. By evening, they'd reached Bun Loyne, threading through mountains in constant switchbacks.

Lochlann stared at the mountain peaks before them. "The land is much like this, even on Skye. We've the mysterious Black Cuillin mountains and the majestic Red Cuillins. Dunvegan itself is flat

173

enough, but you can still see the peaks from our home on a clear day." His eyes unfocused, as if gazing on the invisible mountains even now.

What would it be like to have a settled home? Her parents' wagon had been home all her life, but they had never wintered in the same place twice. If she must live her life with this man, perhaps she could find something good in her plight. "What's your home like, Lochlann?"

"We own a farmhouse on the northwest coast of Skye, within sight of Dunvegan castle, near Borreraig village. My father lives at the castle."

"And do you Travel every summer?"

Donald let out a snort as Lochlann grimaced. "Aye, in the past, before Mam died. We left last August." He glanced at his hands clasped in his lap. "Da and I got into an argument."

Would Éamonn prefer to settle some place? Or would he rather remain a Traveler? She didn't know what she'd like and had never considered settled life. Settled Folk had always been *other*. Not Travelers. Her people had often ignored Settled Folk and sometimes dealt with them out of necessity, but always handled them with caution and a mind for one's purse and safety. In the meantime, soldiers tried to arrest anyone for being a Traveler, like they committed a crime to be free of place. At least if she became Settled Folk, she might move into a world where she'd be less harassed by others.

As if she'd summoned them with her thought, ten soldiers marched toward them along the road. Donald pulled the wagons to one side, watching as they passed. They halted, and the leader stared at Katie. Her hair danced in the wind, stray locks escaping from her tie. She kept her tied hands hidden in her lap, under the edge of her cloak. While she wanted to escape Donald, falling in with English soldiers would be jumping out of the frying pan and into the fire. She'd heard enough stories about them.

The leader of the soldiers nodded to Donald and Lochlann and moved on. Each man glanced at her as he passed. Most gazed upon her with indifference or even kindness. The last one, a dark-haired man with one eye, glared at her with naked hatred. His reaction chilled her to the core, and her skin prickled.

Lochlann sighed with relief as they passed around the bend. "For a moment, I thought they'd be trouble."

Donald gave a curt nod. "Ten are too many to fight. I'm glad they moved on."

As they pulled into Bun Loyne, Katie looked around. The settlement seemed more of a crossroads than anything else, and they might have slept in the wagons but for a wicked wind whipping through the mountain pass. The alehouse had no rooms, only places on the floor near the measly fire. But they ate bread, drank ale, and curled up next to the meager warmth while wind shook the small inn.

Katie kept changing positions, to find a way her body wouldn't ache on the hard floor. She had bruises in so many places. A solid kick from Donald's boot had connected with her right hip. Sleeping on that side hurt. A few blows on her left shoulder ruled out that side, as well. Her back ached from the hard wagon bench. She never could sleep on her stomach.

The sun hadn't yet risen when Lochlann shook her shoulder. "Get up! Quickly now, we're off."

Katie rubbed the sleep from her eyes. "Now? But the sun isn't even up."

"Donald said we must move now. Get up!"

She sat up, straightening her back and moaning at the pain in her muscles. Katie accepted Lochlann's offered hand to help her to her feet. Outside, Donald already had the wagons hooked and the horses harnessed.

As Lochlann packed their tent, Katie went to relieve herself, ripping another strip from her dress. So far, she'd left a half-dozen strips along their trail, and she prayed Éamonn saw them.

When she returned to the wagons, Donald scowled down the dark road. "Hurry up, lazy gits! Now!"

She scrambled to her bench, relieved he hadn't tied her hands. Either he'd forgotten or didn't care.

Why must they flee in the pre-dawn hours? Had he gotten word of Éamonn coming close? At that notion, hope soared in her heart as she craned her neck but only found darkness in the pale starlight. With a *click* of his tongue, Donald got both mares moving. The mule let out a bellow of protest before following.

While they traveled on the dark track, water glittered to the left, with more black mountains in the dim dawn. She nodded off during the harrowing journey. She'd only gotten a few hours' sleep and dozed in and out as the wagons bounced along the road.

Katie could have sworn she heard other hoofbeats, but she must have imagined them. Many sounds lived in the deep of the night. The noises kept to themselves, only intruding upon waking folk with padded feet and the forgotten dream of terrors past. Sometimes, however, they'd reach out and yank someone from sleep's embrace, an abrupt transition into the waking world.

Such a brusque change left a person gasping, with a vague awareness of slithering in the darkness. Something lurked in the gloom, something she couldn't see or hear, questing for her, to hook and drag her into the void. She shuddered, and Lochlann's arm tightened around her shoulders.

Fearsome beasts lived in the wilds. Most stories she'd heard came from the wilds of America, but did Scotland have beasts of their own? She recalled tales of water horses. They looked like beautiful horses, but lured hapless folk into riding them, then drowning the foolish rider.

Irish legend had the Dullahan, a headless rider who rode a black horse and carried his severed head under his arm. Rumored to be a fearsome creature, the Dullahan used a human spine as a horsewhip. If the Dullahan stopped riding, someone died.

Katie prayed the Dullahan didn't follow them in the gloom.

Donald slowed as the first glow of dawn appeared on the horizon. A deep cobalt sky revealed harsh mountains dotted with the faint glitter of mountain ponds. The river cut a deep cleft between them, the road winding in and out of rocky outcroppings. The breeze picked up into a strong wind, skipping through the valley with a howl.

As the sky lightened, Donald turned the group onto a side trail, a crofter's path to an abandoned cottage. The sides looked solid, but thatched roofing drooped at an alarming angle. Still, any shelter meant sleep, and Katie's eyelids drooped.

The cottage hid behind a rocky outcropping, sheltered from the wind. The rocks also hid it from the road.

Donald drove the wagons behind the cottage. He and Lochlann unharnessed the horses to let them graze as Katie tied another strip for Éamonn to find.

The inside of the cottage stank of wet wool and sheep dung. *Beasts must winter here from the worst of the Scottish weather.* Katie swept out the worst of the droppings, but the pong remained. Cleaning the space properly would take a lot of effort, and she felt ready to collapse.

Every muscle aching from fatigue, she shoved her blanket into one corner. She ignored her growling stomach, and collapsed into her blanket. Her bruises made her regret the graceless fall. As she shifted to find a less uncomfortable position, Lochlann and Donald muttered in the opposite corner.

Éamonn's name intruded on her exhaustion, and she pricked her ears to hear. Had he followed her this far? Donald said *Dunvegan*, the name of the castle on Skye. Was that Lochlann sobbing? A grown man, crying? Sure, and he'd never be the strongest of men, but what would make a man cry?

Chapter Twelve

Lochlann:

The next days blurred for Lochlann. A messenger had come to the inn with word of their father's illness. They traveled as quickly as possible, but they'd never be in time. He'd taken a turn for the worse and demanded their presence. But with a day for the messenger to find them, and another two days for the wagons to make their ponderous way to Skye, would their father live long enough to meet his new daughter-in-law? Lochlann prayed he would.

He may not love his father, but they must meet. He'd promised Katie, and their bedding depended on it. Lochlann knew her own father had been much like Donald, brutish and cruel. While his father wasn't much better, Lochlann had hoped he'd welcome her into their family, to give her something she'd never had. He hadn't expected to care so much about her, but he'd failed his father too many times. He mustn't fail her, too.

The last hours of the journey seemed the longest. Wend through the mountains, along the shoreline, ferry across to the island, and then repeat. By the time they arrived at Portree, they were fair knackered. The three of them slept in turns on the wagon bench, but the horses needed to rest, too. Just a few more hours and they'd be home.

Will my father approve of Katie? He'd had many discussions with Donald before they struck the deal, and more after. Their father might decide Katie didn't measure up and disinherit them all in a fit of pique and frustration. And what if the Irishman followed them even now? Would he barge in and make a mockery of the whole marriage? The possibility made his cheeks turn hot with shame.

Lochlann had half a mind to let the girl run back into the arms of the man she obviously lusted after, and to Hell with her. But then he'd have to explain to his father how he'd traded their prize stallion for a woman, and then lost the woman. Worse than lost. He'd have let her go, a move no man with sense would make. No, he must earn his father's respect, even if he'd never get his love.

And if, by some miracle, he ever earned Katie's love, would that be enough to erase the need for his father's love?

Turrets from Dunvegan Castle peeked over the trees, the fortress of the MacLeod, where their father resided. A square, solid structure, with pale golden stonework. A curtain wall built several centuries before surrounded the keep, and the castle commanded a fantastic vantage point on a rocky outcrop next to Loch Dunvegan.

The MacLeod wasn't in residence, as no banner flew from the pole. When they reached the massive gate, they found it barred against all invaders. Two guards stood at their post. "No visitors permitted. Laird's orders."

Lochlann sat up in the wagon seat, querulous from his fatigue. "My father is in the castle. We must get in to see him. He's very ill!" To his shame, his voice cracked.

A sandy-haired guard about Donald's age, scratched his beard. "What do you reckon, James?"

James shrugged. "Aye, well, let them go on in. But the wagons must stay here. We'll watch them."

Lochlann didn't much care for the sound of that. Donald's scowl showed he didn't care for the notion, either.

James leered at Katie, too wearied to even glance up. "Leave the lass to watch over the wagons if you're a-feared we'll do aught to them."

With a snort at that idea, Donald glared at Katie, then Lochlann, and then back to the guards. "I'll go in. Then my brother will, when I return. We can't leave his wife on her own in a strange place, now, can we?"

James pouted, but he had already made the offer, and he couldn't renege on that now. "Fine, if it's what you must do. Go on then. Be quick about your business."

"Donald, what if Da is—" Lochlann couldn't finish.

"If he's gone, then he's gone. We'll bury him and go to the house. If he's still alive, I'll come right back for you."

Lochlann had to be satisfied with that. He stared at his brother's broad back as it disappeared down the long, winding garden path to the castle's main door.

The guards ignored them, other than an occasional glance at Katie. They muttered between themselves, but Lochlann lost interest in them. His wife slumped on the bench.

He gave her an awkward hug. "We'll have time to rest soon. If Da is still alive, he'll tell the guards to let us in. If not, well, if not, we'll go to the house. Our place is only a few miles farther. Perhaps an hours' journey with the wagons."

Katie's voice sounded faint, as if coming from another world. "Another hour?"

"Only if Da has passed. If he's alive, we can rest here."

"Rest. Rest sounds good." She set her head on his shoulder. Her weight felt warm and liquid, as if all her bones had turned to water. He reveled in her trust. She'd offered him no affection since the wedding. He understood her sense of loyalty, but she'd dropped her defenses to trust him this much.

An eternity passed before Donald returned, but when he did, his normal belligerence melted into defeat, as if someone had sucked his soul away. Donald didn't need to say a word for Lochlann to understand they'd arrived too late. Lochlann's need to see his father once again, to pay his respects, warred with his need to get away from the pain and disappointment.

Lochlann choked in his grief until they'd gotten away from the guards. The tears burned behind his eyes, and his throat closed. Katie roused when he moved his arm to take the reins, but then she mumbled and curled to sleep against him.

Both he and Donald let tears fall once they turned the corner. They didn't speak but shared their grief in silence. Now he'd never keep his promise to his father, earn his respect, or earn his love.

An hour later, exhausted and wrung out from grief, they pulled into their farmhouse.

A proper, two-story house, with a slate roof and a chimney on each end loomed into sight. Gray stone, white mortar, and real glass windows, with several outbuildings standing behind. The white front faced the water, a rocky shore on the south edge of Loch Dunvegan. An old ring fort jutted up on a promontory into the loch. This was no crofter's cottage, filled with black smoke and thatch. This was a fine dwelling for a rich family.

The sun shone high now, which seemed wrong to Lochlann. Such a nice day for such a horrible event. He unharnessed the horses without a word, leaving Katie where she lay for the moment. She slept, and he didn't wish to interrupt her rest until he must.

Lochlann glanced back toward the castle, a blur of yellow in the distant trees. "Donald?"

His brother took the first pack from the mule's back.

"Donald? When did he pass?"

His brother grunted as he lifted the last pack. "Just after the messenger left. We'd never have made it no matter how hard we pushed."

That he held no control over their timing didn't lessen his guilt in the slightest. "Did he leave any word?"

Donald unharnessed the mule and sent the beast off to the pasture with a slap on his flank. "A letter, aye. We'll read it once we're settled."

Once they unburdened, brushed, and stabled the horses and mule, they stowed the wagons. Lochlann hefted Katie from the seat and, with some effort, carried her up the wide stairway to what had been his mother's bedroom. His wife didn't stir once. The large room smelled musty and could do with a thorough cleaning. Katie should be able to take that role, once she was rested.

He removed her boots and tucked her into the linen sheets and wool blanket. Though he took off the overdress, he left her in her shift, despite the fabric clinging to her body with sweat and grime. Lochlann gazed at her sleeping face, so lovely. Anger faded from her brow and cheeks and sharp lines softened. He almost wished she'd never wake.

With a sigh, he drew the curtains closed and left her to sleep. She'd probably sleep out the day at least. He craved the same, but not yet.

Lochlann brought bannocks and cheese and left the tray with a pot of ale next to her bedside should she wake hungry. Then he went to find Donald.

His brother had started a fire in the hearth and stared at the glowing peat.

Lochlann brought two pots of ale and handed one over. "Donald? Where's the letter?"

Donald gestured to the table without turning his head. The red wax seal still held the gray outer envelope together. Lochlann glanced back to his brother, whose face flickered in the hearth light. "Do you want to open it?"

Donald remained frozen.

Lochlann walked to the table and picked up the oiled linen envelope. The red wax seal bore the mark of their father's signet ring, a bull's head, a variation on the MacLeod crest. They didn't have their own family crest but sheltered under the protection of the larger clan. The MacCrimmon clan commanded respect, despite its small size. They were the pipers of the land. Great clan chiefs sent their own pipers to MacCrimmon lands to master their craft.

Lochlann stared at the paper, reluctant to open these final words from his father. Donald came behind him and snatched the missive out of his hands.

"Hoi!"

"Just open the bloody thing, will you? It's not like he can argue anymore." Donald broke the seal and read the heavy, dark script. Lochlann read over his brother's shoulder.

Always a precise penman, their father had taken great care in his letters. Someone else must have penned this messy scrawl at his behest. Had he had so little strength at the end, then?

To my Sons:

If you should receive this after my death, please know that my Last Thoughts were of you. I would have wished for you to be here, but alas, it is not to be.

To my eldest son, Donald: My greatest wish is that you should follow in my footsteps and take up the pipes for the MacLeod in our time-honored family tradition. I realize you have a great facilitie others in the family may not have for this work, and our duty is to continue this fealty to the laird. I know you will make me proude from the Heavens.

To my youngest son, Lochlann: I wish you to become Tacksman for the MacLeod, should that Please him. You have a gift for the horses, and such is not to be taken lightly.

I urge both of you to take a wife and continue the Honorable Familie Name.

The growing Unrest in the country can only mean Warre, ultimately, and I should hope you shall Triumph over the Rebels in the End.

I shall watch over you from whichever Realm I now reside in.
Your Father,
Calum MacCrimmon
This 20th Day of May, in the Year of Our Lord, 1745.

Donald had been right. Lochlann could no longer argue with their father. And they couldn't betray his dying wishes, or the clan would shun them, and their names blackened forever. They'd need to become permanent Travelers, never to return to their own home.

Never return to the house they'd grown up in, where all memories of their mother lived.

Lochlann sat like a lump on the old stool by the hearth. His arms and legs grew leaden, as if submerged in water. Anguish dragged him into the despondent earth.

"Well, I guess he got the last word in, after all." Donald's words sounded a mile away. "Is the girl upstairs?"

Lochlann nodded, numb. He'd never speak to his father again. Never get his approval. Never hear the warmth of pride in his father's voice. Never give Katie a warm welcome from his whole family, like she deserved. The peat glowed in a random pattern of hell and brimstone. He considered falling face first into that bit of torture. Would he die fast? Or linger in pain and pity?

"I suppose she's passed out from exhaustion. I think I'm for the same. Get yourself up to your room, Lochlann. You've a wedding night tomorrow."

Donald's words made little sense. He'd married in Ireland. "A wedding night?"

"Yes, ye bampot! You can finally swive the shrew. She made you wait until she met Da, no? Well, that won't happen now. She's no more excuses left."

Katie:
Katie woke in complete confusion. When she fell asleep, she'd been tied to an uncomfortable wagon seat, jouncing along a rutted road in the rain. Now, she lay on a well-stuffed feather bed, with fine blankets of soft wool trapping the warmth. Sunlight streamed through lace curtains in the windows of a fine house. Try as she might, she couldn't recall how she got here.

Vague memories of an interminable ride on the wagons flashed in her mind. A hard, wooden bench banging bruises on her aching backside. Her wrists chaffed and scabbed from days in ropes. A flash of a massive castle, guards, and more traveling. Then she woke.

As she blinked her eyes open, focusing on the carved wooden bedpost, Katie yawned. Then she glanced around, noting the enormous room and heavy furniture. She didn't realize Lochlann's farmhouse would be so grand. Katie swung her feet to the floor, though her abused and neglected muscles screamed when she moved. Ever so slowly, she rolled each joint. Her ankles, legs, waist, shoulders and, one by one, she massaged the kinks out. Standing, she bent at the waist, stretching her arms and legs until she felt almost human, despite the lingering bruises and rope burns.

The cool wooden floor creaked as she walked. She only wore her shift. Had Lochlann undressed her? After noticing the food and drink on the press, a wave of gratitude swept over her. The water remained chilly but soothed her parched throat, and she nibbled on the food, but her stomach roiled, so she couldn't eat much.

Katie glanced out the window. She wasn't on the ground floor. One story up? Two? Water sparkled in the sunlight. An inlet from the ocean or a loch? Waves crashing on a beach argued for the former and the tang of salt on the air cinched the theory. The water looked deep gray-green, dappled with sunlight peeking through scudding clouds. Below her, a carpet of green fields studded with rocky outcrops. Several farmhouses and smaller crofts sprinkled the land. White dots of sheep grazed across the green grass.

The air tasted sweet and cool. Katie took several more breaths and closed her eyes before abandoning her vantage.

At a basin and ewer, she scrubbed at the grime and dust of travel. She would have preferred washing in a stream to slough off layers of dirt, but the ewer must suffice. She must be presentable to her husband's father.

The idea arrested her movements. The father. They stopped at a castle. Had she heard someone saying the father had died?

Katie's mind raced, trying to find some other way to put off the inevitable, but she could think of nothing. Her respite had ended, and her shoulders drooped in defeat. She could no longer postpone their consummation.

Holding back a sob, Katie wished with a deep ache in her bones Éamonn had come, but he hadn't. Either he'd lost his way, or he'd abandoned her. She must make the best of her life.

Éamonn hadn't found her in time, and she must go through with the wedding night. Lochlann treated her kindly, but he wasn't her love. He wasn't the one she wanted to caress, to feel his hands on her skin. *No, I can't think of Éamonn. I need to forget him. He failed me. Lochlann is all I have left.*

Her trunk hulked in one corner of the spacious room. She must have truly passed out. How long had she slept? After pulling out several pieces of clothing, she peeled off her soiled shift and donned a clean one, with stays, petticoats, and a dark wool skirt. She had a dark gray jacket somewhere. Somber colors for a death in the family. Of her father-in-law. Unaccountable tears bubbled at the loss of family she'd never met. Perhaps a father who might have welcomed her. A father who didn't beat her. A father like Turlough was to Éamonn.

She pulled on the jacket, with pale blue embroidery on the cuffs but subdued enough for mourning. Then she attacked her hair.

Matted and tangled, the curly mess resisted her efforts. She had done little to tame her hair in the last harrowing days of the journey. Katie paid for that neglect now. She sat in front of the cracked, faded mirror. Her comb pulled, tore, and jerked until she had an acceptable head of hair. She would have given her left arm for a way to wash the mess. Lacking that, she pulled her curls into a tight bun. A sour old maid glowered at her in the wizened mirror. She pulled a few curls around her face to soften her appearance.

With some restored confidence, Katie descended the stairs.

The steps opened into a great room. Katie glimpsed a kitchen beyond that and a study on the other side. Though furnished and decorated with taste, the room seemed musty and empty. Dust everywhere spoke of neglect, even abandonment. A fire crackled in the hearth, though, and she warmed her hands. The large house felt chilly in more than temperature. Then her stomach growled, evidently settled enough to complain.

The next room she found was the kitchen, with their saddlebags piled on a huge wooden table. A few had been partially unpacked. A half-loaf of wheaten bread lay on the counter. She pounced on it and tore off bits to quiet her growling stomach.

The study contained about twenty books on one wall. A few bound with leather and a couple with wood. Several scrolls lay in one cubbyhole, and a massive oak desk dominated the center of the room.

Searching for more information about her new family, Katie returned upstairs. Three bedrooms lay past the one she woke in, each one leading into the next in a circle. She crept down the hallway, praying she wouldn't encounter either brother. One dusty bedroom held large, sturdy furniture. This must have been their father's room. The other two had few furnishings and looked even dustier. She guessed they must be Lochlann's and Donald's rooms when they lived at home.

Katie glanced outside, catching a hint of movement near an outbuilding. Steadying her gaze, she recognized Donald currying a horse. Beside the stable sat a henhouse with no hens, a pigpen with no pigs, and several sheds.

She'd held a faint hope that Éamonn would be riding up the road to rescue her, but the landscape looked achingly empty, and his failure strengthened her resolve to make the best of her new life.

This must have been a decent farm but left to decay and rot. The windows had genuine glass, but some panes had broken. Someone tacked leather over them to keep out gusts of icy Scottish wind. Stones in the outbuildings crumbled, and the pigpen lay open.

Did the neglect date to Lochlann's mother's death? She peered around the room she'd slept in to get more clues of her dead mother-in-law.

Lacy curtains, a lace doily on the vanity, and dresses in the wardrobe spoke of someone who liked to dress pretty. She must have been tall. Katie would trip over the hems of the dresses. The personal items looked precisely arranged, so Katie didn't touch them. A horsehair brush and matching mirror lay on the vanity, silver inlaid with pearls. Bottles of long-dissipated scent and dusty pieces of sponge lay in one drawer.

What had she looked like? Did she have Lochlann's fair, flyaway hair? Or darker and thick like Donald's? She might have had their dark eyes. Had she been a kind woman?

A sound behind her made her whirl. Donald hulked in the doorway.

Hay stuck out of his sleeve and he smelled of horses. "So, you've decided to wake and face the day, have you? And what a day this is! A fine day for a honeymoon, no?"

Her brother-in-law stepped in and shut the door behind him. Katie's skin crawled as the latch clicked. He advanced a few steps, heavy boots clomping on the wooden floor. She retreated until her back hit the tall press.

"Hm. I'd forgotten how pretty you look when you try. You looked like a muddy rag doll these last few days. This is much better." He traced his finger along her clenched jawline.

She shuddered and clenched her fists. "And whose fault is that, then? You're the one who forced me into such a state!" She spat at him.

He pulled back, eyes wide. "Forced you? I haven't forced you into anything. You just be careful, aye? Or I'll show you just how forceful I can be!" He raised his hand, but she cowered and closed her eyes. Her subservience must have satisfied him as a blow never came.

Katie risked a peek, and he'd lowered his hand but leered at her. "Yes, definitely looking more presentable now. And acting like a good wife." He pulled a curl dangling from her bun and curled it around his finger. She didn't dare move and kept her breathing even despite her hammering heart.

"Too bad Lochlann's got first call on that. He won't appreciate it as much as I would." His finger caressed to her shoulder, and then inched his hand down her jacket. He stopped above her breast, then traced the curve to where her nipple hid under the thick wool. She didn't dare breathe now.

Donald paused at the top button of her jacket. This was her good jacket, with seven round, bone buttons carved into flowers. He flipped the top one open, exposing her stays and shift.

Katie swallowed and glanced at the door. "Where…where's Lochlann?"

Donald gave her a feral grin that chilled her to the bone. "Your groom's gone to the village for supplies. He won't be back for several hours, at least."

He stood between her and the door. She couldn't get past him. She must try another tack. Struck by the memory of his reaction to her foxglove, she coughed and bent over to the side, hacking up as much disgusting phlegm as she could muster. Her throat still felt rough from the trip, and she pretended she had a sore throat.

Donald backed up, his nose wrinkling. "What did you do, swallow a cat?"

She shook her head and went towards the ale bottle, still half-full. Katie sipped and coughed some more. She must stay as far away from the bed as possible.

"If you'll excuse me, I must get some fresh air. The dust is too much." She rushed past him to the door and scrambled to open it. The latch stuck, and her heart pounded in her chest until the door finally opened.

His harsh laughter followed her as she flew down the stairs and outside. She panted, back against the solid stone wall of the stable. That wall felt like a fortress between her and Donald MacCrimmon.

She saw Donald's face in the upstairs window, a cruel smile lingering on his lips. She scooted around the corner where he couldn't see her. She didn't want to be seen, not by that man.

Katie crept into the malting shed, hoping for shelter from prying eyes. The aromatic ghost of whiskey mash lingered in the wooden walls. She felt safer hidden from sight.

Her heart pounded in her chest. She had to get away. But where could she run to? These brothers were the only two people she knew in this country. They'd taken her to the back of beyond, and she had no place to escape to, no one to help her. A sob escaped as she covered her face with her hands.

Would Donald have taken his own brother's wife? That sort took what they wanted and cared little for who was hurt in the process. Donald had struck his own brother for speaking up for her. She trembled at the memory, despite the rising heat of the day, and rubbed her arms, trying to brush off the touch of him while avoiding the yellowing bruises he'd given her.

It must be late morning now, but when had they arrived? Time remained a muzzy haze in her mind. She must have slept through the night. Katie felt better rested than only a few hours would account for.

The horses whickered in the stables, and the mule answered. Someone must be out there. Hoping to catch sight of the visitor, she peered out from the doorway of the malting shed.

Lochlann came up the path, and her heart leapt. He was the only one who could keep her safe now. She'd have to explain what happened, so he'd stay by her side, and make clear to Donald that he'd not have his way with her.

Katie walked out from her hiding spot, and Lochlann's eyes lit up. "Ah, what a lovely sight you are, my wife. You soothe my soul."

"And is your soul troubled, Lochlann?" She wanted to take back the words as soon as she spoke. Of course, a man whose father had just died would be troubled.

With a single nod, he took her hand. He brought it up to his lips for a chaste kiss. "You look wonderful, Katie. Did you sleep well? Are you hungry? Can I get you anything?"

With a weak smile, she waved off his solicitous offers. "No, no, I'm fine. I woke up a little while ago and the house seemed empty. Then Donald came in—"

His joyful expression soured. "Did Donald pester you? Well, I'm back now. You're safe." Such a simple statement, a declaration of protection from all evil in the world, including his own brother. Despite herself, her heart began to thaw.

Éamonn had promised to keep her safe, but he never came. He'd broken his promise.

She'd never experienced such a trust before, certainly not from her father. Lochlann wasn't strong, but she wanted to believe him when he promised to keep her safe. She *had* to believe. There were no other options left for her.

In a meek voice, she answered, "Thank you…husband." Katie squeezed his hand once, and they walked into the house.

He unpacked his bag filled with provisions from the village. Eggs, a side of ham, candles, fresh milk, apples, a large cheese, and loaves of bread. "That should stock the larder for now. Donald's upstairs?"

She glanced at the stairs, and he headed in that direction as Katie put items away in the cupboard. She found a souterrain built into the earth near the outside wall, ideal for keeping food cool. Since she ate when she woke, she didn't yet suffer hunger pangs, but Lochlann might be ready for a meal.

After slicing ham and cheese, she arranged them with bread on a platter. She glanced at the food, wishing she could find a way to poison Donald. This time, she'd use more. But she couldn't hide the foxglove in simple bread and cheese. She'd have to bide her time until her chance came again.

Would Lochlann live here only in winter and travel the rest of the year? Would she go with him, or stay here alone? Katie shuddered at the notion of spending the entire summer alone in such a strange place.

At least the house looked wealthy, charming, and solid, if in need of some thorough cleaning. But she would crave human companionship.

Maybe she could join him on trades. Unless Donald took charge of those expeditions. Ice crawled up her spine. She might be better off rattling about in this big house alone.

Voices drifted downstairs, too muffled to understand the words. The volume rose. Did they argue about her? About their father? She wanted to creep to the stairwell to hear better, but the rumble of thunder distracted her.

Katie never cared for thunderstorms. To keep her mind off the storm, she cleaned. She found clean rags in the kitchen cabinet. First, she wiped crumbs off the table and dust from the shelves. As she moved into the main room, heavy footsteps came down the stairs. Donald.

After halting at the bottom of the stairs, he strode toward her, his boots echoing on the wooden floor. She shrank into the kitchen and ran behind the enormous woodblock table.

He rolled his eyes and let out a sigh of exasperation. "Come on, girl. Time to do your duty at long last." He grabbed her arm, but she scooted away.

Raindrops pattered on the roof. "It isn't nighttime yet!"

"What in the name of the *Cailleach* does that matter? You're awake, you're rested, you've no father to meet, and our mother's long dead. You've run out of time and excuses, girl. Get yourself upstairs, or I'll take you. And I might not take you straight to him! Father wanted the family name to continue, and you were bought for that purpose alone. If my weakling brother can't get sons on you, so help me, I will! Father can't forbid me another wife any longer!"

Lochlann ran down the stairs and yanked her from Donald's grasp. "I'll thank you to keep your hands off my wife, brother."

Donald's lip curled into a sneer. "She's not your wife, brother, not yet. You need to swive her first. Or are you even capable?"

Lochlann let go of Katie, and she scurried to the wall as he swung at Donald's head. The larger man ducked and landed a blow in Lochlann's stomach. Her heart fell as her husband doubled over with a *whoosh*. She let out a sob of dismay.

Just as Donald took this moment to leer at her, Lochlann threw a punch up across his brother's jaw, and the larger man dropped. Lochlann stared down, his eyes wide at what he'd done. Then he shook his head and marched back to Katie. She let him lead her up the stairs as she spared a glance at the still-unconscious Donald.

Lochlann brought her to the lacy bedroom where she'd slept. Hesitating at the doorway, she glanced at him and swallowed. In that room lay a new chapter to her life. She couldn't go back after this. With a long, hopeless look down the stairs, as if expecting Éamonn to burst through at the last minute, she stepped across the threshold.

She stared at the bed she'd slept in the night before. His mother's room. Was that odd? Perhaps this would be the best room, a place where a woman might be more comfortable. The other room, their father's room, must become Donald's now. The very notion of losing her maidenhead in Donald's bed made her shiver. Steeling her nerve, she shut the door behind her.

Lochlann shuffled to the bed and sat, his eyes shifted and sweat beaded on his brow. Could this be his first time, too? The idea hit her like an epiphany. He acted so meek, and she daren't ask. They didn't have that level of friendship, much less intimacy. Donald's implied threat spurred her to walk to the bed and sit next to her husband.

Katie's throat locked, and she swallowed again, trying to keep her fear at bay. Lochlann jumped to his feet, walked to the press, and returned with the ale pot. He'd refreshed the food, too. Apples, cheese, and honeycomb. Too bad she'd lost the foxglove leaves over the last few days of their journey, or she'd have a chance to dose Donald again.

She gave him a weak smile and drank the whole thing, letting out a tiny belch. Though the sky darkened with storm clouds, she wished night had fallen. "It seems wicked to do this in daylight."

With a deep breath, she placed the ale on the floor and took both his hands. His dark eyes looked hopeful and frightened at the same time. "Not so wicked for a husband and his wife."

She swallowed an angry retort and let out a long sigh. She'd need to get his protection, one way or another. If she continued to act the shrew, he'd eventually give up on her, and leave her to Donald's tender mercies. "Lochlann, I promised that I'll do my best to be a good wife. You're a kind man, and I'd much rather be matched to you than, well, other men who are less kind. Oh, dear, I'm making a mess of this." Flushed, she dropped her gaze.

He squeezed her hands. "I know that well, Katie. And I promise to take care of you and protect you."

"Protect me? Including from Donald?"

He stared at the door. "I've not done that well enough, but I will. I've never been good with words. Believe it or not, Donald is the poet in the family."

Katie let out a snort. "Donald? Poetry? You must be jesting."

"No, I'm not! He composes music for the bagpipes, too. You should listen to him play. His tunes are haunting and lovely."

The ice had cracked, but not yet broken. "I don't know if I can fit that image with the Donald I've come to know and hate these past weeks." Katie gave a half-smile, and they both dropped their gazes in the resulting silence.

Their brief connection formed and dropped. The tension grew so thick she might die from suffocation. She must say something. "Well, we should get started, shouldn't we?"

"Yes, well, yes." He stood and pulled her to her feet. They stood too close for a couple moments before he unbuttoned her jacket. She smelled the ale on his breath.

He started at the top, with the same button Donald had flipped open so casually earlier. Trembling, she waited as Lochlann fumbled two more of the strange buttons.

Exasperated at his clumsiness, she undid the rest herself. After shrugging off the jacket, she turned for him to untie her stays. With no one to help her tie them on, they hadn't been pulled tight, which made things easier for him.

He unlaced the eyelets one by one, but she turned back around before he finished half. "You don't have to do each one, Lochlann. Just loosen them, and I can slip out of the stays."

"Oh. I didn't realize."

He must still be inexperienced with women, which almost made her feel sympathy for him. He'd dressed in breeks and a wool jacket which came past his hips, both dark green, with a cream-colored shirt. Katie pulled his jacket off one shoulder, and then the other. He blushed more than she did.

"Lochlann—"

"Katie?"

She clenched her jaw, forcing herself to ask the question. "Is this, I mean, have you done this before?"

He blinked, owlish. "Undress? Of course, I have!"

"No, I mean this." She gestured at the bed, and then herself. Would he force her to say the word?

"Oh. That. Well, not precisely."

Katie placed her hands on her hips. "Not precisely? What in Brid's name does that mean?"

He bowed his head, staring at his feet. "Well, I've kissed, of course, and, well, some other things. But no, I've not lain with a woman. Not like you mean."

Curious about what the *other things* might be, she narrowed her eyes. Even a shy man might hire a bawdy woman. Or did

Donald hire one for him? Lochlann must be at least twenty years old. Had he never spent his need before now? Deirdre once told her men's needs came so strong they often couldn't control them.

Katie wanted to laugh at the idea of soft, timid Lochlann with a pox-ridden old bawd, but she clamped down on the image. Instead, she untied the laces at his wrists and helped him pull his shirt over his head.

His chest looked smooth, with only a few dark blond hairs around his nipples. They contracted against the cold, and gooseflesh prickled his arms. The storm cooled the air in the house. Her own skin prickled, too.

She tried to untie his breeks, but he did that himself. He loosened his belt, stepped out of his breeks, and stood in the center of the room, naked.

Lochlann had a thick torso, in contrast to slim arms and legs. He wasn't ill-favored, but odd-shaped. Not that she'd seen men naked. Clothes hid many things. Blond, fuzzy hair grew on his legs and between them, framing his manhood. Blushing, she turned away and pulled her shift off. Her hair escaped from the bun, crackling as the fabric brushed against it.

She stood with her shoulders back as he studied her, fighting the urge to clutch a blanket close. Her husband took a step closer, and she took one back, only to bark her calves on the bed.

He caressed her cheek. Closing her eyes, Katie enjoyed the soft feather touch. Lochlann's hand moved to her shoulder, and then her arm. His other hand touched her waist, which made her flinch.

Her husband wrapped his arms around her, kissing her and hugging her body close. Bare skin against bare skin grew warm in the chilly room. She enjoyed the kiss more than she'd expected. He opened his mouth and teased her tongue. He tasted like ale and bread.

Moving his hand to her buttocks, he squeezed. Then he eased her onto the bed. Her heartbeat sped up as they crawled under the blankets. "Can we take this slow?"

"Of course, Katie. However you like."

Exploring with his hands, he touched her everywhere. Her breasts seemed like separate creatures, no longer attached to her body. They reacted to his caress, hot and cold shivers coursing through when he took one into his mouth. She let out a moan.

Moving down, his hands cupped her hips again, and she steeled against another fit of tickling. Parting her thighs, he stroked her leg until he came to her cleft. With tentative strokes, he explored her creases.

Older girls had told her disgusting details about a wife's duty. Even Deirdre spoke about things. Katie's parents wrestled under cover of night and bedclothes. And, of course, animals rutted in the spring. But the act between a husband and wife seemed such a mystery.

Lochlann stopped touching and climbed on top of her. Katie couldn't breathe and she grew dizzy. This was it, the point of no return. The old tales spoke of pain. She closed her eyes and clenched her muscles.

"Katie? Are you hurt?"

When she opened her eyes, Lochlann's worried face hovered an inch away. "No, no, I'm just nervous. I'm sorry if I don't know what to do."

Lochlann moved his hands between her legs and pushed her thighs wide. She felt like a wanton. She wanted to pull away, but his weight pinned her in place. He fumbled and shoved his manhood against her, a strange pressure. He pushed rhythmically, but he just chaffed against her leg. Then he pulled back, frowned, and pushed harder. This time, he pierced her. The pain shot up, and she cried out.

"Shh, shh, they say it only hurts a little."

Katie didn't believe him. He plunged harder, in and out. She tried to wriggle away from the pain, but his hands held her shoulders in place. Lochlann shoved his manhood inside her faster. Pain plunged deeper, and she struggled to get away. Katie sobbed, beating at him with her hands, but he closed his eyes and ignored her, stabbing her womanhood again and again. White hot pain filled her as she cried out. Thunder crashed in time with her weeping.

With a powerful, painful thrust, he stopped and shuddered, pulsing inside. His eyes rolled back into his head as he fell on her chest, twitching and moaning, a heavy weight crushing the air from her lungs. He lay as if dead.

Katie gasped out, "Lochlann, I can't breathe!"

With a groan, he pulled himself out of her body and lay next to her. Katie felt slimy, disgusting, and every part of her hurt. She wanted to curl up into a ball and never move again.

Turning to lie on her side, Lochlann curled around her back.

A clash of emotions ran through her. Horror, pain, and betrayal battled with duty and resignation. Katie shoved them all away and let out a long, shuddering breath. *Done is done.* If this is what she must endure to be a good wife, she must learn to do so. Maybe her duty wouldn't hurt so much next time. The storm eased to a drizzle as thunder grumbled in the far distance.

Lochlann put his arm around her and squeezed. "I've heard tell next time we will be better. It won't hurt so much."

The wetness between her legs grew uncomfortable. She needed to clean herself, and at least put her shift back on. She felt dirty and used, soiled goods. Even if Éamonn did finally come rescue her, she'd be lost to him.

Squirming to escape Lochlann's heavy arm, she slid off the bed and walked to the wash basin. She picked up her shift from the floor and pulled the garment over her head. Katie put her hands on her hips and glared at her now-snoring husband. A stain of red from her maidenhead bloomed bright on the linen sheets.

Katie didn't know what her new role would be, or what her new life would be like. However, she must establish her marriage's pecking order. If she wanted to retain her soul, she'd need to take command. She shook her new husband awake. "Come on, Lochlann, no sleeping now! Get up! I need to wash those linens."

An hour later, she placed a hand to her aching back, arching to stretch her muscles. The sun peeked out from the retreating storm clouds as she pulled linens out from soapy water. The washboard got a good workout today.

While she scrubbed the linens and her traveling clothes, as well as the men's clothing, Donald and Lochlann spoke in urgent tones in the main room. Pausing, she strained to hear the words drifting out the open window.

"This is our duty, Lochlann. He expected it of us, and so does the MacLeod."

"I'm a horrible soldier. You know that better than anyone."

"What does that matter? We're MacCrimmons, pipers to the MacLeod. He's at Inverness and has called for Da. With Da dead, his duty falls to us to answer the call. There can be no other way."

Lochlann mumbled his reply.

They must leave again? Would she stay here if they went to war? She didn't want to follow an army. Soldiers led a dangerous life, and she'd heard grisly stories. Tales of good wives taken by the opposing army, forced into prostitution or raped. Maybe even left to die.

Shuddering despite the sun's warmth, she bent to her task. Using the chore to rid her mind of frightening imaginings, she sang. One of the old working songs would do. Rhythmic and mindless, the song helped her pass the time and the task.

Céad beannacht uaim, hù il oro
Go dtí an strath tá a fhios agam, o hi ibh o
Agus go dtí an fána beag, hù il oro
Le birches deas, o.

She sang the second verse in English.

A hundred greetings from me
To the strath I know
And to the little slope
With pretty birches

She jumped when Donald barked at her. "What in nine holy hells is that noise? Finish up, girl, and pack things when they're done. We're off again in the morning."

Her heart racing, she kept her face calm with prim assurance while she hung another petticoat. "But Lochlann just filled the larder! And the clothes won't be dry by then." The day had almost gone, and a long day at that, so near to summer solstice. Still, she refused to return to the road in dank, damp clothing.

"I didn't tell Lochlann we were leaving, and I don't care about the clothes. Leave them out all night if you must, but we leave soon after first light. We must join in the King's army."

Donald turned to her, thunder in his eyes. "And you, if you so much as think about trying to escape back to Ireland or your little paramour, I will hunt you down and beat you both so hard, you'll be nothing but a lump of blood and bones. Do you hear me?" He stomped back into the house.

Katie swallowed down her fear. Even if Éamonn came for her, it was much too late. She'd have to turn him away. Pushing back her tears, she dragged herself back into the house to cook them all supper before bed. She wanted to rest more from their mad journey to Skye and had no wish to be on the road again. If Donald fell ill, he might delay the trip a few days. Katie wished she still had those foxglove leaves.

Part IV
Chapter Fourteen

Katie:

The next week was full of more mind-numbing travel, but at least they'd finally arrived at the soldier's camp. Lochlann and Donald went to check in with the bursar, leaving Katie in a group of camp women.

A large, older woman took Katie under her wing immediately. "Now, child, have ye ever camped with an army before? No? Well, ye'll learn well enough."

Mrs. McKensey showed the younger girl her duties, where to hang washing, which soldiers were handsy when in their cups. Having someone other than Lochlann and Donald to talk to felt wonderful.

Lochlann would march with the general troops, while Donald had gone off with the elite pipers. Less exposure to Donald's temper made Katie sigh with respite. The routine of cleaning, washing, cooking, and mending quickly took over her day, while sleeping in a tent with Lochlann took up her night. They spent a week like this, almost making it a routine.

Katie tried to put off marital relations with him. "The camp's too crowded. I don't want all these strangers to hear us." She blushed and lowered her eyes.

He stroked her arm in supplication. "This is a soldier's camp, with plenty of sounds to mask us. We can stay quiet."

Katie hadn't wanted to do anything on the trip from Skye, either, but with Donald glowering and leering at her in turns, she hadn't been comfortable sleeping outside Lochlann's tent. And sleeping beside her own husband, expecting restraint, seemed cruel. She had a duty as a wife.

"Lying with you in a soldier's camp makes me feel like a dirty animal who ruts constantly."

"There's nothing dirty about marital duties, my wife. I showed you already they can be better than the first time, did I not?"

As they learned from each other, subsequent encounters over the last week had been gentler and slower. She'd learned to enjoy the sensations. His questing hand now caressed her breast with a feather touch. The soft caress was a maddening mix of tickle and pleasure.

Éamonn:
They were a bedraggled mess as they pulled into Borreraig. Éamonn patted the dust and mud from his ripped clothing. Ciaran looked like a herd of cows had run over him, and Deirdre slumped like a rag doll, little more than a miserable lump on her horse.

Éamonn eyed the fancy farmhouse with two stories, all gray stone and white mortar. Real windows, too. The house was an empty shell when they arrived, but the kitchen door hadn't been latched. He crept inside, searching for clues of Katie. Someone had been here today, as the peat in the hearth still smoked.

They must have left that morning. Éamonn slammed his hand against the wall. "Damn it all to hell!"

Deirdre lifted her head when he spoke. She sat in a chair in the main room, a shapeless pile of filthy clothing.

Ciaran paced, a scowl on his face. "We shouldn't be in here. It's bad luck."

Éamonn sat in another chair. "This has to be the house. I saw another of those scraps of cloth outside. Clever girl to leave those."

Strong bitterness colored Deirdre's tone. "Oh, yes, so clever. Clever enough to be taken to a strange country by a husband she never wanted."

He'd had enough of her wild mood swings between simpering lust and cruel cynicism. "She had no say in that! In fact, if you'd passed on my message, we might have escaped before the wedding."

Though Éamonn wished he could rid himself of the girl, he couldn't abandon her here. And his cousin had descended into a dour, moping sot. He answered questions with single words if he answered at all, ever since they arrived in Scotland. He seldom spoke except to comment on dread at a bad omen. Black crows, cats, magpies landing to the left, every imagined threat to their destiny.

Éamonn wished he'd come alone.

The occupants of the house had left in a hurry. Someone had tried to restock the kitchen, and then packed food for traveling. He found fresh milk in the springhouse. Upstairs, drawers gaped open with men's clothing tossed on the floor. Papers scattered across the study desk. Éamonn leafed through the pages, searching for a clue to where the MacCrimmons had taken his Katie. He stopped cold when he recognized something.

A sheet of harp music. While he had no musical talent himself, he'd helped his father copy out music many times. This looked like harp music, and what's more, like his father's handwriting.

Had he found the missing O'Carolan tunes? Éamonn scratched his head, trying to think of why the MacCrimmons would steal them. Could they even read music? Then he glanced into the corner of the study.

A glass case displayed a set of bagpipes. The case had room for a much larger set next to it, but the small pipes hung on hooks, dusty and long unused.

Donald and Lochlann were pipers? Or their father? He couldn't remember ever hearing what their father did.

Pipers worked for a clan chief, from what he'd heard. Such an odd concept, marching onto a battlefield with nothing but a musical instrument as a weapon. Having heard the pipes, though, he understood being terrified as they howled on a foggy, damp morning. The mists would carry the haunting sound until the enemy seemed all around.

He carried the sheets back to the main room. "Ciaran! Ciaran, I found Da's stolen music."

Ciaran perked up, his eyes narrowed. "What music?"

"The pages stolen from his bag. Don't you remember? They were the only transcription he had of some of O'Carolan's tunes. He valued them greatly, and they went missing just before the wedding."

His cousin's gaze darted to the pages. After a moment, he gave a shrug. "Grand! At least we accomplished something out of this mess. Come on, let's go home. We can't find out where they took her. I'm bone tired of this foolish journey."

Éamonn scowled, crushing the papers in his fist. "You didn't have to come."

"And let you take both women? Not on your life. You've always done as you pleased and let others pick up the pieces. This time, I mean to come out ahead."

Deirdre entered with mugs of steaming herbal tea. When had she built a fire? She must have made it as he explored. He sipped the warm liquid as he settled into an overstuffed velvet chair.

Deirdre shot him a glare. "Éamonn, we came too late. She'll have met their father and consummated the wedding. She can't annul the marriage now. You've lost." Deirdre's words hit hard, though she used a wheedling tone as if teasing him out onto the dance floor. She took his arm, pulling him out of the chair.

Despite being annoyed at her words, he was forced accept them. Lochlann must have taken Katie by now, likely in this very house. She'd be wedded and bedded, so he'd lost her. He'd never run his fingers through her red curls or kiss her soft lips. Failure weighed on his shoulders. Éamonn hadn't been fast enough to rescue her.

Heaving a sigh, he stumbled as Deirdre tugged him down the hall. Memory of his vow to Katie pushed back. With an almost audible snap, he stood straight, recalling the blue strips of cloth, proof Katie wanted to be found. She wanted to be rescued. Should he challenge Lochlann to a duel, and leave Katie a widow? He could wed her then. But he had no experience with swords or guns. If Lochlann lived in this fancy house, he'd know how to use a sword.

Could Éamonn even kill someone? Could he use his magic to make Lochlann lose? The notion sickened him, an illness that had nothing to do with using his power. Besides, Katie couldn't love a murderer.

If the MacCrimmons had positions as pipers, they might have gone to war. That offered an opportunity. Deirdre still tugged on his arm, but he yanked out of her grasp. "They can't have gone far since this morning. Someone in the village will know where they've gone."

Ciaran and Deirdre both groaned.

After narrowing his gaze at them both, he threw his hands up and stalked out. He spied a village down the hill and stomped toward it. He didn't care if either of his companions followed. The bright day dimmed with gray clouds.

The village had a smithy and a stone chapel off to one side. No shops, not even an alehouse, so he had few choices. He angled toward the chapel. Priests knew what went on in their parish.

The tiny chapel looked empty. Éamonn walked around the back and spied a man in a dark coat kneeling, pulling weeds from around a tombstone.

"Father?"

The squat, froggy man glanced up. He wore round, wire-rimmed spectacles over enormous bushy gray eyebrows and blinked several times before his eyes focused on Éamonn. The priest spoke in a thick Highland accent. "My, aren't ye the tall one! And how can I help you on this fine day, my lad?"

Fine day? Éamonn squinted at the overcast sky. The priest must have a different definition of fine. "Good afternoon, Father. My name is Éamonn, and I'm searching for my, uh, sister. Her name is Katie, Katie MacCrimmon. She came to the house on the hill in the last day or so. I must have just missed them. Have you any idea where they might have gone?" His guilt at lying to a priest nagged at the back of his mind.

He said the words in a rush. He'd practiced the speech all the way down from the house. The truth wouldn't work. He had no legal claim on Katie, as Deirdre pointed out so often.

"Ah, yes, the young lass with red hair? Lochlann's new bride came as a surprise, but they didn't tarry long enough for us to meet her. Away they flew, just this morning, as you surmised."

The man rose and brushed the dirt from his knees. The cassock hem swept the grass. "Let me see. A messenger from the MacLeod came through yesterday. A letter for Donald, from what one of the village lads said. They might have gone to join His Majesty's Army."

"Army? They've gone to war?" His Majesty's army. The priest must mean the English king, not Prince Charles.

"Indeed. Now, I know I heard someone mention where..." He tapped his lip and glanced off to the side as if reading through an invisible book. "Ah, yes! Inverness, I believe. The MacLeod is stationed at the fort, or at least had been a few weeks ago. Armies don't move fast, though, so they might remain for a while."

Inverness. The place name meant little to Éamonn. His confusion must have shown on his face for the little priest chuckled. "Inverness is sheer on the other side of the country, lad. Back to the mainland, due east, and then northeast along Loch Ness. As I said, they just went this morning. They left their wagons so will travel fast, but if you're determined enough, you might catch them."

202

Éamonn wanted to hug the little man, but he just gave a hearty handshake, "Thank you, Father. Thank you so much!" He rushed back up the hill as the first raindrops fell.

Standing in the doorway, he stopped, panting. Ciaran and Deirdre had disappeared. He spied a tray of bread and a steaming cup of tea on the table. Grateful for a hot drink, he downed it, the warmth spreading through his body. But where had Ciaran and Deirdre gone? Confused, he glanced around outside, then climbed the stairs.

The first room must have been the father's room. A huge oak bed stood in the middle, covered with heavy drapes for comfort. And Ciaran had discovered just how comfortable. His cousin lay passed out on the massive bed, arms and legs sprawled out like a spider. With a groan, Éamonn shut the door. They all needed sleep, as they'd gotten little enough on the road. While he ached to rush after Katie, he must allow them all some rest.

Éamonn glanced into the next room, a woman's room, with frilly white things everywhere. The place looked like a lace-maker's shop. Deirdre lay naked in the center of the soft feather bed. He swallowed his shock as his skin tingled. The tea roiled in his stomach.

While striking a sensuous pose, she ran her hands over her full breasts. His body answered, and he kept a tight grip on the doorframe.

"Don't you want to touch them? What are you afraid of, Éamonn? You remember how soft they are. And the bed is *so* warm." She stroked the feather mattress beside her, peering at him from under lowered lashes.

He couldn't move. Katie. He must think of Katie. Katie MacCrimmon, who might have lost her maidenhood in this very bed, with her husband. As Deirdre rose, he squeezed his eyes shut to summon her face in his mind. Panicking, he couldn't remember the color of her eyes. Were they blue? Green? Moss-green, that's the color. While he filled out the details of her smile and freckles in the image, Deirdre's hand caressed his waist.

Éamonn's eyes flew open to find the still-naked Deirdre latched onto him, her arms locked around his waist as she pulled him away from the doorframe.

"No, Deirdre. Go away." He tried to push power into his words and gripped the door harder, but it did no good.

Deirdre shifted one hand between his legs. With a rhythmic stroke, she convinced his body of what it wanted, a primal hunger, an overpowering need to slake his burning thirst. His grip on the door relaxed. Before he knew it, she'd undressed him. She pulled him into bed and under the gray woolen blanket.

She hadn't lied. The bed felt warm, snug, and soft, like Deirdre. He surrendered at last, caressing her curves with frantic need. He stroked her hips and thighs, his rough hands hard against her smooth, pale skin. Then he put his face between her breasts with a catch in his throat, and she cradled him, murmuring as a mother comforts a crying child.

Deirdre pushed him onto his back and straddled him. She rubbed her cleft over his manhood picking up the rhythm with slow, measured movements. He could barely breathe, his need burned so strong. He tried to shift Deirdre to enter her, but she shook her head with a half-smile. Then she scooted down, putting her mouth around him.

Coherent thought disappeared. The incredible pulling of her warm, wet mouth on his manhood became everything in his world. She used her tongue in spirals and he struggled to hold back his climax. His entire body quaked as she mounted him.

Deirdre sank onto his shaft. Her back arched, and she let out a primal moan. He answered her cry and thrust, grasping her hips. Pushing, he couldn't wait, he couldn't go slowly. He had no control left, not after so many weeks of teasing and wanting. With animal drive, he seized her hips and pumped until his own need exploded.

In anguish and ecstasy, he cried out, "Katie!" as his seed left him a shuddering, quivering mess.

Thunder woke him much later, with Deirdre curled next to him, sleeping like a cat. Flashes of what they'd done taunted him and, with great shame at his own weakness, Éamonn wept.

Éamonn:
He hated himself for his weakness. When he woke the next day, Deirdre still slept in the bed, but he rose and dressed. Then he shuffled to the window and gazed out. The freshness of the landscape after the storm taunted him. What right did the world

have for being sweet and bright, when he'd soiled his promise to Katie and his own honor?

A crow flew past the window, cawing censure at his idiocy. He straightened his spine and resolved to fix things. He couldn't get Katie back, not after what he'd done, but he must at least assure himself that the Scotsman was taking good care of her. Especially since Éamonn had failed in that promise.

The week-long journey to Inverness numbed Éamonn and left them all as tired as when they'd arrived in Borreraig. The night's rest had helped, especially Deirdre, but the flush of renewed vigor faded as they trudged once again across the Highlands. His quest had morphed from one of hope to one of dogged determination, with little chance of joy at the end. And yet he must continue, as he refused to give up without the assurance of Katie's well-being.

They discovered very few villages along the road, and those few seemed wary of strangers. English soldiers must be active in this area, taking suspicions out on innocent crofters and villagers. Most Highlander crofters had to endure stolen sheep, burnt fields, or an accosted wife in these years of warfare. From what Éamonn heard, the Black Watch could be worse. Righteous bandits demanding protection money.

Crofters stared through windows as they passed. Sooty faces with wary eyes that didn't relax. Daughters and wives hid away as soon as any stranger approached. No laughter escaped at the alehouses of an evening. Éamonn found a group of threadbare, skinny men throwing dice now and then, but he had no heart to cheat them from their meager coin.

Without gambling income, they lived rough. They supplemented their waning travel food with hunting, though none had great hunting skills. As they got closer to Inverness, they'd found no food for the last day and had no money to buy more. Deirdre ran out of her supply of tea the day after they'd left Borreraig.

When Éamonn had insisted on pushing on to find Katie, she'd thrown up her hands. "Even after all this, you still want her? Do I mean nothing to you? What spell did she place on you, Éamonn Doherty? You never even kissed her!"

Éamonn rubbed his temples. He felt like he could think more clearly than on Skye, but his head still ached. "I love her, Deirdre. It's always been about Katie, and it always will be. Besides, I promised to protect her."

"She's not your responsibility, Éamonn. She has a husband. *His* job is to protect her."

"I must satisfy myself he's taking care of her, then. I promised, and I refuse to break that vow. I have a duty."

She glared at him, placing her hands on her hips and thrusting her breasts forward. "And what of your duties to me, Éamonn? Do I not warrant your protection? Will you not wed me now that you've bedded me?"

He rolled his eyes and leaned in close, lowering his voice to a whisper. "You're well able to take care of yourself, Deirdre. Haven't you proven that many times over? You don't need me. Obviously, I wasn't your first."

She paled, but then stamped her foot. "But I love you! You can't just use me like that!"

Éamonn let out a snort. "You love nothing, Deirdre. Except the hunt, you do love that. Well, you felled your quarry, and he still doesn't want you."

Her chin quivered as she burst into tears, a dirty trick. Éamonn wanted to gather her into his arms to comfort her, but that's why she used that technique. Her tricks grew easier to resist the farther they got from Skye.

When the tears didn't work, she screamed and kicked, scratched at him, beat him with her fists. *Such a hellcat!* Ciaran drew her away to comfort her, shooting Éamonn a resentful look.

Despite his obsession, he took some time to reconsider the worth of this quest. Deirdre wanted him, that came clear enough, even for his thick skull. *Why can't I settle for the woman I have rather than go on a mad, dangerous quest for a woman already well married to another man?*

Why, indeed. The idea of spending the rest of his life with Deirdre made him recoil. Sure, she had beauty and skill. He had no complaints about that. But when she didn't outright seduce him, she pestered him. She alternated between pitiful sobbing, wheedling, and moping. Her mood swung from intense fury to pathetic whining, like traveling with a sexy, sulky child.

With Katie, she felt part of him. Temper and all, she'd be a proper match to his own mind. Éamonn had played at life. He'd start projects with all the vigor and passion of youth but seldom saw them through. This time, being with Katie felt important to his very being, to the center of his soul, to complete his quest. He must find Katie again so they could be one. Or at least be sure she'd found contentment.

He'd kept each blue ribbon he found, tied to his belt. He stroked them like a magical talisman each time he thought of her.

Éamonn refused to lie with Deirdre again. His body didn't understand his refusal, but she seemed to accept a *no* more easily with each passing day. The girl didn't accept this dismissal, of course. Every evening, she served him his supper, sitting next to him, her thigh touching his by the campfire. Deirdre caressed him with any excuse, her hand lingering on his arm, his collarbone, his back. Every night, she begged him to join her. And every night, he steeled himself from giving in to his animal lust again.

In the morning, he found her crying in Ciaran's arms, and he knew himself for a callous blackguard. He'd been weak once, and he couldn't risk doing so again. When she asked for his help in preparing dinner, he agreed out of guilt and pity, and her misery lessened.

Five days later, they approached Inverness as the farms grew smaller and closer together. A stone castle perched on a promontory near the mouth of the River Ness, with grand houses flanking both sides. Simpler cottages with thatched roofs spread out around this city center. The port swarmed with activity, and seamen ran around the quay like ants to clear cargo from late arrivals. Several king's soldiers marched through the streets, especially into the inns and taverns. This must be the right place.

How to find Katie in all these people? Éamonn poked his head into each alehouse and inn they passed, but her red hair didn't pop out. She might not even be at an inn. Married soldiers might sleep in barracks. Would a soldier even have permission to marry? They must if they joined after having already wed. Despite that, Katie would be a camp follower. The sordid implications of that made Éamonn's skin crawl. He hoped Lochlann stayed strong enough to keep her from the attentions of other soldiers.

Frustrated by too many options, Éamonn settled on camping outside the city. They had no coin for even the lowliest alehouse, and he didn't want to risk harassment. They pulled into a clearing beside the river.

"I'll see if I can scrounge food, Éamonn, and I'll watch out for your girl." Ciaran left without waiting for Éamonn's answer, but he didn't blame his cousin. After five days of travel, each one of them felt exhausted, dirty, and starving.

"You're not going with him, Deirdre? You're more likely to elicit offers of charity than his dour face."

She sidled up to him. "No, I'd rather wait here with you."

Éamonn rolled his eyes and pushed her away. "Deirdre, no. You go with Ciaran. I'll be grand here on my own, to be sure."

"I don't want to go tramping about the dark countryside with him." She put a warm hand on his thigh. His skin prickled and tensed.

Standing, he strode to his horse and pulled out his waterskin. Any excuse to get away from her. He filled it down by the river, balancing on a rock to get the skin into the water.

Her voice at his shoulder almost made him leap into the river. "Why are you afraid of me, Éamonn?"

"In the name of all that's holy, girl! Stop sneaking up on me!"

"You have no reason to fear me. No reason at all." Her voice sounded silky smooth as she caressed his back with both hands. He had to escape this. Pushing back, he leapt off the rock and onto the shore, putting her off balance.

With a cry of indignation, she fell on her rump in the dew-damp grass. "Éamonn! That wasn't nice! Here, now, help me up again." She put her hand out and awaited his help. A sensuous half-smile played across her lips.

"You are perfectly capable of getting up yourself, Deirdre." He stalked back to the camp.

Her exclamation of exasperation faded as he walked away. Taking the harness and saddle off his horse and currying the poor beast down helped him to steady his mind and his desires. Saying no came easier now. He pulled strength from that realization. Maybe because he drew nearer to Katie? Or did his body tire of such spoiled delights? Just being in the habit of saying no helped.

Éamonn regretted that night on Skye. Not that he hadn't enjoyed it, but his betrayal made him unworthy of Katie's love.

Ciaran returned with day-old bread and a hunk of cheese large enough to fill all their shrunken stomachs. They chewed the food in silence. As he finished the last bite, Éamonn turned to Ciaran. "Did you search the soldier camps?"

Ciaran swallowed the lump of bread he'd been chewing. "A large army is camped next to the official barracks in the town with overflows beyond that. The camp woman I got this from told me they've twice as many soldiers as they have berths." He held his bread. "She said they'd been camped a month, and glad of the mild weather. Lots of fights already. I asked about recent arrivals, and she said to check the other side of the camp. That's where the bursar's tent is, where they'd check in."

Éamonn slapped his knees and rose. "Well done, thank you. We'll search for her in the morning, then. Rest well tonight."

Deirdre let out a whine and Ciaran tried to comfort her. She rolled her eyes and stomped off into the darkness. When she returned with bundles of foraged onions and garlic, she set about cooking them a meal in silence.

They didn't even bother setting up tents in the warm, dry evening. They laid blankets and slept under the stars. After rebuffing Deirdre's questing hand, Éamonn stumbled into a dream.

On a lonely moor, Katie stood in the distance. She waved to him, and then ran in the opposite direction, the curly mop of her red hair bouncing farther and farther away until she disappeared in the heather. Éamonn ran toward her, but strange, squid-like creatures attached to both legs. They wore long cassocks. He pulled and jerked, but as soon as he extracted himself from one, three others latched on until long, thin slimy tentacles sucked at his feet. One popped up with round, wire-rimmed glasses and told him he'd catch up with the young lass if he hopped like a frog.

Éamonn tried to jump, but mud splashed everywhere. He fell deeper into the bog. Tentacles crept from his ankles to his knees. They crept higher until reaching his neck.

His eyes flew open with a cry, the fog of sleep still around him. Éamonn shook his head until he woke. Tentacles still squeezed his privates. He glanced down to find Deirdre's hands. She peered at him with a crafty smile. His member stood stiff and ready for action. With iron will, he detached her hand as he had the tentacles in the bog. She resisted his efforts. Her other hand moved to his balls, but he removed that, too. The coming dawn tinged the blue velvet of the star-filled sky.

"You were moaning in your sleep, and it sounded like a horrible dream. I just wanted to comfort you."

He whispered low, so as not to wake Ciaran, "Enough, Deirdre. I don't need your comfort."

"It's never enough, Éamonn. Can't you see? I'm so much better, not to mention closer, than Katie? I want you with all my being." She pressed against him, her breasts straining against her shift. One lock of ink-dark hair fell across her cleavage, pale in the bare dawn. He tore his eyes away from her tempting flesh.

"No. That's a real no, Deirdre, and final. Even if I don't find Katie, or if she can't come to me, I'll still say no. Can't you understand?" He tried to push the power of the brooch into his words, but he'd tried that before. While it may work for a short time, the effect wore off too quickly to matter.

With a pout, she caressed his arm. "You liked me well enough in the past. Don't you remember?"

She pressed her breasts against his shoulder, moving a hand up his chest and then to his breeks. Éamonn pushed her off and scrambled to his feet. "I remember well enough, Deirdre. But we're finished. Get that through your head, will you?" He didn't whisper any longer, and Ciaran stirred.

Deirdre opened her mouth to answer but fell silent as several troops of soldiers marched past them. Ciaran woke as well, and all three rose to watch the column pass south along the road. The jingle of tack and the clatter of wagons spoke of hundreds of soldiers.

After the troops and supply wagons, came the camp followers. Éamonn strained to make out details in the still-dark morning. He spied a red-haired lass, but she looked too tall to be Katie. Another looked short enough, but a kerchief covered her hair.

Then, like a summer sunrise, her wonderfully familiar face shone out from the darkness like a beacon to his heart. He stood frozen in disbelief, to see the fair lass not twenty feet ahead. Bright as a new *doit,* her curls as vibrant and springy as he remembered. She spoke with another woman as they walked.

Éamonn called out as his heart sped, and his feet finally obeyed him to run toward her. "Katie! Katie!"

Her head whipped around. She halted, and her mouth formed an *O.* Confusion and wonder tinged her voice. "Éamonn?"

By all that's holy, she's more beautiful than I remember, a shining star in a sea of darkness. Those still walking shoved and jostled her while she stood staring at him.

Katie stepped out of the stream of people and stepped toward them, eyes wide in disbelief. Éamonn couldn't believe his own eyes after so long chasing his dreams. With gentle anticipation, he took her hands. They felt ice cold.

She shook her head and furrowed her brow, expressions of relief, anger, and confusion warring on her face. "Éamonn, it really is you! But what are you doing here *now*?"

A hundred times he'd imagined their reunion. None of them started like this. In his dreams, they ran toward each other, then hugged each other tight, spinning around like tops. This felt more like a slap in the face.

She waited for an answer, impatience already clouding her expression. "Katie, I came for you. You're everything I've ever wanted in my life."

His love glared at him with wonder. Her voice remained flat. "You came for me."

"Of course, I did! Those fabric strips were very clever, by the way." He gave her his most charming grin.

She pulled her hands from his. "The fabric strips. Not clever enough, evidently! I haven't left any since Skye! You prime idiot, you're too late! I'm wedded and bedded now. Damn you, Éamonn Doherty! Why didn't you come sooner?" Her anger tinged with frustration. A sob caught in her voice.

He tried to take her hands again. "I tried! We came a day behind you at Borreraig. I swear! The hearth still felt warm."

She jerked away, her eyes flashing. Éamonn felt torn between feeling guilt and relishing her fire again. "Well, and you still would have been too late. H-he took me the day before we left." She shuddered and her gaze flicked behind her, as if worried about someone seeing them. What had Lochlann done to her when they consummated the marriage? Or had it been Donald?

A massive surge of jealousy rocked him. "Where is he? Where is Lochlann? I'll—"

"You'll what? Kill him and take me away like a Viking? I'm not a prize to be carried off! He may not be the husband I chose, but he treats me well enough. You have nerve, Éamonn Doherty!" Her eyes sparked in the rising dawn like a vengeful goddess. *Dear God, she looked magnificent in her fury.*

Éamonn's resolve slipped away. "Are you safe, then? Does he protect you? Are you content?"

For a brief second, terror flashed in her eyes, and she swallowed, glancing to either side again, and then at the ground.

Deirdre's voice came from behind him. "Katie?"

Katie gave her sister a disdainful glare. "Deirdre."

Deirdre came up behind Éamonn with a knowing smirk and snaked a possessive arm around his waist. He removed her hand and glared at her, but too late.

Katie's gaze narrowed. "Oh, so that's how things are, are they? Better the one you've got than the one you don't? Well, this all works out, then, doesn't it? You can have him, Deirdre, and joy to you both." Spitting the words with venom, she stomped back toward the line of camp followers.

Éamonn ran after her. "Katie, wait! No, we're not like that! I love *you!*" She kept tromping down the road.

He grabbed her arm and spun her about. "Katie."

The naked fury on her face made him stumble back. "You faithless load of gobshite! I wouldn't take you now if you were the last man on earth. How *dare* you profess your love to me, and then swive my own sister! Can you deny you have?"

Her vitriol stuck him dumb. She must have taken his silence as consent. He couldn't deny her accusation, and his guilt must have shone clear. Katie's expression turned dark and with one last scowl at him, she ran after the group.

A few people glanced back at the fracas.

He watched her retreating form, his heart sinking with each step. Damn Deirdre and her manipulations. She came to him now and tried to hold his hand. He shook her off and, for the first time, had the incredible urge to shake her. Anything to get her clinging, betraying hands off him. Her betraying hands, which had turned Katie away from him. No, that wasn't fair. He'd betrayed Katie, and this was all his fault.

Éamonn clenched his jaw, trying to keep the tears from bursting forth. He had no idea what he should do next, but he couldn't give up yet. *Damn it, this isn't how I meant things to go!* As he marched to their horses, he felt helpless, but he couldn't leave now.

Ciaran grabbed his arm as he saddled his horse. "Éamonn, what else can you do? You have your verdict from her own mouth. You're too late, and she doesn't want you. Face the truth, for once in your blasted life, will you?"

He yanked his arm from his cousin's grip. "This isn't done, not nearly so. Didn't you see? She's terrified of something, and I'll lay long odds it's Donald. I'm not done yet. Go if you like and take Deirdre with you."

Ciaran stared at him with his eyes and mouth wide. Then he turned to stare at Katie. "You might have a point. She looked a lot more nervous than I remember."

Éamonn glanced toward the retreating column of camp followers, his heart aching to hold her. He'd been so close.

With a frustrated growl, Ciaran grabbed Deirdre's arm and tugged. She resisted at first, but then followed him with a sigh.

Ideas swirled through his brain like a maelstrom. What could he do? Follow Katie around like a puppy until her husband shot him? Skulk around in the night, hoping for a kind glance? Spirit her off against her will and beg her to love him? That last thought disgusted him. Even thinking it made him question his own motives. This shouldn't be about what he wanted. This should be what *they* wanted. But they had no *they* any longer.

Perhaps he'd kill Donald. That would fulfill his promise of protection from that threat. But Éamonn had never killed a man.

Chapter Fourteen

Katie:

Katie's heat grew in the chilly dawn as she marched to the safety of the column. Éamonn betrayed her twice over. First, he failed to rescue her in time, and then he must have bedded Deirdre, from his guilty expression. Her own sister! She didn't doubt Deirdre played a large part in that action. But for Éamonn to have succumbed to her sister's all-too-obvious charms infuriated her. His guilt had been so plain on his face. Even if Donald hadn't threatened them both with such vile retribution, she wouldn't be able to erase that image of guilt from her mind.

The triumph in his initial expression made everything worse, as if he'd been the conquering hero. Katie wanted to slap that silly grin away, even punch him until he begged for mercy. The image flashing in her mind made her reel.

Her image morphed into a memory she'd tried to forget, when she'd begged her own father for mercy. Thanks to a stray comment from Deirdre, her father had learned that Katie had run off her latest suitor, an older man from a wealthy trading family. The arse had pushed her against a wall, intent on sampling her affections before he even offered a contract. She'd responded with violent rejection, and he'd run away holding his privates.

When her father learned of this, he'd whipped his belt across her back, laying open great welts that stung for weeks afterward. And when she begged him to stop, he only growled and hit her harder.

Katie shook her aching head to dispel her boiling blood and painful memories. She needed to cool down.

How dare he show up *now,* after she began to fit into this new life? She'd forged a cautious friendship with her husband, and while Lochlann may be spineless, he looked upon her with a puppy-like adoration. Despite being cloying, Katie might build a life with him, given half a chance.

And not a day after her decision, hours even, along came Éamonn, lumbering back into her life like a bear, expecting her to rush into his arms with joy. Well, she wouldn't do that! Éamonn had failed her, and he'd have to deal with his failure. Katie suspected he'd seldom done that before.

The idea of him bedding Deirdre made her angry, confused, and jealous. Something felt broken and lost forever, and the absence of that broken thing haunted her.

Mrs. MacKensey had asked a question, and she hadn't been listening. Katie cocked her head. "I'm sorry, what did you ask?"

"I said, who is yon giant? He's a lovely one, isn't he?"

"Oh, him. Yes, I suppose so. He's not my husband, though."

The older woman gave a saucy wink. "I've seen your husband, lass. That one yonder is much more the man. I saw that well enough."

Katie suspected Mrs. MacKensey had the right idea. But she'd married in the eyes of God and the law. Her anger at Éamonn still simmered.

"Still, you've got your man well and truly wound about your little finger, so you do. Your one would fight you all the way, I'm sure. Ah, but what a battle that would be!" With that, she elbowed Katie in the waist and rambled about other things.

The night before, Lochlann had told her they headed to a manor house south of Inverness. Reports of a large group of Jacobite rebels came, and British soldiers sent to rout them or kill them, as needs be. Lochlann confided that shouldn't tell her all this. He blushed at his wickedness, but the discipline of the army hadn't settled in yet. Besides, he didn't know what house or what town. Lochlann's obvious need to impress his wife with his worldly knowledge seemed pathetic.

They marched all morning and most of the afternoon. A wide field became a camp while troops rested. Women set up camp and prepared to feed their men.

The long, hot, dusty walk exhausted Katie. She'd been traveling for weeks now, but on a wagon or on horseback. Now, she marched with the other followers. Officers had commandeered their horses as soon as they arrived, though Donald kept his, thanks to his status as a piper. He checked on them when they stopped, speaking with Lochlann in whispers. Katie ignored their hurried conference and served them both tea. She smiled at her detested brother-in-law as he sipped and grimaced at the strong taste.

"Mint?" Lochlann asked her. "Where'd you find mint?"

"Catmint. Mrs. MacKensey had some, so I brewed some as soon as we settled." She kept the smile pasted on her face so long her jaw ached. She hoped she'd put enough of the foxglove in Donald's tea to disguise the taste.

After draining the dregs, Donald tossed the dirty mug to her, grabbed his package of travel food, and swung up onto his horse. With a last significant look at Lochlann, he cantered off.

As she prepared Lochlann's pack, she swallowed. "Take care of yourself, Lochlann."

After looking up from his lacing his boots, his eyes grew wide. "I'll come back, I promise." He kissed her on the mouth with sweet tenderness. For a moment, she worried for his safety in the battle. He was her only protection in this world right now, Éamonn's ill-timed return notwithstanding. Besides, Éamonn had bedded her sister. She simply couldn't get the image of his guilty face from her mind.

Then, like millions of women in ages past and days to come, she hunkered down with the other women as they waited for their men to return from battle.

Mrs. MacKensey stirred the stew pot. "It takes courage to go off into battle, especially against a bigger or better armed enemy. To face someone down who's trying to kill you takes power."

Katie stared at her hands. "But they still go."

"Of course, they go, as they must. But waiting for them to come back might be harder. We don't know if they'll come back at all, and you have no control. If they come back, they have wounds in body or soul. Sometimes, their wounds are hard to see, like a breaking of the mind, the spirit, a cleaving of their humanity. Too many of these wounds, and the soldier is a different person, a shell of their former self."

Katie didn't love Lochlann, but she'd learned to care for him, and as her husband, he should be a shield against the world. She relied upon him for support, and she had no other family in this land. A strange feeling to realize she'd miss him, that she must have become reconciled to her fate. Not that she had much choice in the matter, thanks to Éamonn's blundering idiocy. *Damn Éamonn.*

Stewing about Éamonn would be worse than worrying about Lochlann. She must find a constructive task. Grabbing her pack, she rummaged for her needle set. She had plenty of mending, and now would be the perfect time.

Several hours passed with no news of the soldiers. Some few remained with the camp followers, set on guard duty. Mrs. McKensey set up a communal hearth, and Katie nestled her own stewpot in the coals. When Lochlann returned, he'd need food. Better to be prepared.

One woman described the battle at Fort Augustus back in March. "'Twas different from this. A siege rather than a pitched battle. Closeted in the fort, unable t' leave for the troops outside. 'Twas horrifying. I thought for certain we'd all die."

Katie gripped her hands tight. "What happened?"

"Nothing had prepared us, you see. We had a week or two of good food before we'd need to eat the horses. We had fresh water from the well inside. But we'd heard tell of sieges lasting months. I huddled in a corner as dark as I could find, so the rebels might miss me as they passed."

A younger woman piped up, glancing to where their own men had departed, "I never heard tell of soldiers ever *missing* a pretty girl."

A grandmother-aged woman snorted. "Ye might as well just leave off the word *pretty*, my girl. And *young* as well. Some men couldn't care less how a woman looks, as long as he can stick his stick in her." The younger girl paled. Even Katie swallowed against nausea. As much as she'd resisted Lochlann, he'd never been cruel or violent. However, she had no trouble believing such acts of her brother-in-law.

Slipping into the role of an army wife wouldn't be easy but, in some ways, the details seemed similar to being a Traveler. Now she just had to wait.

Had Éamonn headed back to Ireland? While she wanted him to travel to the gates of Hell for not rescuing her in time, at the same time, the idea of him leaving made her heart ache. Katie straightened her spine. Éamonn could be none of her business any longer, nor she any of his.

A commotion outside camp caught their attention. Had their soldiers returned already? She stood and peered to the edge of camp, trying to identify the noise.

Her short stature kept her from seeing what caused the kerfuffle.

Mrs. McKensey climbed a fence to get a better vantage. "I can't see… Wait… No, that's not our men, but… Bloody hell! Everyone, hide! The rebels are coming this way!" She jumped down, grabbed a pouch from the ground, and ran for the trees. Other women scrambled around the same. Like any smart Traveler, Katie kept her few valuables, a couple of coins and a simple necklace Lochlann had gifted her, sewn into the lining of her skirts, so she only had to grab a carving knife before she fled.

The stories about the atrocities committed during war swam through her head with alarming, graphic detail. She thanked God she wore her dark green and brown skirt, not the bright red one. Her bodice was the color of the summer sky, and her shift, cream-colored. Before she'd begun this mad climb up a tree, she'd just washed them. Now, sticky sap and bark stuck in the wool.

As she reached the tree line, Katie discarded one bush as being too spindly to hide her. Most of the tall Scotch pines had no low-hanging branches to grab. One tree had partially fallen, held by the crutch of another tree. She scrambled up the fallen tree to the straight one and kept climbing.

Her skirt snagged on bark and branch. She scratched her arm on the sharp point of another branch as she wiped the sap on her skirt. She halted at a spot shielded from the ground. While trying to calm her labored breathing, she pushed down on the fear that crept up and threatened to smother her. Should someone espy her, she had no escape route.

Lochlann had bought her a Scottish shawl, an *arisaid,* in a muted MacCrimmon plaid. She wrapped the enormous fabric under her, to mask from eyes below. The kerchief she wore over her cleavage might cover her hair. She yanked the fabric free and wrapped it around her head, hiding her red curls just as the rebels came into view, crashing and cursing came through the trees. They flooded the woods, Highlanders dressed in kilts and breeks, shoving through bushes and beating them with sticks. Her heart raced and she tried to remember to breathe.

A tall man with hair as red as hers peered into the trees. When he spied the fallen one, his gaze followed the line straight to her. Katie hid her face and held her breath.

The tree trembled as he climbed. How would she get out of this bloody mess? Bravado and temper were her only weapons... *weapons!* She still had the carving knife! She'd stuck a chunk of wood on the tip and tucked the tool into her pocket before climbing. She bent down to retrieve the knife but couldn't quite reach the low-hanging pouch. With a muffled curse, she bent further, brushing the pocket strings with the tip of her fingers. The man climbed closer as she bent so far, her back spasmed, but she grasped the strings, pulling the pocket up. Her hands got tangled in the strings as she got the knife out and plucked the wood from the tip. While the blade measured only seven inches, she felt much less helpless with its hefty weight in her hand.

A young man who fancied her once had spent several afternoons teaching her how to use a knife, but she might not have the courage. And being perched in the tree complicated matters. After placing the wood back on the end of the knife, she tucked it back into the pocket. She'd have a better chance on the ground. If she knifed the man until he fell, his comrades would hear. Instead, she broke free a stout branch, though she had to work to worry the green wood free.

Now that she had a plan in mind, the man took forever to reach her. She glared down at him, all pretense of hiding gone. He grinned up at her.

When he'd reached ten feet away, she spat out, "Stop! Don't come any closer!" She brandished her branch like a club.

"Ah, lass, don't be daft. I'm after riches, not yer fine self. You'll fetch a fine ransom and worth a whipping about!" He grabbed the next branch and pulled himself up.

"I'm warning you! You'll regret it!"

He gave a wicked chuckle. His large nose poked over his bushy red beard laced with gray. As he reached his hand toward her, she smacked him with the tree branch and kicked at his face. The Highlander grabbed her foot and climbed up her leg to her waist. She kicked with her other foot and connected with his ear.

After securing himself around the tree with his legs, he clutched her waist and plucked her from her perch. She gripped tight to the branch, but he was too strong. Katie wanted to scream, but that would just bring more men. Now, she wished she'd kept her knife handy.

Struggling when slung over someone's shoulder while he descended a tall tree might mean a cracked skull. Katie waited until they reached solid ground before she walloped him. With a chuckle, he set her down. "Hm. Yes, you'll do, darlin'. You're definitely worth the climb!"

Her aching muscles pulled and screamed as she pummeled him. Now she finally had room to pull out her knife, and she whipped the blade out. His eyes grew wide as he stepped back, his arms open. She slashed at his hip, ripping his kilt, but he twisted around before she got near his kidney. "Hey, now! This kitten has claws! Be a good girl and hand over your knife."

"I am not a good girl. Now, get the hell away from me, you bloody highland bastard!" She brandished the knife in front of her, point up but out of his reach, as Fionn had taught her. She quested back with one foot but didn't dare look around. Could she run from him? He had long legs, and he'd catch her in a moment.

Someone grabbed her from behind. She screeched and kicked, flailing with her knife, but couldn't touch her attacker.

The new man plucked the knife with no trouble while she wriggled in his powerful arms. "You've caught yourself a wee hellcat, Angus."

Katie bit his arm hard, and he let out a yelp. "Put me down, you manky gobshite!"

"Are ye sure you want this one? She'll be awhile taming."

"I'm no worried. I'm looking for ransom, not a woman. You know my own Senga would never forgive me if I took that sort of spoils."

"Ah, but what a time that would be! Well, Captain says they're to be left alone until we check on ransoms."

"Here, hand her over, will ye?" The red-haired man slung her over his shoulder again. She ripped at his back with her nails, but his leather armor kept him from harm. Twisting and squirming earned her a smack on the arse, but she was somewhat reassured he didn't mean to rape her. She'd get away later. If she got a later.

Éamonn:

Éamonn stumbled across the battlefield just as the Highlanders swept through with their pitchforks and great swords. Judging from the uniformed bodies littering the ground, the English hadn't won.

He glimpsed blond hair dancing in the wind from one of the bodies and he steadied his gaze. For a moment, Éamonn thought he imagined it but, no, his rival lay on the ground, Lochlann MacCrimmon, wounded.

He rushed to the man's side and watched his chest rise. A nasty rip in his side oozed blood into a large, dark puddle. For a moment, he considered finishing the job some rebel had begun, but he couldn't do that to Katie, besides, the man didn't look like he'd survive his wounds. Éamonn took his hand. "Lochlann? Lochlann, can you hear me?"

The injured man moaned and his eyes fluttered open. Then they widened. "What are ye… Why are ye here?"

"I came to find Katie, but she sent me away." The concession sounded hollow.

Lochlann's voice gurgled, and he coughed. "Nay, ye must take her now."

Éamonn shook his head, gripping Lochlann's hand tighter. "She doesn't want me, Lochlann."

The setting sun colored the field in gold and rose as it dropped below the tree line.

"Take her. Take her from Donald…don't let him…" Lochlann coughed again, blood dribbling down his cheek. "Love her, Éamonn. Even *you* should be able to manage so much, aye?" Lochlann gave a wan smile through the pain.

Éamonn's throat closed. He'd done this man a disservice. Lochlann cared for Katie and might have made her a fine husband. Lochlann stared up, seeing nothing but the sky.

With a swallow, he squeezed his rival's hand as the light began to fade from his eyes. His harsh breathing slowed as sounds of fighting behind him faded to nothing. The Scotsman's chest stopped moving and with a shuddering sigh, Éamonn closed the dead man's eyes.

A snarling voice, barely human, came from behind him. "Murderer!"

Donald MacCrimmon, blood streaking his face, charged him with a sword. Éamonn rolled away, scrambling for his belt knife. He jumped to his feet and crouched, ready for the next attack.

Donald circled him, fiery insanity in his eyes. Éamonn remembered the tales of berserkers, men who lost all sense as they fought. The blood smeared across Donald's face, made him especially inhuman, his dark eyes glittering from the gloaming. The enraged Scotsman groaned, clutching his stomach but didn't break eye contact.

"You killed my brother, you damned murderer!" He circled around Éamonn, who tripped on a body lying in the mud. Donald closed the distance as Éamonn struggled to regain his balance. Gripping Donald's arm, Éamonn tried to keep the wicked weapon from his neck. His other hand kept his attacker's fingers from clawing out his eyes. Éamonn lost an inch with each breath as they grappled and Donald's superior strength came closer to killing him.

He pushed hard into Donald's mind, to calm him with his magic. "We've no reason to fight, Donald. Your brother had already been injured. I did nothing to hurt him."

Donald snarled as his sword got closer to Éamonn's face. "I'll rip your lying heart out and fry it with onions!"

Éamonn saw an opening and jumped out of his grip. Pain in his shoulder told him he hadn't escaped unscathed. He didn't dare check if the wet trickle was blood or sweat.

"Calm down, Donald. We have no quarrel." He pushed his magic so hard he retched in his mouth and gagged it back down.

Donald lowered his sword, and a woman's soul-wrenching scream sliced through the air. The Scot's gaze flicked to his right. Éamonn kept his gaze on the madman when a dark form tackled Donald to the ground.

Ciaran.

The two wrestled in the mud and blood. Éamonn couldn't think, his head pounding like a corps of drummers. The scream must have been Deirdre. She hovered at the edge of the trees but seemed safe enough.

With a horrific grunt, Ciaran and Donald stopped grappling. Éamonn, still crouched on the ground and holding his head, could barely move from the pain. He didn't want to look up but forced himself to do so.

Ciaran had backed away from the highlander and Donald crouched as if ready to pounce on him. He sprang from the ground, knocked Ciaran to the side, and ran toward the camp.

Éamonn drew in several harsh breaths, trying to get control over his shaking hands and thankful that Donald had run away. He hadn't seemed the cowardly type, but Éamonn counted his blessings. Then he realized which direction Donald went.

Katie.

With a roar, Éamonn snatched Lochlann's sword from the ground and launched to his feet, pelting toward Donald. Ciaran watched him run past with a confused expression. His lungs burned as he followed the highlander past dying soldiers and into the sea of white tents.

He slowed, searching for Donald or Katie. Very few things moved here, with everyone either fled or dead. A crack made him turn and he spied his quarry, the highland tartan flashing in the firelight.

Éamonn let out a challenging growl. "Donald!"

The other man turned, a feral smile across his face. "Come and die, Irishman."

Donald poked his sword toward Éamonn, but he batted it away with his own sword, and they settled into a crouch. They circled each other, both arms out as they tested their defenses. Éamonn spied a dark stain on Donald's side. Had Ciaran managed to stab him? If so, he must remember to thank his cousin for helping him. If he survived this part of the fight.

Donald feinted to one side, but Éamonn didn't take the bait. He held the sword steady. He had little experience fighting with a sword, but Donald didn't know that.

He considered telling Donald to give up, using his power, but Donald seemed to be immune to his power. Besides, the suggestion must have a kernel of reasonability, and this situation held none of that.

Someone cried out behind him, but he must concentrate on his foe. Another sound, a shout, came from behind Donald. Others must be filtering back to the camp. Éamonn stepped to the right as Donald did the same, each searching for an opening.

Donald halted, his eyes growing wide, before he turned his head and spewed onto the ground. In that moment of inattention, Éamonn swung Lochlann's sword onto Donald's suddenly exposed neck.

The sword didn't slice all the way through, like he expected. It got caught in the neck bones. Éamonn tugged, trying to free it, as Donald sliced up with his own sword. He had to let go of Lochlann's weapon and dance back. But the damage was done. Donald fell to his knees, coughed up blood, and then fell to the ground, silent in the darkening night.

Éamonn retrieved the sword, stained with blood and gore dripping from the blade. Éamonn wheezed, trying to gain his breath, but Donald didn't move.

Éamonn:

With her husband killed and Katie all alone, Éamonn planned to rescue her from the soldier's camp, but as soon as he arrived, he realized his plan had already failed. From the struggling captives being rounded up, the Jacobites had rousted the camp followers.

She may not want him, but he still had a duty to get her to safety. If Éamonn could just find Katie, he could get her back to Ireland, back to her home, where she belonged. But his luck had deserted him. All he saw were rebel soldiers and their prisoners, none with Katie's lovely fiery hair.

He moved from group to group, searching each woman for her face, listening for her voice, praying for her safety. Every flicker of red caught his eye. He didn't want to imagine what these rebels could be doing to her this very moment, and his search grew frantic.

Just as he was about to give up, he heard her voice, already in someone else's control. She turned toward him, and their gazes locked, but the man who held her jerked her away.

Éamonn considered taking her by force, but he only held a long knife. The man holding Katie stood as tall as he and looked a good four stone more in weight, with a long sword, with other rebels all around, sure to come to his rescue if Éamonn tried to wrest her free. All Éamonn could do was make a plan.

Therefore, he pretended to be a rebel by joining their search for prisoners and a celebratory drink afterward. No one recognized him, of course, but in a group of over two hundred, who knew everyone? His Irish accent would mark him out, but he wasn't the only Irishman to join the cause. Many left Ireland after the Battle of Aughrim fifty years before. Finding his countrymen dotted through the Highlands didn't seem so strange, a logical place for the rebellious sort.

From snippets of conversation, he learned what had happened that afternoon. Rumors of rebels in the manor house became a ruse for an ambush. They lured English soldiers into a pass and an easy slaughter.

Éamonn asked one Scot if any English soldiers escaped, but his neighboring revelers just laughed. "Och, some must have run away, the lily-livered cowards. What true Highlander would run away and leave his comrades to fight off the Devil? None I know, for sure!" The Scotsman raised his cup in a toast, and Éamonn raised his own in tacit agreement.

At least he'd found the prisoners, a couple of crofter cottages with guards posted around them. The few captured officers would be ransomed, but the women and children would only be ransomed if they had wealthy kin. He didn't really want to dwell on the fate of those without wealthy kin. At least he had time and a notion.

As the evening wore on, he pulled out his dice cup and rattled it. This pulled in several gamers and they formed a circle. He had few scruples about using his Fae-given talent to save Katie. He played for higher stakes now than a few coins.

Éamonn won, and often. He threw a few losses, just to head off accusations of cheating, but his markers increased as the night descended. His opponents dwindled until the last man, an officer, threw his cup down.

"All right, I've had enough. You're too lucky by half, friend. Must be yon Irish luck they're always gabbling on about. Well, you've enough markers to buy half the regiment, lad!"

God, how his head ached. "Do you think I might trade them in for something, Alistair?"

His opponent's gaze narrowed as he scratched his three-day beard. "What did you have in mind, Éamonn?"

He held the pile of markers in both hands. "Maybe the pick of the women prisoners?"

Alistair stared at him a long moment and then guffawed into raucous laughter. He slapped Éamonn on the back. "Now here's a lad who knows how to spend his coin! Aye, boy, I can promise you so. We'll have to find out if she's family first, mind you, in case we can get ransom, but take your pick."

Still chuckling, he walked off with Éamonn's markers and spoke with the prisoners' guards. With an enormous sigh of relief, Éamonn gathered his dice and cup, following the guard into one of the holding huts.

The inside had only a low peat fire to cut the gloom. He whispered, "Katie? Katie, are you in here?"

A couple of women answered yes. *Damn!* Katie must be a popular name in the Highlands. "Katie MacCrimmon, I'm searching for." Saying that name galled him.

"Éamonn?" A harsh whisper came from one corner, near the back wall. He stumbled through the lumps in the dark until he found her.

He fumbled for her hand and grasped tight. "Katie? I can get you out of here."

Only her breathing answered him.

"Katie? Did you hear me?"

She snapped back. "I heard you. What do you want from me, Éamonn? I told you already, I'm married and that's the end of us."

Éamonn wished someone else could tell her, but he was the only one here. He must be brave and take the plunge. "I saw Lochlann, Katie. He didn't survive the ambush."

"Ambush? He got ambushed?" Her voice rose, but he shushed her. She sounded pitiful, like a lost child.

Éamonn's stomach turned at the grisly memory and the fight afterward, but she needed to know. "Aye. He asked me to take care of you, Katie. To save you from Donald. His last thoughts were of you." Éamonn swallowed against the words. "He would have been a good husband to you."

In the dim firelight, the sparkle of a tear showed on her cheek.

"Katie, listen to me. I can get you out of here. Will you let me?" He pleaded with all the gods he knew that she'd say yes.

"How?" Her voice came soft now, trembling on the single word.

Éamonn's heart soared that she seemed willing to finally come with him, but then he remembered her response to being sold for a horse. He ducked his head and ruffled his hair, which set off his fae-induced headache again. "Well, I sort of won you."

Her voice rose. "You won me?"

"Shh! Yes, I won you. I played dice and I cashed my winnings in on the first pick of the hostages. That's how I'm getting you out."

"You won me? At *dice?*" She spat the word with indignation.

Éamonn let out an exasperated breath. "Would you rather I traded a horse for you, like Lochlann? Do you want out of here or not, Katie? I could leave you to the tender mercies of the men outside, if you prefer. After they determine who they can ransom off, they'll have their joy of the rest."

Stunned silence followed for several heartbeats. "Fine. What do I need to do, then?"

"When the officer comes and asks you if you've family to ransom, you say your husband died in the fighting, and you've no other family. Then I'm allowed to take you away."

"That's the truth, after all." She sounded defeated and Éamonn ached to gather her into his arms and comfort her.

"Wait, what about Donald? He might...he might claim me." She shrunk back from him, her back against the stone wall. The way she shivered, a frightened mouse, Éamonn could only imagine what Donald had done to the lass. *Damn that brute!* "Donald's dead, too, Katie. You have me now."

"Hmph. Fat lot of good you've done me in the past." Despite her dismissal of his efforts, his heart surged with the return of her fighting spirit.

"I'm here now, aren't I? I'll get you out of here. I promise."

Katie crossed her arms. "And you've promised other things to me in the past, Éamonn. How do I know you'll keep this one?"

Guilt flooded him as a failure. "*Mo cheann dearg*, my heart has hurt every day I've not been able to keep you from harm. You *do* know that, don't you?"

She sat on the ground, her head in her hands. "I don't know anything anymore, Éamonn."

"I won't let you down, I swear by all that's holy."

With a kiss on her forehead, he stayed with her until she sent him from the crowded cottage. Another nod at the guard and he visited the other two cottages. He must appear to be searching for the *best of the bunch* when he told Alistair his choice.

When Alistair brought Katie out to question her, she struggled against the guards. Éamonn couldn't tell if her venomous glares at him were fake, but he took that with a grain of salt. One soldier leered and protested Éamonn's claim, but Alistair stared them down. "He won fair and square, boys. We found plenty of other lovely lasses for the likes of you."

The leering soldier had grabbed Katie's shoulder, but he gave a grimace and shoved her towards Éamonn. "Take her then. She's likely poxed anyhow."

Within an hour, they'd escaped the camp. Once they were out of sight from the last of the soldiers, Katie let out a deep sigh and turned to him. "Now what, oh grand plan master?"

"Back to Ireland as fast as we can. Fighting in a foreign war isn't my idea of a party."

They returned to where Éamonn had left Ciaran and Deirdre with the horses, but they had disappeared. The remains of a campfire and scuffled boot prints showed signs of a struggle. "Damn Ciaran to the nine circles of Hell. Can't he manage to keep from being captured for a couple hours?"

Katie's voice came quiet, either through distrust, anger, or vulnerability, he couldn't be sure. "And what of your Deirdre?"

With a deep sigh, Éamonn sat on a log. "Look, Katie. Let's talk about Deirdre."

"And what should we talk about, Éamonn? You coupled with her. While you went searching for me, you slept with her. And you broke my heart in the process! What else can we talk about?"

He waved his hand. "I haven't touched her in over a week. She, well, she's very persuasive when she wants to be." He rubbed the back of his neck. "I didn't want to, honestly! But she came and rubbed up against me, and touched me—"

Katie snapped at him. "I know exactly what she does! She's my sister, and she's done this to a dozen other men!"

"A dozen?" Deirdre had been no maid, but a dozen?

"At least! You're not so special as you think, Éamonn Doherty. She's mastered the arts of seduction. You're just the latest in a long line of conquests."

Éamonn shook his head from the faceless images crowding within. "Well, I'm done with her, and glad of it. She must have lost her power because I can resist her now. Being one of a dozen makes that even easier."

She crossed her arms and stared out into the night. "Hmph. I'll believe *that* when I see the proof."

"Truly, Katie. Would you like me to pledge my troth to you now? Here? As I never did for your wanton sister?" He got off the log and knelt before her. He held her hand and kissed her knuckles.

"I pledge to thee, Caitriona MacCrimmon, I will love thee with all my heart. I shall protect thee with my body and my soul, and have no others but thee, 'til my dying day. I say this without hope or prayer you'll return my vow, but with a simple truth. I am yours, from this day forward."

Her face seemed but a shadow against the stars in the midnight sky. He wished with his heart for a fire so he could see her expression. She sighed, but not with exasperation. A sweet sigh. He stood and embraced her, as she crumpled against him with a ragged sob. One sob turned into more until she cried with childlike abandon against his chest. "Shh, shh, *mo chroi*. I've got you now."

"What am I to do? I can't deny my love for you. I never stopped. I just shoved my feelings into a convenient hole in my heart. But I... Lochlann..."

"Your husband was a good man. He deserved better than a cold death on a battlefield. We'll honor his memory, yes?"

She sniffed, tears streaking down her face. "He was kind to me."

"And so he should have been. I'm glad he treated you well. I aim to do the same."

Rustling in the bushes made them both spin to face the threat, but it was only Ciaran.

"Ciaran?" His cousin appeared and Éamonn slapped him on the back. "I thought the English took you!" Deirdre emerged from the darkness, eyeing Katie. After a long moment of staring daggers at each other, Katie hugged her sister tight. When they finally parted, Deirdre glanced between Katie and Éamonn, her eyes wide.

Ciaran let out a snort. "They did, but we slipped away, no thanks to you. Some fighting among the drunks pulled some soldiers from their posts. I convinced the other prisoners to overpower the two left. Most of us escaped into the night. A grand caper, all in all."

"If a bunch of prisoners is on the loose, we'd best get going. They'll come searching. Did you save the horses, by any chance?"

Ciaran shook his head, glancing at his feet. "No, they've still got those, and most of our packs. We've got nothing but our clothes."

Éamonn grabbed his own pack from the ground. "Well, we can get more supplies in Inverness. I don't like the idea of walking through the night, but we need a head start. I've bread to tide you over if you're hungry."

Katie snatched the loaf from his hand. "I'm starved!"

Deirdre's voice held a childish mixture of whining and demanding. "Why should we go to Inverness? Shouldn't we head straight back to Campbeltown?"

Éamonn shouldered his pack. "We've got to get supplies first."

Deirdre snorted with derision. "Hmph. No. No, we don't."

"Deirdre, we won't find any towns on the way. This is the highlands of Scotland, not the Dublin Pale."

The dark-haired girl lifted her chin. "We can get plenty of supplies right down the road."

Ciaran crossed himself. "The ambush site? Deirdre, I'm not robbing the dead!" For once, Éamonn agreed with his cousin.

She rolled her eyes. "Why? They aren't using them. Most of the soldiers won't even have family to bury them."

Katie burst into tears. Éamonn rushed to comfort her as Deirdre scowled.

"We need to bury him, Éamonn. He d-deserves that, does he not?"

"He does, Katie, he does. New plan, Ciaran. We go bury Lochlann, and then we find new clothes." He turned to Katie. "Do you want to bury Donald, too?"

Her spine stiffened. "Donald can rot on the cursed ground. I hope his black soul is burning in Hell for eternity." Her voice hardened into a caustic note Éamonn had never heard from her.

Éamonn pulled her into his arms again. "Did he hurt you, *mo chroí?*"

She didn't cry this time, but she spoke with steel in her voice. "He hit me as hard as Da ever did. He didn't take me or anything like that, though I swear he came close. No, the world is better off without the likes of him, no question."

Éamonn:

They watched their steps, anxious not to trod upon a dead body. Pools of blood and body pieces littered the field. A flock of ravens flew away as they approached, squawking in complaint.

Deirdre stopped to examine a finely tooled saddle. "We don't know for certain we're stealing from the dead. Perhaps the owner's just injured. A saddle this nice could feed us all for weeks, and buy us passage back to Ireland."

Éamonn scratched his chin. "That's a fair point. But who could buy it? We couldn't sell it here. Which means we'd have to lug it back to the coast."

In the end, they left the saddle, despite Deirdre's urging. They kept searching until they found Lochlann. Katie and Deirdre washed her husband's body and wrapped him in a mostly clean tent cloth while Ciaran and Éamonn dug a shallow grave, underneath a willow tree. Katie said a few mumbled words as Éamonn kept an eye out for any soldiers.

Once they buried Lochlann, no one had much strength left, so they found a clearing well off the main track and slept. They only had Éamonn's pack and a few supplies Deirdre stole from the battlefield, and Lochlann's sword. Ciaran declared he wouldn't touch those items. No horses, no food, no tools, and only the clothes on their backs. Even Deirdre wouldn't steal bloody clothing from dead bodies.

He lay down next to Katie under a massive oak tree, stretching out his back and with an arm under his head. She was already asleep, her breath even and shallow.

The nightmare came as soon as he shut his eyes. Éamonn couldn't move at all as the tendrils from the bog enveloped every limb, dragging him into the mire. He resisted, but he had no strength and he succumbed to the darkness.

Éamonn woke up first, searching for a brook to refill his waterskin. When he returned, he offered each a drink as they woke.

He must find men to gamble with. He'd saved the few coins from the prior evening, thank God, so he had a stake. But they needed so much. Food, drink, horses, and boat fare. They might pass on buying horses until they returned to Ireland. But Campbeltown lay sheer across the country again, somewhere to the southwest. The few folks they'd met had very little to win, and trying left him so ill he could barely get up the next day.

Katie's skirts had rips and stains from grime and sap, but she had a huge *arisaid* to keep her warm. Her hair looked like a tangled bird's nest. Ciaran looked like death. Deirdre had curled into herself, all sparkle having fled from her eyes. Éamonn felt sorry for the girl, but he steeled himself against pity. That way lay madness.

"The day is bright, and the weather is fine. Let's take advantage while we can. We'll have at least a week's walk back to the ferry port. One step at a time, aye?"

Ciaran exchanged a glance with Deirdre and scowled at Éamonn. "And who put you in charge, I might ask?"

Éamonn blinked several times. "I put myself in charge. Do you have a better idea?"

His cousin dropped his gaze. "Not really, no. I just didn't like the way you ordered us about."

Éamonn grinned and cuffed Ciaran on the shoulder. "Not orders. Common sense, to be sure. First town we find, I'll win us coin so we can sleep in proper beds. Ciaran, would you mind hunting on the way?"

"With what? I lost my traps with my saddle bags."

"Oh, right. Bloody hell."

Deirdre spoke in a flat voice. "Give me foraging time. I can find plants or berries. I'm good with such things."

Éamonn placed a hand on her shoulder. "That's a good idea. Do you want to take time before we leave, or take side trips as we travel?"

"Both." She stood, dusted her skirts off, and disappeared into the trees.

Katie placed a hand on his arm. "She does know her plants and herbs."

"She's the best source we've got at the moment. While she's off, let's take stock of what we have."

He emptied his pack on the ground. His dice and cup, a couple small loaves of horsebread, a hunk of cheese, and dried meat. The waterskin, a clean shirt, breeks, and woolen stockings in much need of darning. The music he'd retrieved from the MacCrimmons' house. His belt knife, a half-bag of oats, and a horse blanket completed the inventory.

He passed out the bread, saving the meat and cheese for when Deirdre returned. Despite her manipulations, she deserved a share of everything.

The morning passed in aching minutes, gray and sodden. Katie scrubbed at the worst of the stains in her clothing while Ciaran slumped on a log.

Éamonn sat next to him. "Ciaran? Talk to me, cousin. What's on your mind?"

"Nothing."

"That's a load of shite. You've been sulky ever since we started. We've succeeded in our quest, and now we're on our way home. Why're you so sour?"

Ciaran glared at him, and if looks could kill, he should have been a quivering mass of burning ashes. Éamonn pulled back, surprised at the venom in his friend's eyes. "What? What have I done to make you so angry?"

Ciaran dropped his gaze again and mumbled.

"Speak up, man!"

He glanced up and said, with great care for enunciation, "Deirdre."

"What about her?"

A flash of anger sparked in Ciaran's eyes. "That's what you did. You took her. You took her like all the women, and now she loves you!"

"By the name of all that's holy, I don't want Deirdre. I never wanted her. She pushed herself on me until I couldn't—"

Ciaran jumped up and shouted in his cousin's face. "That's a load of shite! You're always the one who got the girls. Any time I fancied a lass, they loved you. A flash of your smile and your damned blue eyes, and they panted after you like a bitch in heat! After that, they're spoiled for ordinary men, men like me. It's always you! Why can't you just leave me the one, eh? Just one?"

He huffed like a boar, his face an inch from Éamonn's.

Éamonn kept his voice reasonable. "You can have her, I don't want her! I've got my Katie." He tried a little push with his talent as he placed a hand on Ciaran's shoulder.

He flung Éamonn's hand away. "Sure, and aren't I always to take your castoffs?" With a final scowl, Ciaran stalked off into the woods.

Éamonn didn't know what to do. Everyone seemed angry with him now. This had turned into such a mess.

Well, he must get his little group home, even if none of them spoke to him. When Katie returned, he discussed their route. Heading due west until they came to Loch Ness, then following that south would be the easiest path.

Soon after, Deirdre reappeared with a skirt full of forage. Raspberries, wild strawberries, and dark crowberries. In addition, she found clover, chicory leaves, and dandelions. Fireweed and mushrooms rounded out the haul. Éamonn brought out his meat and cheese, the last bits of bread, and they shared a feast.

Ciaran returned and ignored Éamonn as Deirdre gave him a share of food. He acted solicitous of both the women, laughing and joking with them. After their meal, they trudged down the road, still tired but determined to move.

A few villagers yielded coin to Éamonn's gambling tricks, but he found little joy in cheating these poor crofters. If they hadn't been desperate, he'd never have used the magic. Shame weighed heavy on his shoulders, not only for swindling strangers, but for being with Deirdre, dragging his cousin halfway across this strange country, and for failing the love of his life.

After he earned enough for their food, supplies, and boat fare, he stopped altogether. His weakness after each use of his power grew almost debilitating. The dice themselves lost all their thrill now he could control the outcome. The brooch's magic had gutted one of his oldest joys in life.

Katie still acted prickly and warm in turns, but she stood by his side. He gloried in that minor victory. Ciaran and Deirdre spent more time together. Often the pairs went off on their own after setting up camp. The small bit of privacy kept a cautious peace.

The first night they camped together, as Ciaran and Deirdre retired to their side of the clearing, Éamonn rubbed Katie's tense shoulder. For a moment, she relaxed into the massage, but then snapped her head around. "What do you think you're doing, Éamonn Doherty?"

Surprised, he pulled back. "I think I'm relaxing your shoulders. Is that not working?"

"I'll have you know, Éamonn, I will not allow such intimacy from a man who isn't my husband. Do you understand?"

"As you say, Katie." Éamonn pouted but couldn't argue. She was well within her rights, and he admired her convictions. Instead, they spoke about the journey, getting to know the other's fears and hopes. Katie avoided any mention of her time on Skye, though.

One night, as heavy rain halted their evening progress, the four of them huddled together under a makeshift tent, sharing each other's warmth. Éamonn didn't like being between Deirdre and Katie. The raven-haired girl still tried to touch him any chance she got. He had no wish to wake once again with his manhood hard in her hands. Nor did he have any desire to explain such a situation to Katie.

Just as he drifted off, Katie whispered in his ear, "Éamonn, are you asleep yet?"

He smiled, though he knew she couldn't tell in the inky blackness. "Yes, sound asleep."

"I never thanked you."

"Thanked me? For what?"

"For saving me from the Highlanders. For trying to get me back from Lochlann. For never giving up. For everything."

Éamonn didn't know what to say. He fumbled around until he found her face and stroked her cheek. He could only tell the truth. "The only thing I could do, *mo chroí*. You are my soul's home, after all. And I'll never leave home again."

He had no nightmares that night.

Chapter Fifteen

Katie:

That first night, they bought some ratty tents off the back of a questionable trader's wagon. While they kept most of the rain at bay, the tents leaked and smelled of rot, putting everyone in a foul mood. Curses and glares flew. Luckily, Deirdre found an abandoned crofter's cottage near dusk on the third day on her foraging trip.

The thatch needed work, but the roof kept the now-steady rain off their heads. they even found a bedstead inside, and a table, though not much else. The wind whistled outside, but the cottage should keep them warm. Katie shivered. She hadn't been warm in days.

Their meager stores had grown with Éamonn's efforts, enough to see them started on their trek back to Ireland. He even won enough to purchase an old mule to carry their supplies. A side of ham, several loaves of coarse bread, a bag of apples, and a jug of ale. They each had blankets and a decent cloak.

Éamonn dragged logs into a circle, then tried to get the hearth lit. Katie sat like a shriveled lump and shivering from the damp, despite her cloak. The scent of damp earth and woodsmoke filled her nose. Once the fire flickered to life, he sat next to her, his arm around her shoulders. "Katie? Are you well?"

She just shook her head, shivering. Éamonn lifted her chin. "What's amiss, lass? Have you taken a chill?"

Katie spoke through chattering teeth. "I just c-c-can't seem to get w-warm."

He dragged one log in closer to the fire and pulled her into place. Then he sat behind her, wrapping his legs and arms about her small body to share his warmth. Smoke burned her eyes, but the warmth was worth the sting. His sweat from crafting the firepit and starting the fire and warmed her.

Deirdre snorted, but Katie didn't feel like comforting her sister. While they'd never been especially close, their kinship wore prickly thorns, and Deirdre's seduction of Éamonn made everything even more complicated. She blamed Éamonn, but she knew Deirdre. Seeing her sister so miserable now that Éamonn had dropped her made Katie both smug and sorry. Maybe Ciaran would steady Deirdre. He obviously wanted the task. His slavish devotion made Katie cringe, but Deirdre seemed oblivious to his efforts.

When her shivering eased, Éamonn still clung tight, enveloping her with his arms. She might sink into a deep, dreamless sleep for a week like this.

Éamonn's voice sounded far away. "Katie?"

Her muzzy mind drifted. "Hmm?"

"Must we go back to Ireland?"

That brought her back to her senses. "What are you talking about?"

"Hear me out. What if we stayed right here, and rebuilt this cottage? We'd start a family and live our lives in peace."

Katie's eyes widened. "Are you completely daft? What do you know about farming?"

He didn't answer, and she twisted around to stare at him. "Well?"

"I lived on a farm. Until Da came back from his wanderings, we all worked the land. Remember, he left us. We milked cows, plowed fields, and harvested wheat. Little did we know he'd be gone a full two years. We thought he'd abandoned us. We learned all we could about farming."

"Oh." She felt sheepish now, remembering that tragic story.

He squeezed her shoulders. "What do you say?"

A settled life. Before Lochlann, she'd never even considered such a thing, not with being raised a Traveler. This cottage was a far cry from Lochlann's grand house, bless his soul. Would she own that big farmhouse now, with both brothers dead? But she didn't want it. She wanted nothing to do with anything tainted by Donald. Not now, not ever.

She'd never been greedy, but grubbing in the mud for a subsistence living here was worlds apart from living in a large house with glass windows and feather beds. Besides, any children would crowd them out of this tiny cottage in a few years.

Children.

With a flash of panic, Katie counted the days. No, she couldn't be. Already?

Over three weeks ago, she'd first lain with Lochlann. By her reckoning, she should have had her courses a week ago. Or was it more? *Women are late all the time. It doesn't mean a thing.* But she'd never been late, not once since her courses started.

How could she marry Éamonn, if indeed that's what he wanted, while carrying Lochlann's child? Tears bubbled up inside her. Why could nothing be simple? Never in her life had she cried as much as these last weeks. She'd become a different person, and that convinced her she must be pregnant.

"Katie? Katie, why are you crying? We don't have to stay here. Shh...shh...."

How could she tell him until she knew for certain? Maybe it was nothing. Maybe she wasn't pregnant.

The next day dawned cool, but the sun burned the mist into a glowing morning. Deirdre woke up and tramped around for her daily foraging. She returned with potatoes someone had planted in the garden, perhaps their last act before leaving. Katie hadn't realized the Scots grew them. The tubers made a welcome addition to their stores.

When they got back on the road, Katie gave the lonely cottage one last glance. Could she have made a happy life in that cottage with Éamonn? Or would he leave her when he discovered she carried Lochlann's child?

Should she give in to Éamonn, and lie with him, so he thought the child was his? The sheer manipulation of that idea disgusted her. That was something her sister might do, but Katie didn't want a marriage based on lies.

The sound of horses on the road made them pull to the side to let the other people pass. After the battle, none of them had any wish for confrontation. This morning, they'd already passed a cartful of villagers going to a wool fair, three young men out hunting, and a boy who darted out of the woods with a ball. The lad took one look at them and dashed back out of sight. His antics brought a smile to Katie's lips until she remembered her own possible condition.

Horse hooves clattered around the next bend, so they pulled their mule to the side and waited as English soldiers came into view. Each Traveler kept their faces down as the troop passed. The lead horse stopped, and Katie glanced up to see why.

The officer with a troop of eight redcoats peered at them. "And just what business does this ragtag bunch of beggars have on the King's Road, Martin?"

"I don't know, sir. They might be gypsies. Thieves, mayhap, or even murderers."

"Murderers, aye? Well, we shouldn't let that sort wander around free, should we?"

Éamonn spoke in a meeker voice than she'd ever heard from him. "Please, sir, we're honest folk, Travelers from Ireland. We're just headed back home now."

After staring at each for a long moment, he dismounted. Katie tensed and scooted behind Éamonn.

The officer stared at Deirdre, from the tangled black crown of her head to her muddy, torn shoes. "What do you think, Chambers? Can you find a pretty lass underneath all the Irish grime?"

Chambers grimaced, wrinkling his nose and squinting his eyes. "I think so, sir. Hard to tell, though."

Deirdre shrunk behind Ciaran.

"Here now, we won't hurt you, girl. Just want to get a proper gander, is all." Chambers grabbed her arm. Ciaran protested, but the soldier shoved him aside.

Éamonn spoke up, "Please, sir, we just want to go home. We want no trouble here."

The colonel spat at Éamonn's feet. "I'm not talking to you, you bloody bog-trotter. Now we won't do no harm. Just a kiss, eh?" The Englishman pulled Deirdre out of Chamber's grip and snaked an arm around her waist, pulling her in. He used his other hand to hold her head while he planted a wet, sloppy kiss on her lips. She wriggled and cried out for him to stop, but he laughed and clutched her tighter to his body. He nuzzled her neck, his hands grabbing her breasts. As he buried his face in her cleavage, her cries turned to sobs.

Ciaran burst out. "Stop it! Stop touching her!" He rushed at the colonel, but Chambers tripped him. Ciaran sprawled into the muddy road. Martin dismounted to stand next to his comrade, eyeing Éamonn.

Ciaran tried to scramble to his feet, but Chambers placed a boot on his neck. "That wouldn't be wise, now, would it?"

Katie elbowed Éamonn. "Do something!"

"There are eight of them. If all he wants is a kiss, she's survived worse. But we can't fight them all, Katie."

Despite all her anger, jealousy, and rage at Deirdre, she remained her sister. Born of the same mother, they'd grown up in the same places and survived the brutal attentions of their father.

While mustering all her rage and authority, she stepped out from behind Éamonn to make her own demands for release, but Éamonn pulled her back.

Katie whispered in furious anger. "If you won't stop them, I will!"

Now, the colonel kneaded Deirdre's buttocks and ground his hips against hers. Deirdre stood stock still, tears streaking the dirt on her cheek.

Éamonn whispered back. "I'm keeping you from the same fate, Katie. We've got to bide our time!"

The whispers attracted Martin's attention. "Hey, you two! What's all the discussion about?"

Éamonn pushed Katie back behind him. "Nothing, sir."

"Who is that behind you? I thought her a child, but she's got more curves than this one, sir!" Martin darted over to Katie and yanked her arm.

Katie spat in his face. "Get your stinking paws off me, you rutting bastard!"

Éamonn jerked her back from the soldier's arm and stood eye to eye with the other man. In a firm voice, he urged calm, pouring charm into his words. "Now, gentlemen, everything's grand. We're no threat to you. Now you've gotten your kiss, we'll be on our way."

With his words, an inexplicable peace flowed over Katie. She stared at Éamonn, wondering what he'd done, and the colonel glanced at Éamonn, too. The other soldiers mounted their horses, and Katie let out her breath.

Ciaran gained his feet and inserted himself between Deirdre and the others.

The colonel turned back with one eyebrow lifted, "I want just one more kiss from the lass before I leave."

Ciaran planted his feet and lifted his chin.

The colonel drew his pistol. "Move aside, boy. You don't want any trouble, as your friend said, right?"

Deirdre darted toward the trees.

Éamonn yanked Katie's arm, gesturing for Ciaran and Deirdre to follow with the mule. "We don't want any trouble, that's right, sir. We'll just be going now."

Chambers said, "Sir, we do have to get to Inverness."

"Blast Inverness." The colonel lunged past Ciaran and grabbed Deirdre. Ciaran tackled him, and the pistol fired.

Grabbing Deidre's hand, Éamonn pulled her away from Ciaran and the colonel as they struggled on the ground. The other soldiers dismounted and drew their swords.

With a face punch, Ciaran extracted himself. They ran for the thickest part of the forest.

Éamonn caught Katie's shoulders as he turned to the left. "Split up! Deirdre, stay with Ciaran!" They ran left while Ciaran and Deirdre fled right. She couldn't catch her breath, and her heart might burst from her chest. Thorns and branches ripped her clothes and scratched her skin as they scrambled through the underbrush and trees.

Katie ducked one thick, low branch and jumped another tangle of thorns. Curses came from behind, but they faded. As they emerged from the edge of the forest, a massive moor covered in brown heather spread before them.

Éamonn crawled under a canopy of low heather branches. "Quick, under here!" He disappeared. She followed him into the muck. By the time they'd crawled deep into the heather, they both panted, even more bedraggled and muddy than before.

"Éamonn—"

"Shh. Until we know they're gone. Breathe lightly."

They waited in agony. Every twig or leaf moving in the wind meant danger. She kept expecting a shot from the redcoats and daren't move a muscle. Her stomach ached and her head grew dizzy from holding her breath. She exhaled in slow, shallow breaths but her heart wouldn't stop hammering.

Just as her breath slowed, crunching boots and shouts in the distance made her tense again. Éamonn placed his hand on hers. This grain of reassurance helped more than she expected. She turned her head to see him in the bit of sunlight which worked its way into the heather. He looked drawn, tense, and slightly green.

Mud and blood streaked his cheek. Where had the blood come from? The red-brown smear looked stark against his pale skin.

A branch cracking snapped her attention back to their pursuers.

Through the gaps in the heather, she spied a soldier on the edge of the forest, not far from their hiding spot. He scanned across the moor. She prayed to Brigid he wouldn't think to search under the heather.

The soldier stomped back into the woods. She let out one long, shallow breath and took another glance at Éamonn.

He swallowed and spoke in a bare whisper, "We must remain still until we're certain they've left."

Minutes turned into an eternity under the heather. Every scratch and cut she'd collected on the mad flight now screamed. Her skin felt like a pincushion, poked and sliced into so much ground beef. Her nose itched as buzzing flies and midges tickled and stung. Fighting the urge to sneeze, she rubbed her nose. She daren't sniff.

What seemed like years later, Éamonn let out a breath. "I'll crawl to the edge and scout. Stay here in case I'm taken."

What would she do if they took him? Alone on this blasted heath with no one to help? If the soldiers found him, they'd search for her. She had no safety at all.

"We're grand, Katie. They've gone."

She pushed out of the muddy mess. She craved a river to cleanse the muck and grime, to rid herself of stinging flies.

Katie glanced around. Only twittering birds and buzzing insects surrounded them, with an occasional bough shifting from a summer breeze. "What about Ciaran and Deirdre?"

Éamonn shrugged as he peered through the trees. "They know where we're headed. We'll wait for them in Campbeltown."

Her hand flew up to cover her mouth. "Oh, Éamonn! Our mule and supplies?"

"Even if the soldiers left them, we can't risk going back. Maybe Ciaran and Deirdre can. They headed in the other direction and might circle back. I have my pack, which means I have my dice. We can earn more money. First, we find some folks willing to gamble."

"First, we need to find a river. I'm filthy and itchy."

"Aye, I'll need to be presentable to any dice games. And you, my dear, are a right mess, indeed!"

"Beast. You look no better. What's this?" Seeing a line of red on his thigh, she touched the warm, sticky gash.

Éamonn waved his hand. "A scratch, nothing more. Bloody bastard nicked me with his sword at the last moment. I'll be grand, but I want to wash that out."

Katie:

Even after they found a river and scrubbed their bodies, Éamonn's wound grew red and puffy by the next day. He limped as the day wore on, and his skin turned paler.

They traveled southwest along the road. When travelers came from the other direction, they scattered into the brush. They didn't want to risk altercations, randy soldiers, or highwaymen.

She'd heard from Deirdre that honey kept blood clean. Katie found a honeycomb, risking bee stings to gather sweet, sticky honey to dress the wound.

The first night they had found a hamlet, just four farm crofts, and a storehouse where the village gathered in the evenings. A bit of gambling brought their funds to reasonable levels and earned them a night in a warm, dry stable.

By the third day, pus wept from the gash and Katie's concern about the wound grew. She undressed and washed the wound every time they came to a stream, but his thigh burned hot, tender to the touch.

They found no trace of Ciaran or Deirdre. They doggedly pushed on toward Campbeltown. After the third day, they stumbled into the port town of Oban. Éamonn splurged on a room and collapsed on the narrow cot as soon as they entered. Sweat ran down his face. Katie needed to find the town healer.

After taking coins from his pack, she left the inn to search for someone who might help. She passed an inn and several closed shops before finding the main street. If they hadn't told Deirdre and Ciaran to meet them at Campbeltown, they'd arrange passage from here to Ireland. However, a big port town meant healers.

After the fourth inn, she came across a pair of filthy beggars, sitting with their backs to a cart. A flea-bitten mule gnawed at scraps of grass growing next to the building.

"Katie?"

Katie stopped and turned, incredulous, at her sister's voice. Deirdre had transformed so much, Katie barely recognized her. Her luscious, dark hair looked matted and dirty. Their clothes were nothing but rags. A long cut marred one cheek, with a nasty black scab over her left eye. Ciaran sat, sporting a black eye and several other bruises and cuts.

Katie hugged her sister and almost gagged from her horrible stench. While holding Deirdre at arms-length, she looked her up and down. "Tell me what happened."

Deirdre sobbed, falling back into her arms. Katie gathered her little sister close and rocked her, crooning under her breath.

As Deirdre's tears turned to halting sobs, Katie wiped her face with her skirt, revealing more bruises. "Did they catch you, then?"

Deirdre glanced over at Ciaran and swallowed. He nodded, so she spoke, "They did. They gave us a hard time, but then they left."

Katie caught her sister's gaze, but Deirdre gave a small shake of her head. So, they hadn't done anything worse. She hugged Deirdre tight, and her sister trembled. Katie held her until she stopped shaking.

Ciaran said, "I'm not sure why they stopped. We didn't question the good luck and rushed east as soon as we could."

The spark had fled from Deirdre's eyes, all coy flirting seemed to have drained from her. Confused on how to deal with this change, Katie turned to practical matters. "Éamonn and I arrived last night. We have a little money, but he's got wound fever. I'm searching for a healer."

Deirdre spoke without inflection, "I've got no supplies, but I can forage. If you've coin, we should be able to buy what I'll need."

"Let's get you fed. We'll have to find better clothes, too." Katie's voice sounded over-cheerful to her own ears.

After eating a simple meal and a wash, they found the local herbwoman. Deirdre visited Éamonn's bedside, fumbling in her pack for something. When she pulled out several bundles of herbs, Katie narrowed her eyes.

Her sister had always been canny with herbs and their magic. Katie recognized some, like the foxglove. Now, she spied the moss, rose petals, and lavender Deirdre sprinkled into Éamonn's tea.

Katie touched the closest bundle. "What are those for?"

With a shrug, Dierdre poured hot water from the hearth kettle. "Just some things to ease his pain and bring down the fever."

"Rose petals? I've never heard of them for fever."

The younger sister shot her a sharp glance. "And since when have you been a herbwoman, sister mine? Get yourself downstairs and leave me to my craft."

"Your craft. Which craft is that, Deirdre? Herbwoman or witch? Nurse or wanton?"

Deirdre flicked her hand and stirred the tea. "Believe what you will, Katie. I truly don't care any longer."

Katie couldn't think of anything else to say but vowed to watch Deirdre's actions, as well as Éamonn's reactions. Then she joined Ciaran in the inn's main room.

After a few ales, Ciaran's silence spilled into slurred words. "It was horrible. I couldn't stop them. Oh, I tried, but there were just too many. Why did you both abandon us? We might have fought them off if you stayed."

"We tried to split them up. Some followed us, we heard them. We only escaped by hiding under the heather."

With a snort, Ciaran quaffed his fourth mug of ale. He rubbed his bloodshot eyes. They seemed as hollow and lifeless as Deirdre's. "We held on to the wagon and mule. The soldiers wanted nothing to do with our raggedy things after they tired of us. I'm still not sure what happened. Deirdre grabbed her necklace, mumbled something, and threw it at them. Then they just… left." His voice turned bitter. Katie didn't blame him in the slightest.

He lifted his mug in the air with a half-smile. "And now, Éamonn to the rescue once more."

True, Éamonn's gambling prowess had pulled their feet from the fire several times. But as ill as he was, he in no way resembled a rescuing hero.

They drank in silence. Ciaran simmered with resentment and anger, but she had no way of diffusing his sullen thoughts. What had Deirdre done with her necklace? She didn't even remember her sister wearing a necklace. She must have kept it hidden under her chemise. Katie just hoped Deirdre had the herblore to heal Éamonn.

Éamonn:

Éamonn finally roused enough to sit up and eat after two worrying days. He felt like he'd wasted away to skin and bones.

Katie held his hand when Deirdre came in with broth. "I'll feed him, Katie. You go on downstairs."

Deirdre had gained some weight back and looked less like a starved scarecrow. Katie didn't budge. "Thank you, Deirdre, but

I can feed him. You deserve rest. You've barely slept since we got here."

Deirdre pressed her lips together and placed the tray on a table. She spoke in a clipped tone. "No. I'm the healer, and I'll care for him. You go downstairs. You'll find plenty to keep you company."

Katie's eyes flashed. "And just what is that supposed to mean?"

Deirdre gave an over-sweet smile. "Exactly what I said. You've never had a problem finding companionship."

"Oh, and you're one to talk! At least I was a maid on my wedding night!"

Hands on her hips, Deirdre snapped, "So you've already killed off your first husband, and trying to steal the second one?"

"Steal? I did not steal Éamonn! He was never yours to begin with!"

Deirdre's lips curled into a knowing smile. "He was mine on Skye!"

"Only because you worked some sort of magic spell over him!"

"It wasn't magic!"

Katie growled, "Witch!"

Éamonn didn't have the energy to intervene. He should stop them, but he knew better than to stick his hand between two women fighting.

They glared at each other, almost toe to toe. Ciaran opened the door to peek in but quickly shut it again. Éamonn wished he could follow his cousin to safety.

Deirdre shoved Katie in the shoulder. Katie returned the gesture and, in a moment, they pulled hair, scratched faces, and ripped clothing.

Despite his guilt at being the cause, the fight fascinated him. Women didn't often outright brawl. They sniped well enough without resorting to violence. But occasionally, rage and jealousy needed more than sarcasm and furious insults.

Éamonn loved Katie heart and soul, but he admired Deirdre's inner strength. She had more determination than a score of men he knew. He didn't want either of them hurt.

A grunt brought his attention back to the fracas. They had fallen to the floor, wrestling in a flurry of skirts and arms. Katie elbowed Deirdre in the stomach. The dark-haired sister jerked Katie's hair. Her cry of pain turned to sheer rage as she raked her nails across her sister's cheek.

As weak as he felt, Éamonn couldn't let this go on with blood drawn. He struggled to stand. When his foot caught in the bedding, he tumbled to the wooden floor with a mighty *thump,* distracting both girls.

The fall knocked the wind from him. He scrabbled on the wood to get decent purchase, but his feet still tangled in the blankets. *Well, this is undignified.*

"Éamonn! Éamonn, what are you doing? You'll undo all my healing!" Deirdre's simpering voice hovered near his ear. He cracked one eye to see her kneeling over him, patting his hair like a favorite dog.

"Stop touching him, you bitch. You've no claim on him."

"I've more claim than you. You've not even lain with him! You and your high and mighty ways."

Katie slapped Deirdre, a sharp smack in the silence. "Better than being a witch in league with the devil!"

Deirdre sat back on her heels and stared at nothing, her face turning white.

Her voice turned contrite, "Deirdre—" She put a hand on her sister's shoulder.

Deirdre shrugged her hand away, still gazing out into space. Then she rose and left the room, shutting the door behind her.

Katie sighed and shut her eyes.

Éamonn propped himself up on one elbow. "Are you quite done now?" He hadn't meant to sound judgmental, but his tone came out harsh.

"I never know when to shut up. It's always been a problem. I didn't *mean* to hurt her. Not really. She just makes me so angry!"

Katie helped Éamonn get back onto the bed as he asked with a wry smile, "And jealous?"

"Well, yes, I am jealous if you must know. I've always been envious of her easy ways, her height, her straight hair. She brings out the worst in me."

Éamonn wanted to wipe the sadness from her eyes, and he took her hand. "You have no need to be jealous of me, *mo chroí.* I am yours, for now and always. She may have nursed me back to health, but the memory of you is what kept me going through the fever-dreams. I just imagined your wonderful curly red hair, your sweet smile, and your sharp wit to be at peace and have the desire to hold on."

Katie's lovely smile seemed sad. She pressed into his shoulder, and he tightened his grip. "Éamonn?"

"Yes, *mo chroí*?"

"No, no, it's nothing."

He lifted her chin and gazed into her eyes. "What's nothing?"

"I'll tell you later."

"Hmm." Éamonn believed people could have secrets but shouldn't lie to each other. She'd already been through so much. If she needed time to get used to him again, he must honor that.

They sat for a while in companionable silence. He treasured just being with her, after chasing after the dream of her so long. He held Katie's hand in his own, marveling at how soft her skin felt.

As they went downstairs to have some supper, the main room seemed all but empty. Just one old man in a corner, nursing a mug of ale, and their landlady.

He turned to their hostess as he paid her a doit for their meal. "Have you seen my cousin this evening?"

"Aye, the dark lad? He's off with the lass several hours past."

"Off with?"

"Sure and they left, packs on their backs."

Panic gripped his heart as he exchanged a quick glance with Katie and then ran upstairs to their rooms. Sure enough, all of Ciaran and Deirdre's things were gone. Along with his money and a good portion of their food.

Ciaran:

Whenever he caught a break, another disaster came along to drag him down again. Deirdre seemed in a dour mood since she'd driven those soldiers off, and nothing Ciaran did brought back the delightful, seductively sweet girl he'd fallen for. Their mule went lame, so they needed to find another pack animal.

They also needed to ration the money they'd stolen from Éamonn. While he experienced strong twinges of guilt for that theft, Ciaran knew his cousin would get more funds. The coins they took should get them back down the coast to Campbeltown and it would allow them to travel apart from Éamonn and his too-obvious charms. Ciaran needed more time alone to give Deirdre a chance to fall in love with him, away from his cousin.

The fare across the sea would be cheaper with two people and no horses. But his homesickness grew, and Ciaran still carried the cart and supplies he'd retrieved after the soldier's attack. He considered those things his wages for bearing the brunt of their attentions when Éamonn ran away, like he always did. Besides, he might have to sell more things to pay for passage to Ireland.

No one in Oban planned to sail to Ireland, though. Sailors said a fierce storm lashed the Irish coast. Few captains wanted to chance such a rocky landing in a tempest.

Deirdre had gone to the herbwomen to replenish her herb supplies. With little to do but wait for better weather, he remained restless. Despite the sailor's reports of storms, Ciaran sat on the sea wall, gazing across the calm sea. Waves lapped and broke below his feet. In the distance rose the humped blue forms of the Isle of Mull and Lismore.

And if Éamonn fell to ruin, he'd shed few tears. His cousin had always bested him at everything, whether wooing women or playing dice games. He stood taller, had a broader smile, and those damn blue-green eyes that fascinated the girls so. The only thing Ciaran did better was leatherwork, and Éamonn had a fair hand even at that exacting skill.

And he'd stolen both Katie and Deirdre from him.

Both women falling in love with Éamonn didn't seem fair. Didn't Ciaran deserve one? After all, Katie granted that first fiery kiss. And then along comes Éamonn and sweeps her off her feet. Without even trying, he twisted Deirdre's emotions to the point the girls fought tooth and nail for him.

And to top it all, Éamonn had left them...*abandoned them...* to those vicious soldiers. He still wanted to cry in frustration at his inability to save Deirdre from the beasts, but the best he could do was comfort her and hope it would matter.

Well, all great things must come to an end. And Ciaran knew just how to do that. He slapped his hands on his knees as he formed a plan.

His cousin would need to gamble a lot to earn their fare across the Irish Sea. Éamonn had skill enough to arouse suspicions about cheating. A few whispers in the ears of some sore losers might create a fitting retribution for all the luck Éamonn previously enjoyed. Ciaran had grown so bloody tired of his cousin always winning, whether in gambling or in love. It was high time he lost, and Ciaran had formed a plan to make that happen.

Not long ago, panic about witchcraft burned across the land, leaving in their wake smoking husks of burnt old women and friendless men. People feared what they didn't understand, and men's memories of those fears were long.

Ciaran sat on his sea wall, gazing at the water but not seeing it. Visions of Deirdre swam in his mind. Deirdre of the midnight hair, the rosebud lips, and the enchanting laugh. *His* Deirdre.

What would he do when they returned to Ireland? He'd asked Deirdre to be his wife a dozen times already. Each time, she'd avoided answering, explaining she needed more time. He knew what she didn't say. She wanted more time to win Éamonn back. That made his head spin with jealousy. Reaching into his pack, he yanked out a wineskin and gave it an angry stare. Then he put it back.

Deirdre came up next to him. "It's not every man that thinks the better of that. Here, I'll put it away."

"I can do that, but thanks."

As he placed the wineskin into his pack, the sound of crinkled paper got his attention. Ciaran fingered the fine pieces of vellum Éamonn had rescued from the MacCrimmons' home. They felt dry and smooth, with black, scrawled musical notations. Ciaran couldn't read music. He could barely read anything. But Turlough treasured these pages, and he'd be thrilled to get them back. *If Éamonn doesn't come back, Turlough might accept me as a son rather than a nephew. I'd take Éamonn's place in his heart.*

If only he could take Éamonn's place in Deirdre's heart.

Chapter Sixteen

Éamonn:

The click of the dice, and even without the thrill of anticipation, Éamonn had won again. He missed the pleasure he used to get with each win, but at least he knew he *would* win. The cheating became a necessity since Ciaran and Deirdre stole their coins. Éamonn was just glad he'd finally healed enough that he could spend the evening gambling. He didn't begrudge them the money, despite his stomach doing roiling backflips at using his power. He would have given them funds had they but asked.

Regardless, Éamonn needed more to pay for their fare to Ireland, and gambling gave him his only chance in a strange city with nothing to trade or sell.

Éamonn's latest win resulted in mutters and resentful glances. Nothing unusual in the gambling ring. He pushed pleasant thoughts through his magic, and the grumbling eased. He'd learned finesse with his gift. When he tried, he could affect more people, and for longer. Still, he'd have to back off before things grew ugly. Éamonn gathered his winnings and rose to his feet. Not a huge amount but sufficient to the day.

"Oi, where are you going, mate? We need a chance to earn our dosh back, now."

"Ah, I must go, lads. I've a lady waiting for me, and one should never leave a lady waiting, now, should one?" With a flash of his teeth and a saucy wink, he turned to stride off.

A hand fell on his shoulder and he turned with a scowl to face this new threat. One of his fellow gamblers backed away with his hands up in surrender. A wiry man, a foot shorter than Éamonn, and no match in a fight. "No worries, mate! Just wanted to bring you this. You left it." He handed Éamonn one of his dice.

Abashed, Éamonn accepted the proffered cube. "Thanks, then. Here, I'll be back tomorrow night if you want a chance to win things back, aye?"

"Aye, that'll do." The man walked off with a shrug, and Éamonn heaved a sigh of relief. Thunder growled in the distance and Éamonn glanced up, despite knowing he'd see nothing in the night sky.

He didn't like winning so many nights in the same place. Such a pattern aroused too many suspicions. But with another two nights of decent winnings, they might afford a boat back home. If he could get used to the illness that slammed into him after each night of using his power.

Home. Such an odd concept to a Traveler. He had spent a few years on his uncle's farm. But, in reality, home had always been his father's wagon, wherever that might stop. Now, home became Katie. Without her, his heart hurt, like what he'd heard about homesickness. Her fiery spark kept his soul alive. If she left, he'd be nothing but a dead coal in a cold hearth.

These ideas ran through his mind as he walked into the inn and saw a large man sitting at a round table with Katie. He squinted as the set of the shoulders seemed so familiar.

"Ruari?"

His brother had just brought a huge mug of ale to his lips. After slamming the mug on the table while the liquid sloshed out, he cried out, "Éamonn!"

In his weakened state, his giant of a brother crushed him as they hugged and pounded each other's back. After they pummeled each other, Ruari held him out at arms-length. "When did you get here? But you're so thin? What happened?"

"I arrived yesterday. A sword cut me, and the wound festered like your arm. How *is* your arm? Better, I hope?"

Ruari held his arm at an odd angle. He flexed his shoulder as if just now remembering the wound that had almost robbed him of the limb. "Not so bad. The skin itches, and my muscle aches when the weather changes. It's bad today."

Éamonn pulled up a stool. "How did you find us?"

After Ruari handed her a coin, Katie fetched Éamonn a mug of ale, and the blond man grinned at her with gratitude before taking a long draft.

His brother shrugged. "By accident. I headed toward Skye when I heard about a dice-man who seemed way too lucky, so I thought it might be you. Then I saw Mistress Katie here walking to the inn, and I followed her."

Éamonn clapped his brother on the good shoulder. "It's great to see you, brother, but why did you come? Did Da get an annulment for Katie? Did she tell you that doesn't matter anymore?"

Ruari gave a nod, but his brow furrowed. "She told me she's widowed. Which is good, because Da couldn't get them to do anything. But I have other news."

Éamonn put his mug down. "What? What's wrong, Ruari?"

"It's Da."

He sat straight, a cold thread curling up his spine. "Da? What's wrong with Da?"

"Remember his cough?"

Éamonn searched back through the trials they'd survived the last weeks and remembered his father's cold and gave a cautious nod. "Aye, I remember."

Ruari stared into his ale. "He got worse. He can't get out of bed now, and Cormac said he doesn't have too long left. Da sent me to find you."

The blond man sprang to his feet, his eyes growing wide. "We've got to get back! Damn, I wish we knew where Deirdre disappeared to. She's good at healing. Katie, can you pack our things? Ruari, do you have enough money to get us back to Ireland? I've got some, but not enough for the two of us, much less all three."

Ruari's expression cleared. "I've got some. Let's see if I have enough."

"If not, we'll just have to steal a boat. I must go back for Da."

When they combined their funds, they came up short. And stealing a boat wouldn't be an option once the storm rolled in. He went out in search of a gambling group, but couldn't find any that early in the evening. Éamonn paced in their room, frustrated and out of ideas.

Katie let out an exasperated sigh. "Will you sit your great, lumbering self down, already? I'm getting dizzy with you walking back and forth like a caged cat." She sat cross-legged near the hearth, mending a bramble tear in her skirt. Ruari perched on the edge of the bed. None of them slept with the furious gale battering the wooden building and the knowledge that Turlough might be dying across that wind-tossed sea.

Éamonn kept pacing. Images of his father haunted him, wasting away in his wagon, with no one to care for him, no one to heal him. Éamonn and Ruari weren't there. Ciaran had gone God knows where. Turlough only had Édaín and Síle with him.

Flashes of memory raced unbidden through his mind. The day his father had left them at their uncle's farm to go *wandering*. The first time Éamonn killed a rabbit, and his father showed him how to dress and skin it. The first time he heard Turlough perform for a large crowd and witnessed the joy his father's music gave others.

He'd taken his father for granted. He begged God now for the chance to get back in time to tell his father how much Éamonn loved him, how much he treasured him in his life.

Katie patted the hearth rug. "Come, sit with me by the fire, please?"

Éamonn had too much pent-up energy. "No, I'll go down to the ale room. I need to do something not just sit and twiddle my thumbs."

When he descended, he finally found some dice games going. Despite his best intentions, though, a night of dicing and cards did little to ease his nervous activity. At least it got him *doing*. Anything but stewing on his father dying, alone, far away.

Éamonn didn't pay attention to the dice and lost several rounds. The losses roused his instincts and he made sure he won the next rounds. Suspicious glances from his gaming companions inspired him to push out a wave of peace almost as an afterthought.

Finally, by his calculations, they should have enough to afford the crossing. He tossed the dice on one last throw. Expecting reluctant congratulations, he gathered his winnings. The other gamblers stared at him in silence. With a nervous laugh, Éamonn stood. The others rose with him.

He backed up to give himself room to run. They moved with him.

One large man clapped a meaty hand on his shoulder. "'Ere now, we think you've been a tad too lucky, Irish."

Éamonn shrugged. "Everyone's got a streak now and then. That's no crime." Another few steps backwards, and he came to a wall. *Hell.*

Five burly men surrounded him.

He held up his hands. "Now, boys, I'm sure you all have warm beds to get home to. How about I stand you all a mug of ale?" The inevitable headache pounded, but Éamonn pushed the brooch's magic harder. He reached into his pouch, pulling out several *doits*. The man on the left, the one who had lost the most that night, knocked the coins out of his hand. They scattered across the scarred wooden floor. He growled as his eyes narrowed. Another man let out a nasty laugh and bent to pick them up.

During that distraction, Éamonn ducked past them and pelted toward the inn, his feet sloshing through the mud in the driving rain. One man came close behind him, his panting breath harsh in Éamonn's ears, but he daren't glance back. When he spied the humble building, he sent a prayer of thanks to God. Once inside the inn, he'd have Ruari's help.

He reached the inn door and sucked in deep, desperate breaths. He'd made it. His pursuer had given up. Lucky, too, as he didn't see Ruari. He hoped he'd earned enough for their passage as another night like that might be the death of him.

After several mugs of ale to celebrate his escape and calm his nerves, he stumbled upstairs. His darling wee girl curled up asleep on the narrow cot, while Ruari had set up two pallets on the floor. His brother lay snoring in one, his feet toward the fire. Éamonn banked the fire before he crawled into the second pallet.

In the morning, the storm had blown out, and the day dawned bright with sparkling cool dew on every surface. While Katie and Ruari woke refreshed and energized, Éamonn groaned from his excesses. They packed and descended to the docks.

Éamonn had severely underestimated the cost of passage. Most captains outright laughed at them. One looked at each of them. By the time he looked Ruari up and down, he shook his head. "Too much weight on that one. My boat would capsize at the first squall."

Even with his Fae-given talent, no amount of arguing or pleading would change the captain's mind.

They found a larger sloop with room for about twelve passengers and a receptive captain. "I go to Ballycastle once a week. I'm due out tomorrow as a matter of fact. I prefer to go with a full load, so I'll take ye, despite the short fare. Mind, I expect to get work out of ye for the voyage for that, aye?"

The brothers exchanged a glance. Neither Éamonn or Ruari had any qualms about putting their backs to any task that might allow them to fly across the ocean to their father. Together, they shook hands with the captain.

"Well, be here at dawn tomorrow. We leave on the tide."

Katie:

Impatience flowed out of Éamonn like water. He looked wound so tight, Katie daren't touch him for fear he'd explode. She didn't want him to go gambling again to pass the time, since they had enough funds to leave the next morning. His now well-known reputation as an over-lucky man worried her.

Ruari seemed content to watch seagulls playing in the waves. They all sat on the sea wall at first, but then Éamonn jumped down and tossed stones from the rocky beach into the ocean. He threw each one harder, farther, and sometimes they came close to the birds, which gave raucous squawks and dirty looks as they fluttered to safer waters.

Katie clapped her hands as she got an idea, trying to change him to a positive mood. "Why don't we climb the hill on the other side of town? We might see Ireland from that height."

Éamonn imparted a long-suffering look. "Katie, Ireland's over eighty miles away. On a clear day, you might—might, mind you!—see ten or fifteen miles, if you're on a hill."

She scowled at him, annoyed at his cocksure attitude. "Well, pardon me for not knowing all that! I'm sure a world traveler like yourself knows such things. A poor little button-head idjit like myself is just ignorant." Her family hadn't strayed far from the west coast in their travels.

He stopped throwing stones and came to her on the wall. When standing on the beach, he barely reached her breasts where she perched. He placed a hand on each of her knees, gazing up into her eyes. "Ah, Katie, I didn't mean it to come out like that. I'm just frustrated and eager to be off. You know that, don't you?"

While rolling her eyes, she gave him a half-smile. "Yes, I know that. I just took exception to your tone. Not everyone had a father who traveled the country and taught all he knew."

She regretted speaking of his father as soon as she spoke. Would she never learn to curb her tongue? Both Ruari and Éamonn grew silent. They exchanged a glance and looked out over the water as if searching Turlough out. Éamonn peered up at a hill to their right, gaze narrowing. She looked at the same hill but couldn't see anything special about it. Some stones or an old cottage sat in ruins on the top.

She also regretted being so snappish. She had liked Turlough and knew Éamonn loved and worried for his father. Katie wished time would speed up. Anything to avoid this awkward waiting. Or keep Éamonn from gambling again.

Éamonn let out a deep sigh and patted her on the knee. "I'll be back for supper. I need to take care of something."

She hoped he didn't mean to go dicing. "What's wrong?"

"Nothing's wrong, but I need to go up that hill."

"The hill? Whatever for?"

"I need to see the faery stone. Bide here and rest, eh? I'll not be long."

He might be hours going up the hill and back. She didn't want him to walk back to the inn at night. "But what's so important?"

"Just something I need to do. A ritual my father taught me. Can't you just wait here?"

Katie screwed her face up in skepticism. "Sure and I can, but since when have you been religious, Éamonn Doherty?"

"Not religious, more like a personal ritual." With that, he walked toward the hill.

After watching his retreating form, she gave up. As if time listened to her wish, the sun dipped to the horizon, and the gloaming deepened. Soon, the night would grow too dark to see anything but her own hands. The sky looked dark tonight. She hadn't been paying attention in the last few days to the moon cycles. Such a pity, as she loved the moon. She loved the mysterious glow, a gentler light than the sun, powerful and beautiful. She understood why ancient people worshipped moon goddesses.

Thinking of the moon made her remember her cycle, still missing. Once Éamonn discovered she carried Lochlann's child, he'd abandon her. She placed a hand on her belly and let out a tiny sob.

"What's that?" Ruari's startled tone brought her back from her musings and she noticed him pointing up the hill Éamonn had climbed. Purple sparks danced in the darkness. After jumping off the wall, she strode toward the hill without thinking.

"No, wait! I think I know what that is." Ruari's astonishing comment halted her in her tracks.

"What? What is that?"

Ruari stared up, then shrugged. "Something Da does. At old stones. I don't know what, but he does something with the faeries."

Katie thought Ruari to be beyond such guile, but he must be having her on. "Are you serious? Actual faeries, Fae folk like the Dagda and the Morrigan?" She couldn't keep the disdainful tone out of her words.

"Yes, like them." Said so simply, the fire faded from her sarcasm and cynicism.

Nothing natural made such lights. They flashed blue, purple, and green now, swirling in an elegant spiral dance. A low hum thrummed from the earth. She touched the grass, feeling it tremble beneath her fingers. And then the glowing things vanished, everything pitch dark again. Only a faint hint of deep blue in the western sky betrayed the dying day.

Was Éamonn faery-touched? And his father before him? Shuddering, she recalled all horrible stories from her childhood of Fae exacting revenge on humans. Men afflicted with horrible humpbacks, women struck blind, babies stolen from their cribs and replaced with sickly faery children who died, generations of descendants cursed throughout the ages. Éamonn messed with dangerous powers.

When he climbed down the hill with a jaunty step, she placed her hands on her hips. "What in Brid's name were you doing on the hill, Éamonn? We saw lights."

She couldn't see his face well now that the night had truly fallen, but she could imagine his sheepish expression. "As I said, something Da taught me."

His brother cocked his head. "Did you see the faeries, Éamonn?"

"Faeries? What do you know of the faeries, Ruari?" Éamonn's voice grew cagey.

"Da knew them. He'd call them at the stones. They were his friends."

No one made friends with faeries. Fae folk should be feared, honored, and left alone for the good of body and soul. Leave out a saucer of milk, so they'd drink it and pass on by. Pin iron to a baby to keep them from stealing the child. Never tread on a ring of mushrooms or cut a lone hazel tree. Plant a rowan tree outside your house. Dozens of spells, charms, and rituals kept faeries from paying attention, and for good reason. She'd always been torn between believing the old tales and being skeptical of them.

Éamonn tapped his chin a few times. "Perhaps not friends, but at least they were kind to him. Kind to me, too. They gave me my strength back."

Katie squinted at him in the darkness. "How do you mean?"

"Come to me, and I'll show you."

That sounded more like a sexual invitation than anything else, but she didn't mind, and walked toward his voice.

Suddenly, he lifted her into the air, twirling around until she laughed in delight. "You've gotten stronger! You grew so weak from the fever. How, Éamonn? You were skin and bones when you climbed that hill."

"Da told me I could use the stones to rest, get my energy back. I've gone a few times to find peace but, this time, they rallied in force. They gave me another wondrous gift, before you, uh, just before you got married."

He set her back on the ground, and she stumbled, dizzy from the spin. "Another gift?"

"It's why I'm so lucky with gambling. I can *push* the players, convince them to hold or to place bets. I can make people believe something, convince them of a course, at least for a little while."

What had she gotten herself into here? She stepped back, jostling Ruari. "So, are you a witch?"

Ruari shook his head. "Not a witch. A druid, Da said."

Katie glanced up at the big man. "Druid. They died out hundreds of years ago, Ruari."

"Not all of them. Or they did, but the faeries made more."

"How do you *make* a druid? Druids studied the lore for twenty years or more," she demanded, frustrated now. This talk of magic and faeries and druids confused her. Had she somehow fallen asleep and started dreaming faery tales?

She heard the silly grin in Éamonn's voice, "Apparently, by introducing them to the faeries."

Éamonn placed his hands on her shoulders. "That doesn't matter just now. Let's just get back to the inn and talk later, when we're not standing in the pitch dark, aye?"

Katie jerked away from him. "Hmph. Very well. But I'm still not sure I believe you, Éamonn Doherty. Druids, indeed."

The market stalls closed as they passed, and people went to their evening meal amid farewells. Despite them being visitors, some locals waved as they entered their own homes.

The three ate their supper at the inn, the thin rabbit stew doing little but staving off their appetites. As the night deepened, Éamonn insisted he needed to walk around. Katie didn't like it, but nothing she said changed his mind. After he left, she finished her ale and stared at the door.

After several long moments, Ruari asked, "Do you want me to go after him?"

Katie kept staring. "I don't know. He's not a child. He can take care of himself. But I can't shake this feeling that something's not right."

He gave her a toothy grin and stood. "I'll go catch up. Together, we're a match for anyone."

"Thank you, Ruari. You're a good man and a better friend." She laid a hand on his thick forearm. He covered her hand with his own, twice the size of hers, and patted it a few times before lumbering out the door.

And now, she must wait and worry.

Isn't that the way of women? We wait for men to come back from the day's trade, or from war, or from fishing in a tiny boat on a storm-swept sea as if lives are just for the waiting rather than the doing.

Katie stared at the peat burning in the stone hearth of the main room. It glowed in curls and random patterns like waves in the sea.

She didn't want to think of crossing the sea. So far, Katie had pushed the return trip to the back of her mind, ignoring the quivering fear. This trip would be longer than the first, as they left from a different port. At least she'd be in a larger boat. Ruari told her that would help. And she'd have both brothers to keep her safe. Much good that would do if the thing capsized and dumped them all into a watery grave. A shiver ran down her spine.

The landlady brought her a cup of hot mulled wine. "Are ye cold, mistress? Here, scoot closer to the fire, there's a lamb." Katie flashed the matron a grateful smile before taking a sip.

"Have your lads gone out for the evening, then? You'll be wanting something to keep your mind occupied. Care to spin with me? I've no one else to care for tonight and wouldn't mind the company."

The woman handed her a spindle. Katie eyed the tool with suspicion, but it held flax not wool, so her hands shouldn't itch. The rhythmic motion of the task kept her mind away from the frightening prospect of the morrow's travel.

Still, the soothing rhythm of the work sent her mind wandering. Katie's stomach rumbled, and she placed a hand on it, thinking about the child possibly growing within her. Would Éamonn be willing to raise Lochlann's child as his own? Could he love someone else's child? What would she do if he couldn't?

Katie fell into a spiral of self-doubt and regrets as the fire crackled in the hearth. Hours later, Éamonn and Ruari stumbled in. They each sported a few cuts and bruises, and Éamonn had an impressive new black eye. The landlady rose with a half-grimace and went into the kitchen.

"What in Brid's name happened to you two?" Katie asked, arms crossed. She knew she couldn't trust them to stay out of trouble.

Ruari looked down and shuffled his toe on the floor. "We got attacked."

"Someone attacked you?"

Éamonn explained, touching his swelling cheek. "The only way the cowards could get a drop on Ruari. It must have been someone who'd lost money to me a couple nights ago."

She raised an eyebrow and tapped her toe. "Keep going."

"The three of them came from behind, hit us over the heads, and expected us to go down without a fight. We disappointed them." Éamonn grinned at their success.

Katie just shook her head. "Well, at least you're safe home now."

The landlady returned with a bowl. "Let's get a leech for yon eye, young man." She sat him on a stool. "A few of these handy creatures will take the blood right out. This'll keep it from swelling too badly, you see." She placed three of the dark, slimy creatures under his eye like an exaggerated drawing of a lower eyelash. Katie stifled a giggle, but Ruari had no such restraint.

The landlady sat back, surveying her work. "Ah, yes, that will do nicely. Give them about ten minutes or so. They'll fall off when they're done."

Ruari poked one. "What does that feel like, Éamonn?"

"They tickle, especially when you poke them." He tried not to move his face when he talked, eliciting more laughs. The conversation degraded into stories of past brawls, both won and lost. One of the leeches fell off, making Katie shrink away. As dawn would come early, Katie climbed the stairs to bed and left the brothers to their bragging.

When Éamonn shook her awake, the sun still slept. He lit a single candle, but they'd packed their meager belongings the day before. They just needed to walk down to get to the docks.

As they left the inn, ten men waited outside, carrying torches in the pre-dawn darkness. They muttered and grumbled when Katie emerged. Ruari came next, and then Éamonn.

Several men in front spat out angry words.

"Cheater!"

"Sorcerer!"

"Devil's Man!"

By Brigid's Veil. Éamonn's uncommon luck at dicing had caught up with him after all.

Their landlady stuck her head out of the door, clad in her shift and an enormous white mob cap, and beckoned for them. "Quick, come in through the pub!"

The three scrambled back through the narrow gap and into the stable yard. A back alleyway led down to the docks. With luck, they could make it there before the mob realized where they'd gone.

Ruari pushed aside several obstacles. A clatter of wood sounded too loud to Katie's ears, but she was past caring. She'd had enough of adventure and wanted to flee this troubled land once and for all.

The mob waited for them at the end of the alley, blocking their way. Ruari's eyes darted back and forth. "Should we split up?"

Éamonn spoke over-loud. "No, better we stay together. Come on, back to the other end!" Half the men stayed followed them, but the other half probably went to cut them off at the other end. Panic gripped her and she froze. Éamonn had to yank her arm to get her feet moving.

Instead of running all the way back down the alley, Éamonn cut through the inn, emerging into an empty street. With Ruari and Katie in tow, he cut across to another street and ducked into a new alley. After discovering the back entrance to an abandoned shop, they climbed through the broken door. The walls smelled dank, but darkness hid them. Finding a hiding place behind stairs, they waited.

Katie kept her panting breath shallow, despite her terror. What if those men caught them? People still burned or hanged witches. She gripped Éamonn's arm, her nails digging into his skin. He patted her hand while peering into the inky darkness.

Something clamored outside, shouts and cries of frustration. Glowing torches passed by several times, but no one came into the shop. The front of the shop had been boarded up. Their pursuers might not discover the back entrance. If they did, they'd block any escape. Katie's heart sped up, and her hands shook. She needed to run, escape from this tiny space. Ruari put his arm around her shoulders and held her close. The big man's warmth comforted her and quelled some of her panic.

The shouting grew fainter. They waited longer in case of a ruse. When they finally risked emerging, the darkness had brightened with false dawn. A few stars still twinkled in the clear sky. Rushing down to the docks, Éamonn pointed at their ship, and they ran headlong for the pier.

Someone shouted, "There they are!"

More yells came from behind them. Katie ran faster, not caring that she fell behind Éamonn and Ruari.

Someone yanked her arm, jerking her to the ground, and she fell to her back. Pain shot through her. "Éamonn!" Her voice barely worked.

Ruari and Éamonn halted, glancing. Éamonn spun around and ran headlong into the man who'd pulled her down, knocking him into two others. Ruari waded in, his fist connecting first to one man's jaw and to another's stomach. A third man waved a torch in Ruari's face, forcing him back, but then the big man tackled the torchbearer.

Katie rolled over, coughing and sucking in air. The torch fell from the tackled man's hand, landing close to Katie's head. She rolled away before the flame caught her hair.

She scrambled to her feet just as the first man punched Éamonn in the lower back. Éamonn cried out and fell to his knees as another tried to loop a rope around him.

Ruari faced three men, taunting them, goading them to come at him. None wanted to take on the giant. Éamonn had two opponents now. He tried to join Ruari, so they could fight back-to-back, but the man with the rope cut them off.

Katie grabbed the torch as it sputtered, but the flame didn't die. While the man with the rope tried to loop Éamonn again, she shoved the torch at the attacker's shirt until it caught fire.

He sniffed the air, then bellowed and jumped around, yelling at his friend to put out the flame. Freed from his two opponents, Éamonn joined Ruari, with Katie brandishing her torch like a sword. Faced with poorer odds, the three remaining men backed off. After a few muttered words, they fled down toward the docks.

When they caught sight of the boat, their safe haven, Éamonn caught Katie in a fierce hug and sobbed. "I thought I'd lost you."

Katie got her voice back. "Not today. But we'd best get on the boat right away."

He held Katie's hand as she stepped from the dock to the ship, while Ruari stood at the entrance to the dock. Éamonn whispered to the captain, who stood beside Ruari, forming an impenetrable defensive wall against the mob. She prayed the captain would take their money and get them away from here.

Éamonn picked up their pack. "The captain said he's just waiting for two more passengers, and then we can sail. They should arrive soon, so let's get below. The less visible we are, the better."

Various boxes and trade goods filled the hold. She just hoped none of their attackers had the bright idea of tossing a torch onto the boat.

Scrambling boots above made her jaw clench, but the sailors shouted to untie the lines. The final passengers must have arrived. They'd be off, for good or ill. Katie heaved a sigh of relief and glanced at Éamonn. "Now will you realize you must be more careful with your gambling, gift or no?"

"I usually am. We just needed coin so fast, but I should have been more careful. My talent got a bit out of control."

"Hmph. You have a special talent for getting into trouble, that's a certainty. You're just lucky Ruari saved your hide again. What will you do when he's not around?"

"Not around? Where would he go?"

Katie furrowed her brow. "Well, if we marry, won't he go out on his own?"

Éamonn grabbed a box as the ship rocked on the water. More sailors shouted, and her stomach roiled at the ship's lurching motion. She braced herself against another box.

With a shrug, Éamonn glanced up to the daylight streaming through the hatch, and then over at Ruari, who was standing next to the ladder. "My brother's a solid man, and a true brother, but he's not so great on his own. People take advantage of his good nature and modest wit. I'd rather be around to watch him." He peered at her. "Will that be a problem?"

Ruari was a powerful man, but Éamonn had a point. Despite his size, people would take advantage of him. She enjoyed talking to him. He had no guile or deception. "I like him fine, Éamonn. I don't mind if he stays with us, wherever we go."

While letting out an exaggerated breath, Éamonn grinned. "Oh, good. For a moment, I thought I'd have to choose between you two, and I don't know if I could!" He took both her hands and kissed her knuckles.

Their gazes locked and Katie felt her heat rise. "Have I thanked you yet? For coming for me?"

"Did you ever doubt I would?"

She glanced down at their hands, still clasped. "I have to admit, there were a few moments that I lost faith. But you still came."

He kissed her knuckles again. "I still came. And I would do it again in a moment. You are the only woman I want to spend my life with."

A female voice dripping with sarcasm cut through their tender moment. "Well, if it isn't the two lovebirds. Aren't you just the coziest thing?"

Katie turned to see the nasty smile on her sister's face.

Part V
Chapter Seventeen

Éamonn:

Deirdre and Ciaran climbed down into the hold. Even in the dim light, Éamonn had never seen his cousin's eyes so dead. Ciaran looked as if he had risen from his grave. Deirdre's eyes, in contrast, brimmed with hatred. While Deirdre lashed into Katie, Ciaran spoke to the captain.

Éamonn held his hand out and asked the captain for their fare, but he shook his head. "I don't give refunds to murderers. Just get off my ship." With that, the captain had Katie, Éamonn, and Ruari escorted off the ship.

A moment later, Ciaran and Deirdre stood beside them. They argued with the captain, but he shook his head. "I don't want any of you on my boat. Go away, all of you!"

Éamonn glared at Ciaran for his betrayal and while Ruari clenched his fists, neither gave in to the urge to punch their cousin. A glimmer of life returned to Ciaran's eyes, showing a hint of smug satisfaction before flickering away again. That tiny glimpse made Éamonn shiver.

As they stood on the dock, watching the sailors finish their preparations, voices shouted behind him. He spun around at this new threat. A group of men, malice clear on their frowning faces, blocked the end of the dock.

They were trapped. Éamonn fumbled for Katie's hand. He'd already failed her once. She'd never forgive a second failure.

From the murderous intent in the men's faces, their best chance might be to swim away. But when he glanced at the water, Katie's eyes grew wide. She shook her head, and he discarded that notion. He shot a glare to his cousin, but Ciaran stood with his arms crossed and a huge, satisfied grin on his face. "Looks like your chickens are finally coming home to roost."

The man in front, with a scar on his face and broad shoulders, took a step toward them. Three of his cronies surged forward. Ruari gripped his shoulder almost painfully tight.

Éamonn put up a hand, pouring all his magic into his words. "Stop!"

The three scuffled to a halt, looking at their feet as if surprised.

After clearing his throat, Éamonn spoke in reasonable tones. "We mean you no harm. We just want to go home. You will let us pass."

The closest three smiled, nodding. They stepped aside to let Éamonn, Ruari, and Katie pass. With a swallow against the hard lump in his throat, Éamonn strode by them with all the confidence he didn't possess. However, when they reached the end of the dock, the large man still blocked their way. He must have been too far away to be affected by the magic.

"Where do you bloody well think you're going, *mate?*"

He glanced back at Ruari, who stepped up to stand beside his brother. Shoving away the nausea, Éamonn spoke with more magic. "Let us pass."

The other man just laughed in Éamonn's face. He grabbed, not Éamonn, but Katie, wrenching her away from Éamonn's grip. She let out a scream and pummeled the man's chest as he yanked her close. Her efforts did nothing.

Ruari cocked his arm back and let fly a powerful punch at his nose. The sickening *crack* echoed in the quiet morning. Blood flowed from his nose, dripping on Katie's face. Her screams turned to screeches as she tried to twist out of his grip.

Éamonn threw a punch to the man's gut. But hands from behind pulled him away just after his fist made contact, lessening the strength of the blow. Those men he'd convinced to let them by before had shaken off the Fae magic. Now, they came to help their friend.

More men gathered behind the one holding Katie. He passed her back to them, and Éamonn lost sight of her red, wild curls. "Wait! Wait, we'll come with you. Just don't hurt her."

They allowed Katie to run to Éamonn, and he held her tight in an embrace as she shivered, sobbing on his chest. Then she turned to the assembled men, tears still in her eyes. "How dare you! Why did you attack us? What in Brid's name did you intend to do?"

A few of the younger men shuffled their toes in the dirt, refusing to meet her eyes. However, the big man turned and scowled at her. "We want our money back. This stinking Irishman cheated us. That's what we intended, *girl.*"

She pressed back against Éamonn's solid body but held her chin high. "Well, you are out of luck. We paid all our money to that captain." She pointed behind her to the ship. "And he refused to give any back when he kicked us off. So, if you want your money so bad, get it from him!"

Her entire body quivered with anger. At this moment, Éamonn loved her more than anything in his entire world. She looked amazing in her furious indignation, like some ancient battle goddess ready to smite an entire city.

Despite the lightning bolts coming from her eyes, the surrounding men didn't look convinced. And yet, they couldn't leave, either. He glanced at Ruari, who shrugged.

An older man pushed his way through to them. "Boone, move over. You can't just kill people because you want to. You aren't English."

Boone, the man with big shoulders, grumbled, but moved aside. "They're thieves, Jock."

"They may well be thieves, but we're not lawless. They deserve a proper trial."

Éamonn gritted his teeth. His father could die any day and they wanted to waste time with a trial? But what choice did he have?

After a heated discussion, they agreed Jock's notion would be best. Their captors locked them in a dark room until the magistrate arrived.

Katie paced in the small space, throwing her arms up. "What the bloody hell do we do now?"

"I don't know, *mo chailín rua.* I don't know. We can only hope to have a sane and responsible judge."

"In this rough place? And us Travelers? I'm not holding my breath." She crossed her arms and glowered while he tried to form another plan. He didn't dare fail her again.

Ruari tested the walls and the door, but they didn't give in even to his prodigious strength. Éamonn didn't even bother trying.

Someone walked down the hall and Éamonn scrambled to his feet, unwilling to face his fate sitting down.

When the door opened to reveal Ciaran, he scowled. "Ciaran, didn't I just watch you leave on a boat to Ireland?"

His cousin shrugged as the guard shut the door behind him. A key clicked in the lock. "We got off before he left. We have unfinished business with you."

"Look, I don't know what's been eating at you, but we're blood relations. Cousins. Can't we just be kin and leave the rest behind?" Putting both hands out, as if in supplication, Éamonn took a step forward, pushing his magic through his words.

Ciaran waited until he came close. Then his fist snaked out and punched Éamonn in the gut. Bent over, Éamonn coughed and hacked.

Ruari glowered over Ciaran. "You're my cousin, Ciaran, but Éamonn's my brother. If you have a quarrel with us, take your anger out on me."

Looking the big man up and down as if seeing him for the first time, Ciaran gave a sneer. "Right. Only if I want to become a grease spot on the road. No, Éamonn's the only one who can settle his sins. He needs to face up to his own evil deeds."

Éamonn coughed again and spit out phlegm tinged with blood. His tongue explored a coppery spot in his mouth. "What evil deeds?"

Ciaran lifted his hands and counted off on his fingers. "Hmm, let me see. Should I count them off for you? Stealing Katie. Then, not satisfied with one woman, stealing Deirdre. Messing with so many bad omens I lost count. You stole money from poor innocent folks, though God knows I can't figure out how you're cheating them, I just know you are. And then you abandoned us to the soldiers. Abandoning your father—"

"Now, wait just a moment, Ciaran. I don't cheat, I didn't steal anyone, and I never abandoned you or Father. You're twisting around my actions, and that's not fair."

Ciaran's scowl deepened. "Since when have you *ever* played fair, Éamonn Doherty? You with your towering height and your perfect teeth and easy smile. You always win at everything, and it's never *fair!*"

Éamonn couldn't think of anything to say. He'd never been perfect in anything. Sure, he had luck with the ladies, and at gambling, even before the brooch, but Ciaran had been no slouch either.

After drawing them from his pack, Ciaran brandished several pages in Éamonn's face. "I would have brought this back to your Da." Éamonn recognized the music sheets he'd taken from the MacCrimmon's house. "Then he might have taken me on as a true apprentice. Someone worthy of his teaching. He might have…"

Ciaran sniffed and swallowed. "Might have been like a father to me. But he's dying now, and that will never happen."

Éamonn grabbed at the papers, trying to pull them out of Ciaran's grasp, but the pages ripped. Ciaran's scowl turned into a nasty grin as he ripped the rest of the precious pages in half. Ruari and Éamonn both gasped and tried to catch the falling pieces. They only got a few scraps before Ciaran pulled the rest away.

The smug look on Ciaran's face made Éamonn's patience snap. Two steps brought him close enough for a solid punch to the face, but Ciaran ducked fast. Éamonn doubled over from the gut punch and groaned.

"And you should learn how to fight, cousin. Next time someone accuses you of cheating, you might get your due. Oh, right, you won't have a next time. The judge is on his way, and your trial begins in an hour. I can't wait."

After a few hoarse coughs, Éamonn spit out, "Ciaran, just get out of my life. You're no relation of mine, you snake."

"I'll get out of your life soon enough, Éamonn. Soon enough."

As his footsteps faded back down the hall, Éamonn turned to Katie. "My dear love, if this is our last time together, I must tell you something. You, too, Ruari."

Katie screwed her face together and gripped her knees again. Ruari waited with the patience of a stone wall.

"First, if I can say or do anything to get you and Ruari clear of this, I will. Ciaran's quarrel is with me, not the two of you."

Ruari patted him on the back.

"Second, know this. I love both of you more than my words can say."

He didn't care if Katie noticed tears pushing from behind his eyes. Pulling her to her feet, he hugged Katie close, and she trembled in his arms.

Éamonn had a plan, of course, a plan to convince the judge with his brooch-gifted talent that he was innocent of all charges. But if that didn't work, what then?

A flash of lightning and the rumble of thunder heralded the beginnings of a storm.

Katie continued to shiver, despite him rubbing her arms. He pulled his cloak from under him and wrapped the warm wool around her shoulders, but she still shook. She moaned and jumped as lightning cracked closer.

"Katie? Katie, is something wrong?"

She lifted her head, glaring at him. "Of course, something is wrong, you blethering eejit! Do I always curl up like a baby?" She spat at him, and then moaned again. She uncurled and glanced down at herself. "Oh, Sweet Brid."

Éamonn and Ruari both looked down. A spreading stain of dark blood on her skirts. "Katie? What's happening?"

She closed her eyes and curled back into a ball. Another *boom* of thunder ripped through their cell, making her flinch. "I need a healer, but I think even that would be little help."

"Are you dying? What's wrong? Tell me!"

With a shake of her head, she gripped her stomach again. "I hope not, Éamonn. I suspect…" her expression pinched into a grimace, "I suspect I'm losing the baby."

He pulled back as his eyes grew wide. "Baby? Baby! What baby? When did you… What—"

"Are you a complete eejit? Lochlann's baby, you arse. Who did you think?" She bent again until the latest wave passed.

"Oh." He didn't know what to think about that. He wanted to ease her pain, of course, but he didn't want her to have Lochlann's baby.

Women died in childbirth all the time. She couldn't have been more than a month gone. She didn't even have a bump. Could something that small kill her? But those dark stains kept spreading.

He held her tight, worried that, if he let go, she might die. "Is that why you have been so distant? Because you're carrying his baby?"

She nodded, her jaw clenched.

He hugged her close. "That doesn't matter to me, Katie. I want you, now and forever, whether you have a score of children by someone else. I will love your children, no matter what."

Katie struggled for air. "Stop smothering me! Éamonn, it hurts. Just let me—" Grunting again, she doubled over.

Between waves of pain marring Katie's beautiful face, flashes of lightning, earth-shattering booms of thunder, and the steady drip of water from the ceiling, Éamonn entered an eternity of torture. He couldn't help Katie's pain and God must not be listening to his prayers. *Drip, drip, drip…* He shook his head just to dispel the fatal rhythm. *Drip, drip, moan…* Katie writhed in his lap and didn't wake.

Éamonn clutched her shoulders. "Katie? Katie! Katie, wake up!" She couldn't die, not now. Not when he'd finally found her again, the love of his life. Her body lay limp in his arms. "Help! Someone help us! We need a healer!"

The blood didn't get worse, and the water rinsed her skirts. The stain might pass as a poor dye job, an inexperienced girl's fumble, someone who neglected her dye tubs.

If he lost Katie, all of this would have been for naught. So much for Éamonn on his mad quest for his perfect bride, his lady love, only to return with nothing but a beautiful corpse stained with blood and a dying father to show for his gamble. And he'd have lost everything he held dear.

Éamonn cried for help until his throat turned hoarse, but no one came. The rain eased, and then stopped. Everything still dripped, including his tangled shreds of hope. Hope for rescue. Hope for justice. Hope for a life with his love. Katie groaned and moved, and his heart leapt, but she didn't wake.

Footsteps once again sounded in the hallway. Éamonn prayed they'd sent a healer.

The door opened, and four burly men came in. They tied Ruari's hands first. When they tried to tie Éamonn's, they frowned at Katie, still laying in his lap.

The first man turned to Éamonn. "Did you do this to her? Are we to try you for her murder?"

Through gritted teeth, Éamonn said, "She needs a healer, man! She's losing a baby. Quick, before she bleeds more!"

Still frowning, the man hesitated. Éamonn wanted to smack him, shake him out of his dumbfounded indecision. After an eternity, he yelled down the hall, "Graham! Fetch the midwife. Quick, now! The rest of you, take the prisoners to the church." More guards ran down the hall.

Éamonn kept hold of his love. "No! I can't leave her!"

"You'll do as you're told! Now, go!" Three guards grabbed his arms, pulling him away from Katie. Her head hit the floor with a horrid *thump*. He jerked away from their grip and scooped Katie into his arms again. She moaned, and her eyes fluttered open. They glittered like glass in the dim light, but they looked at him.

This time, five guards pulled him away. He struggled against their grip but couldn't break free. "I'll come back, Katie, I promise! I love you!"

Ruari knelt beside Katie and whispered something in her ear before the guards took his arms. She nodded and closed her eyes.

He blinked as they came out into the daylight, though rain still spit from the dark, sullen sky. Guards marched Éamonn and Ruari through the street. Folks lined up to witness the prisoners' parade to the church.

Dozens of people crowded the church steps. Éamonn scanned the faces for someone he knew, anyone. Their landlady sat near the door with a few merchants he'd bought supplies from. The gamblers scowled at him from the bottom of the steps, but when they noticed his attention, they smiled with smug satisfaction.

Ciaran and Deirdre stood right at the church doors. Deirdre hissed at him as he walked by, and Ciaran scowled, elbowing her in the ribs. She stopped her hissing but glared at Éamonn with poisonous malice.

Their captors halted at the church doors and the judge emerged from inside. He wore a priest's cassock. A man of God might listen to reason, and he'd have little sympathy for gamblers, whether they cried foul or not. Of course, Éamonn was also a gambler, so that might work against him as easily as for him.

The priest turned and addressed the crowd. "These men are accused of cheating their fellow man with the powers of witchcraft, and of the murder of a soldier in the King's Army. Who accuses them?"

Murder? Who did I murder?

Ciaran stood up. "I accuse him. I witnessed him killing a soldier of the King's Army, Lochlann MacCrimmon, in cold blood. I have seen him consort with demons and do the Devil's own work on this Earth." Deirdre nodded beside him, her lips pressed into a thin line.

Oh, bloody hell in a handbasket.

The priest turned to him. "How do you answer these charges?"

Indignation rose within him, eager to burst forth. "I'm innocent of both these charges, Father! This is my cousin, and he's held a personal grudge against me. He's telling lies!" The sky roiled and twisted with his emotions, and a few people glanced up in concern.

Gesturing towards Ciaran, the priest cocked his head. "Is this true, my son?"

"Yes, it's true I'm his cousin. But I'm not lying about the magic! Ask these men. They've lost money to him when he uses witchcraft on his dice!"

The priest frowned and peered at the gamblers. They milled but said nothing. He raised his eyebrows at Ciaran. "None seem to come forth to support your claims, young man. Have you any proof of your accusations other than your word?"

Deirdre stepped up. "He has my word as well! I saw everything."

Éamonn glared at them, standing proudly in their perfidy. "You only accuse me because I rejected you!"

Deirdre narrowed her eyes, pointing a finger at him. "Liar! Cheat! Witch!"

He drew upon his brooch-given gift, pushing his will to the entire crowd, to convince the priest, the spectators, even Ciaran and Deirdre, of the truth of his words. He put all his fear about Katie and her baby into the gift, his desperate flight to find her, all his frustrations of the last weeks. While concentrating on his persuasion power, he pushed and pushed until his head spun and lights danced before his eyes, lights no one else saw. They swirled in purples and gold, a spiral of fairies winking in and out of the rising wind. "I am innocent. I've never consorted with the Devil. I do no witchcraft."

Ciaran spat one word out. "Liar!"

Éamonn took a deep breath and said, with all the authority he could muster, "You both lie!"

Dark clouds roiled above. Black thunderheads billowed, and the wind whipped icy cold. Sparks of what could never be lightning sparkled within the rolling mass. Éamonn gasped and took an involuntary step backward. The mob started a new muttering, one of fear rather than anger.

Lightning crackled from one dark cloud to another, the flash limning the crowd with an otherworldly blue glow.

A sibilant voice rose from the earth, the sky, and the surrounding wind, "Lies!"

The muttering grew louder and some of the gathered crowd darted away. The rest milled about, with faint questions on their tongues and fear in their hearts. The voice grew louder, shaking Éamonn's bones, *"Lies!"*

The voice pushed through Éamonn, but not from his mouth. It must come from the Otherworld, from the faeries who'd gifted him power. He begged his body not to betray him, willed himself not to fall to his knees.

Ciaran and Deirdre's eyes grew wide as the crowd melted away.

The priest's gaze darted from the storm, to Éamonn, and to Ciaran, his eyes widening with fear. "Hear the word directly from the heavens! Do you dare to take the Lord's justice in your own hands? Let him without sin throw the first stone!" His voice rang out over the stragglers. The first heavy drops of icy rain fell, and people scrambled for shelter. The fae lights and voice drove everyone away and soon, no one remained but the priest. Even Éamonn's accusers had vanished, along with Ciaran and Deirdre.

The priest crossed himself and turned to Éamonn, untying both him and Ruari. "Son, I don't know what just happened, but I'm willing to call this a miracle from God and let you go if you give me one promise."

Relief washed through his bones as nausea rushed up. As soon as he said this, the Fae-given illness slammed into his chest. He turned and vomited in the grass, his stomach cramping with intense pain.

Ruari held his shoulders to keep him from losing balance as he dry-heaved until his throat turned raw. Able to breathe again, he turned to the priest. "Anything, Father!"

"Go away. Leave my town and never return. I never want to see the likes of *that* again."

"Aye, Father. I am happy to leave and never come back!"

Katie:

As she dragged herself back from the void, Katie heard familiar voices. They cut through the fog of pain which had clouded her world. Ruari said something in his rumbling voice. And Éamonn, sounding desperate and pleading. Someone else she didn't know gave them instructions.

When she opened her eyes, an unfamiliar room surrounded her, but Éamonn sat by her bedside, clutching her hand. "Katie?"

Her voice didn't seem to work when she tried to answer. He shook his head. "No, don't speak. The healer said you're recovering. As soon as you're well enough, we'll head back to Ireland and be back on our own soil before you know it, aye?"

She placed a hand on her stomach, the question high in her mind. He shook his head. "The healer said that the bleeding was something else."

"So I'm still pregnant?"

He shook his head. "She couldn't tell for certain. It's still too early. You just ejected clotted blood."

Both relief and devastation flooded her as she croaked out her next question. "What about your father?"

He swallowed and glanced at Ruari. "I've heard no news. And how would any messenger find us if anything changed? We won't know until we arrive, I'm afraid."

Katie asked for some water, and he poured her some from an ewer. Then he told her of his promise to the priest in Campbeltown.

"But you didn't leave. You're here still."

"No, we're in the next village, Glenramskill. I found a healer to help you. I didn't want to lose you again." He squeezed her hand and kissed her softly on the lips.

By the time the healer judged her well enough to travel, Éamonn had raised more funds for their passage, being careful to travel to other towns for his gambling nights, and being much more circumspect in his winning. He kept an eye out for Ciaran or Deirdre, but never saw them.

Still, she did not look forward to the voyage, remembering how nauseous she'd been on the first time crossing. At least she didn't face a loveless marriage at the end of this trip. Instead, she had Éamonn's love and support, and that made all the difference in the world.

Éamonn:
Katie survived the journey, but she looked miserable. Éamonn held her shivering body tight the entire trip. By the time they docked, he had had enough of the sea for a lifetime, and knew Katie felt the same. He never wanted to leave his beloved Ireland again.

Ruari, Katie, and Éamonn trekked back to Ballyshannon, rushing as much as they could, praying they'd reach it before their father died. For once, the weather smiled upon them. The final mile felt like the longest part of the long journey.

As they reached the village, Éamonn rushed into the healer's tent. When he entered, he blinked to adjust his eyes to the dim room. Turlough lay on the bed, but he barely recognized his own father.

Turlough had never been a fleshy man. Tall and slim, he had wiry strength, but very little fat. Even that had melted into this skeletal figure, as if his skin stretched over a frame three sizes too large. His face had grown yellow and thin. He coughed into his hand, and blood mixed with his spittle. Éamonn had no healing skill, but coughing blood meant bad things.

Ruari showed hm the ripped remains of the music sheets out. Wondrous delight bloomed in their father's eyes as he recognized the missing Turlough O'Carolan tunes.

"My boys, my dear boys. However did you find them? And what happened to them?"

Éamonn grimaced. "I think Donald stole them. He was one of those Scottish pipers. Then Ciaran stole them from me."

Turlough's eyes grew wide. "Ciaran? But why?"

Éamonn gave a shrug and glanced at Ruari. "He said something about getting you to apprentice him. But that was when he'd gotten us thrown in jail, so I don't trust anything he says anymore."

His father furrowed his brow but then noticed Katie hovering behind Ruari. "Oh, Katie, you are back with us! I'm—" He coughed, and the rattling, racking pain shivered through Éamonn's own bones. "I'm so glad to see you," but his gaze dropped to his hands as he paused, the next words sounding pained. "I am so sorry. I tried as hard as I could, but the council wouldn't approve the annulment."

Katie, her fair face still grimy from the road dust, held his thin hand. "It's fine, Turlough. Lochlann…" she paused to swallow before continuing, "Lochlann was killed in a battle." Her eyes glistened with unshed tears.

Éamonn sniffed back his own impending tears, but nothing helped. "Da? Da, I'll marry her, and we'll have many fine children. We'll name one Turlough, I swear to you."

Turlough shook his head with a half-grin. "Oh, don't do that, son. Turlough is a horrible name to saddle a child with. What if he should have no music? He'll feel forever bound to failure. No, give him a more noble name. Perhaps Brian for Brian Boruma, our great hero."

Ruari placed his hand on his father's, his voice catching. "I love you, Da. Don't go yet, please?"

Katie gripped his arm. "At least stay until Éamonn and I can get married, if you can?"

Turlough glanced at Katie, and then back at Éamonn. "Could you do so quickly, then? I don't have a great deal of time. Cormac's surprised I've held on this long," his voice tapered off into a whisper and shifted to another cough.

Éamonn sniffed back a sob and turned to his beloved. "Katie?"

She wiped at the tears streaming down her face. "Yes, right away, if we can. I 'd be honored to have Turlough witness our wedding."

Turlough waved his hand. "Ah, you're such a delight, my dear. My daughter, soon enough. Come, let me see you more closely."

She knelt beside the bed. Turlough caressed her cheek and then stroked a red curl that had come free from her kerchief. "Aye, you will be a fit bride for my headstrong son, Caitriona O'Malley. Your eyes are full of fire. Don't let him get away with most of what he tries, and you will live a long and happy life together. And remember me on my birthday, will you? A prayer from you will be heeded in Heaven."

Katie sobbed, her face blotchy and red. Ruari wept quietly behind her. Éamonn's own face grew wet from tears as he sniffed in again.

"Now, get thee out and start planning the party! I want to see my new daughter dressed in a fine gown. Éamonn, make sure she has one, will ye not? A bride should feel new and beautiful. Ruari, I've instructions for you as well. Bide while they make the arrangements." He fell into a fit of bloody coughing after this speech.

Éamonn:

Loath to leave even for a few minutes, Éamonn backed out of the room, pulling Katie with him. "Here, Katie. Can you find a shirt that will please him to wear? He loves green, perhaps with embroidered vines?"

She took the coin pouch he thrust at her and dashed off to the village shops. His task would be to arrange for Father Byrne to officiate. He walked to the church, his heart both heavy and light.

The town knew Turlough from his performances at the fair and subsequent case before the council. Some Travelers remained behind, concerned about the respected musician and the case he fought so hard for. Even though the council declined to annul Katie and Lochlann's wedding, several people sympathized and assured him that they felt the decision to be unjust.

As word spread about Éamonn's return, many folks stopped by Cormac's cottage that day. Éamonn made Katie rest from their journey. She told him to rest as well, but he couldn't. How could he waste precious hours sleeping when they'd be the last he'd ever spend with his father?

Passing time with Turlough felt both galvanizing and grueling. Knowing his father neared the end made every word, every moment, precious. He spent time alone with his father, recounting his adventures in Scotland, his experiences at the stones, his adoration of Katie. They spoke of the faery gift, which he'd so casually dismissed at first but had helped him get Katie back, after all. Ruari spent some time with Turlough, filling in what gaps of the torn music he remembered. Sometimes, all three held hands and communed in silent affection.

They'd marry at dusk. Cormac asked his wife, Neala, to help Katie prepare. Neala, being a similar size to Katie, lent the bride her own wedding dress. The gown looked like a treasure, bright with embroidery.

Éamonn stood next to the priest, shifting his weight from foot to foot. Ruari stood beside him, a tentative smile pasted across his face. That disappeared as their sisters carried Turlough out on a cot and propped him up to see.

Éamonn's own anticipation seemed equal parts elation and turmoil. *This is it. I'll finally wed my bride, after all the pain and escapades of the last months.* Lochlann had snatched Katie from his grasp, but he'd found and won her. Now they'd be together forever, and his heart soared in anticipation.

A sigh echoed through the stone church as Katie appeared in the doorway. She glowed, resplendent in the soft, pale-green dress. It set off her freckles, and her red hair sparkled in the dying sunlight, a blaze of glory. Green ivy wound in her cascading hair. Her face looked fresh-scrubbed and so achingly beautiful his heart leapt into his throat.

Cormac escorted her to the altar, and Éamonn took her hands, and they felt cold and clammy, trembling in his grip. She gazed at him, the tears in her eyes reflecting his own.

He didn't hear Father Byrne's words. Katie repeated them, and then Éamonn copied her, but his world muddled in a gold-green haze. He only saw Katie's bright green eyes and her freckles dancing like sparkling faeries at the stone circle.

He fumbled for the ring. The ring! Turlough said he'd give them his mother's wedding ring, but Éamonn couldn't remember if he had. Ruari held his hand out, a delicate band of etched silver in his large palm. With a grateful smile, Éamonn took the ring and placed it on Katie's shaking finger. The thin band fit perfectly, and he grinned as he looked up and met her eyes.

The priest gave them the words to repeat for their vows, and they both repeated them in unison.

> *You are the star of each night, you are the brightness of every morning,*
> *You are the story of each guest, you are the report of every land.*
>
> *No evil shall befall you, on hill nor bank, in field or valley, on mountain or in glen.*
> *Neither above, nor below, neither in sea, nor on shore, in skies above, nor in the depths.*
>
> *You are the kernel of my heart, you are the face of my sun,*
> *You are the harp of my music; you are the crown of my company.*

When he finally kissed Katie, all his worries fled. Her lips tasted of honey and mint. He hugged her so tight, her feet lifted from the floor as the crowd cheered. The sweetest kiss he'd ever received.

As the kiss broke, and he glanced over the crowd, Cormac and Neala grinned wide. Traders who had been at the fair, other merchants, and horse trainers he'd worked with patting each other on the shoulders. *So many Travelers still bide here, two months after the fair?* He felt gratitude their celebration wasn't among strangers.

Turlough had a look of smug satisfaction on his face. At least Éamonn could give his father the gift of seeing his son married to a good woman. God knew he had been a disappointment in so many other areas. He shoved that idea away. He had no time for such things just now.

Just after the wedding, he gathered them all around. First, Turlough gifted Katie a lovely necklace of pale jade beads. "They set off your eyes to a lovely color, *m'iníon*. I bought them for Éamonn's mother when we wed, and she cherished them. Think of me when you wear them, and I'll send you a kiss from Heaven."

To Éamonn he offered nothing material. "The most valuable thing I can give you is advice, my darling son. You already have the brooch, my most precious possession. Use it with wisdom. Pass it on to someone of your blood in the future, someone who seeks the truth. And remember, God gifted you a fine woman. Treat her well, and your life will be joyous."

Most of the leather stock went to Ruari. "I give the business to you, my dear, sweet son, but listen to Éamonn. He's a head for intrigue and business. You've the talent, but he'll keep things running. I love you."

Éamonn wanted to leave before Édaín and Síle got their gifts, but he made himself stay, to cherish every remaining moment of his father's life. He needed to breathe the fresh air before he succumbed once again to despair. How would he live his life without his father, his anchor?

He Síle the few pieces of jewelry he had from their mother and Édaín his harp. "I know you aren't in love with the music like I am, but you can play, and take some comfort from my own spirit in the instrument."

Once the guests dispersed, Turlough beckoned to Éamonn and Katie. "Take me to the stones, Éamonn. I'd like to glimpse the other world once more before I die."

Éamonn wanted to argue Turlough couldn't die yet, that his father had lots of time but, deep in his heart, he knew that for a lie. He wanted to cry and scream to the heavens that it wasn't fair, that his father was a good man, that he deserved a long, healthy life, but every good Irishman knew railing against God's will did no good.

Ruari carried Turlough and with Katie and Éamonn, they trekked through the autumn bog, heavy with muck and mist, and to the hill covered with faery stones. Ruari placed Turlough on the main altar stone.

Turlough's voice croaked out at a whisper, "Ruari, Katie, give me some time alone with the lad?"

Éamonn exchanged a half-smile with Ruari. "They know, Da."

"They do? How's that?" An echo of his father's spark shone through his eyes. "Did I not warn you about telling others?"

"Aye, you did. But Ruari'd already seen you at the stones. He's seen the lights. Then they noticed me on a hill, but I didn't know the sparks would visit me, and on a dark night. So—"

Turlough wrinkled his nose and sighed. "Well, done is done. You both realize, of course, how dangerous this knowledge is?"

Katie placed a hand on his arm. "We do indeed. They almost hanged us for witches in Campbeltown, as I'm sure Éamonn told you."

The older man's lips flattened into a grim line. "Yes, I suppose you do, at that. Well then, let's see what we can do here."

He closed his eyes and, for many tense moments, nothing happened. Éamonn felt the thrumming before he saw anything. The earth rumbled beneath his feet and in his bones. Song hummed in a tuneless voice before the first sparks appeared.

Glimmering lights showered in a fountain over Turlough's head. As the older man glanced around, a smile of wonder on his face, a figure appeared, shining so bright Éamonn had to shield his eyes.

Turlough spoke in the Irish, *"An féidir libh mise a leigheas, mo chairde?" Can you heal me, my friends?*

"Ní féidir linn." We cannot.

The hope that had risen in Turlough's eyes faded as he bowed his head in acceptance. The shimmering creature walked toward Turlough and touched him on the forehead. A green-white glow crackled, traveling down the figure's arm and into Turlough's body.

The bard stood, strength giving his body vitality. He let out a joyful laugh, flinging his arms out and spinning, like a young boy with eternal strength and life. Turlough did a deep-knee bend and then straightened, arms stretched up to the sky. "Ah, such a wonderful feeling! Thank you, my dear friends!"

He sat again on the stone, and the glowing figure faded to darkness. Glistening sparks followed him, and a twinkling laugh surrounded them as the lights died.

Fatigue crept back into Turlough's voice, "We should return."

Éamonn couldn't keep the giddiness from his tone. "Da? What was that all about? Did they… Are you healed?" If the Fae gave him his strength back after his fever, perhaps they could heal his father's ailment.

"No, no son. I'm not healed." Turlough's hacking cough proved his statement. "The Fae only gave me a few moments, enough to feel alive again."

Éamonn's burgeoning dreams crashed. He clutched tight to his father's hand as Ruari carried him back to the healer's cottage.

As the day faded to darkness, Turlough's family sat around him. Harsh coughs punctuated whispered conversations. They stood in a solemn silence with flickering candles. Éamonn sat on his right, his throat tight. Ruari knelt on the other side, face buried in his hands. Katie sniffled at the foot of the bed, holding hands with Síle and Édaín. Turlough's precious harp sat behind Ruari, looming in the dim corner.

Turlough closed his eyes with a long sigh and didn't draw another breath.

Éamonn let loose the tears he'd held back for his father's sake. The whole family mourned him with weeping and wine as the man who was the center of their lives moved on to the next world.

Éamonn:

How can we have a funeral the day after a wedding? Still, he'd forever treasure the memory of that day, the more for his father bearing witness.

When they were planning the wedding, he'd braced himself to ask Katie a difficult question. "Do you mind especially if we wait on our marriage night?"

She glanced up from the vegetables she was cutting for the feast. "Wait?"

"It just doesn't seem right for that yet, not until we've said goodbye to Da. I have my hands full of funeral plans, and it should be… it should be something special for both of us."

Katie placed a gentle hand on his cheek. "Sure, and we've waited this long. What's a few nights more?"

He closed his eyes and covered her hand with his own.

As the eldest, he must sort through his father's possessions and either give them to siblings or sell them off. The priest agreed to bury Turlough in his churchyard, despite not being a local parishioner, as Turlough had become a part of the community.

Éamonn commissioned a stonemason to carve a proper headstone with Turlough's name and dates. The mason said he could add a musical note into one corner. That detail would have pleased Turlough. To have his name forever associated with music was a given, considering his namesake. But his father had a true gift to immortalize.

His father's music would keep his memory alive forever. He and Ruari went through the mess of papers, doing their best to organize them into a reasonable order. He turned to his brother once they had completed their task. "Now what do we do with them?"

Ruari shrugged. "Neither of us are musical."

Éamonn took a deep breath, wishing he had some ideas. Then the bells of the church peeled for Mass and he looked up, his eyes wide. "We can entrust them to the priest. He can read music. He is trustworthy. And he loved Da well. He'd keep them safe."

Father Byrne promised to preserve the sheets and to keep them in trust.

Turlough had already handed out most of his other possessions during that night-long vigil. Only rubbish bits of furniture and household items remained.

Travelers held funerals once a year for all those who'd passed during that time, to enable as many relatives and friends as possible to attend. But Turlough had become a man of both the Settled world and the Traveling community. The Travelers took pride in counting him as their own, but the townspeople also claimed him. His funeral would honor both aspects of the musician's life.

In a procession through the main street, a pair of horses pulled a cart with Turlough's coffin, a simple pine box.

First, his children marched in line, each paired together. Éamonn walked with Síle, their hands clasped tight. Then Ruari with Édaín, then friends and more distant relations. Éamonn's heart ached for Fionnuala and her sweet smile. At least she'd have company with their father in Heaven now. He sniffed back his tears as they came near the grave.

The priest spoke a simple, solemn ceremony and no one begrudged the tears peppering the ground as they lowered Turlough into the earth. A few sparks of color danced in the hole, but Éamonn wasn't sure if anyone else saw them. On this day, he didn't care.

As Father Byrne raised his voice in the final words of the benediction, the visitors dispersed. There'd be libations and memories to celebrate. Éamonn didn't know if he could stay strong but, for his father's sake, he'd try.

Katie:

Hers was the oddest wedding night in history. Even after the funeral and mourning, she didn't feel ready for such relations for several weeks.

When she felt ready to finally consummate their much-delayed marriage, she approached Éamonn shyly. "Éamonn, let's find some time for ourselves today."

He glanced up from the belt pouch he was cutting and then did a double take when he saw her expression. He jumped from the tool bench with a wide grin. "Absolutely! Let's go now! I know just the place."

They paused only long enough to pack a supply of fruit and cheese and rode double down toward the long, sandy beach. It stretched out in front of them as the sun dipped below the horizon, sending shoots of orange and silver across the bay.

Éamonn set up their tent with the door towards the setting sun. They sat on the quilt, holding hands, while magnificent colors painted the wispy peach clouds until they faded into a pale purple twilight.

She turned to him and gazed into his deep blue-green eyes, glittering with intensity. Not trusting herself to speak, she leaned forward and kissed him.

His lips felt tender, and he didn't lean into the kiss at first, as if scared of frightening her off. Then he placed his hand behind her head. They shared a deep, longing kiss. Katie didn't know how long it lasted. Waves lapped on the shore and a seagull cried out. Her heart raced with anticipation.

Pulling back, Éamonn gazed into her eyes again. He placed a tentative hand on her cheek.

Suddenly tired of all this waiting, Katie cocked her head. "Éamonn, do you know what to do?"

"I want your first time to be—" He halted, his eyes growing wide. Did he just realize that this wasn't her first time? He swallowed and opened his mouth but shut it again without speaking.

Katie let out a low chuckle. "It's fine, Éamonn. It just means it won't hurt this time. This is the first time I'll be making love with my husband. Lochlann treated me with kindness, but it wasn't—" She couldn't go on, as she didn't wish to insult the dead.

Éamonn cupped her cheeks in his hands. "I don't care about what Lochlann is or isn't. He's gone. There's no room for three in a marriage bed. All I care about is you and what you feel, *mo chroi*. It was always about you, and it will always be about you."

With these tender words, he kissed her forehead, her nose, and her chin. Then he drew his finger down to her chin. He lifted her face to kiss her again, and then nuzzled her neck. Ticklish, she giggled and squirmed away. He giggled, too, but didn't relent. She laid back and pulled him down to lie next to her on the quilt.

He stared at her and caught his breath. "In the name of all that's holy, I never dreamed this day would come. You are a rare woman, Caitriona Doherty, and I mean to make you know it!"

He kissed her between the breasts, working the stays open. She tried to help, but they fumbled and got in each other's way. As she stripped down to her shift and skirts, she felt sinfully wicked in the open air. Katie sat up, pulling her skirts over her head. The shift came away with it.

Éamonn let out a low whistle. "Bloody hell. I don't know if I'm going to be able to be gentle, Katie. But I'll try."

Katie gave him a sly smile. "Gentle is fine to a point, Éamonn."

He cupped her breast with one hand as she lay back, teasing the nipple of the other with his tongue. Her body twitched as pleasure shot through her body.

When he stopped, she reached up to untie his stock. He untied it himself and pulled his shirt over his head. He stepped out of his breeks as well, and lay against her, skin to skin.

His chest felt warm and dry, with a light dusting of blond hair. As she rubbed her hands along it, the wiry hairs tickled. His leg muscles tensed along hers. His roughened hand moved with feather lightness over her breasts, waist, and hips, down her thigh, and towards her cleft. She struggled not to jerk away at his touch, memories of Lochlann crowding in. Then she shoved those

Epilogue

April 1746

Less than a year later, Katie worked bent over her loom, untangling the flax from the weft. Éamonn sat at the workbench, carving bone buttons. Ruari slammed the door open, startling her to cry out.

"Katie! A letter came for you."

She cocked her head. Who would be writing to her? Ruari handed her a folded paper with a chipped wax seal. She unfolded the square envelope and read the scrawled words inside.

Katie:

I hope this letter finds you. I'm writing to let you know that I'm leaving on a ship tomorrow, emigrating to America. I lost Ciaran at the battle of Culloden, and there's nothing left for me here. I'm sure you'll be pleased. I wish you joy of Éamonn.

Deirdre

Katie stared at the letter, trying to understand the words. They jumbled in her mind and she couldn't make sense of them. Ciaran had died? Was Deirdre being sarcastic in wishing her joy? Or was that an honest sentiment. Perhaps she would never know.

Éamonn read over her shoulder and let out a long sigh. "They joined the Jacobites? And now they're dead. Ruari, Ciaran died."

They all bowed their heads in mourning for Ciaran, sorry for their demise despite their betrayals. She mourned those who'd died in the field. Katie remembered that horrible time waiting to hear if Lochlann lived or died. She may not have loved him, but she'd liked him in the end.

Ruari and Éamonn fell into a discussion about the Jacobites, Culloden, and how that might affect the Irish, but Katie lost interest as their argument droned on. She turned her attention to the restless child in her belly. Katie stood and arched her back, pressing her hand into the muscle.

Éamonn hopped up and massaged her lower back. He'd learned just where to press to give her the best respite. She moaned in relief as he eased the ache. She couldn't wait for this babe to be born, but she had at least another three months to go.

She'd lost Lochlann's baby after all, a month after they got married. She mourned the loss of the last bit of Lochlann, but she got pregnant again. Now she carried Éamonn's babe, and that child should come due soon.

Katie liked this area outside Ardara. Father Byrne's church was within easy travel distance, and Éamonn kept in touch with him. He might harbor lingering guilt over having married her to Lochlann in the first place, but he'd been helpful to them since.

Would she have a boy or a girl? Éamonn wanted a boy. He'd said so many times, though he always hastily assured her he'd love a daughter just as much. A husband wanted a son to carry on his name. Turlough had suggested the name, Brian. She hadn't cared for the name before, but Turlough's wishes held weight. What if she had a girl? Brianna, perhaps? Such a clumsy name. Maybe Brid. She'd have to get out of the habit of swearing to Brid. She let a giggle slip.

"And what's so funny, *mo chroi*? Am I tickling you?" His strong hands moved to her waist, where she was hyper-ticklish.

"No, don't stop. It feels much too good."

They lived well enough above the leather shop. Katie ran the household and even helped sew woolen pieces to sell. Hats, mittens, or horse blankets. She had no great skill with needlework, but she wove well enough if she used gloves against the harsh wool.

Katie insisted Éamonn give up all gambling after the trouble they'd gone through from using his Fae-gift. If he used it to sell leather goods, Katie didn't know. She didn't really want to know.

Ruari was a great help and lived with them, never acting like a third wheel, going out every few nights on his own to give them time alone.

She wasn't certain if Éamonn ever sought out the stone circle on the hill above town. If he did, he never mentioned it. Katie would rather the Fae not take any special interest in their child. She fingered the iron pin she'd asked the blacksmith to craft. The child would wear the pin at all times for protection. For a moment, she thought of Deirdre and her magical spells. Would the fae claim her, as they had Turlough?

She felt guilty thinking of Deirdre and feeling glad her sister was gone to America, and she'd never have to fear her sister walking back into Katie's life and destroying it. And if she never saw her own parents again, it would be too soon. She still heard her sister's voice on the wind sometimes. Ruari and Éamonn were all the family she needed or wanted.

And, of course, their child. Katie put a tender hand over her belly, cupping the curve. Her hope for the future. Perhaps it would be a better world for her son, Brian, or her daughter, Brid. All a parent could do was their best for their child. It was all anyone could do, in the end.

A magical gift of the fae.
When a soothsayer faces her end of days,
can she find her lone heir before more blood is spilled?

Can Orlagh's unflagging devotion survive the brutal conflict on the horizon?

Buy *Misfortune of Vision* to match wits with fate today!
books2read.com/Misfortune-of-Vision

Thank you!

Thank you so much for enjoying Legacy of Luck. If you've enjoyed the story, please consider leaving a review to help others discover Katie and Éamonn's love!

If you would like to get updates, sneak previews, sales, and get a FREE short story and a FAMILY TREE, please sign up for my newsletter.

www.GreenDragonArtist.com

Other Books by This Author

**See all the books available
Through Green Dragon Publishing at
www.GreenDragonArtist.com/books**

Historical Note

Dear Readers,

As you venture into the enchanting world of "Legacy of Luck," I am excited to provide a glimpse into the historical inspirations that weave through the tapestry of this captivating tale.

Set against the backdrop of Ireland in 1746, where legends come alive and destiny unfolds its intricate design, the story revolves around Éamonn Doherty. He is a Traveler, and as such, travels around Ireland trading, working, and attending horse fairs like the one in this book. The brightly painted iconic wagons we know today weren't quite yet in use in 1746, but they did have carts, covered wagons, and tents.

Travelers are called many names. Tinkers, Mincéirí, gypsies, pavees, paddies, pikeys. They are itinerant ethnic groups in Ireland and Scotland, with a long tradition of customs. They speak English but have their own languages such as Shelta, Gammon, or Cant. Ethnically, they are not related to the Romani gypsy tribes from Eastern Europe, though the two groups have some cultural things in common. Their origins are shrouded in the mists of time, but they have been a separate group for probably at least a thousand years, according to DNA testing evidence. Their numbers were greatly increased during the Great Hunger of the 1840s when many folks lost their homes.

Within the community, marriages are often arranged. It is considered a duty for the young lady to agree to the match, under the assumption she is not wise enough to choose a proper match at her age. However, the bride is allowed to refuse a match. Just like in non-Traveler society, however, an abusive father can bring more pressure to agree to a match, as our characters do in this story.

The remote Isle of Skye becomes the stage for a tale of love thwarted by an arranged marriage, prompting Éamonn to embark on a perilous quest to bridge the distance that separates them. Dunvegan Castle is definitely real, and the clan MacLeod used MacCrimmons as their official pipers. There are several scenes at battles, and each one is based on a real battle in the 1746 Jacobite Rebellion. There was a Donald MacCrimmon who participated in the Jacobite rising and killed in a raid. Beyond that, I have created the details of the MacCrimmon brothers to fit the story.

I invite you to immerse yourself in this legendary tale, where the past comes alive, destiny is shaped, and the magic of Éamonn's quest awaits.

About the Author

Christy Nicholas writes under several pen names, including Emeline Rhys, CN Jackson, and Rowan Dillon. She is an author, artist, and accountant. After she failed to become an airline pilot, she quit her ceaseless pursuit of careers that began with the letter 'A' and decided to concentrate on her writing. Since she has Project Completion Compulsion, she is one of the few authors with no unfinished novels.

Christy has her hands in many crafts, including digital art, beaded jewelry, writing, and photography. In real life, she's a CPA, but having grown up with art all around her (her mother, grandmother, and great-grandmother are/were all artists), it sort of infected her, as it were.

She wants to expose the incredible beauty in this world, hidden beneath the everyday grime of familiarity and habit, and share it with others. She uses characters out of time and places infused with magic and myth, writing magical realism stories in both historical fantasy and time travel flavors.

Social Media Links:

Blog: www.GreenDragonArtist.net
Website: www.GreenDragonArtist.com
Facebook: www.facebook.com/greendragonauthor
Instagram: www.instagram.com/greendragonartist9
TikTok: www.tiktok.com/@greendragonauthor

9 781087 932002